*Lost Children Archive*

# Lost Children Archive

### VALERIA LUISELLI

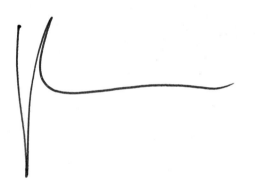

*Alfred A. Knopf*

NEW YORK 2019

THIS IS A BORZOI BOOK PUBLISHED BY ALFRED A. KNOPF

www.aaknopf.com

Knopf, Borzoi Books, and the colophon are registered trademarks of Penguin Random House LLC.

Grateful acknowledgment is made to the following for permission to reprint previously published material:
Alfred A. Knopf, a division of Penguin Random House LLC, and Aragi, Inc.: Excerpt of "Father's Old Blue Cardigan" from *Men in the Off Hours* by Anne Carson, copyright © 2000 by Anne Carson. Reprinted by permission of Alfred A. Knopf, an imprint of the Knopf Doubleday Publishing Group, a division of Penguin Random House LLC, and Aragi, Inc. All rights reserved.

Houghton Mifflin Harcourt Publishing Company: Excerpt of "Little Sleep's Head Sprouting Hair in the Moonlight" from *Collected Poems* by Galway Kinnell. Copyright © 2017 by The Literary Estate of Galway Kinnell, LLC. Reprinted by permission of Houghton Mifflin Harcourt Publishing Company. All rights reserved.

International Editors' Co., on behalf of Bárbara Jacobs and María Monterroso: "El Dinosaurio" by Augusto Monterroso, copyright © 1959 by Augusto Monterroso. Reprinted by permission of International Editors' Co., on behalf of Bárbara Jacobs and María Monterroso.

Library of Congress Cataloging-in-Publication Data
Names: Luiselli, Valeria, [date] author.
Title: Lost children archive : a novel / by Valeria Luiselli.
Description: First edition. | New York : Alfred A. Knopf, 2019.
Identifiers: LCCN 2018018390 | ISBN 9780525520610 (hardcover) | 9780525520627 (ebook) | 9781524711504 (open market)
Subjects: LCSH: Family life. | Immigrant children—United States—Social conditions. | Illegal alien children—United States—Social conditions. | Immigrant children—Legal status, laws, etc.—United States. | Illegal alien children—Legal status, laws, etc.— United States. | United States—Emigration and immigration—Government policy. | BISAC: FICTION / Literary. | FICTION / Family Life.
Classification: LCC PQ7298.422.U37 L67 2019 | DDC 863/.7—dc23
LC record available at https://lccn.loc.gov/2018018390

Jacket photographs courtesy of the author
Jacket design by Jenny Carrow

Manufactured in the United States of America
First Edition

*To Maia and Dylan, who showed me childhood all over again.*

# CONTENTS

# PART I

## *Family Soundscape*

# RELOCATIONS

An archive presupposes an archivist, a hand that collects and classifies.

—ARLETTE FARGE

*To leave is to die a little.*
*To arrive is never to arrive.*

—MIGRANT PRAYER

## DEPARTURE

Mouths open to the sun, they sleep. Boy and girl, foreheads pearled with sweat, cheeks red and streaked white with dry spit. They occupy the entire space in the back of the car, spread out, limbs offering, heavy and placid. From the copilot seat, I glance back to check on them every so often, then turn around again to study the map. We advance in the slow lava of traffic toward the city limits, across the GW Bridge, and merge onto the interstate. An airplane passes above us and leaves a straight long scar on the palate of the cloudless sky. Behind the wheel, my husband adjusts his hat, dries his forehead with the back of his hand.

## FAMILY LEXICON

I don't know what my husband and I will say to each of our children one day. I'm not sure which parts of our story we might each choose to pluck and edit out for them, and which ones we'll shuffle around and insert back in to produce a final version—even though plucking, shuffling, and editing sounds is probably the best summary of what my husband and I do for a living. But the children will ask, because ask is what children do. And we'll need to tell them a beginning, a middle, and an end. We'll need to give them an answer, tell them a proper story.

The boy turned ten yesterday, just one day before we left New York. We got him good presents. He had specifically said:

No toys.

The girl is five, and for some weeks has been asking, insistently:

When do I turn six?

No matter our answer, she'll find it unsatisfactory. So we usually say something ambiguous, like:

Soon.

In a few months.

Before you know it.

The girl is my daughter and the boy is my husband's son. I'm a biological mother to one, a stepmother to the other, and a de facto mother in general to both of them. My husband is a father and a stepfather, to each one respectively, but also just a father. The girl and boy are therefore: step-sister, son, stepdaughter, daughter, step-brother, sister, stepson, brother. And because hyphenations and petty nuances complicate the sentences of everyday grammar— the us, the them, the our, the your—as soon as we started living together, when the boy was almost six and the girl still a toddler, we adopted the much simpler possessive adjective our to refer to them two. They became: our children. And sometimes: the boy, the girl. Quickly, the two of them learned the rules of our private grammar, and adopted the generic nouns Mama and Papa, or sometimes simply Ma and Pa. And until now at least, our family lexicon defined the scope and limits of our shared world.

## FAMILY PLOT

My husband and I met four years ago, recording a soundscape of New York City. We were part of a large team of people working for New York University's Center for Urban Science and Progress. The soundscape was meant to sample and collect all the keynotes and the soundmarks that were emblematic of the city: subway cars screeching to a halt, music in the long underground hallways of Forty-Second Street, ministers preaching in Harlem, bells, rumors and murmurs inside the Wall Street stock exchange. But it also attempted to survey and classify all the other sounds that the city produced and that usually went by, as noise, unnoticed: cash registers opening and closing in delis, a script being rehearsed in an empty Broadway theater, underwater currents in the Hudson, Canada geese flocking and shitting over Van Cortlandt Park, swings swinging in Astoria playgrounds, elderly Korean women filing wealthy fingernails on the Upper West Side, a fire breaking through an old tenement building in the Bronx, a passerby yelling a stream of motherfuckers at another. There were journalists, sound artists, geographers, urbanists, writers, historians, acoustemologists, anthropologists, musicians, and even bathymetrists, with those complicated devices called multibeam echo sounders, which were plunged into the waterspaces surrounding the city, measuring the depth and contours of the riverbeds, and who knows what else. Everyone, in couples or small groups, surveyed and sampled wavelengths around the city, like we were documenting the last sounds of an enormous beast.

The two of us were paired up and given the task of recording all the languages spoken in the city, over a period of four calendar years. The description of our duties specified: "surveying the most linguistically diverse metropolis on the planet, and mapping the entirety of languages that its adults and children speak." We were good at it, it turned out; maybe even really good. We made a perfect team of two. Then, after working together for just a few months, we fell in love—completely, irrationally, predictably, and headfirst, like a rock might fall in love with a bird, not knowing who the rock was and who the bird—and when summer arrived, we decided to move in together.

The girl remembers nothing about that period, of course. The boy says he remembers that I was always wearing an old blue cardigan that had lost a couple of buttons and came down to my knees, and that sometimes, when we rode the subway or buses—always with freezing air pouring out—I'd take it off and use it as a blanket to cover him and the girl, and that it smelled of tobacco and was itchy. Moving in together had been a rash decision—messy, confusing, urgent, and as beautiful and real as life feels when you're not thinking about its consequences. We became a tribe. Then came the consequences. We met each other's relatives, got married, started filing joint taxes, became a family.


INVENTORY

In the front seats: he and I. In the glove compartment: proof of insurance, registration, owner's manual, and road maps. In the backseat: the two children, their backpacks, a tissue box, and a blue cooler with water bottles and perishable snacks. And in the trunk: a small duffle bag with my Sony PCM-D50 digital voice recorder, headphones, cables, and extra batteries; a large Porta-Brace organizer for his collapsible boom pole, mic, headphones, cables, zeppelin and dead-cat windshield, and the 702T Sound Device. Also: four small suitcases with our clothes, and seven bankers boxes (15″ x 12″ x 10″), double-thick bottoms and solid lids.

## C O V A L E N C E

Despite our efforts to keep it all firmly together, there has always been an anxiety around each one's place in the family. We're like those problematic molecules you learn about in chemistry classes, with covalent instead of ionic bonds—or maybe it's the other way around. The boy lost his biological mother at birth, though that topic is never spoken about. My husband delivered the fact to me, in one sentence, early on in our relationship, and I immediately understood that it was not a matter open to further questions. I don't like to be asked about the girl's biological father, either, so the two of us have always kept a respectful pact of silence about those elements of our and our children's pasts.

In response to all that, perhaps, the children have always wanted to listen to stories about themselves within the context of us. They want to know everything about when the two of them became our children, and we all became a family. They're like anthropologists studying cosmogonic narratives, but with a touch more narcissism. The girl asks to hear the same stories over and over again. The boy asks about moments of their childhood together, as if they had happened decades or even centuries ago. So we tell them. We tell them all the stories we're able to remember. Always, if we miss a part, confuse a detail, or if they notice any minimal variation to the version they remember, they interrupt, correct us, and demand that the story be told once more, properly this time. So we rewind the tape in our minds and play it again from the beginning.

## F O U N D A T I O N A L   M Y T H S

In our beginning was an almost empty apartment, and a heat wave. On the first night in that apartment—the same apartment we just left behind—the four of us were sitting in our underwear on the floor of the living room, sweaty and exhausted, balancing slices of pizza on our palms.

We'd finished unpacking some of our belongings and a few extra things we'd bought that day: a corkscrew, four new pillows, window cleaner, dishwashing soap, two small picture frames, nails, hammer. Next we measured the children's heights and made the first marks on the hallway wall: 33 inches and 42 inches. Then we'd hammered two nails into the kitchen wall to hang two postcards that had hung in our former, respective apartments: one was a portrait of Malcolm X, taken shortly before his assassination, where he's resting his head on his right hand and looking intently at someone or something; the other was of Emiliano Zapata, standing upright, holding a rifle in one hand and a saber in the other, a sash around one shoulder, his double cartridge belt crosswise. The glass protecting the postcard of Zapata was still covered in a layer of grime—or is it soot?—from my old kitchen. We hung them both next to the refrigerator. But even after this, the new apartment still looked too empty, walls too white, still felt foreign.

The boy looked around the living room, chewing pizza, and asked:

Now what?

And the girl, who was two years old then, echoed him:

Yes what?

Neither of us found an answer to give them, though I think we did search hard for one, perhaps because that was the question we'd also been silently threading across the empty room.

Now what? the boy asked again.

Finally, I answered:

Now go brush your teeth.

But we haven't unpacked our toothbrushes yet, the boy said.

So go rinse your mouths in the bathroom sink and go to sleep, my husband replied.

They came back from the bathroom, saying they were scared to sleep alone in the new bedroom. We agreed to let them stay in the living room with us, for a while, if they promised to go to sleep. They crawled into an empty box, and after puppying around for the fairest division of cardboard space, they fell into a deep, heavy sleep.

My husband and I opened a bottle of wine, and, out the window, we smoked a joint. Then we sat on the floor, doing nothing, saying nothing, just watching the children sleep in their cardboard box. From where we were sitting, we could see only a tangle of heads and butts: his hair damp with sweat, her curls a nest; he, aspirin-assed, and she, apple-bottomed. They looked like one of those couples who've overstayed their time together, become middle-aged too fast, grown tired of each other but comfortable enough. They slept in total, solitary companionship. And now and then, interrupting our maybe slightly stoned silence, the boy snored like a drunk man, and the girl's body released long, sonorous farts.

They'd given a similar concert earlier that day, while we rode the subway from the supermarket back to our new apartment, surrounded by white plastic bags full of enormous eggs, very pink ham, organic almonds, corn bread, and tiny cartons of organic whole milk—the enriched and enhanced products of the new, upgraded diet of a family with two salaries. Two or three subway minutes and the children were asleep, heads on each of our laps, tangled humid hair, lovely salty smell like the warm giant pretzels we'd eaten earlier that day on a street corner. They were angelic, and we were young enough, and together we were a beautiful tribe, an enviable bunch. Then, suddenly, one started snoring and the other stared farting. The few passengers who were not plugged into their telephones took note, looked at her, at us, at him, and smiled—difficult to know if in compassion or complicity with our children's public shamelessness. My husband smiled back at the smiling strangers. I thought for a second I should divert their attention, reflect it away from us, maybe stare accusingly at the old man sleeping a few seats from us, or at the young lady in full jogging gear. I didn't, of course. I just nodded in acknowledgment, or in resignation, and smiled back at the subway strangers—a tight, buttonhole smile. I suppose I felt the kind of stage fright that comes up in certain dreams, where you realize you went to school and forgot to put on underwear; a sudden and deep vulnerability in front of all those strangers being offered a glimpse of our still very new world.

But later that night, back in the intimacy of our new apartment, when the children were asleep and were making all those beautiful noises all over again—real beauty, always unintentional—I was able to listen to them fully, without the burden of self-consciousness. The girl's intestinal sounds were amplified against the wall of the cardboard box and traveled, diaphanous, across the almost empty living room. And after a little while, from somewhere deep in his sleep, the boy heard them—or so it seemed to us—and replied to them with utterances and mumbles. My husband took note of the fact that we were witnessing one of the languages of the city sound-scape, now put to use in the ultimately circular act of conversation:

A mouth replying to a butthole.

I suppressed the desire to laugh, for an instant, but then I noticed that my husband was holding his breath and closing his eyes in order to not laugh. Perhaps we were a little more stoned than we thought. I became undone, my vocal cords bursting into a sound more por-cine than human. He followed, with a series of puffs and gasps, his nasal wings flapping, face wrinkling, eyes almost disappearing, his entire body rocking back and forth like a wounded piñata. Most people acquire a frightening appearance in mid-laughter. I've always feared those who click their teeth, and found those who laugh with-out emitting a single sound rather worrisome. In my paternal fam-ily, we have a genetic defect, I think, which manifests in snorts and grunts at the very end of the laughing cycle—a sound that, perhaps for its animality, unleashes another cycle of laughter. Until every-one has tears in their eyes, and a feeling of shame overcomes them.

I took a deep breath and wiped a tear from my cheek. I real-ized then that this was the first time my husband and I had ever heard each other laugh. With our deeper laughs, that is—a laugh unleashed, untied, a laugh entire and ridiculous. Perhaps no one really knows us who does not know the way we laugh. My husband and I finally recomposed ourselves.

It's mean to laugh at the expense of our sleeping children, yes? I asked.

Yes, very wrong.

We decided that what we had to do, instead, was document them, so we took out our recording gear. My husband swept the space with his boom pole; I zoomed my handheld voice recorder up close to the boy and the girl. She sucked her thumb and he mumbled words and strange sleep-utterances into it; cars drove by out-side in the street into my husband's mic. In childish complicity, the two of us sampled their sounds. I'm not sure what deeper reasons prompted us to record the children that night. Maybe it was just the summer heat, plus the wine, minus the joint, times the excite-ment of the move, divided by all the cardboard recycling ahead of us. Or maybe we were following an impulse to allow the moment, which felt like the beginning of something, to leave a trace. After all, we'd trained our minds to seize recording opportunities, trained our ears to listen to our daily lives as if they were raw tape. All of it, us and them, here and there, inside and outside, was registered, collected, and archived. New families, like young nations after vio-lent wars of independence or social revolutions, perhaps need to anchor their beginnings in a symbolic moment and nail that instant in time. That night was our foundation, it was the night where our chaos became a cosmos.

Later, tired and having lost momentum, we carried the chil-dren in our arms into their new room, their mattresses not much larger than the cardboard box where they been sleeping. Then, in our bedroom, we slid onto our own mattress and wedged our legs together, saying nothing, but with our bodies saying something like maybe later, maybe tomorrow, tomorrow we'll make love, make plans, tomorrow.

Goodnight.

Goodnight.

## MOTHER TONGUES

When I was first invited to work on the soundscape project, I thought it seemed somewhat tacky, megalomaniacal, possi-bly too didactic. I was young, though not much younger than I am now, and still thought of myself as a hard-core political journalist. I also didn't like the fact that the project, though it was orchestrated by NYU's Center for Urban Science and Progress, and would even-tually form part of their sound archive, was in part funded by some huge multinational corporations. I tried to do some research on their CEOs—for scandals, frauds, any fascist allegiances. But I had a little girl. So when I was told that the contract included medical insurance, and realized that I could live on the salary without having to do the myriad journalistic gigs I was taking on to survive, I stopped researching, stopped acting as if I was privileged enough to worry about corporate ethics, and signed the contract. I'm not sure what his reasons were, but at around the same time, my husband—who was then just a stranger specialized in acoustemology and not my husband or our children's father—signed his.

The two of us gave ourselves completely to the soundscape project. Every day, while the children were in daycare and school, respectively, we went out into the city, not knowing what would happen but always sure we'd find something new. We traveled in and out of the five boroughs, interviewing strangers, asking them to talk in and about their native tongues. He liked the days we spent in transitional spaces, like train stations, airports, and bus stops. I liked the days we spent in schools, sampling children. He'd walk around the crowded cafeterias, his Porta-Brace sound bag hanging from a strap around his right shoulder, his boom held up at an angle, recording the cluster of voices, cutlery, footsteps. In hallways and classrooms, I'd hold my recorder up close to each child's mouth as they uttered sounds, responding to my prompts. I asked them to recall songs and sayings they heard in their homes. Their accents were often anglicized, domesticated, their parents' languages now foreign to them. I remember their actual, physical tongues—pink, earnest, disciplined—trying to wrap themselves around the sounds of their more and more distant mother tongues: the difficult position of the tongue's tip in the Hispanic erre, the quick tongue-slaps against the palate in all the polysyllabic Kichwa and Karif words, the soft and downward curved bed of the tongue in the aspirated Arabic h.

The months passed, and we recorded voices, collected accents. We accumulated hours of tape of people speaking, telling stories, pausing, telling lies, praying, hesitating, confessing, breathing.

TIME

We also accumulated things: plants, plates, books, chairs. We picked up objects from curbsides in affluent neighborhoods.

Often, we realized later that we didn't really need another chair, another bookshelf, and so we put it back outside, on the curbside of our less-affluent neighborhood, feeling that we were participants in the invisible left hand of wealth redistribution—the anti–Adam Smiths of sidewalks and curbsides. For a while, we continued to pick up objects from the streets, until we heard on the radio one day that there was a bedbug crisis in the city, so we stopped scavenging, quit redistributing wealth, and winter came, and then came spring.

It's never clear what turns a space into a home, and a life-project into a life. One day, our books didn't fit in the bookshelves anymore, and the big empty room in our apartment had become our living room. It had become the place where we watched movies, read books, assembled puzzles, napped, helped the children with their homework. Then the place where we had friends over, held long conversations after they'd left, fucked, said beautiful and horrible things to each other, and cleaned up in silence afterward.

Who knows how, and who knows where the time had gone, but one day, the boy had turned eight, then nine, and the girl was five. They had started going to the same public school. All the little strangers they had met, they now called their friends. There were soccer teams, gymnastics, end-of-year performances, sleepovers, always too many birthday parties, and the marks we had made on the hallway wall of our apartment to register our children's heights suddenly summed up to a vertical story. They had grown so much taller. My husband thought they grew tall too fast. Unnaturally fast, he said, because of that organic whole milk they consumed in those little cartons; he thought that the milk was chemically altered to produce premature tallness in children. Maybe, I thought. But possibly, also, it was just that time had passed.

## TEETH

How much more?
How much longer?

I suppose it's the same with all children: if they are awake inside a car, they ask for attention, ask for bathroom stops, ask for snacks. But mostly they ask:

When will we get there?

We usually tell the boy and girl it'll be just a little while. Or else we say:

Play with your toys.

Count all the white cars that pass.

Try to sleep.

Now, as we halt at a tollbooth near Philadelphia, they suddenly wake up, as if their sleep were synchronized—both between the two of them and, more inexplicably, with the car's varying accelerations. From the backseat, the girl calls out:

How many more blocks?

Just a little while till we make a stop in Baltimore, I say.

But how many blocks till we get all the way to the end?

All the way to the end is Arizona. The plan is to drive from New York to the southeastern corner of the state. As we drive, southwest-bound toward the borderlands, my husband and I will each be working on our new sound projects, doing field recordings and surveys. I'll focus on interviews with people, catch fragments of conversations among strangers, record the sound of news on the radio or voices in diners. When we get to Arizona, I'll record my last samples and start editing everything. I have four weeks to get it all done. Then I'll probably have to fly back to New York with the girl, but I'm not sure of that yet. I'm not sure what my husband's exact plan is either. I study his face in profile. He concentrates on the road ahead. He'll be sampling things like the sound of wind blowing through plains or parking lots; footsteps walking on gravel, cement, or sand; maybe pennies falling into cash registers, teeth grinding peanuts, a child's hand probing a jacket pocket full of pebbles. I don't know how long his new sound project will take him, or what will happen next. The girl breaks our silence, insisting:

I asked you a question, Mama, Papa: How many blocks till we get all the way there?

We have to remind ourselves to be patient. We know—I suppose even the boy knows—how confusing it must be to live in the timeless world of a five-year-old: a world not without time but with a surplus of it. My husband finally gives the girl an answer that seems to satisfy her:

We'll get all the way there when you lose your second bottom tooth.

## TONGUE TIES

When the girl was four and had started going to public school, she prematurely lost a tooth. Immediately after, she started stuttering. We never knew if the events were in fact causally related: school, tooth, stutter. But in our familial narrative, at least, the three things got tied together in a confusing, emotionally charged knot.

One morning during our last winter in New York, I had a conversation with the mother of one of my daughter's classmates. We were in the auditorium, waiting to vote for new parent representatives. The two of us stood in line for a while, exchanging stories about our children's linguistic and cultural stalemates. My daughter had stuttered for a year, I told her, sometimes to the point of noncommunication. She'd begin every sentence like she was about to sneeze. But she had recently discovered that if she sang a sentence instead of speaking it, it would come out without a stutter. And so, slowly, she had been growing out of her stuttering. Her son, she told me, had not said a word in almost six months, not in any language.

We asked each other about the places we were from, and the languages that we spoke at home. They were from Tlaxiaco, in the Mixteca, she told me. Her first language was Trique. I had never heard Trique, and the only thing I knew about it was that it is one of the most complex tonal languages, with more than eight tones. My grandmother was Hñähñu and spoke Otomí, a simpler tonal language than Trique, with only three tones. But my mother didn't learn it, I said, and of course I didn't learn it either. When I asked her if her son could speak Trique, she told me no, of course not, and said:

Our mothers teach us to speak, and the world teaches us to shut up.

After we voted, right before saying goodbye, we introduced ourselves, though it should have been the other way around. Her name was Manuela, the same as my grandmother's name. She found the coincidence less amusing than I did. I asked her if she might be willing to let me record her one day, and told her about the sound documentary my husband and I were almost finished working on. We had not yet sampled Trique—it was a rare language to come by. She agreed, hesitantly, and when we met in the park next to the school a few days later, she said she would ask for one thing in exchange for this. She had two older daughters—eight and ten years old—who had just arrived in the country, crossing the border on foot, and were being held in a detention center in Texas. She needed someone to translate their documents from Spanish into English, at little or no cost, so she could find a lawyer to defend them from being deported. I agreed, without knowing what I was getting myself into.

## PROCEDURES

First it was just translating legal papers: the girls' birth certificates, vaccination records, one school report card. Then there was a series of letters written by a neighbor back home and addressed to Manuela, giving a detailed account of the situation there: the untamable waves of violence, the army, the gangs, the police, the sudden disappearances of people—mostly young women and girls. Then, one day, Manuela asked me to go to a meeting with a potential lawyer.

The three of us met in a waiting room in the New York City Immigration Court. The lawyer followed a brief questionnaire, asking questions in English that I translated into Spanish for Manuela. She told her story, and the girls' story. They were all from a small town on the border of Oaxaca and Guerrero. About six years ago, when the younger of the two girls turned two and the older was four, Manuela left them in their grandmother's care. Food was scant; it was impossible to raise the girls with so little, she explained. She crossed the border, with no documents, and settled in the Bronx, where she had a cousin. She found a job, started sending money back. The plan was to save up quickly and return home as soon as possible. But she got pregnant, and life got complicated, and the years started speeding by. The girls were growing up, talking to her on the telephone, hearing stories about snow falling, about big avenues, bridges, traffic jams, and, later, about their baby brother.

Meanwhile, the situation back home became more and more complicated, became unsafe, so Manuela asked her boss for a loan, and paid a coyote to bring the girls over to her.

The girls' grandmother prepared them for the trip, told them it would be a long journey, packed their backpacks: Bible, water bottle, nuts, one toy each, spare underwear. She made them matching dresses, and the day before they left, she sewed Manuela's telephone number on the collars of the dresses. She had tried to get them to memorize the ten digits, but the girls had not been able to. So she sewed the number on the collars of their dresses and, over and over, repeated a single instruction: they should never take their dresses off, never, and as soon as they reached America, as soon as they met the first American, be it a policeman or a normal person, they had to show the inside of the collar to him or her. That person would then dial the number sewed on the collars and let them speak to their mother. The rest would follow.

And it did, except not quite as planned. The girls made it safely to the border, but instead of taking them across, the coyote left them in the desert in the middle of the night. They were found by Border Patrol at dawn, sitting by the side of a road near a checkpoint, and were placed in a detention center for unaccompanied minors. An officer telephoned Manuela to tell her that the girls had been found. His voice was kind and gentle, she said, for a Border Patrol officer. He told her that normally, according to the law, children from Mexico and Canada, unlike children from other countries, had to be sent back immediately. He had managed to keep them in detention, but she was going to need a lawyer from now on. Before he hung up, he let her speak to the girls. He gave them five minutes. It was the first time since they'd left on the journey that she'd heard their voices. The older girl spoke, told her they were okay. The younger one only breathed into the phone, said nothing.

The lawyer we met with that day, after listening to Manuela's story, said sorry, she could not take on their case. She said the case was not "strong enough," and gave no further explanation. Manuela and I were escorted out of the courtroom, along corridors, down elevators, and out of the building. We walked out onto Broadway, into the late morning, and the city was buzzing, the buildings high and solid, the sky pristine blue, the sun bright—as if nothing catastrophic were happening. I promised I'd help her figure it out, help her get a good lawyer, help in any way possible.

## JOINT FILING

Spring came, my husband and I filed our taxes, and we delivered our material for the soundscape project. There were over eight hundred languages in New York City, and after four years of work, we had sampled almost all of them. We could finally move on—to whatever came next. And that was exactly what happened: we started to move on. We were moving forward, but not quite together.

I had gotten involved further with the legal case against Manuela's two girls. A lawyer at a nonprofit had finally agreed to take on their case and, although the girls were still not with their mother, they had at least been transferred from a brutal, semi-secure detention facility in Texas to a supposedly more humane setting—a former Walmart supercenter converted into an immigration detention center for minors, near Lordsburg, New Mexico. To keep up with the case, I had been studying a bit more about immigration law, attending hearings in court, talking to lawyers. Their case was one among tens of thousands of similar ones across the country. More than eighty thousand undocumented children from Mexico and the Northern Triangle, but mostly from the latter, had been detained at the US southern border in just the previous six or seven months. All those children were fleeing circumstances of unspeakable abuse and systematic violence, fleeing countries where gangs had become parastates, had usurped power and taken over the rule of law. They had come to the United States looking for protection, looking for mothers, fathers, or other relatives who had migrated earlier and might take them in. They weren't looking for the American Dream, as the narrative usually goes. The children were merely looking for a way out of their daily nightmare.

At that time, the radio and some newspapers were slowly starting to feature stories about the wave of undocumented children arriving in the country, but none of them seemed to be covering the situation from the perspective of the children involved in it. I decided to approach the director of NYU's Center for Urban Science and Progress. I presented a rough idea of how to narrate the story from a different angle. After some back-and-forth, and a few concessions on my part, she agreed to help me fund a sound documentary about the children's crisis at the border. Not a big production: just me, my recording instruments, and a tight time line.

I initially hadn't noticed, but my husband had also started to work on a new project. First, it was just a bunch of books about Apache history. They piled on his desk and on his bedside table. I knew he'd always been interested in the subject, and he often told the children stories about Apaches, so it wasn't strange that he was reading all those books. Then, maps of Apache territory and images of chiefs and warriors started filling the walls around his desk. I began to sense that what had been a lifelong interest was becoming formal research.

What are you working on? I asked him one afternoon.

Just some stories.

About?

Apaches.

Why Apaches? Which ones?

He said he was interested in Chief Cochise, Geronimo, and the Chiricahuas, because they'd been the last Apache leaders—moral, political, military—of the last free peoples on the American continent, the last to surrender. It was, of course, a more than compelling reason to undertake any kind of research, but it wasn't quite the reason I was waiting to hear.

Later, he started referring to that research as a new sound project. He bought some bankers boxes and filled them with stuff: books, index cards full of notes and quotes, cutouts, scraps, and maps, field recordings and sound surveys he found in public libraries and private archives, as well as a series of little brown notebooks where he wrote daily, almost obsessively. I wondered how all of that would eventually be translated into a sound piece. When I asked him about those boxes, and the stuff inside them, as well as about his plans, and how they fit with our plans together—he just said that he didn't know yet but that he'd soon let me know.

And when he did, a few weeks later, we discussed our next steps. I said I wanted to focus on my project, recording children's stories and their hearings in the New York immigration court. I also said I was considering applying for a job at a local radio station. He said what I suspected he'd say. What he wanted was to work on his own documentary project, about the Apaches. He had applied for a grant and had gotten it. He also said the material he had to collect for this project was linked to specific locations, but this soundscape was going to be different. He called it an "inventory of echoes," said it would be about the ghosts of Geronimo and the last Apaches.

The thing about living with someone is that even though you see them every day and can predict all their gestures in a conversation, even when you can read intentions behind their actions and calculate their responses to circumstances fairly accurately, even when you are sure there's not a single crease in them left unexplored, even then, one day, the other can suddenly become a stranger. What I didn't expect my husband to say was that, in order to be able to work on his new project, he needed time, more time than just a single summer. He also needed silence and solitude. And he needed to relocate more permanently to the southwest of the country.

How permanently? I asked.

Possibly a year or two, or maybe more.

And where in the southwest?

I don't know yet.

And what about my project, here? I asked.

A meaningful project, was all he said.

ALONE TOGETHER

I suppose my husband and I simply hadn't prepared for the second part of our togetherness, the part where we just lived the life we'd been making. Without a future professional project together, we begun to drift apart in other ways. I guess we—or perhaps just I—had made the very common mistake of thinking that marriage was a mode of absolute commonality and a breaking down of all boundaries, instead of understanding it simply as a pact between two people willing to be the guardians of each other's solitude, as Rilke or some other equanimous, philosophical soul had long ago prescribed. But can anyone really prepare? Can anyone tackle effects before detecting causes?

A friend had told us during our wedding party, some years earlier, with that oracular aura of some drunk men right before they fade, that marriage was a banquet to which people arrived too late, when everything was already half eaten, everyone already too tired and wanting to leave, but not knowing how to leave, or with whom.

But I, my friends, can tell you how to make it last forever! he said.

Then he closed his eyes, sunk his beard into his breast, and passed out in his chair.


ITEMIZATION

We spent many difficult evenings, after putting the children to bed, discussing the logistics around my husband's plan to relocate more permanently to the southwest. Many sleepless nights negotiating, fighting, fucking, renegotiating, figuring things out. I spent hours trying to understand or at least come to terms with his project, and many more hours trying to come up with ways to dissuade him from pursuing his plan. Losing temperance one night, I even hurled a lightbulb, a roll of toilet paper, and a series of lame insults at him.

But the days passed, and preparations for the trip began. He searched online and bought things: cooler, sleeping bag, gadgets. I bought maps of the United States. One big one of the whole country, and several others of the southern states we'd probably cross. I studied them late into the night. And as the trip became more and more concrete, I tried to reconcile myself to the idea that I no longer had any other choice but to accept a decision already taken, and then I slowly wrote my own terms into the deal, trying hard not to itemize our life together as if it were now eligible for standard deductions, up for some kind of moral computation of losses, credits, and taxable assets. I tried hard, in other words, not to become someone I would eventually disdain.

I could use these new circumstances, I said to myself, to reinvent myself professionally, to rebuild my life—and other such notions that sound meaningful only in horoscope predictions, or when someone is falling apart and has lost all sense of humor.

More reasonably, regathering my thoughts a little on better days, I convinced myself that our growing apart professionally did not have to imply a deeper break in our relationship. Pursuing our own projects shouldn't have to conduce to dissolving our world together. We could drive down to the borderlands as soon as the children's school year finished, and each work on our respective projects. I wasn't sure how, but I thought I could start researching, slowly build an archive, and extend my focus on the child refugee crisis from the court of immigration in New York, where I had been centering all my attention, to any one of its geographic points in the southern borderlands. It was an obvious development in the research itself, of course. But also, it was a way for our two projects, very different from each other, to be made compatible. At least for now. Compatible enough at this point, in any case, for us to go on a family road trip to the southwest. After that, we'd figure something out.

## ARCHIVE

I pored over reports and articles about child refugees, and tried to gather information on what was happening beyond the New York immigration court, at the border, in detention centers and shelters. I got in touch with lawyers, attended conferences of the New York City Bar Association, had private meetings with non-profit workers and community organizers. I collected loose notes, scraps, cutouts, quotes copied down on cards, letters, maps, photographs, lists of words, clippings, tape-recorded testimonies. When I started to get lost in the documental labyrinth of my own making, I contacted an old friend, a Columbia University professor specializing in archival studies, who wrote me a long letter and sent me a list of articles and books that might shine some light on my confusion. I read and read, long sleepless nights reading about archive fevers, about rebuilding memory in diasporic narratives, about being lost in "the ashes" of the archive.

Finally, after I'd found some clarity and amassed a reasonable amount of well-filtered material that would help me understand how to document the children's crisis at the border, I placed everything inside one of the bankers boxes that my husband had not yet filled with his own stuff. I had a few photos, some legal papers, intake questionnaires used for court screenings, maps of migrant deaths in the southern deserts, and a folder with dozens of "Migrant Mortality Reports" printed from online search engines that locate the missing, which listed bodies found in those deserts, the possible cause of death, and their exact location. At the very top of the box, I placed a few books I'd read and thought could help me think about the whole project from a certain narrative distance: *The Gates of Paradise,* by Jerzy Andrzejewski; *The Children's Crusade,* by Marcel Schwob; *Belladonna,* by Daša Drndić; *Le goût de l'archive,* by Arlette Farge; and a little red book I hadn't yet read, called *Elegies for Lost Children,* by Ella Camposanto.

When my husband complained about my using one of his boxes, I complained back, said he had four boxes, while I had only one. He pointed out that I was an adult so could not possibly complain about him having more boxes than me. In a way he was right, so I smiled in acknowledgment. But still, I used his box.

Then the boy complained. Why couldn't he have a box, too? We had no arguments against his demand, so we allowed him one box.

Naturally, the girl then also complained. So we allowed her a box. When we asked them what they wanted to put in their boxes, the boy said he wanted to leave his empty for now:

So I can collect stuff on the way.

Me too, said the girl.

We argued that empty boxes would be a waste of space. But our arguments found good counterarguments, or perhaps we were tired of finding counterarguments in general, so that was that. In total, we had seven boxes. They would travel with us, like an appendix of us, in the trunk of the car we were going to buy. I numbered them carefully with a black marker. Boxes I through IV were my husband's, Box VI was the girl's, Box VII was the boy's. My box was Box V.

APACHERIA

At the start of the summer break, which was only a little more than a month away, we'd drive toward the southwest. In the meantime, during that last month in the city, we still played out our lives as if nothing fundamental were going to change between us. We bought a cheap used car, one of those Volvo wagons, 1996, black, with a huge trunk. We went to two weddings, and both times were told we were a beautiful family. Such handsome children, so different-looking, said an old lady who smelled of talcum powder. We cooked dinner, watched movies, and discussed plans for the trip. Some nights, the four of us studied the big map together, choosing routes we'd take, successfully ignoring the fact that they possibly mapped out the road to our not being together.

But where exactly are we going? the children asked.

We still didn't know, or hadn't agreed on anything. I wanted to go to Texas, the state with the largest number of immigration detention centers for children. There were children, thousands of them, locked up in Galveston, Brownsville, Los Fresnos, El Paso, Nixon, Canutillo, Conroe, Harlingen, Houston, and Corpus Christi. My husband wanted the trip to end in Arizona.

Why Arizona? we all asked.

And where in Arizona? I wanted to know.

Finally, one night, my husband spread the big map out on our bed and called the children and me into our room. He swiped the tip of his index finger from New York all the way down to Arizona, and then tapped twice on a point, a tiny dot in the southeastern corner of the state. He said:

Here.

Here what? the boy asked.

Here are the Chiricahua Mountains, he said.

And? the boy asked.

And that is the heart of Apacheria, he answered.

Is that where we're going? the girl asked.

That's right, my husband replied.

Why there? the boy asked him.

Because that's where the last Chiricahua Apaches lived.

So what? the boy retorted.

So nothing, so that's where we're going, to Apacheria, where the last free peoples on the entire American continent lived before they had to surrender to the white-eyes.

What's a white-eye? the girl asked, possibly imagining a terrifying something.

That's just what the Chiricahuas called the white Europeans and white Americans: white-eyes.

Why? she wanted to know, and I was also curious, but the boy snatched back the reins of the conversation, steering it his way.

But why Apaches, Pa?

Because.

Because what?

Because they were the last of something.


PRONOUNS

It was decided. We would drive to the southeastern tip of Arizona, where he would stay, or rather, where they would stay, for an undetermined amount of time, but where she and I would probably not stay. She and I would go all the way there with them, but we'd probably return to the city at the end of the summer. I would finish the sound documentary about refugee children and would then need to find a job. She would have to go back to school. I couldn't simply relocate to Arizona, leave everything behind, unless I found a way and a reason to follow my husband in this new venture of his without having to abandon my own plans and projects. Though it wasn't even clear to me if, beyond this summer road trip together, he indeed wanted to be followed.

I, he, we, they, she: pronouns shifted place constantly in our confused syntax while we negotiated the terms of the relocation. We started speaking more hesitantly about everything, even the trivial things, and also started speaking more softly, like we were tiptoeing with our tongues, careful to the point of paranoia not to slip and fall on the suddenly very unstable grounds of our family space. There is a poem by Anne Carson called "Reticent Sonnet" that doesn't help solve this at all. It's about how pronouns are "part of a system that argues with shadow," though perhaps she means that we—people, and not pronouns—are "part of a system that argues with shadow." But then again, we is a pronoun, so maybe she means both things at the same time.

In any case, the question of how the final placement of all our pronouns would ultimately rearrange our lives became our center of gravity. It became the dark, silent core around which all our thoughts and questions circulated.

What will we do after we reach Apacheria? the boy would ask repeatedly in the weeks that followed.

Yes, what next? I'd ask my husband later, when we crawled into bed.

Then we'll see what next, he would say.

Apacheria, of course, does not really exist anymore. But it existed in my husband's mind and in nineteenth-century history books, and, more and more, it came to exist in the children's imaginations:

Will there be horses there?

Will there be arrows?

Will we have beds, toys, food, enemies?

When will we leave?

We told them we'd leave on the day after the boy's tenth birthday.

## COSMOLOGIES

During our last days in the city, before we left for Apacheria, our apartment filled with ants. Big black ants in the shape of eights, with a suicidal drive for sugar. If we left a glass of something sweet on a kitchen counter, the following morning we'd find twenty ant corpses floating in it, drowned in their own hedonism. They explored kitchen counters, cabinets, the sink—all normal haunts for ants. But then they moved on to our beds, our drawers, and eventually our elbows and necks. One night I became convinced that if I sat silent long enough, I could hear them marching inside the walls, taking over the apartment's invisible veins. We tried sealing every crevice in the molding between the walls and floors with tape, but it peeled off after a few hours. The boy came up with the much better idea of using Play-Doh to seal cracks, and for a while it did the trick, but the ants soon found a way in again.

One morning, the girl left a dirty pair of panties on the bathroom floor after her shower, and when I picked them up a few hours later to put them in the laundry basket, I noticed that they were alive with ants. It seemed like a deep violation of some sort, a bad sign. The boy found the phenomenon fascinating; and the girl, hilarious. Over dinner that night, the children reported the incident to their father. I wanted to say that I thought those ominous ants foreshadowed something. But how could I explain that to the family, to anyone, without sounding crazy? So I shared only half my thought:

A catastrophe.

My husband listened to the children's report, nodding, smiling, and then told them that ants, in Hopi mythology, are considered sacred. Ant-people were gods who saved those in the upperworld from catastrophes by taking them down to the underworld, where they could live in peace and freedom until the danger had passed and they were able to return to the upperworld.

Which catastrophe are the ants here to take us away from? the boy asked him.

I thought it was a good question, involuntarily poisonous, perhaps. My husband cleared his throat but didn't answer. Then the girl asked:

What's a catastrophe?

Something very bad, the boy said.

She sat silent for a moment, looking at her plate in deep concentration and pressing the back of her fork against her rice to flatten it down. Then, looking up at us again, very serious, she delivered a strange agglutination of concepts, as if the spirit of some nineteenth-century German hermeneutist had possessed her:

The ants, they come marching in, eat my upperworldpanties, they take us where there's no catastrophes, just good trophies and tooshiefreedom.

Children's words, in some ways, are the escape route out of family dramas, taking us to their strangely luminous underworld, safe from our middle-class catastrophes. From that day on, I think, we started allowing our children's voices to take over our silence. We allowed their imaginations to alchemize all our worry and sadness about the future into some sort of redeeming delirium: tooshiefreedom!

Conversations, in a family, become linguistic archaeology. They build the world we share, layer it in a palimpsest, give meaning to our present and future. The question is, when, in the future, we dig into our intimate archive, replay our family tape, will it amount to a story? A soundscape? Or will it all be sound rubble, noise, and debris?

## PASSING STRANGERS

There's a part in Walt Whitman's *Leaves of Grass* that used to be a kind of ur-text or manifesto for my husband and me when we were still a new couple, still imagining and working out our future together. It begins with the lines:

> *Passing stranger! you do not know how longingly I look upon*
>   *you,*
> *You must be he I was seeking, or she I was seeking, (it comes to*
>   *me as of a dream,)*
> *I have somewhere surely lived a life of joy with you,*
> *All is recall'd as we flit by each other, fluid, affectionate, chaste,*
>   *matured,*
> *You grew up with me, were a boy with me or a girl with me,*
> *I ate with you, and slept with you . . .*

The poem explained, or so we thought, why we had decided to devote our lives, alone but together, to recording the sounds of strangers. Sampling their voices, their laughter, their breathing, despite the fleetingness of the encounters we had with each of them, or perhaps on account of that very fleetingness, we were offered an intimacy like no other: an entire life lived parallel, in a flash, with that stranger. And recording sound, we thought, as opposed to filming image, gave us access to a deeper, always invisible layer of the human soul, in the same way that a bathymetrist has to take a sounding of a body of water in order to properly map the depth of an ocean or a lake.

That poem ends with a vow to the passing stranger: "I am to see to it that I do not lose you." It's a promise of permanence: this fleeting moment of intimacy shared between you and me, two strangers, will leave a trace, will reverberate forever. And in many ways, I think we kept that promise with some of the strangers we encountered and recorded over the years—their voices and stories always coming back to haunt us. But we never imagined that that poem, and especially that last line, was also a sort of cautionary tale for us. Committed as we were to collecting intimacies with strangers, devoted as we were to listening so attentively to their voices, we never suspected that silence would slowly grow between the two of us. We never imagined that one day, we would somehow have lost each other amid the crowd.

## SAMPLES & SILENCE

After all that time sampling and recording, we had an archive full of fragments of strangers' lives but had close to nothing of our own lives together. Now that we were leaving an entire world behind, a world we had built, there was almost no record, no soundscape of the four of us, changing over time: the radio in the early morning, and the last reverberations of our dreams merging with news of crises, discoveries, epidemics, inclement weather; the coffee grinder, hard beans becoming powder; the stove sparking and bursting into a ring of fire; the gurgling of the coffeemaker; the long showers the boy took and his father's insistent "Come on, hurry up, we'll be late"; the paused, almost philosophical conversations between us and the two children on their way to school; the slow, careful steps the boy takes down empty school corridors, cutting class; the metallic screech of subways halting to a stop, and the mostly silent ride on train cars during our daily commutes for field recordings, inside the grid or out into the boroughs; the hum of crowded streets where my husband fished for stray sounds with his boom while I approached strangers with my handheld recorder, and the stream of all their voices, their accents and stories; the strike of a match that lit my husband's cigarette and the long inward hiss of his first inhalation, pulling in smoke through clenched teeth, then the slow relief of an exhalation; the strange white noise that large groups of children produce in playgrounds—a vortex of hysteria, swarming cries—and the perfectly distinct voices of our two children among them; the eerie silence that settles over parks after dusk; the tousle and crackle of dry leaves heaped in mounds at the park where the girl digs for worms, for treasures, for whatever can be found, which is always nothing, because all there is under them are cigarette butts, fossilized dog turds, and miniature ziplock stash bags, hopefully empty; the friction of our coats against the northern gusts come winter; the effort of our feet pedaling rusty bicycles along the river path come spring; the heavy pant of our chests taking in the toxic vapors of the river's gray waters, and the silent, shitty vibes of both the overeager joggers and the stray Canada geese that always overstay their migratory sojourns; the cannonade of instructions and reprimands fired by professional cyclists, all of them geared up, male, and middle-aged: "Move over!" and "Look left!"; and in response to that, our voices either softly mumbling, "Sorry sir, sorry sir," or shouting loud heartfelt insults back at them—always abridged or drowned, alas, by the gushing winds; and finally, all the gaps of sound during our moments spent alone, collecting pieces of the world the way we each know how to gather it best. The sound of everything and everyone that once surrounded us, the noise we contributed, and the silence we leave behind.

## FUTURE

And then the boy turned ten. We took him out to a good restaurant, gave him his presents (no toys). I got him a Polaroid camera and several boxes of film, both black-and-white and color. His father got him a kit for the trip: a Swiss Army knife, a pair of binoculars, a flashlight, and a small compass. At his request, we also agreed to deviate from the planned itinerary and spend the next day, the first of our trip, at Baltimore's National Aquarium. He'd done a school project about Calypso, the five-hundred-pound turtle with a missing front flipper that lives there, and had been obsessed with her ever since.

That night, after dinner, my husband packed his suitcase, I packed mine, and we let the boy and the girl pack theirs. Once the children were asleep, I repacked for them. They'd chosen the most unlikely combinations of things. Their suitcases were portable Duchampian disasters: miniature clothes tailored for a family of miniature bears, a broken light saber, a lone Rollerblade wheel, ziplock bags full of tiny plastic everything. I replaced all of it with real pants, real skirts, real underwear, real everything. My husband and I lined up the four suitcases by the door, plus our seven boxes and our recording materials.

When we'd finished, we sat in our living room and shared a cigarette in silence. I had found a young couple to whom to sublet the apartment for the next month at least, and the place already felt more theirs than ours. In my tired mind, all I could think of was the list of all the relocations that had preceded this one: the four of us moving in together four years ago; my husband's many relocations before that one, as well as my own; the relocations of the hundreds of people and families we had interviewed and recorded for the city soundscape project; those of the refugee children whose story I now was going to try to document; and those of the last Chiricahua Apache peoples, whose ghosts my husband would soon start chasing after. Everyone leaves, if they need to, if they can, or if they have to.

And finally, the next day, after breakfast, we washed the last dishes and left.

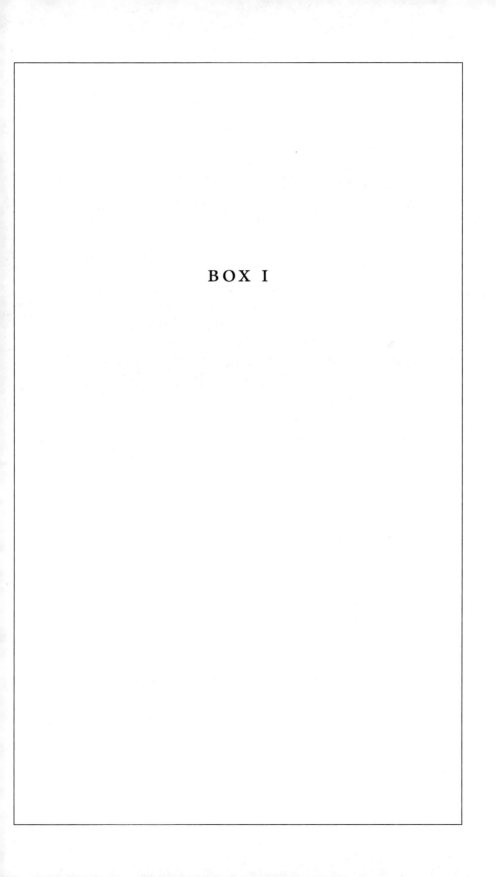

BOX I

§ FOUR NOTEBOOKS (7¾″ x 5″)

"On Collecting"
"On Archiving"
"On Inventorying"
"On Cataloguing"


§ TEN BOOKS


*The Museum of Unconditional Surrender,* Dubravka Ugrešić
*Reborn: Journals and Notebooks, 1947–1963,* Susan Sontag
*As Consciousness Is Harnessed to Flesh: Notebooks and*
    *Journals, 1964–1980,* Susan Sontag
*The Collected Works of Billy the Kid,* Michael Ondaatje
*Relocated: Twenty Sculptures by Isamu Noguchi from Japan,*
    Isamu Noguchi, Thomas Messer, and Bonnie Rychlak
*Radio Benjamin,* Walter Benjamin
*Journal des faux-monnayeurs,* André Gide
*A Brief History of Portable Literature,* Enrique Vila-Matas
*Perpetual Inventory,* Rosalind E. Krauss
*The Collected Poems of Emily Dickinson*


§ FOLDER (FACSIMILE COPIES, CLIPPINGS, SCRAPS)

*The Soundscape,* R. Murray Schafer
Whale sounds charts (in Schafer)
Smithsonian Folkways Recordings World of Sound
    Catalog #1
"Uncanny Soundscapes: Towards an Inoperative Acoustic
    Community," Iain Foreman, *Organised Sound* 16 (03)
"Voices from the Past: Compositional Approaches to Using
    Recorded Speech," Cathy Lane, *Organised Sound* 11 (01)

# ROUTES & ROOTS

*Buscar las raíces no es más que una forma*
*subterránea de andarse por las ramas.*
*(Searching for roots is nothing but a subterranean*
*way of beating around the bush.)*

—JOSÉ BERGAMÍN

*When you get lost on the road*
*You run into the dead.*

—FRANK STANFORD

It's past noon when we finally get to the Baltimore aquarium. The boy escorts us through the crowds and takes us straight to the main pool, where the giant turtle is. He makes us stand there, observing that sad, beautiful animal paddling cyclically around her waterspace, looking like the soul of a pregnant woman—haunted, inadequate, trapped in time. After a few minutes, the girl notices the missing flipper:

Where's her other arm? she asks her brother, horrified.

These turtles only need one flipper, so they evolved to having only one, and that's called Darwinism, he states.

We're not sure if his answer is a sign of sudden maturity that's meant to protect his sister from the truth or a mismanagement of evolutionary theory. Probably the latter. We let it pass. The wall text, which all of us except the girl can read, explains that the turtle lost the flipper in the Long Island Sound, where she was rescued eleven years ago.

Eleven: my age plus one! the boy says, bursting into a flame of enthusiasm, which he normally represses.

Standing there, watching the enormous turtle, it's difficult not to think of her as a metaphor for something. But before I can figure out for what, exactly, the boy starts lecturing us. Turtles like Calypso, he explains, are born on the East Coast and immediately swim out into the Atlantic, all alone. They sometimes take up to a decade to return to coastal waters. The hatchlings start their journey in the east and are then carried by the warm currents of the Gulf Stream into the deep. They eventually reach the Sargasso Sea, which, the boy says, gets its name from the enormous quantities of sargassum seaweed that float there, almost motionless, trapped by currents that circle clockwise.

I've heard that word before, Sargasso, and never knew what it meant. There's a line of an Ezra Pound poem I've never quite understood or remembered the title of: "Your mind and you are our Sargasso Sea." It leaps back to me now, while the boy continues to talk about this turtle and her journey in the North Atlantic seas. Was Pound thinking barren? Was he thinking waste? Or is the image one of ships cutting through centuries of rubbish? Or is it just about human minds trapped in futile cycles of thought, unable to ever free themselves from destructive patterns?

Before we leave the aquarium, the boy wants to take his first Polaroid picture. He makes his father and me stand in front of the main pool, our backs to the turtle. He holds his new camera steady. The girl stands next to him—she, holding an invisible camera—and as we freeze, upright, and smile awkwardly for them, they both look at us as if we were their children and they the parents:

Say cheese.

So we grin and say:

Cheese.

Cheese.

But the boy's picture comes out entirely creamy white, as if he'd documented our future instead of the present. Or maybe his picture is a document not of our physical bodies but of our minds, wandering, oaring, lost in the almost motionless gyre—asking why, thinking where, saying what next?

## M A P S

If we mapped our lives back in the city, if we drew a map of the daily circuits and routines the four of us left behind, it would look nothing like the route map we will now follow across this vast country. Our daily lives back in the city traced lines that branched outward—school, work, errands, appointments, meetings, bookstore, corner deli, notary public, doctor's office—but always those lines circled around, brought back and reunited in a single point at the end of day. That point was the apartment where we had lived together for four years. It was a small but luminous space where we had become a family. It was the center of gravity we had now, suddenly, lost.

Inside the car, although we all sit at arm's length from one another, we are four unconnected dots—each in our seat, with our private thoughts, each dealing silently with our varying moods and unspoken fears. Sunk in the passenger seat, I study the map with the tip of a pencil. Highways and roads vein the enormous piece of paper, folded several times (it's a map of the entire country, too big to be fully unfolded inside the car). I follow long lines, red or yellow or black, to beautiful names like Memphis, to names unseemly— Truth or Consequences, Shakespeare—to old names now resignified by new mythologies: Arizona, Apache, Cochise Stronghold. And when I glance up from my map, I see the long, straight line of the highway thrusting us forward into an uncertain future.

## ACOUSTEMOLOGY

Sound and space are connected in a way much deeper than we usually acknowledge. Not only do we come to know, understand, and feel our way in space through its sounds, which is the more obvious connection between the two, but we also experience space through the sounds overlaid upon it. For us, as a family, the sound of the radio has always charted the threefold transition from sleep, where we were each alone, to our tight togetherness in the early morning, to the wide world outside our home. We know the sound of the radio better than anything. It was the first thing we heard every morning in our apartment in New York, when my husband got out of bed and turned it on. We all heard the sound of it, bouncing off somewhere deep in our pillows and in our minds, and walked slowly from our beds into the kitchen. The morning then filled with opinions, urgency, facts, the smell of coffee beans, and we were all sitting at the table, saying:

Pass the milk.

Here's the salt.

Thank you.

Did you hear what they just said?

Terrible news.

Now, inside the car, when we drive through more populated areas, we scan for a radio signal and tune in. Whenever I can find news about the situation at the border, I raise the volume and we all listen: hundreds of children arriving alone, every day, thousands every week. The broadcasters are calling it an immigration crisis. A mass influx of children, they call it, a sudden surge. They are undocumented, they are illegals, they are aliens, some say. They are refugees, legally entitled to protection, others argue. This law says that they should be protected; this other amendment says that they should not. Congress is divided, public opinion is divided, the press is thriving on a surplus of controversy, nonprofits are working overtime. Everyone has an opinion on the issue; no one agrees on anything.

## PRESENTIMENT, THAT LONG SHADOW

We agree to drive only until dusk that day, and the days that will follow. Never more than that. The children become difficult as soon as the light wanes. They sense the end of daytime, and the presentiment of longer shadows falling on the world shifts their mood, eclipses their softer daylight personalities. The boy, usually so mild in temperament, becomes mercurial and irritable; the girl, always full of enthusiasm and vitality, becomes demanding and a little melancholic.

## JUKEBOXES & COFFINS

The town is called Front Royal, in Virginia. The sun is setting, and white supremacist something is playing full blast in the gas station where we stop to fill the tank. The cashier crosses herself quickly and quietly, avoiding eye contact, when our total comes to $66.60. We had planned to find a restaurant or a diner, but after this, back in the car, we decide we'd rather pass—unnoticed. Less than a mile from the gas station, we find a Motel 6 and pull into the parking lot. Checkout is prepaid, there's coffee in the reception area twenty-four hours a day, and a long, clinical corridor leads to our room. We fetch a few basics from the trunk of the car. When we open the door, we find a room flooded with the kind of light that makes even soulless spaces like this one feel like a lovely childhood memory: flower-stamped bedsheets tucked tight under the mattress, dust particles suspended in a beam of sunlight that comes in through slightly parted green velvet curtains.

The children occupy the space immediately, jump between the

two beds, turn the television on, turn it off, drink water from the tap. For dinner, sitting on the edges of our beds, we eat dry cereal from the box, and it tastes good. When we're done, the children want to take a bath, so I fill the tub halfway for them, and then step outside the room to join my husband, our door left ajar in case one of the kids calls us in. They always need help with all the little bathroom routines. At least as far as it concerns bathroom habits, parenthood seems at times like teaching an extinct, complicated religion. There are more rituals than rationales behind them, more faith than reasons: unscrew the lid off the toothpaste tube like this, squeeze it like that; unroll only this amount of toilet paper, then either fold it this way or scrunch it up like this to wipe; squirt the shampoo into your hand first, not directly on your head; pull the plug to let the water drain only once you're outside the bathtub.

My husband has taken out his recording gear, and is sitting by the door of our room, holding up his boom. I sit next to him quietly, not wanting my presence to modify whatever he's trying to sample. We sit there, cross-legged on the cement floor, resting our backs against the wall. We open beer cans and roll cigarettes. In the room next door, a dog barks relentlessly. From another room, three or four doors down, a man and his teenage daughter appear. He is slow and large; she is toothpick-legged, dressed only in a swimsuit and an unzipped jacket. They walk to a pickup parked in front of their door and step up. When the motor roars, the dog stops barking, then resumes more anxiously. I sip my beer, following the pickup as it drives away. The image of those two strangers—father, daughter, no mother—getting into a pickup and driving together to a possible swimming pool for night practice in some town nearby reminds me of something Jack Kerouac said about Americans: After seeing them, "you end up finally not knowing any more whether a jukebox is sadder than a coffin." Though maybe Kerouac had said it of Robert Frank's pictures in his book *The Americans,* and not of Americans in general. My husband records a few more minutes of the dog barking, until, summoned by the children—in urgent need of help with the toothpaste and towels—we step back inside.

CHECKPOINT

I know I won't be able to sleep, so when the children are finally tucked into bed, I go outside again, walk down the long corridor to our car, and open the trunk. I stand in front of our portable mess, studying the contents of the trunk as if reading an index, trying to decide which page to go to.

Well stacked on the left side of the trunk are our boxes, five of them, with our archive—though it's optimistic to call our collected mess an archive—plus the two empty boxes for the children's future archive. I peek inside Boxes I and II, both my husband's. Some of the books in them are about documenting or about keeping and consulting archives during any documentary process; others are photography books. In Box II, I find Sally Mann's *Immediate Family*. Sitting down on the curbside, I flip through it. I've always liked the way she sees children and what she chooses to see as childhood: vomit, bruises, nakedness, wet beds, defiant gazes, confusion, innocence, untamed wildness. I also like the constant tension in those pictures, a tension between document and fabrication, between capturing a unique fleeting instant and staging an instant. She wrote somewhere that photographs create their own memories, and supplant the past. In her pictures there isn't nostalgia for the fleeting moment, captured by chance with a camera. Rather, there's a confession: this moment captured is not a moment stumbled upon and preserved but a moment stolen, plucked from the continuum of experience in order to be preserved.

It comes to me that maybe, by shuffling around in my husband's boxes like this, once in a while, when he's not looking, and by trying to listen to all the sounds trapped in his archive, I might find a way into the exact story I need to document, the exact form it needs. I suppose an archive gives you a kind of valley in which your thoughts can bounce back to you, transformed. You whisper intuitions and thoughts into the emptiness, hoping to hear something back. And sometimes, just sometimes, an echo does indeed return, a real reverberation of something, bouncing back with clarity when you've finally hit the right pitch and found the right surface.

I search inside my husband's Box III, which at first glance seems like an all-male compendium of "going a journey," conquering and colonizing: *Heart of Darkness, The Cantos, The Waste Land, Lord of the Flies, On the Road, 2666,* the Bible. Among these I find a small white book—the galleys of a novel by Nathalie Léger called *Untitled for Barbara Loden.* It looks a little out of place there, squeezed and silent, so I take it out and head back to the room.

## ARCHIVE

In their beds, they all sound warm and vulnerable, like a pack of sleeping wolves. I can recognize each one by the way they breathe, asleep: my husband next to me, and the two children next to each other in the contiguous double bed. The easiest to make out is the girl, who almost purrs as she sucks arrhythmically at her thumb.

I lie in bed, listening to them. The room is dark, and the light from the parking lot frames the curtains in a whiskey orange. No cars pass on the highway. If I close my eyes, disquieting visions and thoughts churn inside my eye sockets and spill over into my mind. I keep my eyes open and try to imagine the eyes of my sleeping tribe. The boy's eyes are hazel brown, usually dreamy and soft, but can suddenly ignite with joy or rage and blaze, like the meteoric eyes of souls too large and fierce to go gentle—"gentle into that good night." The girl's eyes are black and enormous. Come tears, and a red ring appears instantly around their edges. They are completely transparent in their sudden mood shifts. I think when I was a child, my eyes were like hers. My adult eyes are probably more constant, unyielding, and more ambivalent in their small shifts. My husband's eyes are gray, slanted, and often troubled. When he drives, he looks into the line of the highway like he's reading a difficult book, and furrows his brows. He has the same look in his eyes when he's recording. I don't know what my husband sees when he studies my eyes; he doesn't look very often these days.

I turn on my bedside lamp and stay up late, reading the novel by Nathalie Léger, underlining parts of sentences:

"violence, yes, but the acceptable face of violence, the kind of banal cruelty enacted within the family"

"the hum of ordinary life"

"the story of a woman who has lost something important but does not know exactly what"

"a woman on the run or in hiding, concealing her pain and her refusal, putting on an act in order to break free"

I'm reading the same book in bed when the boy wakes up before sunrise the next morning. His sister and father are still asleep. I have hardly slept all night. He makes an effort to seem like he's been awake for a long time, or like he'd never fallen asleep and we'd been having an intermittent conversation all the while. Wrenching himself up, in a loud, clear voice, he asks what I'm reading.

A French book, I whisper.

What's it about?

Nothing, really. It's about a woman who's looking for something.

Looking for what?

I don't know yet; she doesn't know yet.

Are they all like that?

What do you mean?

The French books you read, are they all like that?

Like what?

Like that one, white and small, with no pictures on the cover.

GPS

This morning we'll drive across the Shenandoah Valley, a place I don't know but had just seen last night—all partial slivers and borrowed memories—through Sally Mann's photographs taken in that same valley.

To appease our children, and fill the winding hours as we make our way up the mountain roads, my husband tells stories about the old American southwest. He tells them about the strategies Chief Cochise used to hide from his enemies in the Dragoon and Chiricahua Mountains, and how, even after he died, he came back to haunt them. People said that, even today, he could be spotted around the Dos Cabezas Peaks. The children listen most attentively when their father tells them about the life of Geronimo. When he speaks about Geronimo, his words perhaps bring time closer to us, containing it inside the car instead of letting it stretch out beyond us like an unattainable goal. He has their full attention, and I listen, too: Geronimo was the last man in the Americas to surrender to the white-eyes. He became a medicine man. He was Mexican by nationality but hated Mexicans, whom Apaches called Nakaiye, "those who come and go." Mexican soldiers had killed his three children, his mother, and his wife. He never learned English. He acted as an interpreter between Apache and Spanish for Chief Cochise. Geronimo was a sort of Saint Jerome, my husband says.

Why Saint Jerome? I ask.

He adjusts his hat and begins to explain something, in professorial detail, about Saint Jerome's translation of the Bible into Latin, until I lose interest, the children fall asleep, and we both fall silent, or perhaps fall into a kind of noise, distracted by sudden demands of the route: highways merging, speed checks, roadwork ahead, dangerous curves, a tollbooth—look for spare change and pass the coffee.

We follow a map. Against everyone's recommendations, we decided not to use a GPS. I have a dear friend whose father worked unhappily in a big company until he was seventy years old and had saved enough money to start his own business, following his one true passion. He opened a publishing house, called The New Frontier, which made thousands of gorgeous little nautical maps, tailored carefully and lovingly for the ships that sailed the Mediterranean. But six months after he opened his company, the GPS was invented. And that was it: an entire life gone. When my friend told me this story, I vowed never to use a GPS. So, of course, we get lost often, especially when we're trying to leave a town. We realize now that for the past hour or so, we've been driving in circles and are back in Front Royal.

STOP

On a road called Happy Creek, we get pulled over by a police car. My husband turns off the engine, takes off his hat, and rolls down his window, smiling at the policewoman. She asks for his license, registration, and proof of insurance. I frown and mumble in my seat, incapable of restraining the visceral, immature way my body responds to any form of reprimand from an authority figure. Like a teenager washing dishes, I reach heavily and wearily into the glove box and collect all the documents the policewoman requests. I slap them into my husband's hands. He, in turn, offers them to her ceremoniously, as if he were giving her hot tea in a porcelain cup. She explains that we've been pulled over because we failed to stop fully at the sign, and she points to it—that bright red octagonal object over there, which clearly pins the intersection between Happy Creek Road and Dismal Hollow Road and signals a very simple instruction: Stop. Only then do I notice this other street, Dismal Hollow Road, its name written in black capital letters on the white aluminum signpost, the name a more accurate label for the place it designates. My husband nods, and nods again, and says, sorry, and again, sorry. The policewoman returns our documents, convinced now we are not dangerous, but before she lets us go, she asks a final question:

And how old are these lovely children, may God bless them?

Nine and five, my husband says.

Ten! the boy corrects him from the backseat.

Sorry sorry sorry, yes, they're ten and five.

I know the girl wants to say something, too, to intervene somehow; I sense it even though I'm not looking at her. She probably wants to explain that soon she will be six instead of five. But she doesn't even open her mouth. Like my husband, and unlike me, she has a deep, instinctive fear of authority figures, a fear that expresses itself in both of them as earnest respectfulness, even submissiveness. In me, this instinct comes out as a sort of defiant defensive unwillingness to admit to an error. My husband knows this, and he makes sure I never talk in situations where we have to negotiate ourselves out of something.

Sir—the policewoman says now—in Virginia, we care for our children. Any child under the age of seven has to ride in a proper booster seat. For the child's safety, may God bless her.

Seven, ma'am? Not five?

Seven, sir.

Sorry, officer, so sorry. I—we—had no idea. Where can we buy a booster seat around here?

Contrary to my expectations, instead of claiming her right to rhetorical usufruct of his admitted wrongs, instead of using his defeat as a trampoline from which to spring her own power into a concrete infliction of punishment, she suddenly parts her lips, layered in bright pink lipstick, and offers a smile. A beautiful smile, in fact—shy but also generous. She gives us directions to a shop, very precise directions, and then, modulating her tone, offers us advice on which exact booster seat to buy: the best ones are the ones without the back part, and we must look for the ones with metal buckles, not plastic. In the end, though, I convince my husband to not stop to buy the booster seat. In exchange, I agree to use the Google Maps GPS, just this once, so we can get out of the maze of this town and back onto a road.

MAP

We drive onward, southwest-bound, and listen to the news on the radio, news about all the children traveling north. They travel, alone, on trains and on foot. They travel without their fathers, without their mothers, without suitcases, without passports. Always without maps. They have to cross national borders, rivers, deserts, horrors. And those who finally arrive are placed in limbo, are told to wait.

Have you heard from Manuela and her two girls, by the way? my husband asks me.

I tell him no, I haven't. Last time I heard from her, right before we left New York, her girls were still at the detention center in New Mexico, waiting either for legal permission to be sent to their mother or for a final deportation order. I've tried to call her a couple of times, but she doesn't pick up. I imagine she's still waiting to hear what will happen to her daughters, hoping they will be granted refugee status.

What does "refugee" mean, Mama? the girl asks from the backseat.

I look for possible answers to give her. I suppose that someone who is fleeing is still not a refugee. A refugee is someone who has already arrived somewhere, in a foreign land, but must wait for an indefinite time before actually, fully having arrived. Refugees wait in detention centers, shelters, or camps; in federal custody and under the gaze of armed officials. They wait in long lines for lunch, for a bed to sleep in, wait with their hands raised to ask if they can use the bathroom. They wait to be let out, wait for a telephone call, for someone to claim or pick them up. And then there are refugees who are lucky enough to be finally reunited with their families, living in a new home. But even those still wait. They wait for the court's notice to appear, for a court ruling, for either deportation or asylum, wait to know where they will end up living and under what conditions. They wait for a school to admit them, for a job opening, for a doctor to see them. They wait for visas, documents, permission. They wait for a cue, for instructions, and then wait some more. They wait for their dignity to be restored.

What does it mean to be a refugee? I suppose I could tell the girl:

A child refugee is someone who waits.

But instead, I tell her that a refugee is someone who has to find a new home. Then, to soften the conversation, distract her from all this, I look for a playlist and press Shuffle. Immediately, like a current sweeping over us, everything is shuffled back into a more light-hearted reality, or at least a more manageable unreality:

Who is singing this fa fa fa fa fa song? the girl asks.

Talking Heads.

Did these heads have any hair?

Yes, of course.

Long or short?

Short.

We're almost out of gas. We need to find a detour, find a town, my husband says, anywhere that we might find a gas station. I take the map out of the glove box and study it.

## CREDIBLE FEAR

When undocumented children arrive at the border, they are subjected to an interrogation conducted by a Border Patrol officer. It's called the credible fear interview, and its purpose is to determine whether the child has good enough reasons to seek asylum in the country. It always includes more or less the same questions:

Why did you come to the United States?

On what date did you leave your country?

Why did you leave your country?

Did anyone threaten to kill you?

Are you afraid to return to your country? Why?

I think about all those children, undocumented, who cross Mexico in the hands of a coyote, riding atop train cars, trying to not fall off, to not fall into the hands of immigration authorities, or into the hands of drug lords who would enslave them in poppy fields, if they don't kill them. If they make it all the way to the US border, they try to turn themselves in, but if they don't find a Border Patrol officer, the children walk into the desert. If they do find an officer or are found by one, they are put in detention and held to an interrogation, asked:

Why did you come to the United States?

Be careful! I shout, looking up from the map toward the road. My husband jerks the steering wheel. The car swerves a little, but he regains control.

Just focus on the map and I'll focus on the road, my husband says, and swipes the back of his hand across his forehead.

Okay, I answer, but you were about to hit that rock, or raccoon, or whatever that was.

Jesus, he says.

Jesus what?

Jesus Fucking Christ, he says.

What?

Just get us to a gas station.

Unplugging her thumb from her mouth, the girl grunts, puffs, and tells us to quit it, punctuating our amorphous, flaky, ungrammatical yapping with the resolve of her suddenly civilized annoyance. Without losing her poise, she sighs a deep, weary period right into our stream of words, clearing her throat. We stop talking. Then, when she knows she has our full, silent, contrite attention, she footnotes a piece of final advice to round up her intervention. She sometimes speaks to us—though she's still only five years old, not even six yet, and still sucks her thumb and occasionally wets her bed—with the same forgiving air psychiatrists exude when they hand out prescriptions to their weak-minded patients:

Now, Papa. I think it's time you smoked another one of your little sticks. And you, Mama, you just need to focus on your map and on your radio. Okay? Both of you just have to look at the bigger picture now.

## QUESTIONS & ANSWERS

No one looks at the bigger map, historical and geographical, of a refugee population's migration routes. Most people think of refugees and migrants as a foreign problem. Few conceive of migration simply as a national reality. Searching online about the children's crisis, I find a *New York Times* article from a couple of years back, titled "Children at the Border." It's an article set up as a Q&A, except the author both asks the questions and replies to them, so perhaps it's not quite a Q&A. To a question about where the children are from, the author answers that three-quarters of them are from "mostly poor and violent towns" in El Salvador, Guatemala, and Honduras. I think of the words "mostly poor and violent towns" and the possible implications of that schematic way of mapping the origins of children who migrate to the United States. These children are utterly foreign to us, they seem to imply. They come from a barbaric reality. These children are also, most probably, not white. Then, after posing the question of why the children are not deported immediately, the reader is told: "Under an anti-trafficking statute adopted with bipartisan support . . . minors from Central America cannot be deported immediately and must be given a court hearing before they are deported. A United States policy allows Mexican minors caught crossing the border to be sent back quickly." That word "allows" in the final sentence. It's as if, in answer to the question "Why are the children not deported immediately?" the author of the article tried to offer relief, saying something like, don't worry, at least we're not keeping the Mexican children, because luckily there's a policy that "allows" us to send them back quickly. Like Manuela's girls, who would have been deported immediately, except some officer had been kind enough to let them pass. But how many children are sent back without even being given a chance to voice their credible or incredible fears?

No one thinks of the children arriving here now as refugees of a hemispheric war that extends, at least, from these very mountains, down across the country into the southern US and northern Mexican deserts, sweeping across the Mexican sierras, forests, and southern rain forests into Guatemala, into El Salvador, and all the way to the Celaque Mountains in Honduras. No one thinks of those children as consequences of a historical war that goes back decades. Everyone keeps asking: Which war, where? Why are they here? Why did they come to the United States? What will we do with them? No one is asking: Why did they flee their homes?

NO  U-TURN

Why can't we just go back home? asks the boy.

He is fidgeting with his Polaroid in the backseat, learning how to handle it, reading the instructions, grunting.

There's nothing to take pictures of anyway, he complains. Everything we pass is old and ugly and looks haunted.

Is that true? Is everything haunted? asks the girl.

No baby, I say, nothing is haunted.

Though perhaps, in a way, it is. The deeper we drive into this land, the more I feel like I'm looking at remains and ruins. As we pass an abandoned dairy farm, the boy says:

Imagine the first person who ever milked a cow. What a strange person.

Zoophilia, I think, but I don't say it. I don't know what my husband thinks, but he doesn't say anything either. The girl suggests that maybe that first cow milker thought that if he pulled hard enough— down there—the bell around the cow's neck would ding-dong.

Chime, the boy corrects her.

And then suddenly milk came out, she concludes, ignoring her brother.

Adjusting the mirror, I see her: an ample smile, at once serene and mischievous. A slightly more reasonable explanation comes to me:

Maybe it was a human mother who had no milk to give her baby, so she decided to take it from the cow.

But the children are not convinced:

A mother with no milk?

That's crazy, Mama.

That's preposterous, Ma, please.


PEAKS & POINTS

As a teenager, I had a friend who would always look for a high spot whenever she had to make a decision or understand a difficult problem. A rooftop, a bridge, a mountain if available, a bunk bed, any kind of height. Her theory was that it was impossible to make a good decision or come to any relevant conclusion if you weren't experiencing the vertiginous clarity that heights impose on you. Perhaps.

As we climb the mountain roads of the Appalachians, I can think more clearly, for the first time, about what has been happening to us as a family—to us as a couple, really—over the last months. I suppose that, over time, my husband started feeling that all our obligations as a couple and as a family—rent, bills, medical insurance—had forced him to take a more conventional path, farther and farther away from the kind of work he wanted to devote his life to. And that, some years later, it finally became clear to him that the life we'd made together was at odds with what he wanted. For months, trying to understand what was happening to us, I felt angry, blamed him, thought he was acting on whimsy—for novelty, for change, for other women, for whatever. But now, traveling together, physically closer than ever before but far from the scaffolding that had sustained the daily work in progress of our familial world and distanced from the project that had once brought us together, I realize I had been accumulating similar feelings. I needed to admit my share: although I hadn't lit the match that started this fire, for months I had been leaving a trail of dry debris that was now fueling it.

The speed limit on the roads across the Appalachians is 25 miles per hour, which irritates my husband but which I find ideal. Even at this speed, though, it took me a few hours to notice that the trees along the mountain path are covered in kudzu. We had passed acres of woodland blanketed in it on our way up toward this high valley, but only now do we see it clearly. My husband explains to the children that kudzu was brought over from Japan in the nineteenth century, and that farmers were paid by the hour to plant it on harvested soil, in order to control erosion. They went overboard, though, and eventually the kudzu spread across the fields, crept up the mountains, and climbed up all the trees. It blocks the sunlight and sucks out all the water from them. The trees have no defense mechanism. From the higher parts of the mountain road, the sight is terrifying: like cancerous marks, patches of yellowing treetops freckle the forests of Virginia.

All those trees will die, asphyxiated, sucked dry by this bloody rootless creeper, my husband tells us, slowing down as we hit a curve.

But so will you, Pa, and all of us, and everyone else, the boy says.

Well, yes, his father admits, and grins. But that's not the point.

Instructively, the girl then informs us:

The point is, the point is, the point is always pointy.


VALLEYS

We wind up and down the narrow, sinuous road, across the Blue Ridge Mountains, and head west into a narrow valley cradled between two arms of the range, once more looking for a gas station. When we start to lose signal again, I turn off the radio, and the boy asks his father for stories, stories of the past in general. The girl interrupts now and then, asks him very concrete questions.

What about Apache girls? Did they exist?

What do you mean? he says.

You only talk about Apache men, and sometimes Apache boys, so were there any girls?

He thinks for a moment, and finally says:

Of course. There's Lozen.

He tells her that Lozen was the best Apache girl, the bravest. Her name meant "dexterous horse thief." She grew up during a tough time for the Apaches, after the Mexican government had placed a bounty on Apache scalps, and paid large sums for their long black hair. They never got Lozen's, though; she was too quick and too smart.

Did she have long or short hair?

She wore her hair in two long braids. She was known to be a clairvoyant, who knew when danger was upon her people and always steered them out of trouble. She was also a warrior, and a healer. And when she got older, she became a midwife.

What's a midwife? the girl asks.

Someone who delivers babies, says my husband.

Like the postwoman?

Yes, he says, like the postwoman.


FOOTPRINTS

In the first town we pass through, deep into Virginia, we see more churches than people, and more signs for places than places themselves. Everything looks like it's been hollowed out and gutted from the inside out, and what remains are only the words: names of things pointing toward a vacuum. We're driving through a country made up only of signs. One such sign announces a family-owned restaurant and promises hospitality; behind it, nothing but a dilapidated iron structure beams beautiful in the sunlight.

After miles of passing abandoned gas stations, bushes sprouting through every crack in the cement, we come to one that seems only partly abandoned. We park next to the single operational fuel dispenser and step out of the car to stretch our legs. The girl stays inside, seeing her chance to sit behind the wheel while my husband fills the tank. The boy and I fiddle with his new camera outside.

What am I supposed to do? he asks.

I tell him—trying to translate between a language I know well and a language I know little about—that he just needs to think of photographing as if he were recording the sound of an echo. But in truth, it's difficult to draw parallels between sonography and photography. A camera can capture an entire portion of a landscape in a single impression; but a microphone, even a parabolic one, can sample only fragments and details.

What I mean, Ma, is what button do I press and when?

I show him the eyepiece, lens, focus, and shutter, and as he looks around the space through the eyepiece, I suggest:

Maybe you could take a picture of that tree growing out through the cement.

Why would I do that?

I don't know why—just to document it, I guess.

That doesn't even mean anything, Ma, document it.

He's right. What does it mean to document something, an object, our lives, a story? I suppose that documenting things—through the lens of a camera, on paper, or with a sound recording device—is really only a way of contributing one more layer, something like soot, to all the things already sedimented in a collective understanding of the world. I suggest we take a picture of our car, just to try out the camera again and see why the pictures are coming out all hazy white. The boy holds the camera in his hands like a soccer ball about to be kicked by an amateur goalkeeper, peeks into the eyepiece, and shoots.

Did you focus?

I think so.

Was the image clear?

Kind of, yes.

It's no use; the Polaroid comes out blue and then slowly turns creamy white. He claims the camera is broken, has a factory error, is probably just a toy camera, not a real camera. I assure him it's not a toy, and suggest a theory:

Perhaps they're coming out white not because the camera is broken or just a toy camera but because what you're photographing is not actually there. If there's no thing, there's no echo that can bounce off it. Like ghosts, I tell him, who don't appear in photos, or vampires, who don't appear in mirrors, because they're not actually there.

He's not impressed, not amused, doesn't find my echo-thing the-ory convincing, or even funny. He shoves the camera into my belly and jumps back into his seat.

Back in the car, the discussion about the problem with the pic-tures continues for a little longer, the boy insisting I've given him a broken camera, useless. The boy's father tries to chime in, mediat-ing. He tells the boy about Man Ray's "rayographs," and the strange method with which Ray composed them, without a camera, plac-ing little objects like scissors, thumbtacks, screws, or compasses directly on top of photosensitive paper and then exposing them to light. He tells him how the images Ray created with this method were always like the ghostly traces of objects no longer there, like visual echoes, or like footprints left in the mud by someone who'd passed by long ago.

NOISE

In the late hour, we reach a village perched high in the Appala-chians. We decide to stop. The children have started to behave like nasty medieval monks in the car—playing disquieting verbal games in the backseat, games that involve burying each other alive, killing cats, burning towns. Listening to them makes me think that the theory of reincarnation is accurate: the boy must have hunted witches in Salem in the 1600s; the girl must have been a fascist sol-dier in Mussolini's Italy. History is playing out in them, repeating itself in microscales.

Outside the only grocery store in the village, a sign announces: Cottage Rentals. Ask Inside. We rent a cottage, small but com-fortable, removed from the main road. That night, in bed, the boy has an anxiety attack. He doesn't call it that, but he says he can't breathe properly, says his eyes won't stay shut, says he can't think in a straight line. He calls me to his side:

Do you really think that some things aren't there? he asks. That we see them but they're not actually there?

What do you mean?

You said so earlier.

What did I say?

You said what if I see you and this room and everything else but nothing is really here, so it can't make echoes, so it can't be photographed.

I was only joking, love.

Okay.

Go to sleep, all right?

Okay.

Later that night, I stand in front of the open trunk of our car with a flashlight, just staring, trying to pick a box to open—a box in which I will find a book to also open and read. I need to think about my sound project, and reading others' words, inhabiting their minds for a while, has always been an entry point to my own thoughts. But where to start? Standing in front of the seven bankers boxes, I wonder what any other mind might do with that same collection of bits and scraps, now temporarily archived in a given order inside those boxes. How many possible combinations of all those documents were there? And what completely different stories would be told by their varying permutations, shufflings, and reorderings?

In my husband's Box II, under some notebooks, there's a book titled *The Soundscape,* by R. Murray Schafer. I remember reading it many years ago and understanding only a meager portion of it but understanding at least that it was a titanic effort, possibly in vain, to organize the surplus of sound that human presence in the world had created. By separating and cataloging sounds, Schafer was trying to get rid of noise. Now I flip through the pages—full of difficult graphs, symbolic notations of different types of sounds, and a vast inventory that catalogs the sounds of what Schafer referred to as the World Soundscape Project. The inventory ranges from "Sounds of Water" and "Sounds of Seasons," to "Sounds of the Body" and "Domestic Sounds," to "Internal Combustion Engines," "Instruments of War and Destruction," and "Sounds of Time." Under each of these categories, there is a list of particulars. For example, under "Sounds of the Body" there is: heartbeat, breathing, footsteps, hands (clapping, scratching, etc.), eating, drinking, evacuating, lovemaking, nervous system, dream sounds. At the very end of the inventory is the category "Sound Indicators of Future Occurrences." But, of course, there are no particulars listed under it.

I put the book back in its box and open Box I, digging around inside it carefully. I take out a brown notebook, on the first page of which my husband has written "On Collecting." I jump to a random page and read a note: "Collecting is a form of fruitful procrastination, of inactivity pregnant with possibility." A few lines down there's a quote copied from a book by Marina Tsvetaeva: "Genius: the highest degree of being mentally pulled to pieces, and the highest of being—collected." The book, *Art in the Light of Conscience,* belongs to me, and that sentence was probably something I once underlined. Seeing it there, in his notebook, feels like a mental petty theft, like he's snatched an inner experience of mine and made it his own. But I'm somehow proud of being looted. Finally, from the box, though it's unlikely that it'll help me think about my sound project or about soundscaping in general, I take Susan Sontag's *Reborn: Journals & Notebooks, 1947–1963.*

## CONSCIOUSNESS & ELECTRICITY

I stay up on the porch outside the cottage, reading Sontag's journals. My arms and legs, a feast for the mosquitoes. Above my head, beetles smack their stubborn exoskeletons against the single lightbulb; white moths spiral up around its halo, then plummet down. A small spider spins a trap in the intersection of a beam and a column. And in the distance, a redeeming constellation of fireflies—intermittent—landscapes the dark immensity beyond the rectangle of the porch.

I don't keep a journal. My journals are the things I underline in books. I would never lend a book to anyone after having read it. I underline too much, sometimes entire pages, sometimes with double underline. My husband and I once read this copy of Sontag's journals together. We had just met. Both of us underlined entire passages of it, enthusiastically, almost feverishly. We read out loud, taking turns, opening the pages as if consulting an oracle, legs naked and intertwined on a twin bed. I suppose that words, timely and arranged in the right order, produce an afterglow. When you read words like that in a book, beautiful words, a powerful but fleeting emotion ensues. And you also know that soon, it'll all be gone: the concept you just grasped and the emotion it produced. Then comes a need to possess that strange, ephemeral afterglow, and to hold on to that emotion. So you reread, underline, and perhaps even memorize and transcribe the words somewhere—in a notebook, on a napkin, on your hand. In our copy of Sontag's journals, underlined once, twice, sometimes boxed-in and marked at the margins:

> "One of the main (social) functions of a journal or diary is precisely to be read furtively by other people, the people (like parents & lovers) about whom one has been cruelly honest only in the journal."
> "In a time hollowed out by decorum, one must school oneself in spontaneity."
> "1831: Hegel died."
> "We sit in this rat hole on our asses growing eminent and middle-aged . . ."
> "Moral bookkeeping requires a settling of accounts."
> "In marriage, I have suffered a certain loss of personality—at first the loss was pleasant, easy . . ."
> "Marriage is based on the principle of inertia."
> "The sky, as seen in the city, is negative—where the buildings are not."
> "The parting was vague, because the separation still seems unreal."

This last line is underlined in pencil, then circled in black ink, and also flagged in the margin with an exclamation mark. Was it me or him who underlined it? I don't remember. I do remember, though, that when I read Sontag for the first time, just like the first time I read Hannah Arendt, Emily Dickinson, and Pascal, I kept having those sudden, subtle, and possibly microchemical raptures—little lights flickering deep inside the brain tissue—that some people experience when they finally find words for a very simple and yet till then utterly unspeakable feeling. When someone else's words enter your consciousness like that, they become small conceptual light-marks. They're not necessarily illuminating. A match struck alight in a dark hallway, the lit tip of a cigarette smoked in bed at midnight, embers in a dying chimney: none of these things has enough light of its own to reveal anything. Neither do anyone's words. But sometimes a little light can make you aware of the dark, unknown space that surrounds it, of the enormous ignorance that envelops everything we think we know. And that recognition and coming to terms with darkness is more valuable than all the factual knowledge we may ever accumulate.

Rereading passages underlined in this copy of the Sontag journals, finding them once again powerful years later, and reunderlining some—especially the meditations around marriage—I realize that everything I'm reading was written in 1957 or 1958. I count with my fingers. Sontag was only twenty-four then, nine years younger than I am now. I am suddenly embarrassed, like I've been caught laughing at a joke before the punch line or have clapped between movements at a concert. So I skip to 1963, when Sontag has turned thirty-something, is finally divorced, and maybe has more clarity about things present and future. I'm too tired to read on. I mark the page, close the book, turn off the porch light—mobbed with beetles and moths—and head to bed.


ARCHIVE

I wake up early the next morning in the cottage and make my way to the kitchen and living room area. I open the door to the porch, and the sun is rising behind the mountain. For the first time in years, there are slices of our private space that I'd like to record, sounds that I again feel an impulse to document and store. Perhaps it's just that new things, new circumstances, have an aura of things past. Beginnings get confused with endings. We look at them the way a goat or a skunk might stare stupidly toward a horizon where there's a sun, not knowing if the yellow star there is rising or setting.

I want to record these first sounds of our trip together, maybe because they feel like the last sounds of something. But at the same time I don't, because I don't want to interfere with my recording; I don't want to turn this particular moment of our lives together into a document for a future archive. If I could only, simply, underline certain things with my mind, I would: this light coming in through the kitchen window, flooding the entire cottage in a golden warmth as I prepare the coffeemaker; this soft breeze blowing in through the open door and brushing past my legs as I turn on the stove; that sound of footsteps—feet little, bare, and warm—as the girl gets out of bed and approaches me from behind, announcing:

Mama, I woke up!

She finds me standing by the stove, waiting for the coffee to be ready. She looks at me, smiles, and rubs her eyes when I say good morning back to her. I don't know anyone for whom waking up is such good news, such a joyful event. Her eyes are startlingly large, her chest is bare, and her panties are white and puffy, too big around her. Serious and full of decorum, she says:

I have a question, Mama.

What is it?

I want to ask you: Who is this Jesus Fucking Christ?

I don't answer, but I hand her a huge glass of milk.


ORDER

The boy and his father are still asleep, and the two of us—mother, daughter—find a seat on the couch in the cottage's small but luminous living room. She sips her milk and opens her sketchbook. After a few failed attempts at drawing something, she asks me to make four squares for her—two at the top, two at the bottom— and instructs me to label them in this order: "Character," "Setting," "Problem," "Solution." When I finish labeling the four squares and ask what they're for, she explains that at school, they taught her to tell stories this way. Bad literary education begins too early and continues for way too long. I remember how one day, when the boy was in second grade and I was helping him with homework, I suddenly realized he probably didn't know the difference between a noun and a verb. So I asked him. He looked up at the ceiling theatrically, and after a few seconds said yes, of course he knew: nouns were the letters on the yellow cards above the blackboard, and verbs were the ones on the blue cards below the blackboard.

The girl concentrates on her drawing now, filling in the squares I made for her. I drink my coffee, and open Sontag's journals again, rereading loose lines and words. Marriage, parting, moral book-keeping, hollowed out, separation: Did our underlining these words foreshadow it? When did the end of us begin? I cannot say when or why. I'm not sure how. When I told a couple of friends, shortly before the four of us went on this trip, that my marriage was possibly ending, or at least was in a moment of crisis, they asked:

What happened?

They wanted a precise date:

When did you realize, exactly? Before this or after that?

They wanted a reason:

Politics? Boredom? Emotional violence?

They wanted an event:

Did he cheat? Did you?

I'd repeat to all of them that no, nothing had happened. Or rather, yes, everything they listed had probably happened, but that wasn't the problem. Still, they insisted. They wanted reasons, motivations, and especially, they wanted a beginning:

When, when exactly?

I remember going to the supermarket one day shortly before we left on this trip. The boy and girl were arguing over the better flavor of some squeezable pureed snack. My husband was complaining about my particular choice of something, maybe milk, maybe detergent, maybe pasta. I remember imagining, for the first time since we had moved in together, how it would be to shop for just the girl and me, in a future where our family was no longer a family of four. I remember my feeling of remorse, almost instant, at having the thought. Then a much deeper feeling—maybe a blow of nostalgia for the future, or maybe the inner vacuum of melancholia, sucking up presentness and spreading absence—as I placed the shampoo the boy had chosen on the conveyer belt, vanilla scented for frequent use.

But surely it was not that day, in that supermarket, that I understood what was happening to us. Beginnings, middles, and ends are only a matter of hindsight. If we are forced to produce a story in retrospect, our narrative wraps itself selectively around the elements that seem relevant, bypassing all the others.

The girl is finished with her drawing and shows it to me, full of satisfaction. In the first square, she has drawn a shark. In the second, a shark surrounded by other sea animals and algae, the surface of the water above them, the sun at the very top in a distant corner. In the third square, a shark, still in the water, looking distraught and facing a kind of underwater pine tree. In the fourth and last square, a shark biting and possibly eating another big fish, maybe also a shark.

So what's the story? I ask.

You tell it, Mama, you guess.

Well, first there is a shark; second, he's in the sea, where he lives; third, the problem is there's only trees to eat, and he's not a vegetarian because he's a shark; and fourth, finally, he finds food and eats it up.

No, Mama. All wrong. Sharks don't eat sharks.

Okay. So what's the story? I ask her.

The story is, character: a shark. Setting: the ocean. Problem: the shark is feeling sad and confused because another shark bit him, so he goes to his thinking-tree. Solution: he finally figures it out.

Figures what out? I ask her.

That he just has to bite the other shark back for biting him!

## CHAOS

The boy and his father finally wake up, and over breakfast, we discuss plans. My husband and I decide we need to get going again. The children complain, say they want to stay longer. This isn't a normal vacation, we remind them; even if we can stop and enjoy things once in a while, the two of us have to work. I have to start recording material about the crisis at the southern border. From what I can gather by listening to the radio and fishing for news online whenever I can, the situation is becoming graver by the day. The administration, backed by the courts, has just announced the creation of a priority docket for undocumented minors, which means that the children who are arriving at the border will get priority in being deported. Federal immigration courts will process their cases before any others, and if they don't find a lawyer to defend them within the impossibly narrow span of twenty-one days, they will have no chance, and will receive a final removal order from a judge.

I don't say all that to our children, of course. But I do tell the boy that what I'm working on is time sensitive, and I need to get to the southern border as quickly as possible. My husband says he wants to get to Oklahoma—where we will visit an Apache cemetery—as soon as possible. Sounding like a 1950s suburban housewife, the boy tells us that we're always "putting work before family." When he's older, I tell him, he'll understand that the two things are inseparable. He rolls his eyes, tells me I'm predictable and self-involved—two adjectives I've never heard him use before. I reprimand him, tell him he and his sister have to do the breakfast dishes.

Do you remember when we had other parents? he asks her as they start with the dishes and we start packing up.

What do you mean? she answers, confused, passing him the liquid soap.

We had parents, once upon a time, better than these ones that we have now.

I listen, wonder, and worry. I want to tell him that I love him, unconditionally, that he does not have to demonstrate anything to me, that I'm his mother and want him near me, always, that I also need him. I should tell him all that, but instead, when he gets like this, I grow distant, circumspect, and maybe even unbiologically cold. It exasperates me not to understand how to ease his anger. I usually externalize my messy emotions, scolding him for little things: put on your shoes, brush your hair, pick up that bag. Most of the time, his father also turns his own exasperation inward, but he doesn't scold him; doesn't say or do anything. He just becomes passive—a sad spectator of our family life, like he's watching a silent movie in an empty theater.

Outside the cottage, as we make final preparations to leave, we ask the boy to help reorganize the things in the trunk, and he throws a bigger tantrum. He screams horrible things, wishing he belonged to a different world, a better family. I think he thinks we are here, in this world, to thrust him toward unhappiness: eat this fried egg you hate the texture of; let's go, hurry up; learn to ride this bicycle that you fear; wear these pants that we bought just for you even though you don't like them—they were expensive, so be grateful; play with that boy in the park who offers you his ephemeral friendship and his ball; be normal, be happy, be a child.

He screams louder and louder, wishing us gone, wishing us dead, kicking the car's tires, tossing rocks and gravel into the air. When he spins off into a spiral of rage like this, his voice sounds distant to me, remote, foreign, as if I were listening to it on an old analog recorder, through metal wires and across static, or as if I were a line operator listening to him in a faraway country. I recognize the familiar ring of his tone somewhere in the background, but I cannot tell whether he is reaching out to us in a desire to make contact, yearning for our love and undivided attention, or if he is somehow telling us to stay away, to fuck off from his ten years of life in this world and let him grow out of our little circle of familial ties. I listen, wonder, and worry.

The tantrum continues, and his father finally loses patience. He walks over to him, grabs him firmly by the shoulders, and shouts. The boy wriggles out of his clutch and kicks his father in the ankles and knees—not kicks intended to harm or hurt, but kicks nonetheless. In response, his father takes off his hat, and with it, smacks him twice, maybe three times, on the butt. Not a painful punishment, but a humiliating one, for a ten-year-old: a hat-spanking. What follows is expected but also disarming: tears, sniffing, deep breaths, and stuttered words like okay, sorry, fine.

When the boy has at last calmed down, his sister walks up to him, and with a little hopefulness and a little hesitancy, asks him if he wants to play with her for a while. She needs him to confirm to her that they still share a world. That they are together in this world, inextricably bound, beyond their two parents and their flaws. The boy turns her away at first, gently but firmly:

Just give me a moment.

Yet in the end, he's still small, still susceptible to our fragile, private family mythologies. So when his father suggests we delay our departure so that they can all play the Apache game before we leave, the boy is overcome by a deep, primal happiness. He collects feathers, prepares his plastic bow and arrow, dresses his sister up as an Indian princess, taking care to tie a cotton belt around her head, not too tight and not too loose, and then runs around in circles howling like a madchild, wild and unburdened. He fills our life with his breath, with his sudden warmth, with his particular way of exploding into roaring laughter.

ARCHIVE

In the slow float of midmorning light, the children play the Apache game with their father. The cottage is at the crest of a hill in a high valley that undulates down toward the main road, invisible to us. No houses can be seen, just farmland and grassland, sprinkled here and there with wildflowers we do not know the names of. They are white and violet, and I make out a few orange patches. Farther away in the distance, a confederacy of cows grazes, looking quietly conspiratorial.

From what I can make out, sitting on the porch bench, the game consists of nothing more than collecting little sticks from the forest proper, bringing them back, and fixing them into the ground one next to the other. Intermittently, little disputes spice the game: the girl suddenly says she wants to be a cowgirl, not an Indian princess, not any type of princess. My husband tells her this game has no white-eyes. They quarrel. In the end, she agrees hesitantly. She'll carry on being an Apache, but only if she can be Lozen and if she's still allowed to wear that cowgirl hat we found in the cottage, instead of the ribbon, which keeps slipping off.

I sit on the porch, half reading my book, looking up at the three of them now and then. They look memorable from where I'm sitting; look like they should be photographed. I almost never take pictures of my own children. They hate being in pictures and always boycott the family's photographic moments. If they are asked to pose for a portrait, they make sure their disdain is apparent, and fake a wide, cynical smile. If they are allowed to do as they please, they make porcine grimaces, stick out their tongues, contort themselves like Hollywood aliens in midseizure. They rehearse antisocial behaviors in general. Maybe it's the same with all children. Adults, on the contrary, profess almost religious reverence toward the photographic ritual. They adopt solemn gestures, or calculate a smile;

they look toward the horizon with patrician vanity, or into the lens of the camera with the solitary intensity of porn stars. Adults pose for eternity; children for the instant.

I step back into the cottage to look for the Polaroid and the instruction booklet. I'd promised the boy I'd study them, because surely we were doing something wrong if the camera was indeed real yet his pictures still came out all white. I find them both—camera, instructions—in his backpack, among little cars, rubber bands, comics, his shiny red Swiss Army knife. Why is it that looking through someone's things is always somehow so sad and also endearing, as if the deep fragility of the person becomes exposed in their absence, through their belongings? I once had to look for an ID my sister had forgotten in her drawer and was suddenly wiping away tears with my sleeve as I went through her well-ordered pencils, colored clips, and random Post-it notes addressed to herself—visit Mama this week, talk more slowly, buy flowers and long earrings, walk more often. Impossible to know why items like these can reveal such important things about a person; and difficult to understand the sudden melancholy they produce in that person's absence. Perhaps it's just that belongings often outlive their owners, so our minds can easily place those belongings in a future in which their owner is no longer present. We anticipate our loved ones' future absence through the material presence of all their random stuff.

Back on the porch, I study the instruction booklet for the camera. The children and their father are now gathering rocks, which they place between the sticks fixed in the ground, alternating rock, stick, rock. The camera instructions are complicated. New Polaroid film has to be shielded from the light as soon as the photograph is expelled from the exit slide, the booklet explains. Otherwise, the film burns. The children and their father are taking over Texas, defending it from the American army, handing it over to their Apache fellows, and fencing it off, rock, stick, rock. Color film takes thirty minutes to develop; black-and-white film takes ten. During this time, the picture has to remain horizontal and in total darkness. A single ray of light will leave a trace, an accident. The instructions recommend keeping a developing Polaroid picture inside a special black-box, available from the store. Otherwise, it can be placed between the pages of a book and kept there until all its colors and shades are fully fixed.

I don't have a special black-box, of course. But I have a book, Sontag's journals, which I can leave open by my side and where I can place the Polaroid as soon as it comes out of the camera. I flip the book open to a random page, in preparation: page 142. Before I lay the book back down next to me, I read a little bit, just to make sure the page I found augurs something good. I've never been able to resist a superstitious impulse to read a page opened at random, any page, as if it were the day's horoscope. One of those coincidences so small, yet so extraordinary: the page before me is a strange mirror of the exact moment I am witnessing. The children are playing the Apache game with their father, and Sontag describes this moment with her son: "At 5:00 David cried out—I dashed to the room & we hugged & kissed for an hour. He was a Mexican soldier (& therefore so was I); we changed history so that Mexico got to keep Texas. 'Daddy' was an American soldier."

I pick up the camera, look around the field through the lens. I finally find the children—focus, refocus, and shoot. As soon as the camera spits out the shot, I take it with my index finger and thumb and tuck it between pages 142 and 143.


DOCUMENT

The picture comes out in shades of brown: sepia, ecru, wheat, and sand. Boy and girl, unaware of me, a few feet from the porch, stand next to a fence. He is holding a stick in his right hand, and she points toward a clearing in the woods behind the cottage, perhaps suggesting they look for more sticks. Behind them is a narrow path, and behind that, a row of trees that follow the declination of the hill from the cottage toward the main road. Though I can't explain exactly why or how, they look as though they're not really there, like they are being remembered instead of photographed.

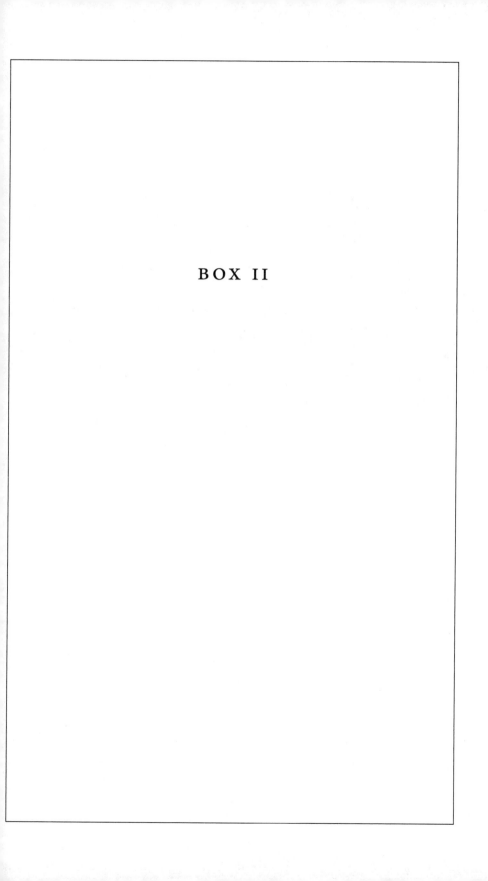

BOX II

§ FOUR NOTEBOOKS (7¾" X 5")

"On Soundscaping"
"On Acoustemology"
"On Documenting"
"On Field Recording"


§ SEVEN BOOKS

*Sound and Sentiment,* Steven Feld
*The Americans,* Robert Frank (introduction by Jack Kerouac)
*Immediate Family,* Sally Mann
*Ilf and Petrov's American Road Trip,* Ilya Ilf and Evgeny
    Petrov
*The Soundscape,* R. Murray Schafer
*A Field Guide to Getting Lost,* Rebecca Solnit
*In the Field: The Art of Field Recording,* Cathy Lane and
    Angus Carlyle, eds.


§ THREE COMPACT DISCS (BOXED SETS)

*Voices of the Rainforest,* Steven Feld
*Lost & Found Sound,* The Kitchen Sisters
*Desert Winds,* Scott Smallwood


§ FOLDER "ABOUT SOUND MAPS"
(NOTES, CLIPPINGS, FACSIMILES)

"Sound Around You" project, University of Salford, UK
*The Soundscape Newsletter,* vols. I–X, World Forum for
    Acoustic Ecology
"NYSoundmap," the New York Society for Acoustic Ecology
"Fonoteca Bahia Blanca," Argentina

# UNDOCUMENTED

An exile feels that the state of exile is a constant, special sensitivity to sound.

—DUBRAVKA UGREŠIĆ

Hearing is a way of touching at a distance.

—R. MURRAY SCHAFER

Inside the car, the air is familiar and the smell our own. As we head southwest across the Appalachians, toward North Carolina, the world outside seems more foreign than ever before. My husband keeps his eyes steady on the road, which winds and curves higher into the mountains, and we all listen to the radio. A boy, maybe nine or ten, judging by the sound of his voice, is being interviewed by a reporter in a detention center in Nixon, Texas.

How did you travel to the United States? the reporter asks.

His voice calm and composed, the boy replies in Spanish, saying that he came on the Bestia. I translate his response for my husband.

Like Manuela's daughters! the boy calls out from the backseat.

That's right, I tell him.

The reporter explains that as many as half a million migrants annually ride on the rooftops of trains, which people call the Bestia, or beast, and says that the boy he's interviewing today lost his little brother on one of those trains. The news report then switches to the boy again. His voice is no longer calm. Now it's breaking, hesitating, trembling. The boy says that his little brother fell off the train shortly before it reached the border. As he begins to explain what happened, exactly, I switch off the radio. I feel a dull, deep nausea—a physical reaction to the boy's story and his voice, but also to the way that news coverage exploits sadness and desperation to give us its representation: tragedy. Our children react violently to the story; they want to hear more but also don't want to hear more. They won't stop asking:

What happened next?

What happened to the little boy?

To distract them, my husband tells them Apache stories, tells them about how the Chiricahua tribe consisted of four different bands, tells them about the smallest band, which was also one of the most powerful, because it was led by a man who was six and a half feet tall, called Mangas Coloradas.

But did an Apache children band exist? the girl interrupts my husband.

What do you mean?

I mean, did they also have a children band? she says.

The boy rephrases her question, translates for her:

I think she means: Were there any bands that were only made up of children?

Their father, his eyes on the road, takes a sip of coffee from a cardboard cup and hands it over to me to put down again in the cup holder before he replies.

There was one that he knows of, he tells them, his gray eyes trying to find theirs in the rearview mirror. They were called the Eagle Warriors. It was a band of young Apache children led by an older boy. They were fearsome, they lived in the mountains, they ate birds that had fallen from the sky and were still warm, they had the power to control the weather, they could attract rain or push a storm back. He tells the children that these young warriors lived in a place called Echo Canyon, a place where the echoes are so loud and clear that even if you whisper, your voice comes right back to you, crisp.

I don't know if what my husband is telling them is true, but the story resonates with me. I can perfectly imagine the faces of those child warriors as we drive slowly forward across Appalachia. Our children listen to him in silence, looking out the window into the dense forests, possibly also imagining these children warriors. As we turn on a closed curve, the forest clears, and we see a cluster of storm clouds—and intermittent lightning—gathering above the high peaks to the southwest.

## STORIES

Traveling in the tight space of the car, we realize how little we know our two children, even though of course we know them. We listen to their backseat games. They are strangers, especially when we add them together. Boy and girl, two startlingly distinct individuals whom we often just consider a single entity: our children. Their games are random, noisy, uncanny, like a television suffering a high fever.

But now and then they find a better pace, establish a softer energy between them. They talk more slowly, thoughtfully. Sometimes they pick up the lost thread of their father's Apache stories, or of the stories about the children stuck at the border, and enact possible outcomes:

If we are forced to stop hunting wild game, we shall raid their ranches and steal their cows!

Yeah, let's steal the white cows, the white, the white-eyes' cows!

Be careful with bluecoats and the Border Patrol!

We realize then that they in fact have been listening, more attentively than we thought, to the stories of Chief Nana, Chief Loco, Chihuahua, Geronimo—the last of the Chiricahuas—as well as to the story we are all following on the news, about the child refugees at the border. But they combine the stories, confuse them. They come up with possible endings and counterfactual histories.

What if Geronimo had never surrendered to the white-eyes?

What if he'd won that war?

The lost children would be the rulers of Apacheria!

Whenever the boy and girl talk about child refugees, I realize now, they call them "the lost children." I suppose the word "refugee" is more difficult to remember. And even if the term "lost" is not precise, in our intimate family lexicon, the refugees become known to us as "the lost children." And in a way, I guess, they are lost children. They are children who have lost the right to a childhood.

BEGINNINGS

The lost children's stories are troubling our own children. We decide to stop listening to the news, at least when they are awake. We decide to listen, instead, to music. Or, better, to audiobooks.

"When he woke in the woods in the dark and the cold of the night . . . ," says the voice of the man on the car speakers, "he'd reach out to touch the child sleeping beside him." I press Stop as soon as it pauses at the end of the sentence. My husband and I agree that Cormac McCarthy, although we both like him, and even if we especially like *The Road,* seems a little too rough for the children. Also, we agree that whoever is reading for this audiobook version is an actor acting—tries too hard, breathes too loud—instead of a person reading. So I press Stop. Then I scroll down and press Play on another audiobook.

"I came to Comala because I had been told that my father, a man named Pedro Páramo, lived there," a mistranslation of the first line of *Pedro Páramo*—I think Juan Rulfo really writes "because they told me" and not "because I had been told"—that passive voice and that extra layer of pastness blurring the novel's calculated austerity and temporal ambiguity. I scroll down again, then press Play.

"I am an invisible man." It's a barren, perfect first sentence. But no, not Ralph Ellison's *Invisible Man,* either. What we want is to overlay the stretch of the drive ahead with a voice and a narrative that may glove itself upon the landscape, and not something that will jerk our minds elsewhere while we move across this humid entanglement of creepers upon forests. Next. Play.

"In the town there were two mutes, and they were always together." This one I would want to listen to, but I gather no quorum from the two traitors in the backseat. My husband does not want it either, says Carson McCullers's only achievement was that one novel's title and only the title: *The Heart Is a Lonely Hunter.* He is wrong, and I say so, throwing back my disagreement with a little bit of poison, asking him if he doesn't think that first line is exactly about the two of us, and if we might not want to listen to the rest of it as if visiting an oracle. He does not laugh or smile. Next book.

"I first met Dean not long after my wife and I split up." Pause. We discuss this one at greater length. My husband thinks Kerouac's *On the Road* would be a perfect choice. Even if the children won't get the meaning, he says, we can all enjoy the rhythm of it as we drive. I remember reading Kerouac in my early twenties, when I dated a bookseller. He was a Kerouac fan, and gave me all of his books, one by one. I read them like I had to finish an infinite bowl of lukewarm soup. Every time I was about to finish, the bowl would be refilled. Later into my twenties, I reread a few of Kerouac's books, started getting them, and grew to like some things in his prose: his untidy way of tying sentences together, his way of speeding through the story as if he's not imagining or remembering it but catching up with it, and his way of ending paragraphs like he's cheating on a test. But I don't want to give my husband this victory, so I say:

I would rather listen to evangelical radio than to *On the Road.*

Why? he asks.

It's a good question, so I look for a good reason. My sister, who teaches literature in Chicago, always says that Kerouac is like an enormous penis, pissing all over the USA. She thinks that his syntax reads like he's marking his territory, claiming inches by slamming verbs into sentences, filling up all silences. I love that argument, though I don't know if I quite understand it, or if it's even an argument. So I don't put it forward. We're approaching a tollbooth, and I dig around for spare change. We halt, pay a machine—not a person—and drive on. Kerouac's America is nothing like this America, so bony, desolate, and factual. I use the distraction to move beyond our Kerouac discussion, a dead-end street, no doubt. And as we gain speed again, I scroll down and press Play on the next audiobook.

"The boy with fair hair lowered himself down the last few feet of rock and began to pick his way towards the lagoon." After listening to its opening sentence, we all agree: this is it, this is what we'll listen to, *Lord of the Flies,* read by William Golding himself. We know it's no fairy tale, no sugarcoated portrait of childhood, but it's—at least—fiction. Not a fiction that will separate us and the children from reality, but one that might help us, eventually, explain some of it to them.

We listen to the reading for a few hours, and probably take some wrong turns, and get lost for a while, and so we listen to the reading some more, until we cannot listen anymore, cannot drive anymore, cannot sit anymore. We find a motel in a town called Damascus, near the Virginia–Tennessee border. I have no idea why it's called that, but as we pull into the parking lot, and I read a sign that says Free Wi-Fi & Cable TV, it's clear to me that some appropriations of names are more unsettling than others.

Outside the motel room, while the rest prepare for bed, I roll myself a cigarette and try to call Manuela. She doesn't pick up, but I leave a message, asking how things are moving forward with the case, saying please call me when you have some time.

## NARRATIVE ARC

The girl asks the waitress for crayons and paper while we wait for our breakfasts in a diner booth the next morning, and then asks me if I can draw four squares for her, and label them the same way I did in the cottage the other day. I'll do it, I say, but only if she's willing to let me make the game a little more challenging for her.

How? she asks, skeptical.

I'll draw eight squares instead of four, I say, and you figure out what to do with the rest.

She's not convinced, grumbles, crosses her arms and digs her elbows into the table. But when her brother says he wants to try it out, she says:

Okay, fine, fine, fine: eight squares.

My husband reads a newspaper, and the children concentrate on their drawings, piecing together a more difficult plot, working out how to arrange and rearrange information in an eightfold space.

When I sat through courtroom hearings in the New York City Immigration Court, listening to and recording children's testimonies, my recorder on my lap, hidden under a sweater, I felt that I knew exactly what I was doing, and why I was doing it. When I hovered in hallways, offices, or waiting rooms, the recorder in my hand, talking to immigration lawyers, priests, police officers, people in general, sampling the sounds of that raw legal reality, I trusted that I would eventually come to understand how to arrange all the pieces of what I was recording and tell a meaningful story. But as soon as I pressed Stop on my recording device, put all my stuff into my bag, and went back home, all the momentum and certainty I had had slowly dissolved. And when I re-listened to the material, thinking of ways to put it together in a narrative sequence, I was flooded by doubts and problems, paralyzed by hesitance and constant concerns.

The food finally arrives, but the children aren't interested. They are too caught up in working out how to finish their last few squares. I observe them with pride, and maybe a little envy, a childish feeling, wishing I also had a crayon and was participating in the eight-square story game. I wonder how I'd distribute all the concerns I have.

Political concern: How can a radio documentary be useful in helping more undocumented children find asylum? Aesthetic problem: On the other hand, why should a sound piece, or any other form of storytelling, for that matter, be a means to a specific end? I should know, by now, that instrumentalism, applied to any art form, is a way of guaranteeing really shitty results: light pedagogic material, moralistic young-adult novels, boring art in general. Professional hesitance: But then again, isn't art for art's sake so often an absolutely ridiculous display of intellectual arrogance? Ethical concern: And why would I even think that I can or should make art with someone else's suffering? Pragmatic concern: Shouldn't I simply document, like the serious journalist I was when I first started working in radio and sound production? Realistic concern: Maybe it is better to keep the children's stories as far away from the media as possible, anyway, because the more attention a potentially controversial issue receives in the media, the more susceptible it is to becoming politicized, and in these times, a politicized issue is no longer a matter that urgently calls for committed debate in the public arena but rather a bargaining chip that parties use frivolously in order to move their own agendas forward. Constant concerns: Cultural appropriation, pissing all over someone else's toilet seat, who am I to tell this story, micromanaging identity politics, heavy-handedness, am I too angry, am I mentally colonized by Western-Saxon-white categories, what's the correct use of personal pronouns, go light on the adjectives, and oh, who gives a fuck how very whimsical phrasal verbs are?

## COPULA & COPULATION

My husband wants us to listen to Aaron Copland's *Appalachian Spring* while we drive up and down this meandering road through the Cherokee National Forest, toward Asheville, North Carolina. It will be instructive, he says. So I roll down the window, breathe in the thin mountain air, and agree to search for the piece on my phone. When I finally catch some signal, I find a 1945 recording—apparently the original—and press Play.

For miles, as we make our way up to the very cusp of the mountain range and across the skyline drive, we hear *Appalachian Spring* over and over, and then once more. Making me pause, play, and pause again, my husband explains each element of the piece to the children: the tempo, the tonal links between movements, the overall structure of the composition. He tells them it's a programmatic piece, and says it's about white-eyes marrying, reproducing, conquering new land, and then driving Indians out of that land. He explains what a programmatic composition is, how it tells a story, how each section of instruments in the orchestra—woodwinds, strings, brass, percussion—represents a specific character, and how the instruments interact just like people talking, falling in love, fighting, and making up again.

So the wind instruments are the Indians, and the violins are the bad guys? asks the girl.

My husband confirms this, nodding.

But what are the bad guys, Pa, really? she asks him, demanding more details to put all this information together in her little head.

What do you mean?

I mean are they beasts, or cowboys, or monsters, or bears?

Republican cowboys and cowgirls, my husband tells her.

She thinks for a moment as the violins strike a higher pitch, and finally concludes:

Well, I am a cowgirl sometimes, but I'm not ever a Republic.

So, Pa—the boy wants to confirm—this song takes place in these same mountains we are driving through right now, yes?

That's right, his father says.

But then, instead of helping the children understand things in more subtle historical detail, he adds a pedantic coda:

Except it's not called a song. It's just called a piece, or in fact a suite.

And while he explains the exact differences between those three things—song, piece, suite—I stop listening to him and focus on the very cracked screen of my irritating little telephone, where I type in "Copland Appalachian," and find an official-enough-looking page that contradicts my husband's whole story, or at least half of it. Yes, this Copland piece is about people getting married, reproducing, and so on. But it's not at all a political piece about Indians and white-eyes, and the violins in the orchestra are certainly not Republicans. Copland's *Appalachian Spring* is just a ballet about a marriage between two young and hopeful pioneers in the nineteenth century who might—eventually—grow old, and less hopeful. More than a political piece about the two of them fucking Indians over— as was, no doubt, a widespread practice in those times, carried over to today, though in different ways—it's really just a ballet. It's a ballet about two pioneers who (1) privately want to fuck each other, and (2) eventually, and who knows why, publicly want to fuck each other up.

I find a video recording of the ballet, choreographed and danced by Martha Graham. Before it begins, a voice reads these words written by Isamu Noguchi, who designed and sculpted all the props for the choreography: "There is joy in seeing sculpture come to life on the stage in its own world of timeless time. Then the air becomes charged with meaning and emotion, and form plays its integral part in the reenactment of a ritual. Theater is a ceremonial; the performance is a rite." I think of our children, and how they, in their backseat games, constantly reenact bits and pieces of stories they hear. And I wonder what kind of world and what kind of "timeless time" their private performances and rituals bring to life. What is clear to me, in any case, is that everything they reenact in the space of the back of the car indeed charges our world, if not with "meaning and emotion," with a weird electricity.

As her compact, perfect, square little body swiftly dances, Martha Graham narrates the interior lives of the characters using a precise body lexicon—contraction, release, spiral, fall, recovery— threading all her movements into clear phrases. Her phrases are so impeccably danced that they seem to spell out a clear meaning, even when if you try to translate them back into words, that meaning immediately fades away again—as usually happens when anyone tries to explain dance or music.

Gradually, watching this video recording of the ballet and its reenactment of a ritual, I being to understand one of the deeper layers of the story Copland tells in the piece—about how the failure of most marriages can be explained as a change from a regular transitive verb (to fuck the other person) to a phrasal transitive verb (to fuck the other person up). Graham contracts, tucking her pelvis into her torso and spiraling toward the right side of her body. Her shoulders follow the spiral, and she leaves her neck and head behind, in counterpoint to the rest of her mass. Once the body has reached a contortion limit, she lunges forward with her right leg, then pitch-kicks her left leg upward and falls to the ground in a sequence: her outer-step, the first to buffer the weight of the body; then the ankle; then the outer calf muscle; and finally the knee. Her entire torso reacts to the fall, feigning a kind of faint over the bent leg, arms stretched out to her front, body spread out on the brown wooden floor of the stage—a stage decorated sparingly by Noguchi. Her body, in fact, looks like one of Noguchi's later abstractions: a rock that is also a liquid. Now she's beaten, disjointed, entirely fucked up after reenacting the savage daily ritual of a marriage gone sour.

Generosity in marriage, real and sustained generosity, is hard. If it implies accepting that our partner needs to move one step farther away from us, and maybe even thousands of miles away, it's almost impossible. I know I have not been generous with my husband's future project—this idea of his, the inventory of echoes. I have indeed been trying to fuck him up for it, all this time. The problem—my problem—is that I'm probably still in love with him, or at least cannot imagine life without witnessing the everyday choreography of his presence: his distracted, aloof, sometimes reckless but completely charming way of walking around a space when he's collecting sounds and the grave expression on his face when he re-listens to sampled material; his beautiful, brown, bony long legs and slightly curved upper back; the little curly hairs on his nape; and the process, both meticulous and intuitive, by which he makes coffee in the mornings, makes sound pieces, and sometimes makes love to me.

Toward the end of the sequence, Graham contracts to pull herself back to vertical, and just when she's spiraling her right leg forward, using the flat platform of her strong, square foot to prop herself up again, I lose internet signal and can't watch the rest.

## ALLEGORY

We didn't expect what we find when we drive into Asheville later that afternoon. We thought, ignorantly and a little condescendingly, that we were going to a godforsaken little town. Instead, there's a small, buzzing, vibrant city. Walking along the main street, well groomed and lined with saplings, we see storefronts full of possibilities, though I'm not sure of what—possibilities, perhaps, of furnishing imaginary future lives. In the terrace cafés, we see pale young men with long beards, and lovely girls with feathered hair and freckled cleavages. We see them drinking beer from Mason jars, smoking rolled cigarettes, frowning philosophically. They all look like those actors in Éric Rohmer movies, pretending that it's perfectly normal—despite being too beautiful and too young—to be deeply engaged in a discussion about mortality, atheism, mathematics, and possibly Blaise Pascal. Along the sidewalks, we also see languid, camel-faced junkies, holding up cardboard signs and cuddling their robust bulldogs. We see reformed Harleys, crosses hanging heavy on their graying chests. We see big Italian machines in cafés, brewing good coffee. I wonder what kind of rhapsody Thomas Wolfe would compose about Asheville now. Finally, we see a bookstore, and we walk in.

We realize as we cross the threshold that there's a book-club meeting in progress. The four of us assume the silent, respectful role of spectators who have walked into a theater in the play's second act. The two children find small chairs to sit on in the children's section, and my husband concentrates on the history section. I pace slowly around the bookshelves, inching my way toward the book-club meeting. They're discussing a fat volume, placed vertically in the center of the table, like a totem. Stamped on a poster next to the book is the face of a handsome man, too handsome, maybe: tousled hair, a weather-scarred complexion, melancholy eyes, a cigarette tucked between his fingers.

I don't like to admit it, but faces like this one remind me abstractly of a face I once loved, a face of a man I was maybe not loved by in return, but with whom I at least had a beautiful daughter before he disappeared. This face perhaps also reminds me of future men whom I could love and might be loved by but won't have enough lives to try. Past men are the same as possible future men, in any case. Men whose rooms are spartan, whose T-shirts are self-consciously threadbare around the neck, whose handwritten notes are full of small, crooked letters, like battalions of ants trying to line up into meaning, because they never learned good penmanship. Men whose conversation is not always intelligent but is alive. Men who arrive like a natural disaster, then leave. Men who produce a vacuum toward which I somehow tend to gravitate.

Despite the quotidian repetition, says one book-club member, with an air of professorial authority, the author is able to hinge on the value of the real.

Yes, says another book-club attendee, like in the marriage scene.

I agree, says a young woman. It's about carving out everyday detail and finding the kernel of the real in the very heart of boredom. She has hyperthyroidal eyes and bony hands that cling anxiously to her copy of the book.

I think it's more about the impossibility of fiction in the age of nonfiction, says a soft-spoken woman whose contribution passes unacknowledged.

More than a book club, this sounds like a graduate seminar. I understand nothing of what they say. I take a book randomly from the shelf, Kafka's *Diaries*. I open it and read: "October 18, 1917. Fear of night. Fear of night." I think, instantly, I should buy this book, today. Now an older man speaks to the group, sounding as though he's about to offer the conclusive exegesis:

The book presents truth-telling as a commodity, and it questions the exchange value of truth presented as fiction, and conversely, the added value of fiction when it's rooted in truth.

I repeat his sentence in my mind, to maybe understand it better, but I get lost in the "conversely" part. I went to university, though only for a while, with professors who spoke like that. I had to bear their amphetamine-fueled, connect-the-dots, rhizomatic, and thoroughly self-satisfied language. I hated them. But when I peek between the shelves, I notice that the man who said this looks less like a professor and more like the young post-post-Marxist scholars-to-be whom I used to study and sleep with in my brief passage through university, and suddenly I feel a bit nostalgic, perhaps even find him endearing. Another club member continues:

I read in a blog that he became addicted to heroin after he wrote this; is that true?

Some nod. Some sip at their water bottles. Some leaf through their weatherworn copies of the book. The bewildering consensus among them seems to be that the value of the novel they are discussing is that it is not a novel. That it is fiction but also it is not.

I open the *Diaries* again, at random: "My doubts stand in a circle around every word, I see them before I see the word."

I have never asked a bookseller for a book recommendation. Disclosing desires and expectations to a stranger whose only connection to me is, in abstract, the book, seems too much like Catholic confession, if only a more intellectualized version of it. Dear bookseller, I would like to read a novel about the banal pursuit of carnal desire, which ultimately brings unhappiness to the ones who pursue it, and to everyone else around them. A novel about a couple trying to rid themselves of each other, and at the same time trying desperately to save the little tribe they have so carefully, lovingly, and painstakingly created. They are desperate and confused, dear bookseller; don't judge them. I need a novel about two people who simply stop understanding each other, because they have chosen to not understand each other anymore. There should be a man who knows how to untangle his woman's hair but who decides not to one morning, perhaps because now other women's hair has become interesting, perhaps because he has simply grown tired. There should be a woman who leaves, withdrawing either slowly or in a single sad and elegant coup de dés. A novel about a woman who leaves before she loses something, like the woman in Nathalie Léger's novel I'm reading, or like Sontag in her twenties. A woman who begins to fall in love with strangers, possibly only because they are strangers. There is a couple who loses the ability to laugh together. A man and a woman who sometimes hate each other, and will, if they are not stopped short by a better part of themselves, block out the last ray of innocence left in the other. A novel with a couple whose only engaging conversations are about revisiting past misunderstandings, layers and layers of them, all merged into one enormous rock. Dear bookseller, do you know the myth of Sisyphus? Do you have any version of it? An antidote? A piece of advice? A spare bed?

Do you have a good map of the southwestern United States? I finally ask the bookseller.

We buy the map he recommends—detailed and enormous— though we really don't need another map. My husband buys a book on the history of horses, the boy chooses an illustrated edition of Golding's *Lord of the Flies,* as a companion to the audiobook we've been listening to, and the girl, a book called *The Book with No Pictures.* I don't buy Kafka's *Diaries,* but I buy a book of the collected photographs of Emmet Gowin, which I hardly looked through but which was on the last display table before the counter and seemed—suddenly—indispensable. It's too big to store in any of our bankers boxes, so for now it will live under my feet in the passenger's seat. I also buy Marguerite Duras's *The Lover,* which I read when I was nineteen but have never read in English, as well as the screenplay of *Hiroshima Mon Amour,* annotated by Duras with stills from Resnais's film.

POINT OF VIEW

The next day, finally, the boy learns the Polaroid's mechanism. It's almost noon—we overslept and had a big, slow breakfast— and we are in a gas station right outside Asheville. The boy and I are standing next to the car while his father fills up the tank and checks the wheels. From the top of my box, I've grabbed the small red book called *Elegies for Lost Children.* The boy aims, focuses, and shoots, and as soon as the picture slips out, he puts it in between the pages of the book, which I'm holding open for him. We jump back in the car, and for the next ten or fifteen minutes as we drive out of Asheville—taking Route 40 toward Knoxville—the boy sits completely still and silent with the book on his lap, as if he were guarding a sleeping puppy.

As we wait, I flip through the pages of the Emmet Gowin book. A strange emptiness and boredom is why I like his documentation of people and landscapes. I read somewhere, probably in a wall text in a museum, that he used to say that in landscape photography, both the heart and the mind need time to find their proper place. Perhaps because of his strange name, Emmet, I always thought he was a woman, until I knew he was a man. I still liked him after that, though perhaps not as much. I still liked him more than Robert Frank, Kerouac, and everyone else who has attempted to understand this landscape—perhaps because he takes his time looking at things instead of imposing a point of view on them. He looks at people, forgotten and wild, lets them come forth into the camera with all their lust, frustration, and desperation, their crookedness and innocence. He also looks at landscapes, man-made and embellished but somehow also abandoned. The landscapes that he photographs become visible more slowly than his family portraits. They are less immediately compelling and much more subtle. They come into focus only after you have held your breath long enough in front of them, like when we're driving through a tunnel and out of superstition everyone in the car holds their breath and then, when we reach the other side, the world opens up in front of us, immense and ungraspable, and there is a single moment of silence, mindful but without thoughts.

The boy's picture comes out perfectly this time. He hands it to me from the backseat, ecstatic:

Look, Ma!

A perfect little document, rectangular and in sepia: two unleaded gasoline dispensers and, in the background, a row of Appalachian pine trees, no kudzu. An index, not so much of the things photographed but of the instant the boy finally learned to photograph them.

SYNTAX

The peaks of the Great Smoky Mountains are only half visible, looming ghostlike in the distance, covered in a fog that seems to emanate from them. It's early afternoon, and the children are asleep in the backseat. I tell my husband a story about my parents, a story I've heard several times in my life, though only from my mother's viewpoint. The story has always fascinated me. In the early eighties, my parents traveled to India. They were young, they loved each other, they weren't yet married. They had a twenty-four-hour layover in London on their way to Delhi and slept at a friend's house. This friend worked in technology, and he owned a prototype of a compact disc player, which would be released, successfully, on the world market a few years later. The next morning, before they left again for the airport, their friend gave them the compact disc player, a set of headphones, and the single disc he owned. They would return everything on their way back from India—this was the deal.

During the first part of the trip, they didn't use the player, because it would not switch on. Then, in a smoky hotel by the Ganges, in Varanasi—which my parents always still called Benares—my father lay on the cot, fidgeting with the machine until he finally figured out how to make it work. He simply flipped the batteries, aligning pluses and minuses. On their way from Varanasi to Katmandu, on a sleeper bus in which they did not sleep at all, my parents took turns with the machine, listening to the music, ecstatic, looking out the dark window, humming, whistling, pointing, counting stars, maybe, talking extremely loud to the other when wearing the headphones as the bus climbed and climbed. In Katmandu, they hardly used the player—there was too much around them to be listened to, too much to be absorbed, photographed, noted down.

A few days later, they continued from Katmandu to a small town at the foothills of the Himalayas. They camped. They made love—although this is hard for me to picture. They took photos of each other, all of which are still in a chest in a basement somewhere. In front of the great misty mountains early one morning, they made a fire, prepared coffee, and took the compact disc player out of a backpack. They were sitting on a frosty lawn, their backs to the tent, the sun rising in front of them beyond the mountains. First my mother took a turn with the compact disc player, then my father. But then, in the middle of this almost sacred moment they were sharing but maybe not entirely sharing, my father, his eyes closed, uttered a name. It was not the name of my mother, nor of his mother, nor of anyone whose name sounded like anyone's mother's. It was the name of a stranger, the name of a woman, another woman. It was only a word, one small word. But it was so heavy and unexpected, a cold truth falling suddenly from the bright sky, hitting, opening a chasm, parting the earth between them. My mother then snatched the compact disc player from my father's hands, the headphones from his ears, and walked toward some rocks. She threw all of it against those rocks. Wires, pieces, batteries—the compact disc player was destroyed, maimed, mangled, its blameless electronic heart broken to pieces against the Nepalese Himalayas. The disc inside the player survived, intact. I always wonder what they had been listening to at that moment.

And then what happened? my husband asks me.

Nothing. They flew back to London and returned the broken machine to their friend.

But what did they say to him?

No idea. I suppose they just said they were sorry.

And then?

Then they got married, had my sister and me, then eventually got divorced and lived happily ever after.

## RHYTHM & METER

We've finally descended from the Great Smoky Mountains and approach a populated valley. The landscape changes so dramatically, it's hard to believe we're still in the same country, on the same planet. In less than an hour, we've gone from fog-clad peaks and a vast expanse of countless shades of green—hues nuanced toward blues into grays and purples—to a succession of monochrome parking lots, enormous and mostly empty, surrounding their respective motels, hotels, diners, supermarkets, and drugstores (the ratio of parking space to space for human bodies bewilderingly biased in favor of the former). We make a quick stop for a late lunch in a place called Dolly Parton's Stampede, and make sure to leave before the start of their afternoon show, which, according to the menu, features music, comedy, pyrotechnics, and live animals.

Back in the car, the children demand that we play an audiobook. The boy wants to continue listening to *Lord of the Flies*. "When he woke in the woods in the dark and the cold of the night . . . ," says

the voice of the man in the car speakers, every time, when I connect
my phone to the sound system. I guess it's because that book is at
the top of the playlist, but I can't figure out why it just starts playing
by itself, like some diabolical toy. The children complain from the
backseat. I press Stop and tell them to be patient with me as I search
for *Lord of the Flies*.

The girl says she doesn't want to listen to that story anymore, says
she doesn't get it, and that when she does get it, it's too scary anyway. The boy tells her to hush up, and be more mature, and learn
to listen to things. He tells her that *Lord of the Flies* is a classic, and
she needs to understand the classics if she wants to understand anything about anything. I want to ask him why he thinks that, but I
don't, not now. I wonder at times if the children are indeed getting
any of it, or if they're even supposed to get it. Perhaps we expose
them to too much—too much world. And perhaps we expect too
much from them, expect them to understand things that they are
maybe not ready to.

When my husband and I were just beginning to work on the city
soundscape project, four years ago, we interviewed a man named
Stephen Haff. On the ground floor of a building in Brooklyn, this
man had opened up a one-room schoolhouse called Still Waters
in a Storm. His students, immigrants or children of immigrants,
mostly of Hispanic origin, were between five and seventeen years
old, and he taught them Latin, taught them classical music, taught
them how to scan poems and understand rhythm and meter. He'd
helped them, even his youngest ones, learn parts of *Paradise Lost* by
heart and understand it, and was at that time guiding a group of fifteen children in a collective translation, from Spanish into English,
of *Don Quixote*. In their version, though, Don Quixote was not an
old Spanish man but a group of children who had migrated from
Latin America to the United States. It takes courage, and a little
bit of lunacy, to do things like that. But especially, I thought then
and still think now, it takes clarity of mind and humility of heart
to understand that children can indeed read *Paradise Lost,* and
learn Latin, and translate Cervantes. During a sampling session for
the soundscape, my husband and I recorded one of Stephen Haff's
younger students—a little girl, eight or nine years old—while she

argued passionately with the rest over the exact way to translate the words "When life itself seems lunatic, who knows where madness lies? Perhaps to be too practical is madness. To surrender dreams—this may be madness."

I suppose that after listening to her, we both decided, even though we never really spoke about it, that we should treat our own children not as lesser recipients to whom we, adults, had to impart our higher knowledge of the world, always in small, sugar-coated doses, but as our intellectual equals. Even if we also needed to be the guardians of our children's imaginations and protect their right to travel slowly from innocence toward more and more difficult acknowledgments, they were our life partners in conversation, fellow travelers in the storm with whom we strove constantly to find still waters.

Finally, I find the *Lord of the Flies* file and press Play, picking up from where we'd stopped last time. Piggy's glasses are being stepped on, crushed, and without them he's lost: "The world, that understandable and lawful world, was slipping away." As the sun sets and we drive through Knoxville, we decide to sleep in a motel farther away from the city, perhaps midway between Knoxville and Nashville. We're world-weary, and we don't want to see too many other people or have to think about how to interact with them.

## CLIMAX

There is never a climax unless there is sex, or unless there's a clear narrative arc: beginning, middle, end.

In our story, there had once been a lot of sex, but never a clear narrative. Now if there's sex, it has to be in motel rooms, where the children are sleeping on the bed next to ours. It feels like singing into a bottle. I don't want to have sex tonight; he does. I will have my period soon, and I was once told by a witch doctor that couples who have sex right before the woman's period later act violently toward each other. So I suggest we play a name game instead. He drops a name of someone we know:

Natalia López.

Okay, Natalia.

Do you like her breasts?

A little.

Just a little?

I adore them.

What are they like?

Fuller than mine, rounder.

Her nipples?

Of a much lighter color than mine.

What do they smell like?

Like skin.

Would you like to touch her now?

Yes.

Where?

Her waist, the little hairs on her coccyx, her inner thighs.

Have you ever kissed her?

Yes.

Where?

On a sofa.

But where on her body?

Face.

What is her face like?

Freckled, angled, bony.

Her eyes?

Small, fierce, honey brown.

Her nose?

Andean.

Mouth?

Monica Vitti.

At the end of the game, he's maybe angry but also turned on, and I am turned on but turned off from him, thinking of another body.

He rolls around to his other side, his back to me now, and I switch on the bedside lamp. I peruse my two new Marguerite Duras books while he wriggles around under the sheet in sporadic, silent complaints. In the English version of *The Lover*, Duras describes her young face as "destroyed." I wonder if it should rather be "dilapidated," "devastated," or even "unmade," like a bed after sex. He tugs at the sheet. I think the French word Duras uses is "défait," unmade, though it could also be "détruit."

I don't think it's true that we really come to know and memorize the faces and bodies we love—even those we sleep with every day, and have sex with almost every day, and sometimes study with wistful chagrin after we've fucked them, or them us. I know I once stared into a spread of freckles on Natalia's left shoulder and thought I knew it, every possible constellation in it. But in truth, I don't remember if it was the right or left shoulder, or if the freckles were in fact moles, or if by joining the dots together you got a map of Australia, the paw of a cat, or the skeleton of a fish, and in further truth, this lyrical shit only mattered while the person mattered.

I put down *The Lover* and look through the annotated screenplay of *Hiroshima Mon Amour*. In the prologue, Duras describes an embrace between two lovers as "banal" and "commonplace." I underline the two words, such rare adjectives for the noun they modify. Then, on page 15, I underline a description of a shot where there are two pairs of bare shoulders and arms, perspiring and covered in a kind of ashy dew. The description specifies that "we get the feeling that this dew, this perspiration, has been deposited by the atomic mushroom as it moves away and evaporates." Then comes a succession of images: a hospital hallway, stills of buildings that remain standing in Hiroshima, people walking inside a museum in an exhibition about the bombing, and finally, a group of schoolchildren leaning over a reproduction in scale of the city reduced to ashes. I fall asleep with these images playing circularly in my mind, and probably dream nothing.

The next morning, I wake up, pee, and notice the small-scale nuclear mushrooms of menstrual drops expanding in slow motion in the bowl of the toilet. So many years of this monthly experience and—still—I gasp at the sight.

SIMILES

Years ago, when I was about three months' pregnant with the girl, I visited my sister in Chicago. We had dinner at a Japanese restaurant with a friend of hers, whose job it was to make space suits. The three of us—my sister, her friend, and I—were each emerging from recent circumstances of heartbreak, and were therefore entirely self-centered, orbiting obstinately around our own pain. We were stuck in the mud of our personal narratives, each of us trying to deliver stories too wound up and knotted in yarns of detail—he called me on Tuesday and then on Thursday; she took three hours to answer my SMS; he forgot his wallet on my bed—to be of interest or make sense to anyone else. Not entirely disconnected from reality, though, we probably soon realized that our empathy toward one another, and therefore the possibility of a real conversation, was impaired by the radical solipsism that amorous disappointment brings. So, after a few general statements exchanged over slurped miso soups—sex after marriage, solitude, unrequited desire, the relentless social pressure to subsume personhood under motherhood—we steered toward our professional lives.

In response to my question, my sister's friend said she had just started a small company that was now providing NASA with some of the best space suits in the industry. I was immediately curious, inquired further. She had gained a reputation as a seamstress and welder making removable wolf masks for Cirque du Soleil some years back, so someone connected to NASA had reached out and asked her to design a complicated mechanism for a removable space glove. I listened to these details, in disbelief at first, thinking she was maybe constructing some kind of elaborate and strangely sarcastic metaphor from the debris of our earlier attempt at conversation. But as she continued to speak, I realized she was really just talking about very concrete things, simply describing her craft to us. My sister distributed three small ceramic dishes, and I poured soy sauce into each of them. With the years, her friend's skills had become more refined, and she had gone from sleeves, to helmets, to entire suits. Now she was working on a TMG for female astronauts.

TMG? I asked.

A thermal micrometeoroid garment designed especially for women, she said, and dipped a California roll in soy sauce. For the last month, she'd been trying to figure out how to factor in menstruation.

So the question is—where do you put all that blood?

Her question was of course rhetorical. She knew what she was talking about, understood the needs of people floating in space, including women, as well as the constraints and possibilities of her materials. She went on to explain—and now she was talking to us like we were potential investors sitting around an oval conference table—that it was always better not to fight nature, said it was always preferable to join them if you couldn't beat them, as the saying went. So the thermal micrometeoroid garment included, she said, an undergarment that absorbed menstrual fluids seamlessly, but also beautifully, into the suit. Once expelled, these fluids would then slowly disperse in an arrangement similar to the one on tie-dyed T-shirts, changing colors and creating unique patterns as the astronaut's menstrual moon evolved from the shedding of the uterus's lining into the maturing of a new egg. I looked at her in awe, and probably muttered something to express my admiration. When she finished explaining the project, she smiled wide, and I smiled back, and with the tip of her chopstick, she signaled that I had something stuck between my two front teeth.

## REVERBERATIONS

So what's the plan, Papa? asks the boy.

It's early in the morning, before sunrise, and though it's raining, they are getting ready to go out to record some samples around the motel. His father tells him that the plan is simply to work on the inventory of echoes.

I'm still not sure what he means, exactly, by an "inventory." I suppose he means he'll be picking up passing sounds and voices that may eventually, during montage, suggest a story. Or perhaps he will never organize them into a story. He'll simply walk around places and among people, asking questions now and then, maybe asking nothing, raising his boom to pick up whatever comes his way. Maybe everything will remain unnarrated, a collage of environments and voices telling the story on their own, instead of a single voice forcing it all together into a clean narrative sequence.

But what are we going to actually do? the boy asks his father as they put on their shoes.

Collect sounds that are usually not noticed.

But what kinds of sounds?

Maybe the rain falling on this tin roof, some birds if we can, or maybe just insects buzzing.

How do you tape an insect buzzing?

You just do.

He tells the boy they'll be using a stereo mic on the boom, while trying to get as close as possible to sources. He wants all the sounds to be raw, subtle suggestions in a constant, homogeneous background. But that has to be done after, he tells him, during the mixing, when you can actually level the sounds. Before that, he tells the boy, when you're still recording those kinds of sounds, you want to get as close to the source as possible.

So we get close to insects and record? That's it?

Kind of, yes.

Lying in bed, awake but with my eyes closed, I listen to them speak as they prepare to go out. I wonder how everything my husband is saying to the boy might apply to documenting sounds and voices for my own sound piece. I'm not sure that I'd ever be able to—or should—get as close to my sources as possible. Although a valuable archive of the lost children would need to be composed, fundamentally, of a series of testimonies or oral histories that register their own voices telling their stories, it doesn't seem right to turn those children, their lives, into material for media consumption. Why? What for? So that others can listen to them and feel—pity? Feel—rage? And then do what? No one decides to not go to work and start a hunger strike after listening to the radio in the morning. Everyone continues with their normal lives, no matter the severity of the news they hear, unless the severity concerns weather.

The boy and his father finally step out of the room, into the rain that is now pouring down, and close the door. I turn around on the bed, trying to fall asleep again. I turn, and turn again, and cover my head with the pillow my husband left spare, still warm and a little sweaty. I try to talk myself back into sleep, to talk myself out of the feeling that a chasm is opening up underneath me, or maybe inside of me, swallowing me. How do you fill the emotional voids that appear when there are sudden, unexpected shifts? Which reasons, which narratives, will be the ones that save you from falling, from wanting to not fall? I turn around again, wishing myself back into sleep. I cover my head tighter with the pillow, reach deeper into my mind, looking for reasons, making lists of things, making plans, looking for answers, solutions, wishing for darkness, silence, emptiness, wishing.

## INVENTORY

The morning matures, bright and full of day-sounds. The girl is still asleep, but I cannot fall back into sleep. Outside the window of the motel room, behind the blanket of clouds that hover close above this small portion of the world, the sun climbs its regular path, stirring up steam and humidity but failing to illuminate space, clarify thought, and incite bodies to spring into wakeful action. Once more, I turn heavily onto my side. On his side of the bed, my husband has left one of the books from his boxes, *The Soundscape*, by R. Murray Schafer. I pick it up, lie flat, and hold the book above my sleepy face, flipping it open. From between the pages, a small note slips out and feathers down onto my chest. It's a note addressed to my husband, undated:

> I love the idea of an "inventory of echoes"—it so beautifully resounds the Bosavi dual power of forest agency, being at once acoustemic diagnostic of the h/wealth of a living world, and the "gone reflections/reverberations" of those who have "become" its birds by achieving death. See you soon, I hope.
>
> Yours, Steven Feld

I remember this name, Steven Feld. My husband learned to record and think about sound with a bunch of ethnomusicologists, linguists, and ornithologists, sampling sounds in rain forests and deserts. As a student, he read and listened to the work of Steven Feld, an acoustemologist who, like Murray Schafer, thought that the sounds people make, in music or in language, were always echoes of the landscape that surrounded them, and spent a lifetime sampling examples of that deep and invisible connection. In Papua New Guinea, Feld had first recorded funerary weeping and ceremonial songs of the Bosavi people in the late 1970s, and he later understood that the songs and weeping he had been sampling were actually vocalized maps of the surrounding landscapes, sung from the shifting, sweeping viewpoint of birds that flew over those spaces, so he started recording birds. After listening to them for some years, he realized that the Bosavi understood birds as echoes or "gone reverberations"—as absence turned into a presence; and, at the same time, as a presence that made an absence audible. The Bosavi emulated bird sounds during funeral rites because birds were the only materialization in the world that reflected absence. Bird sounds were, according to the Bosavi, and in Feld's words, "the voice of memory and the resonance of ancestry."

Feld's ideas had formed my husband's worldview—or rather, his world-ear—and he had eventually sought him out, following him to Papua New Guinea, where he helped him record bird songs and song paths along the rain forests, trying to map the soundscape of the dead through their reverberations in birdsong. My husband trailed behind Feld carrying a bag full of recording instruments. They would walk for hours, until Feld decided to stop, enclose his ears in his headphones, turn on the recorder, and start pointing a parabolic microphone into the trees. There were always local children following them around, curious, perhaps, about all the gadgets and cables these men needed in order to listen to the sounds of the forest. The kids would laugh hysterically as Feld pointed his microphone aimlessly up, down, around. My husband would be standing behind him, also listening for sounds under his headphones, shadowing Feld's movements. Sometimes a child would pull Feld's arm and help him point in the right direction. Everyone stood still, under the shadow of an enormous tree, waiting. And all of a sudden, the invisible presence of myriad birds would flood their ear-space, bringing into existence an entire layer of the world, previously ignored.

## HOMO FABER

When I first met my husband, while we were working on the New York City soundscape project, I found his ideas about soundscaping intriguing, and his past life recording bird songs and song paths in rain forests fascinating, but I never quite understood the methods he used for sampling sounds in our project: no direct interviews, no preplanned anything, just walking around listening to the cityscape as if waiting for a rare bird to fly past. He, in turn, never understood or came to terms with the sound tradition that I was educated in, a tradition much more journalism-based and narrative-driven. All those radio journalists, he always used to say, unzipping their pants to take out their long shotgun mics and record *their* story! I disagreed with him, though he was sometimes so convincingly charismatic—especially when he was being nasty—that I often found myself, if not agreeing, at least laughing with him.

When we were in better spirits, we were able to joke about our differences. We'd say that I was a documentarist and he was a documentarian, which meant that I was more like a chemist and he was more like a librarian. What he never understood about how I saw my work—the work I did before we met and the work I was probably going to go back to now, with the lost children's story—was that pragmatic storytelling, commitment to truth, and a direct attack on issues was not, as he thought, a mere adherence to a conventional form of radio journalism. I'd come of age as a professional in a very different sound-setting and political climate. The way I learned to record sound was fundamentally about not fucking it up, about getting the facts of the story as right as possible without getting killed because, alas, you got too close to the sources, and without getting the sources killed because, alas, they got too close to you. My apparent lack of greater aesthetic principles was not a blind obedience to funders and funding, as he often said. My work was simply full of patchwork solutions, like those old houses where everything is falling apart and you just have to solve things, urgently, no time for turning questions and their possible answers into aesthetic theories about sound and its reverberations.

In other words, the ways in which we each listened to and understood the sounds of the world around us were probably irreconcilable. I was a journalist, had always been, even though I had ventured outside my sound-range for a while and was now confused about how to return to my work, about how to reinvent a method and form, and find meaning again in what I did. And he was an acoustemologist and soundscape artist who had devoted his life to sampling echoes, winds, and birds, then found some economic stability working on a big urban project, but was now going back to what he'd always wanted to do. For the past four years, working on the city soundscape project, he had complied with more conventional ways but never really abandoned his ideas about sound; and I had immersed myself in the project, learned from it, and enjoyed not feeling burdened, for a change, by concerns about the immediate political consequences of what I was recording. But I was now gravitating back to the problems and questions that had always haunted me. We were both back to chasing our old ghosts—that, at least, we still shared. And now that we were each venturing out on our own again, and somehow also returning to the places we had each come from, our paths were dividing. It was a deeper chasm than we'd expected.

## HOMO FICTIO

For now, there's a bridge connecting us, and it's the book called *The Book with No Pictures,* which the girl got in Asheville. It's a simple story, though it's metafictional. It's about reading a book with no pictures, and why that might be better than reading one with pictures. The boy and his father have come back from their recording session, and it's still raining too hard. We agree it's not safe to drive in this weather. So we read. We read *The Book with No Pictures* out loud, over and over again, legs and elbows tangled together on the bed, leaving the door of our motel room wide open because we want to hear the rain and let some of its mood come in, but also because the children laugh so uncontrollably with every page of the book that it seems right to let something of this moment, larger than the sum of us, leave the room and travel.

## EXEGESIS

Later that afternoon, when the rain has finally turned into a mere drizzle, we get back in the car, heading toward Nashville. Every day, we drive forward, though it sometimes feels like we're on a treadmill. Inside the car, there is a sort of cyclical current of voices, questions, attitudes, and predictable reactions. Between my husband and me, silence is steadily growing. "When he woke in the woods in the dark and the cold of the night . . ." The line comes up again. I pause the recording and look for a music playlist. We each get to pick one song. I choose Odetta's version of Dylan's "With God on Our Side," which I think is so much better than the original. My husband picks "Straight to Hell," in the original version by The Clash. The boy wants The Rolling Stones, and picks "Paint It Black"—and I acknowledge his good taste in music. The girl wants "Highwayman," by the band The Highwaymen, with Willie Nelson, Johnny Cash, and two others whom we don't know and always forget to look up. We play the song a couple of times as we drive, unraveling the lyrics as if we were dealing with Baroque poetry. My theory is that it's a song about fiction, about being able to live many lives through fiction. My husband thinks it's a song about American history, and American guilt. The boy thinks it's a song about technological developments in means of transportation: from horseback riding, to schooners, to spaceship navigation. He may be right. The girl doesn't have a theory yet but is clearly trying to work it out:
What is a blade?
It's the part of the knife that cuts things.
So the highwayman used his knife?
Yes.
To cut people apart?
Well, perhaps, yes.
So was he an Indian or a cowboy?
He was neither.

Then he was a policeman.

No.

Then he was a white-eye.

Maybe.


FUTURE PRESENT

As we drive farther west into Tennessee, we pass more and more abandoned gas stations, empty churches, closed motels, stores and factories that have shut down. Looking out the window and through the lens of his camera, the boy asks me again:

So what does it mean, Ma, to document stuff?

Perhaps I should say that documenting is when you add thing plus light, light minus thing, photograph after photograph; or when you add sound, plus silence, minus sound, minus silence. What you have, in the end, are all the moments that didn't form part of the actual experience. A sequence of interruptions, holes, missing parts, cut out from the moment in which the experience took place. Because experience, plus a document of the experience, is experience minus one. The strange thing is this: if, in the future one day, you add all those documents together again, what you have, all over again, is the experience. Or at least a version of the experience that replaces the lived experience, even if what you originally documented were the moments cut out from it.

What should I focus on? the boy insists.

I don't know what to say. I know, as we drive through the long, lonely roads of this country—a landscape that I am seeing for the first time—that what I see is not quite what I see. What I see is what others have already documented: Ilf and Petrov, Robert Frank, Robert Adams, Walker Evans, Stephen Shore—the first road photographers and their pictures of road signs, stretches of vacant land, cars, motels, diners, industrial repetition, all the ruins of early capitalism now engulfed by future ruins of later capitalism. When I see the people of this country, their vitality, their decadence, their loneliness, their desperate togetherness, I see the gaze of Emmet Gowin, Larry Clark, and Nan Goldin.

I try an answer:

Documenting just means to collect the present for posterity.

What do you mean, posterity?

I mean—for later.

I'm not sure, though, what "for later" means anymore. Something changed in the world. Not too long ago, it changed, and we know it. We don't know how to explain it yet, but I think we all can feel it, somewhere deep in our gut or in our brain circuits. We feel time differently. No one has quite been able to capture what is happening or say why. Perhaps it's just that we sense an absence of future, because the present has become too overwhelming, so the future has become unimaginable. And without future, time feels like only an accumulation. An accumulation of months, days, natural disasters, television series, terrorist attacks, divorces, mass migrations, birthdays, photographs, sunrises. We haven't understood the exact way we are now experiencing time. And maybe the boy's frustration at not knowing what to take a picture of, or how to frame and focus the things he sees as we all sit inside the car, driving across this strange, beautiful, dark country, is simply a sign of how our ways of documenting the world have fallen short. Perhaps if we found a new way to document it, we might begin to understand this new way we experience space and time. Novels and movies don't quite capture it; journalism doesn't; photography, dance, painting, and theater don't; molecular biology and quantum physics certainly don't either. We haven't understood how space and time exist now, how we really experience them. And until we find a way to document them, we will not understand them. Finally, I tell the boy:

You just have to find your own way of understanding space, so that the rest of us can feel less lost in time.

Okay, Ma, he says, but how much longer till we get to our next stop?

## TROPES

We had planned to stay a few days in Nashville, visiting recording studios, but instead, we drive right through it and sleep in a motel near Jackson. Then, the next morning, we do something entirely predictable, at least for people like us—foreign but not entirely so—which is to play "Graceland" over and over as we cross Memphis into Graceland, trying to figure out where the Mississippi Delta is, exactly, and why it might shine like a national guitar, or if the lyrics even say "national guitar." The boy thinks it's "rational" guitar, but I don't think he has it right. Our entrance, played against the background of the song, has an epic quality, but of the quiet sort. Like a war being lost silently but with resilience.

The boy notes, first, that we are singing off-key, and second, that the boy mentioned in the song is only a year younger than him, nine years old. Also like him, he says, the boy in the song is the son of his dad's first marriage. I wonder how that line in the epicenter of the song—the one about how losing love is like a window suddenly open in someone's heart—would sound to us a few months from now, and if the boy's father and I would show resilience and integrity, and behave like rational guitars.

As soon as the song ends, we are thrust back to the world-weary line that always pops up in the speakers: "When he woke in the woods in the dark and the cold of the night he'd reach out to touch the child sleeping beside him." And so I turn off the radio and look out the window toward the city, broken, abandoned, but also beautiful.

### NOUNS

Unhappiness grows slowly. It lingers inside you, silently, surreptitiously. You nourish it, feeding it scraps of yourself every day—it is the dog kept locked away in the back patio that will bite your hand off if you let it. Unhappiness takes time, but eventually it takes over completely. And then happiness—that word—arrives only sometimes, and always like a sudden change of weather. It found us on our tenth day into the trip. I had called a number of motels in Graceland. None picked up, except one. An old lady answered the phone, her voice like a distant fire, crackling its way into my ear:

Elvis Presley Boulevard Inn, at your service.

I wondered if I was misunderstanding her when she said:

Yes, ma'am, plenty room here, and a new ghee-tar pool.

But we find exactly that: a motel all to ourselves. A motel with a swimming pool in the shape of an electric guitar. A motel in which instead of a bedside Bible, there is an Elvis Presley songbook. A motel with Elvis Presley everything everywhere, from the hand towels in the rooms to the salt and pepper shakers in the breakfast area. The boy and his father stay behind in the parking lot, rearranging the daily puzzle of our luggage, and the girl and I run up to the room to pee. We climb stairs, walk past eerie Elvis wax statues, hundreds of pictures and cartoons, an Elvis piñata, an all-Elvis jukebox, small statuettes, yellowing T-shirts with the King's face nailed to the walls. By the time we make it to our room, we have understood, she in her own terms, that we are in some sort of temple or mausoleum. She's understood that this man is or was something important. She looks up at a photograph of a thirty-something-year-old Elvis Presley hanging on the wall between the two double beds in our new room and asks:

Is that Jesus Fucking Christ, Mama?

No, it's Elvis.

Mama, could you leave Papa and marry Elvis? If you wanted.

I try not to laugh, but I do. I say I will consider it. But then I tell her:

I would, except he is dead, my love.

This poor young man is dead?

He is.

Like Johnny Cash is dead?

Yes.

Like Janis Joplin is dead?

Yes.

When the boy and my husband walk in with bags and suitcases, we all change into our swimsuits and run down to the guitar pool. We forget the towels, and the sunscreen—but then again, we are the type of family that has never taken a picnic blanket to a picnic, or beach chairs to a beach.

The girl, so cautious and philosophical in all her daily activities, becomes a wild beast in the water. She is possessed, delirious.

Beats on her own head and stomach like one of those post-hippie drummers who's been on LSD for too many decades. Her laughter thunders in her open mouth, all milk teeth and perfect pink gums. She howls as she jumps into the pool. Wriggles her way to freedom from our nervous clutches. Discovers, underwater, that she does not know how to surface. So we fish her out and hold her tight and say:

Don't do that again.

Be careful.

You don't know how to swim yet.

We don't know how to embrace her boundless enthusiasm, or her volcanic bursts of vitality. It's hard for the rest of us, I think, to keep up with the dashing, reckless train of her happiness. Hard, for me at least, to let her be, when I keep on feeling that I have to save her from the world. I'm constantly imagining that she'll fall, or get burned, or be run over. Or that she'll drown, right now, in this guitar-shaped swimming pool in Memphis, Tennessee, her face, in my mind, all blue and swollen. A friend of mine calls this "the rescue distance"—the constant equation operating in a parent's mind, where time and distance are factored in to calculate whether it would be possible to save a child from danger.

But at some point, like flipping a switch, we all stop calculating grim catastrophes and let go. We tacitly agree to follow her, instead of expecting her to stay back with us, in our safe incapacity for life. We howl, ululate, roar, we plunge and resurface to float on our backs, looking up at the cloudless sky. We open our eyes wide inside the burning chlorine-water; we emulate shitty fountain-statues, spouting water from our mouths. I teach them a choreography for "All Shook Up" that I vaguely remember being taught by a childhood friend: a lot of shoulder shaking and some hip back-and-forth in the "ughs" of the song. And then, when the spell the girl has cast on us finally evaporates, we all sit by the edge of the pool, dangling our feet in the water and catching our breath.

Later that night, lying in the dark of our motel bedroom, my husband tells the two children an Apache story, about how Apaches learned their war names. We listen to him, silent. His voice rises and whirls around the room, carried across the thick hot air that the ceiling fan stirs—its cheap veneer blades squeaking a bit. We lie faceup, trying to catch a breeze. Except the girl. She lies on her tummy and sucks her thumb, her suck-rhythm in syncopation with the cyclical rattle of paddles bobbling in the ceiling fan. The boy waits for his father to finish the story, and then he says:

If she were an Apache, her war name would be Loud Thumb.

Me? the girl asks, unplugging her thumb from her mouth and raising her head in the dark, not convinced but always proud to be talked about.

Yes, Loud Thumb or Suck Thumb.

No, no. My war name would be Grace Landmemphis Tennessee. Or Guitar Swimming Pool. Either or.

Those are not Apache names, right, Pa?

No, they are not, my husband confirms. Guitar Swimming Pool is not an Apache name.

Well, then I want to be Grace Landmemphis, she says.

It's Graceland, comma, Memphis, you moron, the boy informs her from the heights of his now ten-year-old superiority.

Fine, then. So I'll be Memphis. Just Memphis.

She says this with the authoritative assurance of bureaucrats closing their plastic windows, taking no more requests, no more complaints, and then plugs her thumb back into her mouth. We know this side of her: when she's made up her stubborn little mind, there's no way to convince her otherwise, so we defer, respect her resolve, and say no more.

What about you? I ask the boy.

Me?

He would be Swift Feather, his father immediately suggests.

Yes, that's right, Swift Feather. And Ma? Who's she? he asks.

My husband takes his time to think about it, and finally says:

She would be Lucky Arrow.

I like the name, and I smile in acknowledgment, or in gratitude. I smile at him for the first time in days, maybe weeks. But he can't see me smile because the room is dark and his eyes are probably closed anyway. Then I ask him:

And you? What would your war name be?

The girl chimes in, without taking her thumb out of her mouth, lisping, thething, and fumming her words:

Pa, he's the Elvis. Or the Jesus Fucking Christ. Either or.

My husband and I laugh, and the boy reprimands her:

You're gonna go to hell if you keep saying that.

He probably chastises her more because of our praising laughter than because of the content of her statement. She certainly does not know why she should be censured. Then, taking her thumb out of her mouth, she asks:

Who's your favorite Apache, Pa? Geronimo?

No. My favorite is Chief Cochise.

Then you get to be Papa Cochise, she says, like she's handing him a gift.

Papa Cochise, my husband whispers back.

And softly, slowly, we fall asleep, embracing these new names, the ceiling fan slicing the thick air in the room, thinning it. I fall asleep at the same time as the three of them, maybe for the first time in years, and as I do, I cling to these four certainties: Swift Feather, Papa Cochise, Lucky Arrow, Memphis.

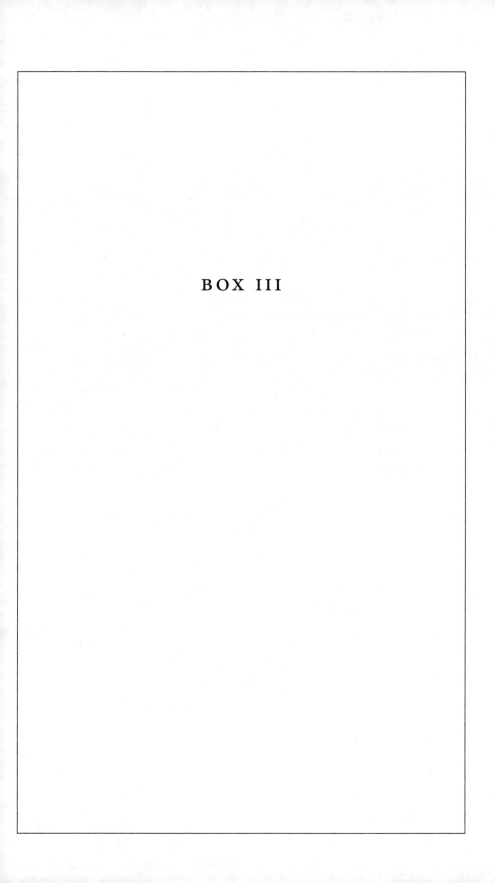

BOX III

§ FOUR NOTEBOOKS (7¾″ X 5″)

"On Reading"
"On Listening"
"On Translating"
"On Time"

§ NINE BOOKS

*The Cantos,* Ezra Pound
*Lord of the Flies,* William Golding
*On the Road,* Jack Kerouac
*Heart of Darkness,* Joseph Conrad
*New Science,* Giambattista Vico
*Blood Meridian* & *All the Pretty Horses* & *Cities of the Plain,*
    Cormac McCarthy
*2666,* Roberto Bolaño
*Untitled for Barbara Loden,* Nathalie Léger
*The New Oxford Annotated Bible,* God?

§ FOLDER (MUSICAL SCORES)

*Metamorphosis,* Philip Glass
*Cantigas de Santa Maria* (Alfonso el Sabio), Jordi Savall

# MISSING

Light poles flicker beside us, aluminum and white neon. The sun is rising behind our car, coming up from under the inch of concrete at the far eastern tip of Route 50. As we drive west across Arkansas, chicken fences stretch out endless. Behind the fences are lonely ranches. Lonely people in those ranches, maybe. People reading, sleeping, fucking, crying, watching television. People watching the news or reality shows, or perhaps just watching over their lives—over a sick boy, a dying mother, over a cow in labor, and eggs hatching. I look out through the windshield, and wonder.

My phone rings as we are driving past a soy field. It's Manuela, finally calling me back after a long silence. The last time I talked to her was nearly three weeks ago, right before we left the city. She doesn't have good news. The judge ruled against the petition for asylum that the lawyer had filed for the girls, and after that, the lawyer dropped the case. She was told that her two daughters would be transferred from the detention center where they had been waiting, in New Mexico, to another detention center, in Arizona, from where they would be deported. But the day they were supposed to be transferred, they disappeared.

What do you mean, disappeared? I ask.

The officer who called her to deliver the news, she tells me, said the girls were put on a plane back to Mexico City. But the girls never arrived there. Manuela's brother had made the trip from Oaxaca to the capital and waited at the airport for eight hours, and the girls never walked out.

I don't understand, I say. Where are the girls now?

She tells me she doesn't know, says that everyone she has talked to tells her that the girls are probably still in the detention center. Everyone tells her to wait, be patient. But she thinks the girls aren't in any detention center. She says she's sure the girls ran away, that maybe someone in the detention center, someone friendly, helped them escape, and that the two of them are possibly on their way to her.

Why do you think that? I ask, wondering if she is losing her grip.

Because I know my blood, she says.

She tells me she's waiting for someone to call her and tell her something. After all, the girls must still have their dresses with them, so they have her telephone number. I don't question her further about it, but I ask:

What are you going to do next?

Look for them.

And what can I do to help?

After a brief silence, she says:

Nothing now, but if you get to New Mexico or Arizona, you help me look.


VIGIL

A few months before the four of us left on this trip, during the period in which I was going to the New York federal immigration court at least once a week, I met a priest, Father Juan Carlos. Having studied at an all-girls Anglican boarding school, I have never been too fond of priests, or nuns, or religion in general. But this priest I immediately liked. I met him outside immigration court one day. I was standing in line, waiting to be let into the building; he was standing to one side of the line, wearing sunglasses even though it was too early in the day to wear sunglasses, and was handing out flyers, smiling at everyone.

I took a flyer from him, read the information. If you were at risk of being deported, it said, you could visit his church any weekend and sign up for sanctuary assistance. And if you had an undocumented family member who had disappeared, you could contact him 24/7 by calling the emergency telephone number written below. I called the number the next day, saying I didn't have an emergency but wanted to ask what this flyer was all about. In a priestly way, perhaps, his explanation was more allegorical than practical, but at the end of our conversation, he invited me to join him and a few others during their weekly vigil the following Thursday.

The vigil was held at 6:00 p.m., outside a building on Varick Street. I arrived a couple of minutes late. Father Juan Carlos was there, with another twelve people. He greeted me, shaking my hand formally, and introduced me to the rest of the group. I asked if I could record the gathering on my sound recorder. He said yes, the others nodded in agreement, and then, ceremoniously but with a candid simplicity uncommon in men accustomed to podiums, he began speaking. He pointed to the sign hanging by the main entrance of the building, which announced Passport Agency, and said that few people knew that the building, which occupied an entire block of the city's grid, was not actually just a place where you got a passport but also a place where people without passports were being held. It was a detention center, where Immigration and Customs Enforcement agents locked people away after detaining them on the streets or raiding their homes at night. The daily federal quota for undocumented people, he said, was 34,000, and was steadily growing. That meant that at least 34,000 people had to be occupying a bed each day in any one of the detention centers, a center just like this one, across the country. People were taken away, he continued, locked up in detention buildings for an indefinite amount of time. Some were later deported back to their home countries. Many were pipelined to federal prisons, which profited from them, subjecting them to sixteen-hour workdays for which they earned less than three dollars. And many of them were simply—disappeared.

At first, I thought Father Juan Carlos was preaching from a kind of Orwellian dystopic delirium. It took me some time to realize that he wasn't. It took me some time to notice that the rest of the people there that day, mostly Garifunas from Honduras, were family members of someone who had, in fact, disappeared during an ICE raid. When Father Juan Carlos finished speaking, he said we'd all now walk twice around the building. Everyone started walking in a line, in complete silence. They were all there to claim their disappeared, there to protest silently against a bigger, deeper silence. I followed them, at the end of the line, my recorder raised above my head, recording that silence.

We walked half a block south, one block west, one block north, one block east, half a block south. And then once more. After the second round, we all stood still on the sidewalk for a few minutes, until the priest instructed us to place the palms of our hands against the wall of the building. I tucked my recorder into my jacket pocket and followed the rest. The concrete felt cold and rough against my hands. Cars whipped past, behind the line of us, along Varick Street. Father Juan Carlos then asked, in a louder, more severe voice than before:

Who are we missing?

One by one, the twelve people standing in the line, their hands firmly pressed against the building's walls, their backs to the busy street, each called out a name:

Awilda.

Digana.

Jessica.

Barana.

Sam.

Lexi.

As each person in the line called out the name of a missing relative, the rest of us repeated the name out loud. We pronounced each one clear and loud, though it was hard to keep our voices from breaking, hard to keep our bodies from shaking:

Cem.

Brandon.

Amanda.

Benjamin.

Gari.

Waricha.

ERASED

Winona, Marianna, Roe, Ulm, Humnoke—I look at the road map, following the names of places we'll pass today. We've been driving for almost two weeks now, and my husband thinks we've been moving too slowly, stopping too often and overstaying in towns. I had been enjoying that rhythm, the slow speed on secondary roads across parks, the long stops in diners and motels. But I know he's right—our time is limited, my time especially, and it's running out. I should get to the borderlands as quickly as possible, too—to New Mexico or Arizona. So I agree when he suggests we drive more hours and stop less frequently. I think about other families, like us and also unlike us, traveling toward a future impossible to envision, the threats and dangers that it poses. What would we do if one of us simply disappeared? Beyond the immediate horror and fear, what concrete steps would we follow? Whom would we call? Where would we go?

I look back at our own children, asleep in the backseat. I hear them breathe, and I wonder. I wonder if they would survive in the hands of coyotes, and what would happen to them if they had to cross the desert on their own. Were they to find themselves alone, would our own children survive?

## FALLINGS

In 1909, Geronimo fell off his horse and died. Of all the things my husband tells the children about him, this fact is the one that both torments and fascinates the children most. Especially the girl. Ever since she heard the story, she brings it back up—now and then, unexpectedly and unprompted, as if it were a casual conversation starter.

So, Geronimo fell off his horse and died, right?

Or:

You know how Geronimo died? He fell off his horse!

Or:

So Geronimo never died, but one day, he died, because he fell off his horse.

Now, as we speed toward Little Rock, Arkansas, she wakes up and tells us:

I dreamed of Geronimo's horse. I was riding it and it was going so fast, I was about to fall off.

Where are we? the boy asks, also waking up, their strange sleep synchronicity.

Arkansas.

What's in Arkansas?

I realize I know very little about Arkansas. I know about the poet Frank Stanford, who shot himself through the heart—three times—in Fayetteville, Arkansas, and fell to the ground. The morbid question of course being not why but how three times. I don't share this story with the family.

Then there's the slightly more comic than tragic death of the Czech writer Bohumil Hrabal, who did not die in Arkansas, but who was for some reason beloved by ex-president Bill Clinton, who lived in Little Rock when he served as Arkansas's governor—so there is that connection. I once saw a photograph of a beer-red, chubby-grinned Bill hanging on the wall of a bar in central Prague. He did not look out of place there, as dignitaries always do in restaurant pictures. He could have been the brother of the owner of the bar, or one of the regulars. Hard to think that the man in that picture, full of bonhomie, was the same man who laid the first brick in the wall dividing Mexico and the United States, and then pretended it never happened. In the photograph, he is shaking hands across the table with Hrabal, whose *Dancing Lessons for the Advanced in Age* Clinton might have read and liked. I had read the book during that trip to Prague. I read it in a state of quiet awe, and underlined and memorized strange and simple lines that I still remember:

> "the minute I saw you I could tell you were supersensitive"
> "he was a whoreson"
> "a composer . . . once tore a chandelier out of the ceiling in his
>     grief"
> "a giant of a girl, but beautiful"
> "the world was as deserted as a star"

More than his books, more than his harsh humor and Decameronian tableaux of human tragicomedy, more than anything, it is the story of Hrabal's own death that has haunted me, always. He died like this: recovering from bronchitis in a hospital room, while trying to feed the pigeons, he fell out of the window.

But Hrabal does not live in Arkansas, so I don't tell the family about him either.

ITEMS

In Little Rock, we see cars, malls, big houses—places presumably occupied by people, but we don't see people, not on the street. At the city limits, there is a Walmart. We see many things there, as is to be expected during a visit to any superstore. Except there really are way too many things, more than normal, a puzzling number of things, some of which I am sure no one has ever seen before or even imagined. For instance, an itemizer. What is an itemizer, really? What does it do? What does it look like? Who might need one? Only this much is clear from the box: it has spring-latch and roller-mounted drawers (with adjustable dividers), has anti-skid strips, and comes with a lock mount, and its units can be stacked. An itemizer "eradicates the need to crawl inside the van every time by placing things at your fingertips." I would imagine that if you gave an itemizer to someone brilliant and slightly intolerant to stupidity—say, Anne Carson, Sor Juana Inés de la Cruz, or Marguerite Yourcenar—they'd write a perfect poem about reindeer walking in the snow.

In the Walmart, we also discover that Walmart is the place where people are. These I like instantly: an old man and his granddaughter choosing avocados, judging each by its smell. The old man tells the girl they have to be smelled "not in the belly but right in the navel," and then goes on to do a demonstration of avocado-navel smelling. This one I instantly dislike: a woman in Crocs who walks slowly, dragging her feet, smiles distractedly at people waiting in line, pretending to be lost or a little confused, and then—cuts the line!

We buy boots. The discounts are incredible. We buy beautiful, cheap, large, cow-family boots. Mine are not cowgirl boots. Mine are imitation-leather punk-lady boots—$15.99—and I put them on immediately, even before I pay, to the indignation of the children, who cannot conceive of usage before payment.

I feel like an astrolady in them as we walk out of the store, someone leaving footprints on the moon-gravel in a tremendous parking lot, walking across "a world as deserted as a star" as Hrabal would surely have said of this Walmart in particular. The boy says we have to keep the empty shoeboxes in the trunk, in case we need them, or in case he needs them, for later. I wonder if I've passed on to him my documentary fever: store, collect, archive, inventory, list, catalog.

What for? I ask

For later, he says.

But I convince him we have enough boxes, reminding him that he already has an empty box he hasn't even used.

Why haven't you used your box yet, by the way? I ask, to distract him and steer the conversation in another direction.

Because, Ma, it's for later, he says.

And he says it with such authority, like a real archivist who knows exactly what he's doing, that I just keep quiet and smile at him.

That afternoon, we drive to the western border of Arkansas, to a town called De Queen, just a few miles from the border with Oklahoma, and there we find a decent-enough motel on a street called Joplin Avenue. Our children are thrilled by the idea of it, Joplin. The girl, instead of asking for a story, takes out her copy of *The Book with No Pictures* and reads theatrically to the family as she flips through the pages: "This is the story of Janis Joplin, the great witch of the night . . ." She makes me both proud and worried sometimes—five years old and a Joplin fan—but maybe more proud than worried. She and the boy are both exempted from brushing their teeth before going to bed just this one time.

## DICKS, WHISKEY

The lights in the room are turned off, the children asleep in their bed. My husband and I quarrel on our own bed. A routine exchange: his poisonous adjectives whispered sharply across his pillow to mine, and my silence like a dull shield in his face. One active, the other passive; both of us equally aggressive. In marriage, there are only two kinds of pacts: pacts that one person insists on having and pacts that the other insists on breaking.

Why is there always a little hum of hate running alongside love? a friend once wrote to me in an email, paraphrasing someone. I don't remember if she said it was Alice Munro or Lydia Davis. After the fight, he sleeps and I don't. A slow rage creeps and flowers in my sternum, burning deep but contained, like a fire smoldering in a fireplace. Slowly, a distance stretches between his sleep and my sleeplessness. I remember Charles Baudelaire said something about everyone being like convalescents in a sickroom, always wishing they could swap beds. But which bed, where? The other bed in this room is warm and pleasant with the children's breathing, but there is no space for me there. I close my eyes and try to thrust myself into thoughts of other places and other beds.

More and more, my presence here, on this trip with my family, driving toward a future we most probably won't share, settling into motel bedrooms for the night, feels ghostly, a life witnessed and not lived. I know I'm here, with them, but also I am not. I behave like those visitors who are always packing and repacking, always getting ready to leave the next day but then don't; or like ancestors in bad magical realist literature, who die but then forget to leave.

I cannot stand the guttural sounds of my husband breathing, he so calm in his nasty, guiltless dreams. So I get out of bed, write a note—"Back later"—in case someone wakes up and worries, and then leave the room. My boots walk me out, out from one godless dark to another. The boots provide a weight, a gravity that I've lately ceased to feel under my feet. One of the metal buckles slaps the faux leather flank of a boot in a rhythmical slap, walk, heel, toe—fuck, I'm probably making too much noise. I try to ghost my way down the motel corridor, feeling like a teenage junkie. A neon tube flickers above the door to the empty reception. Under my arm I've tucked a book, which I may or may not read if I find a bar or an open diner.

I don't have to go too far. Just a mile or so down the highway is the Dicks Whiskey Bar, which I have trouble pronouncing properly in my head—is it a possessive noun or just a plural form? The waitresses are dressed in pioneer costumes, and in the restroom, there are barrels for sinks. A cover version of "Harvest Moon" is playing in the background, seemingly on repeat. At the bar, I find a stool and take a seat. I've always felt inadequate on barstools because my legs are not long enough for my feet to touch the ground, so a remote bone and muscle memory is triggered: I'm four years old again, dangling my legs from my chair, waiting for a glass of milk and maybe some attention amid the morning rush of a house with a loud older sibling, knowing that even if I yell, no one will listen. Older siblings don't listen, and the barman never listens. But I shift a little on my stool and discover that my astrolady boot heels latch on perfectly to the bottom rod between the legs of the stool. So I suddenly feel grounded, present, adult enough to be there. I rest my crossed forearms on the zinc bar and order a whiskey.

Neat, please.

Two places from me I notice a man, also alone, writing notes in the margins of a newspaper page. His legs are long and thin, and his feet touch the ground. He has well-outlined sideburns, a sad crease across his forehead, a strong chin, wild bushy hair. The kind of man, I tell myself, who would have swept me under his charm when I was younger and less experienced. He's wearing a weathered white tank shirt and denims. And as I study his brown naked arms, a shoulder dotted with a darker birthmark, a thick vein that pulses in his neck, and a spiral of small hairs behind his ear, I tell myself no, this man is not at all interesting. Lined up next to his drink—also whiskey, neat—he has four pens, all the same color (in addition to the one he's using to underline something in the newspaper article he's so invested in). I repeat to myself, no, he's not interesting, he's just beautiful, and his beauty is of the most vulgar kind: indisputable. And as I sweep my eyes down along his flank toward his hip, I find myself completely incapable of not asking him:

Can I use one of your pens or do you need all five of them?

And as he hands one of the pens over to me, he smiles with a childish bashfulness, and looks at me with a gaze that reveals both a fierceness and a fundamental decency—not of manners and mores, but of a deeper, more simple noble type. For a man this beautiful, I realize, that kind of gaze is rare. Handsome men are habituated to attention, and they look at other men or women with the cold self-satisfaction that an actor displays in front of a camera. Not this man.

We end up talking to each other, at first following all the ready-made prompts and platitudes.

What brings us here?

He tells me he's on his way to a town called Poetry, which I think is probably a lie, a lie that reveals too much sentimentalism. I don't think a place by that name exists, but I don't question him about it. In return for his lie, I tell him I'm on my way to Apacheria—the same kind of vague, fictitious answer.

What do we each do?

Our answers are evasive, veiled behind an almost overacted mysteriousness that reveals nothing more than insecurity. We try a little harder now. I tell him I do journalism, mostly radio journalism, and I've been trying to work on a sound documentary about refugee children, but my plan for now is, once I reach Apacheria, to go look for two lost girls in New Mexico or possibly Arizona. He says he used to be a photographer but now prefers painting, and is going to Poetry, Texas, because he's been commissioned to paint a series of portraits of the town's eldest generation.

Then we talk politics, and he explains the term "gerrymandering" to me, a term I've never understood even after years of living in the United States. He draws a series of squiggly lines on a paper napkin, the resulting image of which looks like a dog. I laugh, tell him he's a terrible explainer, and I still don't understand the concept, but I fold the gerry-napkin and tuck it into one of my boots.

Slowly, though not so slowly, our conversation leads us toward darker, maybe truer spaces. He is the opposite of me, in circumstance. He's unentangled; I'm a knot. There's my children and his childlessness. His plans for eventual children and my plans for no more. Hard to explain why two complete strangers may suddenly decide to share an unbeautified portrait of their lives. But perhaps also easy to explain, because two people alone in a bar at two in the morning are probably there to try to figure out the exact narrative they need to tell themselves before they go back to wherever they'll sleep that night. There's a compatibility in our loneliness, and an absolute incompatibility of our mutual situations, and a cigarette shared outside, and then the sudden compatibility of our lips, and his breath in my cleavage, and the tip of my fingers around his belt, just inside his pants. My heartbeat races in a way I know well but have not felt in many years. The absolute physicality of desire takes over. He suggests we go back to his motel, and I want to.

I want to, but I know better. With men like this one, I know I'd play the role of lonely hunter; and they, the role of inaccessible prey. And I'm both too old and too young to pursue things that walk away from me.

So there is one last whiskey and then some scribbles—geographic advice and telephone numbers—that we jot down on our respective napkins. His, probably lost the morning after, in the routine emptying out of pockets for the sake of carrying less weight; mine kept in one of my boots, as a kind of reminder of a road not taken.

## GUNS & POETRY

The next morning, in a gas station outside Broken Bow, we buy coffees, milks, cookies, and a local newspaper called *The Daily Gazette*. There's an article titled "Kids, a Biblical Plague" about the children's crisis at the border, which I read through, baffled by its Manichean representation of the world: patriots versus illegal aliens. It's hard to come to terms with the fact that a worldview like that has a place outside of superhero comic strips. I read some sentences out loud to the family:

"Tens of thousands of children streaming from chaotic Central American nations to the U.S."

". . . this 60,000 to 90,000 illegal alien children mass that has come to America . . ."

"These children carry with them viruses that we are not familiar with in the United States."

I think of Manuela's girls, and it's hard not to be overcome by rage. But I suppose it's always been like that. I suppose that the convenient narrative has always been to portray the nations that are systematically abused by more powerful nations as a no-man's-land, as a barbaric periphery whose chaos and brownness threaten civilized white peace. Only such a narrative can justify decades of dirty war, interventionist policies, and the overall delusion of moral and cultural superiority of the world's economic and military powers. Reading articles like this one, I find myself amused at their unflinching certitude about right and wrong, good and bad. Not amused, actually, but a little bit frightened. None of this is new, though I guess I am simply accustomed to dealing with more edulcorated versions of xenophobia. I don't know which is worse.

There's only one place to eat at this time in Boswell, Oklahoma, and it's called the Dixie Café. The boy is the first to jump out of the car, getting his camera ready. I remind him to take the little red book from the top of my box, as well as the big road map, which I left there last night, because the glove box was too full. He runs to the back of the car, fetches everything, and waits for us outside the café, the map and book tucked under his arm and his camera ready in his hand. He takes a picture as the rest of us take our time, climbing out sluggishly, putting on our new Walmart boots.

The only other patrons in the Dixie Café are a woman with a face and arms the texture of boiled chicken, and a toddler in a high chair to whom she's feeding fries. We order four hamburgers and four pink lemonades, and spread our map out on the table while we wait for the food. We follow yellow and red highway lines with the tips of our index fingers, like a troupe of gypsies reading an enormous open palm. We look into our past and future: a departure, a change, long life, short life, hard circumstances beyond, here you will head south, here you will encounter doubt and uncertainty, a crossroads ahead.

Only this we know: in order to reach New Mexico and, eventually, Arizona, we can either drive west across Oklahoma or southwest across Texas.

Was Oklahoma also once part of Mexico, Ma? the boy asks.

No, not Oklahoma, I answer.

Arkansas?

No.

And Arizona?

Yes, I say, Arizona was Mexico.

So what happened? the boy wants to know.

The United States stole it, says my husband.

I nuance his answer. I tell the boy that Mexico kind of sold it, but only after losing the war in 1848. I tell him it was a two-year war, which Americans call the Mexican-American War and Mexicans call, perhaps more accurately, the American Intervention.

So will there be many Mexicans in Arizona? the girl now asks.

No, the boy tells her.

Why?

They shoot them, her brother says.

With bows and arrows?

Guns, he says. And as he says this, he mimics a sniper, shoots the plastic containers of ketchup and then mayonnaise, and is about to squirt some ketchup on Arizona when his father snatches the bottle from him.

We go back to studying the map. My husband wants to spend a couple of days in Oklahoma, where the Apache cemetery is. He says that stop is one of the central reasons for this trip. It's incompatible with his wish, but I want to go through Texas. From where I'm sitting, leaning into the table, the state spreads magnanimous under my eyes. I follow the line of a highway with the tip of my index finger. I pass places like Hope, Pleasant, Commerce, de-route toward Merit, south to Fate, and then to Poetry, Texas, which, to my amazement, does indeed exist. The girl says she wants to go back to Memphis. The boy says he doesn't care, he just wants his food to come now.

The drinks arrive, and we sip in silence, listening to the woman at the other table. She is talking loud and slow to, or maybe at, her toddler about price discounts in the local supermarket while she hands him long fries dipped first in ketchup, then in mayonnaise. The toddler replies with inhuman burbles and shrieks. Bananas, ninety-nine cents a pound. The toddler shrieks. And milk, a carton of milk for seventy-five cents. He gurgles. Then she looks at us, sighs, and tells him that them fore'ns are more and more common these days, and that's okay, it's okay with her as long as they're not troublemakers. She hands him a fry with so much mayo-ketchup on the tip that it bends over sadly, like a dysfunction.

All of us turn around at the same time when another family—father, mother, baby in stroller—walks into the diner. They are of a more discreet type, except for the baby, who is rather big. Maybe even uncannily colossal. It seems difficult to say that someone that size is a baby. But judging by its lumpy features, its almost hairless head, its pixelated movements, it is, by all means, a baby. The toddler, holding a fry up in the air, full of enthusiasm, shouts out from his high chair:

Baby!

No, no, that ain't no baby—the mother tells him, wagging no-no with another French fry.

Baby! the toddler insists.

No-no, that ain't no baby, m'boy, no-no-no. That thing's huge. Scary huge. Like them tomatoes we saw over at the supermarket. Not God's tomatoes.

She does not at all mind the fact that she is very much shouting across the room, past her toddler, past us, and that the family of the more discreet sort have of course taken note of her opinion, which really is also our opinion, except now we don't dare exteriorize it, not even in whispers. When the burgers come, I try the mayo-ketchup combination on my fries and find it rather pleasant.

By the time we pay the check, it's been decided. We'll drive from Boswell to a town called Geronimo, just to see it and understand why it's called that. Then we'll drive to Lawton, which is just a few miles from the cemetery where Geronimo is buried—although there are all sorts of theories about his body having been trafficked elsewhere, by some secret society at Yale. My husband has been planning this visit to the cemetery for months. It's only about a four-hour drive from where we are now to Lawton, so we can make a few stops on the way there, sleep for one night in Lawton, and then visit the cemetery the morning after.

ARCHIVE

A Tamil friend who was born in Tulsa had warned me: driving deeper into Oklahoma is like falling asleep and sinking into deeper and stranger layers of someone's troubled subconscious.

Near Tishomingo, in southern Oklahoma, we pass a sign that the boy reads aloud:

Swimming Site Ahead! Fun Guaranteed!

The children insist, so we agree to stop for a swim. There are several cars parked in front of a small artificial lake, the parking area larger than the lake itself. My husband takes out his recording gear while the rest of us gather some basics. By the shore, we lay out two towels, and the children slip out of their clothes and run into the water in their underwear. The lake is shallow enough, near the shore, for them to play by themselves, so I sit on one of the towels and supervise them from there, occasionally distracted by the other people around us.

A middle-aged woman passes in front of me. She's strolling along the shore with a thin, elderly man—possibly her father. They have two tiny dogs, which hop and bounce a few feet in front them. One of the dogs keeps tripping on rocks, or roots, or maybe on its own legs, and lets out loud yelps. Every time, the woman asks: "Are you okay, cupcake? Are you okay, darling?" The dog does not reply. But the elderly man does: "Oh, I'm just fine, dear. Thanks for asking."

To my left, there's a man spread-eagled in a yellow inflatable boat, drinking beer. His wife, a small, bony woman, reads a magazine, sitting cross-legged on a towel. From time to time, she speaks headlines and sentences out loud: "Scientists Say This Diet Reduces Alzheimer's Risk by 53%!" "You've Been Cutting Cake Wrong Your Whole Life: Here's the Surprising Best Way!" When she gets tired of reading, she stands up and brings her husband another beer, which maybe he orders through telepathic communication, because somehow she's always on time with a new beer when the old one is just about finished. They have a Labrador, which retrieves things that the man in the yellow boat throws into the lake. Now the dog is retrieving rocks—something I've never before seen a dog retrieve.

My husband is in the lake, water to his knees, Porta Brace around his right shoulder and boom raised high. The man in the boat notices him and asks if he's checking for radiation. My husband smiles back at him politely and says he's just recording the sound of the lake. In response, the man snorts and clears his throat. He and his wife are not there alone, I realize. They are the parents of the three children playing near ours: two girls who chuckle uncontrollably, and one chubby boy with an almost invisible nose and an oversized life vest. Every now and then, the boy screams, "Broccoli, broccoli!" I think, at first, maybe their Labrador is called Broccoli. But as I listen more carefully, I understand the boy is referring to the vegetable and not the family's pet. The mother replies, appeasing him from under her magazine: "Yes, love, we'll give you some broccoli when we get back home."

Also witnessing the Labrador scene is a large woman with a pink towel around her neck. She sits on a folding chair half in the water, smoking cigarettes. Everything about her would be normal enough, except that her chair is placed so that she faces the cars in the parking area and not the lake. All of a sudden, she speaks, questioning the family about how they intend to wash their dog later on without making a mess. The man in the yellow boat answers, unhesitant: "Hose." And the woman bursts into hoarse, phlegm-gurgling laughter.

I finally make up my mind to join our children; I change into my swimsuit under my towel and crawl into the lake in an amphibian position—on my belly and using my hands to glide myself forward. Right before I sink my face into the cold water, I see a staunch man with a lovely round bald head riding into the distance on a standing paddleboard. He seems like the only person in this strange human constellation who is perfectly happy.


WESTERNS

People start asking us where we're from, what we do for a living, and what we're doing all the way "out here."

We drove here from New York, I say.

We do radio, my husband says.

We are documentarists, I sometimes say.

Documentarians, he corrects me.

We're working on a sound documentary, I tell them.

A documentary about nature, he follows.

Yes! I add. About the plants and animals of these lands.

But the farther out we drive, the less these little truths and lies about us seem to appease people's need for an explanation. When my husband tells an inquisitive stranger in a diner that he was also born in the south, he gets a cold nod and raised eyebrows in return. Then, in a gas station outside a town called Loco, I get asked about my accent and place of birth, and I say no, I was not born in this country, and when I say where I was born, I don't even get a nod in return. Just cold, dead silence, as if I've confessed a sin. Later, we begin to see fleeting herds of Border Patrol cars, like ominous white stallions racing toward the southern border. And when Border Patrol officers in a town named Comanche ask us to show our passports, we show them, apologetically, and display big smiles, and explain that we're just recording sounds.

Why are we there and what are we recording? they want to know.

Of course I don't mention refugee children, and my husband says nothing about Apaches.

We're just recording sounds for a documentary about love stories in America, we say, and we are here for the open skies and the silence.

Handing back our passports, one of the officers says:

So you came all the way out here for *the inspiration.*

And because we won't contradict anyone who carries a badge and a gun, we just say:

Yes, sir!

After that, we decide not to tell anyone where I was born. So when—once we've finally arrived in the town called Geronimo— a man with a hat and gun tucked tight into his belt asks us who we are and what we all are doing, and tells us that whatever we are looking for, we're not going to find there, and then asks why the heck our son is taking Polaroid pictures of his signpost outside his liquor store, we know we should just say, Sorry, sorry, and then jump back in the car and drive off. But instead, for whatever reason, perhaps boredom, perhaps fatigue, perhaps simply being too immersed at this point in a reality so far from the framework of what we see as normal, we think it's a good idea to stick around a bit and maybe make conversation. And I stupidly think it's a good idea to lie:

We're screenwriters, sir, and we're writing a spaghetti Western.

Then, to our bewilderment, he takes off his hat, smiles, and says:

In that case, you're no strangers.

And he invites us to sit around the plastic table on the little porch outside his liquor store, and offers us a cold beer. To one side of the table, on top of a plastic chair, there's a muted TV playing a commercial about some malady and its even more terrifying remedy, the cord tense and running through a half-open window, presumably connected to a plug inside the store.

Twisting the tip of his tongue into a w, the man whistles, and his wife and son come out immediately from inside. He introduces her to us as Dolly. Then he tells his son, a boy about the age of ours whom he calls Junior, to go play with our children, and points to the empty lot in front of the porch—a barren space full of segments of chicken fence, half-fallen pyramids made of empty beer cans, and an array of uncanny toys (many baby dolls, some with their hair cut short). Our children walk behind Junior toward the lot. Then Dolly—a young, muscular woman with long arms and silky hair—brings us beer in white plastic cups. From the porch, I watch my children for a few minutes as they try to negotiate the rules of a rather violent game with the boy. His hair is cut in exactly the same way as some of those baby dolls'.

We should be scared in the marrow of our bones, I realize, when our host starts to question our professionalism. It's hard to tell if he's questioning us about it on the basis of our appearance, or merely because of our obvious lack of knowledge about spaghetti Westerns. He, it turns out, is an expert in the genre.

Do we know *The Sheriff of Fractured Jaw*? And *The Taste of Violence*? And *Gunfight at High Noon*?

We don't. Our plastic cups are soon refilled, and my hand—sweaty—reaches over to take a long gulp of the newly poured beer. I keep looking at his muted TV screen, on top of which is a plaster mold of someone's malformed denture, trying to remember where I'd seen or read a similar image—perhaps Carver, perhaps Capote—while my husband rummages in the back of his mind for names of directors of and actors in spaghetti Westerns. He is visibly struggling to win at least one point in credibility with our host. But he's not managing too well, so I interrupt him:

My favorite Western is Bela Tarr's *Sátántangó*!

What's that you say? the man replies, studying me.

*Sátántangó*, I repeat.

I remembered this title from so long ago, when I was still in my post-teenage effluvium of intelligence, pretension, and marijuana. I've never actually finished watching *Sátántangó* (it lasts seven hours). So I was completely misusing what little cinematographic education I have and taking a chance—emboldened by my third quick cup of beer. Lucky for us, the man says he's never watched it, so I can retell the movie's plot in a convincingly Western key. I tell it so slowly and in such painfully precise detail that I'm sure our hosts will grow tired of us, find us too boring to cope with, and let us go. But the man is suddenly uplifted by the spirit of Bela Tarr. He has a terrifying, drunken idea:

Why don't we rent it online and watch it together in our house?

We could all stay for dinner and even sleep over if it got late "and crazy"—he says these last words with a wide grin, teeth too perfect to be real. They have plenty of room for visitors. I play out the possibility in my mind, flashes of horror: dinner would be microwaved, the movie would be successfully rented, the seven of us would sit around another TV set, and the movie would begin. My previous plot summary would in no way be reflected on the screen. So the man, first annoyed and then maybe enraged, would switch it off. He'd have realized we'd been lying to him all along. And in the end, we'd all get murdered and be buried in that empty lot where the three kids are still playing now.

We suddenly hear our son wailing, so his father and I rush toward the empty lot to see what's happened. He's been stung by a bee and is screaming, rolling on the dusty ground in pain. His father picks him up, and both of us exchange glances and nod at each other. I seize the opportunity to overreact, and pretend to be very upset and worried. My husband says, following my lead, that we have to rush to a clinic, because the boy is allergic to many things, and we can't take the chance with bees. The man and his wife both seem to take allergies seriously, so they help us back into our car and give us directions to the nearest clinic. As we are waving goodbye, the man suggests we take the children to the UFO museum in Roswell, after the boy gets better, that is, but as a reward for him acting like a "real man" despite the pain and possible life-threatening danger. And we say yes, yes, thank you, yes, thank you, and drive off into the blue-green dusk.

We drive fast, without looking back, while the pain of the bee sting slowly subsides in the boy's body, and the mild intoxication of all those quick beers wears off from our consciousness, and the children want us to promise we'll take them to that UFO museum anyway, even if the bee sting crisis is now over and wasn't so bad after all, and we are feeling so guilty as parents that we promise, yes, yes we will take you, and we talk about what we will see in that museum until our two children fall asleep, and we drive in silence as night settles in, and find a parking spot in front of a motel outside Lawton, carry the two of them from the car to their bed, and then fall asleep on our own bed, hugging each other for the first time in weeks, hugging each other with all our clothes on, boots included.

## PRISONERS

It was 1830, he begins to tell the children as we stand in line at a Dunkin' Donuts in Lawton the next morning. Andrew Jackson was the president of the United States at the time, and he passed an act in Congress called the Indian Removal Act. We get back in the car with donuts, coffees, and milks, and I study our map of Oklahoma, looking for the roads to Fort Still, where Geronimo and the rest of the last Apaches are buried. The Fort Still cemetery for prisoners of war should be about half an hour's drive from where we are.

Geronimo and his band were the last men to surrender to the white-eyes and their Indian Removal Act, my husband tells the children. I don't interrupt his story to say so out loud, but the word "removal" is still used today as a euphemism for "deportation." I read somewhere, though I don't remember where, that removal is to deportation what sex is to rape. When an "illegal" immigrant is deported nowadays, he or she is, in written history, "removed." I take my recorder from the glove compartment and start recording my husband, without him or anyone noticing. His stories are not directly linked to the piece I'm working on, but the more I listen to the stories he tells about this country's past, the more it seems like he's talking about the present.

Geronimo and his people surrendered in Skeleton Canyon, he continues. That canyon is near Cochise Stronghold, which is where we are going to arrive, soon, at the very end of this trip. In the final surrender, which happened in 1886, there were fifteen men, nine women, three children, and Geronimo. After that, General Miles and his men set out across the desert surrounding Skeleton Canyon and herded Geronimo's band like they were herding sheep aboard death ships. They walked north, for ninety or a hundred miles, to what are now the ruins of Fort Bowie, nestled between the Dos Cabezas and Chiricahua Mountains, near where Echo Canyon is.

Where the Eagle Warriors lived? the boy interrupts to ask.

Yes, exactly, his father confirms.

Then they walked another twenty miles or so to the town of Bowie, he tells the children, who are probably a bit lost in the geography. There, in Bowie, Geronimo and his people were crammed into a train car and sent east, far away from everything and everyone, to Florida. But a few years later, they were crammed back into a train car and sent to Fort Still, where most of them died out, slowly. The last Chiricahuas were buried there, in the cemetery we're driving to today.

We pass empty lots, a Target, an abandoned diner, two urgent care centers right next to each other, a sign that announces a gun show, and finally reach a streetlight, where an elderly couple and a little girl are selling puppies.

Are you still with me? my husband asks the children as he stops at the red light.

Yes, Pa, says the boy.

But Papa? the girl says. Can I say something, too?

What is it?

I just want to say that I'm getting bored of your Apache stories, but no offense.

Okay, he says, smiling, no offense taken.

I want to hear more, Pa, says the boy.

During the war, their father continues, the aim was to eliminate the enemy. Wipe the enemy out completely. They were very cruel, very bloody wars. The Apaches would say: "Now we've taken the warpath."

But always for vengeance, right, Pa? Never just like that with no reason?

Right. Always for vengeance.

Turn left at the next exit, I interrupt.

I'm trembling, he tells me. He says he's not sure if it's the Dunkin' Donuts coffee or pure excitement. Then he continues talking. He tells the children that when any of the great chiefs, like Victorio, Cochise, and Mangas Coloradas, declared war on the white-eyes, they brought together all the warriors from all the Apache families and, together, they formed an army. Then they would attack towns, and destroy them completely.

I'm trembling, look, he repeats softly.

His hands are, indeed, shaking a little. But he continues telling the children this story.

When they wanted to loot, the strategy was a little different. The looting was done by only seven or eight warriors, the best of them, and always on horseback. They'd ride onto ranches and steal cows, grain, whiskey, and children. Especially whiskey and children.

They'd take the children? asks the girl.

Yes, they would.

A quarter of a mile, I whisper, my eyes navigating back and forth between the map and the road signs.

And what would they do to the children? asks the boy.

Sometimes they killed them. But if they showed certain signs, if they demonstrated that they could become great warriors, they were spared. They were adopted and became part of the tribe.

Didn't they ever try to run away? the boy asks.

Sometimes they tried. But often, they liked their lives with their new family much better than their old lives.

What? Why?

Because children's lives then weren't the same as they are today. Children worked all day on the farm, they were always hungry, they had no time to play. With the Apaches, life was hard, too, but it was also more exciting. They rode horses, they hunted, they participated in ceremonies. They were trained to become warriors. On the farm with their parents, all they did was work in the field and with the animals, all day, every day the same thing. Even when they were sick.

I would have stayed with the Apaches, the boy declares after giving it some thought.

Me too? the girl asks.

And immediately, she answers her own question:

Yes, me too. I would have stayed with you, she tells her brother.

We are approaching the gates to the military base. Always, we'd thought it was called Fort Still, but now we see the sign ahead:

Welcome to Fort Sill, the boy reads aloud. It's Fort Sill and not Fort Still, Pa. You have to say it without a t. For your inventory, you have to get the name right.

What a pity, says his father, Fort Still is so much better for a cemetery.

Checkpoint, the boy reads.

And then he asks:

There's a checkpoint?

Of course, his father tells him. We are entering territory of the United States Army.

The thought of entering army territory makes me uneasy. As if I were immediately guilty of a war crime. We roll down our windows, and a young man, possibly still in his late teens, asks us for our IDs. We hand them over—me, my passport; my husband, his driver's license—and the young man looks at them routinely, without paying too much attention. When we ask him for directions to Geronimo's grave, he looks into our real faces for the first time and smiles a sweet kind of smile, perhaps surprised by our question.

Geronimo's tomb? Keep going on Randolph, all the same road, follow it all the way to Quinette.

Quintet?

Yeah, make a right on Quinette. You'll see the signs there that say Geronimo. Just follow them.

Once the windows are closed and we start driving down Randolph Street, the boy asks:

Was that man an Apache?

Maybe, I say.

No, the girl says, he sounds just like Mama, so he can't be an Apache.

We follow the instructions—Randolph, then Quinette—but there are no signs that say Geronimo. On lawns and along paths, we see war relics and decorative artillery, planted like shallow-rooted saplings: howitzers, mortars, shells, rockets. A toddler-sized missile painted pink points to the sky like the phallus of a wild colt, ready, eager, and disquietingly cute. The girl confuses it for a play rocket ship, and we don't contradict her. We pass barracks converted into libraries and into museums, old and new houses, playgrounds, tennis courts, an elementary school. It's an idyllic town, protected from the world outside, perhaps not too different from the thousands of university cloisters sprinkled throughout the country, like the one my sister lives in now, where young people trade a lifetime of family efforts for credits, which become scores, which become a piece of paper that will not guarantee them anything else, nothing at all except a lifetime of living in phantasmagoric limbos between half-voluntary deployments, job searches, applications, and inevitable redeployments.

Do they live in a tomb or a tomba? the girl asks.

What? None of us understand the question.

Do Geronimo and the rest of the bunch live in a tomb or in a tomba?

At the same time, we all say:

A tomb!

But it's still some miles before we see the signs that point us to the tomb. It's the boy who spots it first, concentrating hard to fulfill the task handed down to him. He points and cries out:

Turn right! Geronimo's Grave!

The road winds up and down, over train tracks and across little bridges, leading farther and farther away from the schools, the houses, the war relics, the playgrounds, and into this woodland, as if even now the Apaches were a threat to be kept at a distance. As if Geronimo could still come back and retaliate any day.

We are approaching a clearing in the woods, dotted symmetrically with gray and whitened tombstones, and the girl shouts out:

Look, Papa, over there, the tombas!

We pull over in front of a large sign, which the boy reads aloud as we unbuckle our seat belts:

Apache Prisoner-of-War Cemeteries.

We unlock doors, step out of the car.

On a metal plaque fixed onto a stone at the entrance to the cemetery, there is some kind of explanation of what we're about to see. The boy is in charge, he knows, of reading site-specific information.

He stands in front of it and reads aloud, his prosody well attuned to the necrological hypocrisy of the plaque. It explains that three hundred Chiricahua Apaches rest in that cemetery, where they were buried as prisoners of war after they surrendered to the US Army in 1894, and commemorates "their industry and perseverance on their long road to a new way of life."

## ELEGIES

We all walk into the cemetery in silence, trailing behind my husband, who takes us directly to Geronimo's tomb as if he knows his way around. The tomb stands out from all the rest— a kind of pyramid made of stones stuck together with cement, and crowned with a marble reproduction of an eagle, only slightly smaller than life size. At the feet of the eagle are cigarettes, a harmonica, two pocketknives; and hovering above it, tied to a branch, are handkerchiefs, belts, and other personal relics that people leave as offerings.

My husband has taken out his recording instruments and stands, immobile, facing Geronimo's grave. Though he doesn't ask us for solitude or for silence, we all know that we have to give him some space now, so the three of us walk onward, among the graves, first together, then dispersing. The girl runs around, looking for flowers. She plucks them, then deposits them on graves, over and over. The boy zigzags around tombstones, concentrating on taking pictures of some of them. He is serious in his task. He gazes around, finds a tomb, raises the camera to frame it, focuses, shoots. Once the picture is spat out by the camera, he places it inside the little red book tucked under his arm. A short while later, summoned by his father, he brings the book and camera back to me and joins him under a row of trees bordering a slow stream that marks the northern limits of the cemetery. The boy helps him collect sounds. I finally find some good shade under an old cedar, and sit down. The girl is still running around, plucking and distributing flowers, so I open the little red book, *Elegies for Lost Children,* ready to read for a while in silence. A couple of pictures slip out from between its pages—the book has been getting fatter and fatter with the boy's Polaroids. I pick them up and slide them between the pages toward the end, and then flip back carefully to the first pages of the book.

The foreword explains that *Elegies for Lost Children* was originally written in Italian by Ella Camposanto, and translated into English by Aretha Cleare. It is the only work by Camposanto (1928–2014), who probably wrote it over a span of several decades, and is loosely based on the historical Children's Crusade, which involved tens of thousands of children who traveled alone across, and possibly beyond, Europe, and which took place in the year 1212 (though historians disagree about most of this crusade's fundamental details). In Camposanto's version, the "crusade" takes place in what seems like a not-so-distant future in a region that can possibly be mapped back to North Africa, the Middle East, and southern Europe, or to Central and North America (the children ride atop "gondolas," for example, a word used in Central America to refer to the wagons or cars of freight trains). Finally tired and perhaps bored, the girl comes to join me under the cedar, so I close the book and put it in my handbag. I try to take my mind off what I've been reading and concentrate on her. While the boy and his father finish up collecting sounds, the two of us practice cartwheels, handstands, and forward rolls.


## HORSES

It's already late afternoon when we leave the cemetery, so we decide to find a place to sleep somewhere nearby. The boy is out after a few minutes, before we even reach the military checkpoint on our way out of Fort Sill. The girl makes an effort to stay awake a bit longer:

Mama, Papa?

Yes, love? I say.

Geronimo fell off his horse! Right?

That's right, my husband says.

She fills the space in the car with the warmth of her cub breath, and talks to us from the backseat—long, incomprehensible stories that remind me of some of Bob Dylan's later song lyrics, post Christian conversion. Then, quite suddenly, she maybe tires of being in the world, becomes quiet, looks out the window, and says nothing. Perhaps it is in those stretched-out moments in which they meet the world in silence that our children begin to grow apart from us and slowly become unfathomable. Don't stop being a little girl, I think, but I don't say it. She looks out the window and yawns. I don't know what she's thinking, what she knows and doesn't know. I don't know if she sees the same world we see. The sun is setting, and the brutalized, almost lunar Oklahoma landscape stretches on indefinitely. Always defend yourself from this empty, fucked-up world, I want to say to her; cover it with your thumb. But of course I don't say any of this.

She is silent. We pass the military checkpoint, and she scans the view outside the window, then scans us from who knows which long distance to make sure we're not looking at her when she slips her thumb into her mouth. She sucks her thumb and, in the backseat, a different silence settles. Her thoughts are slowing down, her body's muscles yielding, her respiration layering quietude over unrest. Slowly she is absent, erased from us, slipping back deep into herself. Her thumb, sucked, pumped, swells with saliva, then slowly slips out as she slides into sleep. She closes her eyes, dreams horses.

## ECHOES & GHOSTS

As we drive on, heading north toward the Wichita Mountains, I close my eyes and try to join my children in their sleep. But my mind twists and spirals down into the thought of children lost, other children who are lost, and I remember the two girls, alone, imagine them walking across the desert, possibly not too far from here.

It comes to me that I have to record the sound documentary about lost children using the *Elegies*. But how? I need to make some voice notes, I know. Perhaps, like my husband, I should also be collecting sounds in the spaces we pass through along this trip. Am I also chasing ghosts, like he is? All this time, I have not quite understood what my husband meant when he said his inventory of echoes was about the "ghosts" of Geronimo, Cochise, and the other Apaches. But seeing him earlier today, walking patiently around the cemetery holding up his boom, and the boy trailing after him carrying the Porta Brace, his shoulder slightly raised up against the weight of his father's heavy gear, both of them wearing huge headphones, trying to catch the sounds of wind brushing past branches, insects buzzing, and, especially, birds emitting all their strange, varied sounds—I think I finally begin to understand. I think his plan is to record the sounds that now, in the present, travel through some of the same spaces where Geronimo and other Apaches, in the past, once moved, walked, spoke, sang. He's somehow trying to capture their past presence in the world, and making it audible, despite their current absence, by sampling any echoes that still reverberate of them. When a bird sings or wind blows through the branches of cedars in the cemetery where Geronimo was buried, that bird and those branches illuminate an area of a map, a soundscape, in which Geronimo once was. The inventory of echoes was not a collection of sounds that have been lost—such a thing would in fact be impossible—but rather one of sounds that were present in the time of recording and that, when we listen to them, remind us of the ones that are lost.

We finally arrive in Medicine Park, where we rent a spartan little cabin, with a pleasant porch overlooking a stream. It has a basic kitchen, a bathroom, and four army-like cots, on which we deposit the sleeping kids and then deposit ourselves, our bodies landing on them rather than getting into them, heavy and unresisting like felled trees, and fall sleep.

ARCHIVE

The next morning, I'm up before dawn, ready to work and record some voice notes. Everyone is asleep, so I pee and wash my face quietly, take my handbag, and walk outside. The air is cool against my face as I walk to the car, parked next to the garbage containers just in front of the cabin. From the glove box, I take out my recorder and the big map I use to guide us through our daily routes.

I sit on the porch stoop, the light above the door to the cabin turned on because it's still dark out. First, I study the map, locate where we are now. We're much farther away from home than I thought—a vertigo swells slow in my stomach, like a crescent moon tide. I switch on my recorder and record a single voice note:

We're much closer to the end of the trip now than to the starting point.

Then, from my handbag, I take out the *Elegies*, fat with the boy's pictures tucked between its pages. One by one, I take the pictures out and place them in a little pile next to me. Some of them are good and even very good, and I speak rough descriptions of some of them into my recorder. The last picture, of a tomb, is beautiful but brutal. I record:

The arch of Chief Cochise's tombstone can be made out perfectly, but the name engraved on it is erased somehow, impossible to make out.

I flip through the pages of the book one last time, making sure there are no more pictures between them, and then I study it. I look at its spare cover once more, skim through the text on the back cover, and finally open it up to the first lines of the story:

(THE FIRST ELEGY)

M ouths open to the sky, they sleep. Boys, girls: lips chapped, cheeks cracked, for the wind whips day and night. They occupy the entire space there, stiff but warm, lined up like new corpses along the metal roof of the train gondola. From behind the rim of his blue cap, the man in charge counts them—six children; seven minus one. The train advances slowly along tracks parallel to an iron wall. Beyond, on both sides of the wall, the desert stretches out, identical. Above, the swart night is still.

ARCHIVE

I read those first lines once, then twice—both times getting a little lost in the words and syntax. So I flip back a few pages, to the editor's foreword, which I'd left unfinished. I read the rest of the foreword, rushing over some parts and zooming in on some details here and there: the book is written in a series of numbered fragments, sixteen in total; each fragment is called an "elegy," and each elegy is partly composed using a series of quotes. Throughout the book, these quotes are borrowed from different writers. They are either "freely translated" by the author or "recombined" to the point that some are not traceable back to their original versions. In this first English edition (published in 2014), the translator has decided to translate all borrowed quotes directly from the author's Italian and not from the original sources. Once I reach the end of the foreword, I reread the first elegy to myself again, and then begin reading the second one, out loud and into my recorder:

(THE SECOND ELEGY)

They had told them some things about the future, the relatives who saw the children off. "Don't you go heavy with weeping," said one boy's mother when she kissed his hair outside the door of their house one dawn. And a grandmother warned her granddaughters to beware, to look out for the "winds from sternward." And a widowed neighbor recommended: "Never cry in your sleep, for you'll lose your lashes."

The children came from different places, the six who now sleep atop the train car. They all arrived from distant points on a map, other lives, their unconnected stories now locked by circumstance to one another in the firm line of the tracks. Before they boarded the train, they walked to school, strolled along in parks and on sidewalks, strayed within their city's grids alone, and sometimes not alone. They had never crossed paths before; their lives never should have intersected, but did. Now, as they ride in the back of the beastly train, all clustered next to one another, their stories draw a single straight line moving up across the barrenlands. If someone were to map them, the six of them, but also the dozens like them and the hundreds and tens of thousands that have come and will follow on other trains like this one, the map would plot a single line— a thin crack, a long fissure slicing the wide continent in two. "Swartest story stretched over wretched lives there," a woman said to her husband when the horn of a distant train blew through the open window of their kitchen.

While the children travel, asleep or half sleeping, they do not know if they are alone or if they are together. The man in charge sits cross-legged next to them, taking puffs from a pipe and blowing smoke into the dark. The dry leaves nested in the bowl of his pipe hiss when he inhales, then kindle orange like a tangle of electric circuits in a sleeping city seen from far above. A boy lying next to him moans and swallows a gulp of thick saliva. The wheels of the train spit sparks, a dry branch snaps in the dark, the pipe pit crackles again, and from the metallic intestines of the train, a sound like a thousand souls shrieking can be heard all the while, as if to pass through the desert, it had to crush nightmares in clusters.

HOLES

My thinking was that if I recorded some fragments from this book, reading them out loud, I'd be able to work out how to put my sound project together, to understand the best way to tell the story of the other lost children, the ones arriving at the southern border. My eyes move along the ink lines of the page; my voice, low and steady, speaks the words: gulp, spit, snap, crackle, crush; my recorder registers each one of them in digital bytes; and my mind converts the sum of them into impressions, images, future borrowed memories. I take a pencil from my bag and make a note on the last page of the book: "Must record a document that registers the soundmarks, traces, and echoes that lost children leave behind."

Now I hear the voices and footsteps of my own children coming from inside the cabin. They've woken up, so I stop the recording, put the boy's pictures back inside the book, and then put both the book and the recorder into my handbag. The boy and girl come out to the porch and ask:

What are you doing out here?

When is breakfast?

What will happen today?

Can we go swimming?

They've discovered a brochure in the cabin, which invites guests to visit Medicine Park's "gem," a swimming hole called Bath Lake less than a mile from the cabin.

It's only two dollars each, the boy says, pointing with his finger at the information on the brochure.

And it's in walking distance, he adds.

For breakfast there's bread and ham. Then we hang towels around our necks, I hang my handbag on my shoulder, and we all walk down a narrow path to the public swimming hole. We pay our eight dollars, and we stretch our towels out on some rocks. I don't feel like getting into cold water, so I say that I still have my period, tell them to go ahead without me. The three of them race to the water, and I sit in the sunlight, watching them from a distance, like a ghost of myself.


ERASED

What there was, between Arkansas and Oklahoma, was hours of tape and more hours of things not on tape.

What there was, along highways and across thunderstorms, was my husband, drinking his coffee silently or talking to the children as we drove. Sometimes, my wish for all this to end, and to get as far away from him as possible. Other times, my desire, trailing after him, hoping he might suddenly change his mind, tell me that he'd drive back to New York with us at the end of the summer, or ask me to stay with him and the boy, say he could not let me and the girl go.

What there was, between us, was silence. What there was, was Manuela's phone call, about her two girls, who were not there with her yet and who knows where they were. Sometimes, when I shut my eyes to sleep, there was a telephone number sewed on the collars of the dresses that Manuela's girls had worn on their journey north. And once I was asleep, there was a swarm of numbers, impossible to remember.

What there was, between Memphis and Little Rock, was the story of Geronimo, falling from his horse, over and over again.

What there was in Little Rock, Arkansas, was Hrabal leaning out of a hospital window, bread crumbs in his palm, the pigeons scattering as his body falls out and hits the ground.

There was also Frank Stanford, falling into or out of his mind, three dry gunshots.

In Broken Bow there was news of children falling from the sky—a deluge.

What there was in Boswell was frightening.

What there was in Geronimo was a Western.

What there was in Fort Sill were names on tombstones, and names not there anymore, erased, in a photograph.

There was also that book, *Elegies for Lost Children,* in which a group of children were riding atop a train, their lips chapped, their cheeks cracked.

Everything that was there between Arkansas and Oklahoma was not there: Geronimo, Hrabal, Stanford, names on tombstones, our future, the lost children, the two missing girls.

All I see in hindsight is the chaos of history repeated, over and over, reenacted, reinterpreted, the world, its fucked-up heart palpitating underneath us, failing, messing up again and again as it winds its way around a sun. And in the middle of it all, tribes, families, people, all beautiful things falling apart, debris, dust, erasure.

But finally, there is something. There is this one certainty. It arrives like a blow to my face as we speed along an empty highway into Texas. The story I have to record is not the story of children who arrive, those who finally make it to their destinations and can tell their own story. The story I need to document is not that of the children in immigration courts, as I once thought. The media is doing that already, documenting the crisis as well as possible—some journalists leaning more toward sensationalism, their ratings escalating; others adamant about shaping public opinion, this way or that; and a few others simply committed to questioning and fathoming. I am still not sure how I'll do it, but the story I need to tell is the one of the children who are missing, those whose voices can no longer be heard because they are, possibly forever, lost. Perhaps, like my husband, I'm also chasing ghosts and echoes. Except mine are not in history books, and not in cemeteries. Where are they—the lost children? And where are Manuela's two girls? I don't know, but this I do know: if I'm going to find anything, anyone, if I'm going to tell their story, I need to start looking somewhere else.

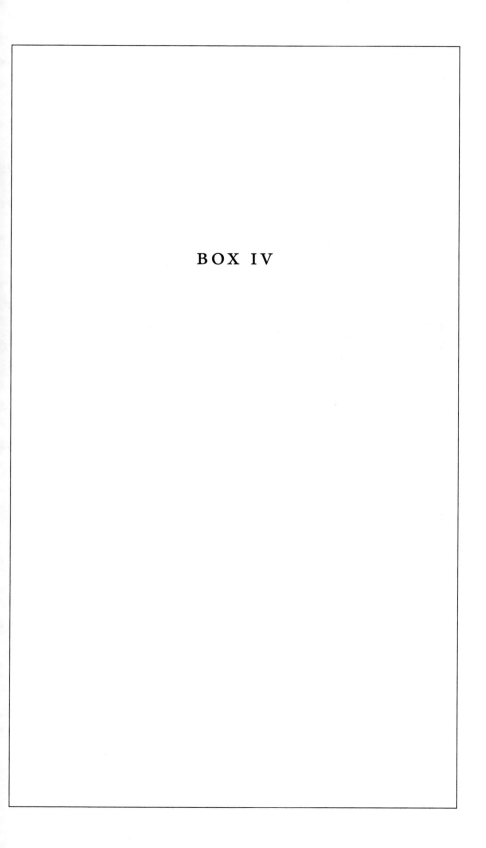

BOX IV

§ FOUR NOTEBOOKS (7¾" X 5")

"On Mapping"
"On History"
"On Reenactment"
"On Erasing"

§ EIGHT BOOKS

*The North American Indian,* Edward S. Curtis
*From Cochise to Geronimo: The Chiricahua Apaches,*
    *1874–1886,* Edwin R. Sweeney
*Lt. Charles Gatewood & His Apache Wars Memoir,* Charles
    Gatewood (Louis Kraft, ed.)
*Geronimo: His Own Story. The Autobiography of a Great*
    *Patriot Warrior,* Geronimo and S. M. Barrett
*Mangas Coloradas: Chief of the Chiricahua Apaches,* Edwin R.
    Sweeney
*A Clash of Cultures,* Robert M. Utley
*The Horse, the Wheel, and Language: How Bronze-Age Riders*
    *from the Eurasian Steppes Shaped the Modern World,*
    David W. Anthony
*Cochise, Chiricahua Apache Chief,* Edwin R. Sweeney

§ ONE BROCHURE

"Desert Adaptations (The Sonoran Desert Species)," National
    Park Service

§ FOUR MAPS

New Mexico
Arizona
Sonora
Chihuahua

§ ONE TAPE

*Hands in Our Names,* Karima Walker

§ ONE COMPACT DISC

*Echo Canyon,* James Newton

§ FOLDER (5 STEREOGRAPHS / COPIES)

Postcard (!) of five men, ankles chained, H. D. Corbett
    Stationery Co.
Two young men, chained
San Carlos Reservation, seven people outside adobe house
Geronimo holding rifle
Geronimo and fellow prisoners on their way to Florida by
    train, September 10, 1886

# REMOVALS

*And it is we who travel, they who flee,*
*We who may choose exile, they who are forced out.*

—JAMES FENTON

*Away and away the aeroplane shot,*
*till it was nothing but a bright spark; an aspiration;*
*    a concentration;*
*a symbol . . . of man's soul; of his determination . . .*
*    to get outside his body.*

—VIRGINIA WOOLF

## STORMS

Everyone says they're empty. Everyone says—vast and flat. Everyone—mesmerizing. Nabokov probably said somewhere—indomitable. But no one had ever told us about the highway storms once you reach the tablelands. You see them from miles away. You fear them, and still you drive straight into them with the dumb tenacity of mosquitoes. Forward, until you reach them and dissolve into them. Highway storms erase the illusory division between the landscape and you, the spectator; they thrust your observant eyes into what you observe. Even inside the hermetic space of the car, the wind blows right into your mind, through stunned eye sockets, clouds your judgment. The rain that falls down looks like it falls up. Thunder blasts so hard it reverberates inside your chest like a sudden uncontrollable anxiety. Lightning strikes so close you don't know if it comes from outside or from inside you, a sudden flash illuminating the world or the nervous mess in your brain, cell circuits igniting in incandescent ephemeral interactions.

## PRIVATE LANGUAGES

We pass the storm, but the rain continues as we drive across the northernmost tip of Texas, heading west toward New Mexico. We play a game now. The game is about names, about knowing the exact names of things in the desertlands we are driving toward. My husband has given the children a catalog of plant species, and they have to memorize names of things, things like saguaro, difficult names like creosote, jojoba, mesquite tree, easier names like organ pipe cactus and teddy bear cholla, names of things that can be eaten, prickly pears, nopales, and then names of animals that eat those things, spadefoot toad, sidewinder snake, desert tortoise, coyote, javelina, pack rat.

In the backseat, the boy reads them all aloud, saguaro, creosote, one by one, jojoba, mesquite, and his sister repeats them after him, teddy bear cholla, sometimes giggling when she finds that her tongue, nopales, cannot wrap itself around a word, spadefoot, sidewinder, and sometimes roaring out her frustration. When we stop for coffees and milks, in a diner by the side of the road, their father tests them. He points to the picture of a species, covering the name underneath the image, and the children have to call out the right name, taking turns. The boy has learned almost all the species by heart. Not the girl. No matter what object my husband points at, she invariably, and without hesitation, shouts:

Saguaro!

And the rest of us, sometimes grinning, sometimes losing patience, answer:

No!

Back in the car, she places the tip of her index finger on the window, pointing to nowhere and everywhere, and says:

Saguaro!

She says the word like she's discovered a new star or planet. But there are no saguaros here, not yet, because this is not the real desert yet, my husband explains. She's not convinced and continues to count saguaros in the wet empty plains, but softly now, to herself, her sticky index finger dotting the foggy window with prints, and slowly mapping, indeed, the constellation of all her saguaros.


ALIENS

Later that day, in a gas station near Amarillo, Texas, we overhear a conversation between the cashier and a customer. As she rings him up, she tells him that the next day, hundreds of "alien kids" will be put on private planes, funded by a patriotic millionaire, and they'll be deported, back to Honduras or Mexico or somewhere in "South America." The planes, full of "alien kids," will leave from an airport not far from the famous UFO museum in Roswell, New Mexico. I'm not sure if when she says the words "alien kids" and "UFO museum," she's stressing the irony of it or is completely unaware of it.

With a quick internet search, back in the car, we confirm the rumor. Or if not confirm, I at least find two articles that support it. I turn toward my husband, tell him we need to go to that airport. We have to drive there and be there when the deportation takes place.

We won't make it on time, he says.

But we will. We are only a few hours away from the first town on the New Mexico–Texas border, a town called Tucumcari, where we can stop to sleep. We can wake up before dawn the next day and drive the two hundred miles or so south to that airport near Roswell.

How will we find the exact airport? he asks.

We just will.

And then what?

Then we'll see, I say, mimicking a type of answer my husband often gives.

Then we'll visit the UFO museum! says the boy from the backseat.

Yes, I say, then the UFO museum.

## GAMES

My back is sweaty against the cracked black leather of the passenger's seat, my body stiff from sitting in the same position for so long. In the back of the car, the children play. The boy says they're both thirsty, lost and walking in the endless desert, says they're both so thirsty and so hungry it feels like hunger is ripping them apart, eating them from the inside, says that hardship and hopelessness are now overtaking them. I wonder where his mind plucks those words from. From *Lord of the Flies*, I suppose. In any case, I want to tell him this reenactment game is silly and frivolous because—because what do they know about lost children, about hardship or hopelessness or getting lost in deserts?

Whenever the boy starts pretending, in the backseat, that he and his sister have left us, run away, and that they're also lost children now, traveling alone through a desert, without adults, I want to stop him short. I want to tell them to stop playing this game. Tell them that their game is irresponsible and even dangerous. But I find no strong arguments, no solid reasons to build a dike around their imagination. Maybe any understanding, especially historical understanding, requires some kind of reenactment of the past, in its small, outward-branching, and often terrifying possibilities. He continues, and I let him continue. He tells his sister that they're walking under the blazing sun, and she picks up his image, says:

We're walking in the desert and it's like we're walking on the sun and not under it.

And soon we will die of thirst and hunger, he says.

Yes, she replies, and the beasts will eat us up unless we get to Echo Canyon soon!

## GRAVITY

Almost every day, we drive, and drive some more, listening to and sometimes recording sounds stretched out across this vast territory, sounds intersecting with us, stories overlaid on a landscape that uncoils, the landscape always flatter, drier. We've been driving for more than three weeks now, though at times it seems like it was just a few days ago that we left our apartment; and at other times, like right now, it seems like we left a lifetime ago, the four of us already very different from the persons we were before we began this trip.

The boy speaks up from the backseat. He asks me to play the David Bowie song about astronauts. I ask him what song, which album, but he doesn't know. He says it's that song about two astronauts talking to each other as one of them is being launched into space. I look for possible songs on my phone, find "Space Oddity," press Play.

Yes, that's it! he says, and asks for more volume.

So I play it loud, as I look out the car window into the impossibly vast skies over Texas. Ground Control speaks to Major Tom, who is about to be launched into space. I imagine other lives—different, but maybe not that different from mine. Some people, when they sense that their lives have reached a stalemate, dynamite everything and start over. I admire those people: women who leave men, men who leave women, people who are able to detect the moment when the life they once chose to live has come to an end, despite possible future plans, despite the children they may have, despite next Christmas, the mortgage agreement they signed, the summer vacation and all the reservations made, the friends and colleagues whom they will have to explain things to. I've never been good at it—acknowledging an ending, leaving when I must. "Space Oddity" is blasting from the car's old speakers, which crackle a bit, a chimney around which we gather. Bowie's voice jumps back and forth between Ground Control and Major Tom—between the one who stayed behind and the one who left.

More louder! the girl shouts, loving the spell this song casts.

Play it again! the boy says after the song finishes.

We play "Space Oddity" more times than I ever imagined I could listen to a song. When they ask for one more round, after the fifth or sixth, I turn back to look at the children scoldingly from my seat, ready to tell them I can no longer take it, can no longer put up with one more replay of the same song. But before I can say anything, I notice that the boy is putting imaginary astronaut helmets on himself and the girl, and then lip-synching into an invisible walkie-talkie:

Copy, copy, Ground Control to Major Tom!

I smile at them both, but they don't smile back. They're too focused on holding fast to imaginary steering wheels, ready to be launched in a capsule into space, ejected from the back of the car, maybe, into the wide-open country now stretching out behind and beyond us as we drive deeper into someplace. I know that I've begun to drift outward, from the nucleus of them, farther away from the center of gravity that once held my everyday life in orbit. I'm sitting in this tin can, falling away from my daughter and son, and they are my Ground Control, falling away from me, the three of us being pulled apart by gravity. I'm not quite sure anymore who my husband is in the picture. He is silent, remote, persistent in his task behind the wheel. The sun has set, the light is blue gray, and he focuses on the road ahead as if underlining a long sentence in a difficult book. If I ask him what he's thinking, he usually says:

Nothing.

I ask him now what he's thinking and wait for an answer, studying his lips. They're dry, and chapped, and could be kissed. He thinks a little, wets his lips with the tip of his tongue:

Nothing, he says.

## SHADOW LINE

Fear—in daytime, under the sun—is something concrete, and it belongs to the adults: speeding on the highway, white policemen, possible accidents, teenagers with guns, cancer, heart attacks, religious fanatics, insects large and medium.

At night, fear belongs to children. It's more difficult to understand its source, harder to give it a name. Night fear, in children, is a small shift of quality and mode in things, like when a cloud suddenly passes in front of the sun, and the colors dim to a lesser version of themselves.

At night, our children's fear is the shadow that a moving curtain projects onto the wall, the deeper dark in the corner of the room, the sounds of wood expanding and water pipes shifting.

But it is not that, even. It is much larger than that. It is behind all that. Too far out of their grasp to be faced, let alone dominated. Our children's fear is a kind of entropy, forever destabilizing the very fragile equilibrium of the adult world.

Long straight roads, empty and monotonous, led us from Oklahoma through the northern tip of Texas and brought us to a stretch of concrete right off Route 66. The town is Tucumcari, New Mexico, and here we found an inn that had once been a bathhouse. I am not sure if that means it was a bordello. The gas station owner described paradise when we asked him about nearby lodging: simple elegance, rocking chairs, family-friendly. What we found, instead, when we parked the car, was a cemetery of bathtubs and broken chairs on a sloped lawn leading up to a porch with webs of old hammocks hanging over empty flowerpots. We found cats in overwhelming numbers. The inn looked like a bad omen. The children were right to point out that the space was:

Creepy.

Dirty.

Saying:

Let's go back home.

What about ghosts, Ma?

Why is there a scarecrow lady in the hallway, in a gown, on a rocking chair?

What are the hats and masks and crosses in the rooms for?

Motel nights are getting longer and more full of past and future ghosts, full of night fears. We have two adjacent rooms in this inn, and my husband has gone to sleep, early, in ours. As I tuck the children into bed, they ask:

What's gonna happen, Mama?

Nothing will happen, I reassure them.

But they insist. They cannot sleep. They're scared.

Can I chupe my thumb, Mama?

Can you read us a story, please, before we go to sleep?

We've read *The Book with No Pictures* too many times, and it doesn't make us laugh anymore, only the girl. So we pick the illustrated edition of *Lord of the Flies*. The girl falls asleep almost immediately, sucking at her thumb. The boy listens attentively, his eyes wide and keen, and not at all prepared for the dreamless sleep that dark nights should confer on children. Some lines we read out loud linger in the room like shadows:

"Maybe there is a beast . . . maybe it's only us."

"We did everything adults would do. What went wrong?"

"The world, that understandable and lawful world, was slipping away."

"What I mean is . . . maybe it's only us . . ."

My husband once told me that when the boy was small, still a baby, right after his biological mother had died, he would wake up almost every night from nightmares, crying inside the rickety crib where he slept. My husband would walk over to the boy, pick him up, and, holding him in his arms, sing him some lines from a poem he liked, by Galway Kinnell:

*When I sleepwalk*
*into your room, and pick you up,*
*and hold you up in the moonlight, you cling to me*
*hard,*
*as if clinging could save us. I think*
*you think*
*I will never die, I think I exude*
*to you the permanence of smoke or stars,*

*even as*
*my broken arms heal themselves around you.*

The boy clings to my arm now as I try to turn the page of the book. It's like a bedtime tug-of-war, except that the ropes are invisible, solely emotional. Before I can continue reading, he asks:

But what if also we were left alone, without you and Papa?

That would never happen.

But it happened to Manuela's two girls, he says. And now they're lost, right?

How do you know about that? I ask him, perhaps naively.

I heard you talking to Pa about it. I wasn't spying. You always talk about it.

Well, that won't happen to you.

But just suppose.

Suppose what?

Suppose you and Pa were gone, and we were lost. Suppose we were inside *Lord of the Flies.* What would happen then?

I wonder what my sister, who understands books better than life, would say if she were confronted with a question like this one. She's so good at explaining books and their meanings, beyond the obvious. Maybe she'd say that all those books and stories devoted to adult-less children—books like *Peter Pan, The Adventures of Huckleberry Finn,* that short story by García Márquez, "Light Is Like Water," and of course *Lord of the Flies*—are nothing but desperate attempts by adults to come to terms with childhood. That although they seem to be stories about children's worlds—worlds without adults—they are in fact stories about an adult's world when there are children in it, about the way that children's imaginations destabilize our adult sense of reality and force us to question the very grounds of that reality. The more time one spends surrounded by children, disconnected from other adults, the more their imaginations leak through the cracks of our own fragile structures.

The boy repeats the question, demanding an explanation of one sort or another:

So what would happen, Ma?

I know I have to reply from my vantage point as mother, my role as a voice that serves as a scaffolding to his world, which is still unfinished, still under construction. He doesn't need to hear about my own fears or philosophical doubts. What he needs is to explore this frightening possibility—alone, no parents—in order to make it less frightening. And I need to help him enact it in his head so that he can maybe find the imaginary solution to his imaginary problem and feel a little more in control of whatever is frightening him.

Well, that's a good question, because that's exactly what this book is about.

What do you mean? Why? What's it about?

I think it's about human nature, I say.

I hate it when you say those kinds of things, Ma.

Okay. So the author, William Golding, was writing this book after the Second World War, and he was disappointed with the way people were always quarreling and looking for more power without even understanding why. So he imagined a situation, like an imaginary scientific experiment, where a group of boys were stranded on an island and had to fend for themselves to survive. And in his imaginary experiment, he concluded that human nature would lead us to really bad things, like savagery and abuse, if we were deprived of the rule of law and a social contract.

What does deprived mean?

Just—without.

So what is human nature deprived of the rule of law? I wish you wouldn't talk like that, Ma.

It just means the way we behave naturally, without the institutions and laws that make up something called the social contract. So the story of these boys is really just a fable of what happens among adults during times of war.

I know what a fable is, Ma, and this book is not like a fable.

It is. Because the boys are not really boys. They're adults imagined as boys. Maybe it's more like a metaphor.

Okay, fine.

But you get what I'm saying, right? You understand?

Yes, I get it. You're saying human nature is war.

No, I'm saying that was Golding's idea about human nature. But that's not necessarily the only possible idea about human nature.

Can't you just get to the point?

The main point, the point the book is trying to make, is simply that problems in society can be traced back to human nature. If A, then B. If humans are naturally selfish and violent, then they will always end up killing and abusing each other, unless they live under a social contract. And because the boys in *Lord of the Flies* are naturally selfish and violent, and are deprived of a social contract, they create a kind of nightmare that they can't wake up from, and end up believing their own games and follies are true, and eventually start torturing and killing one another.

So back to the human nature part. If you and Papa and every adult disappeared, what would happen with our social contract?

What do you mean?

I mean, would my sister and I end up doing what the *Lord of the Flies* boys did to each other?

No!

Why not?

Because you are brother and sister, and you love each other.

But I sometimes hate her, even if she is my sister. Even if she is little. I would also never let anything bad happen to her. But maybe I would let something a little bit bad happen. I don't know what my human nature is. So what would happen to our social contract?

I smell the top of his head. I can see his eyelashes moving up and down as his lids slowly begin to get heavier.

I don't know. What do you think would happen? I say.

He just shrugs, and sighs, so I assure him that nothing bad would ever happen. But what I don't say is that his question hangs as heavily on me as it does on him. What would happen, I wonder? What does happen if children are left completely alone?

Tell me what's happening in that other book you are reading, he says.

You mean the red one, *Elegies for Lost Children*?

Yes, the one about those other lost children.

He listens attentively while I tell him about the freight trains, and the monotonous sound of thousands of footsteps, and the desert, inanimate and calcined by the sun, and a strange country, under a strange sky.

Would you read some of it to me?
Now? It's really late, my love.
Just one chapter.
But just one, okay?
Okay.

(THE THIRD ELEGY)

The children always wanted to ask:
   When will we get there?
How much longer?
When can we stop to rest?
But the man in charge would not take questions. He had made
that clear at the beginning of the journey, long before they boarded
the train, long before they reached the desert, when there were still
seven of them, not six. He had made it clear the day they crossed
the angry brown river aboard the enormous tire tube, black and
rubbery, which a tubeman oared. The tubeman, eyes hollow like
exhausted stars, hands cracked, had helped the seven children sit
around the edges of the tire tube, and then collected the fee from
the man in charge. Standing on a plank of wood stretched out
across the tire tube, he stuck the end of his oar against the muddy
riverbank and pushed. The tube slid into the brown waters.
   The tire tube, before carrying the children across the river, had
been the intestine of a tire, a tire that had belonged to a truck, a
truck that had carried merchandise across countries and national
borders, a truck that had traveled back and forth, many times, along
many roads, many miles, until one day, on a sinuous mountain road,
it crashed into another, similar truck in the bend of a sharp curve.
Both trucks went tumbling down the cliff and hit the bottom with
a loud, metallic blast that reverberated far into the quiet stillness of
that night. The noise was heard by some in a nearby village, and the
next morning, there were several villagers there, investigating the
scene, looking for survivors, although there were none, and rescuing vestiges. From one truck, they rescued boxes of juice, music
cassettes, a cross that had hung from a rearview mirror. From the
other, bags and bags of powder. "Maybe it's cement," one villager

said. "You foolish idiot," another answered, "this is not cement." The days passed and villagers came and went, and went and came, from their homes to the site of the accident, taking everything they could, everything that might be useful to them or sellable to another. And most things were; almost everything was useful, except the two bodies of the deceased drivers, still gripping their steering wheels, each day more decomposed, more unnamable, less human. No one knew what to do with them, and no one ever went to claim them, so one day, an elderly lady from the village came and gave them a final blessing, and two young men dug them graves and planted white crosses on the ground under which they could rest in peace. Before they left, the two young men looked around the site, to see if there was anything else for them to take, and there was almost nothing left, except the trucks' tires, twenty each. From the tires they extracted all the tubes, deflated them, and then sold them to the village's tricycle vendor, who pedaled four hours every day from the village to the side of the big brown river, where he sold his merchandise: cold water, sandwiches, sweet bread, buttons, shoe-laces, and, for some profitable weeks, forty tire tubes that would be reinflated and used as rafts to carry people from one side of the river to the other.

Now the tire tube slid across the brown river, and the seven chil-dren were sitting around its unsteady rim, leaning slightly forward to keep balanced, arms around their backpacks. They'd taken their shoes off and had them clamped between their fingers to keep them from getting wet in the current below. The mighty river flowed under their eyes like an unrestful dream. "There will be no joy in the brilliance of sunshine there," the grandmother of the two girls had said when she described the long stretch of waterway they would have to cross. And indeed there was none, no joy in the rays that beamed down on their foreheads, no beauty in the glittering lights crowning the little waves and many river-folds.

The elder of the two girls had dared to ask the man in charge, her question breaking up with hesitance:

How much longer—long—how to the shore?

She was looking away from the water, perhaps imagined sinking, being swallowed by it. It was the kind of river that looked back at you "vengefully, like a dying snake," her grandmother had warned them both before they set off, following the man in charge. The man now looked at her from under his cap, the shadow long under its blue brim, darkening and lengthening his features. Before answering her question, he snatched one tennis shoe from her unsteady hands and let it drop into a spiraling current in the empty center of the tube. The tubeman continued to oar. The shoe spooned up some water but remained afloat, resisting the pull and shoring up against the inner rubber wall of the tube. Looking down at the shoe from his spot, and then toward the other shore, the man in charge spoke to her but also to everyone:

You are this shoe, and you'll reach the other side when it reaches the other side, if it reaches the other side before sinking to the bottom.

He continued to talk this way and the girl looked at her sister, younger and perhaps less afraid than she was. She signaled to her to close her eyes while he continued to speak, and the older one closed her eyes but the younger one didn't. She looked up at the sky instead and followed two eagles in flight, thinking they looked like gods floating above them, taking care of them, maybe, looking after them while they still had to be stuck to earth. The older one kept her eyes shut, trying to not hear him, trying to hear nothing but the splashing thump of the float against the waters, rising and falling. He uttered threats that filled all of them with terror, threats like "sink to the bottom" and "blue in the face" and "food for the little fish." They all understood then, while they were slowly being ferried across the river, being cut off forever from everything they'd once known, that they were really going nowhere.

HERE

Finally, everyone is asleep: the children in their room and my husband in ours. I walk out to the porch of the old bathhouse. I'm tired but not sleepy, so I want to read for a little longer. Sitting myself down on a rocking chair—unraveled wicker and rickety chipped wood—surrounded by old bathtubs and sinks, I take my hand recorder and the little red book from my handbag. I press Record and read on:

(THE FOURTH ELEGY)

Once, on the northern bank of the river, they'd all walked in a single line, and the man in charge tapped them on the head with the end of a stick and said: girl one, girl two, boy three, boy four, boy five, boy six, boy seven. They'd walked into the thick of the jungle, where they heard many other footsteps, heard leaves full of voices. Some, they were told, were the voices of others like them. Real voices like theirs, coming from all directions, bouncing off tree trunks and passing through thickets. Other voices, no one knew or would say where and what and how. These they had feared. They belonged to the long or recently extinguished, the man in charge told them. They belonged to souls perhaps rising from dark fossae, he said, dead but still stubbornly reverberating aboveground: few youths, the old, tender girls, many men and women. All the "impetuous, impotent dead," he said. All of them "unburied, cast on the wide earth." And though they did not understand his long words, they walked under their shadow the rest of the way.

For ten suns, they traveled on foot. They marched the full stretch from the break of day to noon, when they stopped for a brief meal, and then took to the path again from the long-shadowed hours of the afternoon till the moon was high, or else till the littler ones with flatter feet could no longer take another step. Very often the little ones fell, or threw themselves to the ground, their legs and feet not yet ready, not strong enough, not accustomed. But even the older ones, with higher arches and thick-muscled insteps, could hardly make themselves walk firmly beyond the hour of sunset, so they were quietly thankful when others lagged, or fell, and forced the march to a halt.

When midnight came, all of them fell to the ground, and were ordered by the man in charge to sit in a circle and make a fire. Only then, when the flames were burning high, were they finally allowed to take their shoes off. All unshod, they held their aching foot-soles tight in their hands, wondering how much longer before they reached the train yard. Some sat silent, some howled out their pain shamelessly, one vomited behind his shoulder in horror at the sight of his blood-drenched socks and peeling skin. But the next day at dawn, and the next, they always all stood up and walked some more.

Until one afternoon at the tenth setting sun, they'd finally come to the clearing in the jungle where the train yard was. The clearing was not a yard but also not a proper station. It was a waiting-place of some sort, more like hospital emergency rooms, because the people there were not waiting the way people usually wait for a train. With a little fear and a little relief, the children saw countless people lingering and loitering, men and women, either alone or in groups, some other children, a few elderly, all waiting for help, for answers, for anything they might be offered. There amid those strangers, they found a spot, stretched out tarp tatters and old blankets, reached into their backpacks for water, nuts, a Bible, a sack of green marbles.

Once they were settled in, the man in charge told them not to move from their spot and drifted to a nearby town, strayed in and out of taverns, to and from sad whores and motel beds, snorting long white trails lined up on a pewter dish, short bumps on a credit card, flakes inside a crack in a wooden bar; he'd fallen into stubborn arguments and asked for another drink, dispensing bills and demanding services, hurling insults, then advice, then apologies at sudden foes and instant fellows until, finally, he fell asleep, open-mouthed, on an aluminum table, a string of his saliva meandering like a lazy river between domino tiles and cigarette ash. Above him, an airplane passes, leaves a straight long scar on the palate of the cloudless sky.

In the meantime, the children waited. They sat butt-flat on yard gravel among strangers, or ventured a little between tracks, and waited with the others. Though not everyone in the yard, they noticed, was waiting for a train. There were food vendors, who accepted as little as five cents in exchange for a reused water bottle and a loaf of buttered bread. There were garment traders, letter writers, lice pickers, and ear cleaners, but also priests with long black robes reading words from inside Bibles, fortune-tellers, entertainers, and penitents. With their eyes and ears, they followed a grim young man who warned them and anyone else willing to listen: "Alive enter you, exit you a mummy." Waving a half-missing arm wrapped in soiled bandages, he repeated his deathly sentence like a curse on the children, but he delivered it with a wide-open smile while balancing on a track, heel-toe and heel-toe, looking a little like the circus funambulists in the children's towns, before their towns had been abandoned and the circuses no longer passed through.

Later, they saw a shamefaced penitent who long ago had planted a seed in a little mound of soil on the palm of his hand, and the seed had become a small tree, and its roots now clutched and twisted around his outstretched hand and forearm. One girl had almost paid the penitent five cents to let her touch the miracle tree, but the others had restrained her, said don't be gullible, it's all a trick.

An old blind man had approached them near nightfall and sat with them in silence for a while. Before leaving, though, he'd stood in front of them like a retired schoolmaster and murmured instructions in the dark. They were complicated and confusing instructions, about the trains they'd ride during the journey ahead. He, like the rest of the yard people, knew that the safest train cars to ride were the gondolas. He told them the tank cars were round and slippery, the boxcars were almost always closed and locked, and the hopper cars were a deathtrap you'd climb into and rarely climb back out of. He said the train would come one day soon, and they should pick a gondola. Don't think of home, don't think of people, gods, or consequences, he'd told them. Don't pray or talk or wish anything. And before bowing goodbye, the old blind man had pointed toward some distant star and said, "Thence outward and away," and repeated, "Thence outward and away." Then he'd vanished into the dark.

At sunrise the next day, the man in charge had not come back. Those who came were the chanting men and women who flocked in opportunistic bands of threes or fives between the groups of waiting travelers, offering shoe repairs for cheap, and cloth-mending for almost nothing. They chanted, twenty-five cents for rubber soles, twenty-five cents for superglue on rubber soles, chanted, twenty,

twenty for leather, twenty for hammer and nail service on leather soles, chanted, fifteen, fifteen for cosmetic repairs and needlework.

One of the boys, boy four, paid a man fifteen cents to patch a hole on the flank of his boot with a square piece of fabric cut out from the sleeve of his own canvas jacket. The rest of the children called him an idiot, called him retarded, called him a mule, said he should have sold the jacket or traded it for something better instead. Now he had a patched shoe and a torn jacket, they said, and what good were they? But he knew that the boots had been new while the jacket was an old hand-me-down, so he quietly swallowed their disapproval and looked the other way.

The man in charge still had not returned when the morning had passed and the yellowing light of the afternoon was falling, almost pleasant, on the train yard. The children were playing with some marbles one had brought when a scrotum-faced woman, neck speckled with warts and stray hair, and eyes like a welcome mat on which too many shoes had been wiped, appeared out of the shadows before them and grabbed for their palms, foretelling demented bits of stories that they could not afford to hear complete:

"I see a wine-red glow in the shallows, boy."

"By a rock-pool, you, young man, will grow logy with vine-must."

"They'll buy you, little tiny one, for a little slave-money, while the rest go northward."

"And you, girl. You'll glow like a dying firefly inside a glass cage."

She promised to tell them the rest of the stories for fifty cents each, which was double the cost of shoe repairs. And if they wished her to intercept fortune in their favor, it would cost seventy-five cents, which was many times more than a whole serving of water and bread. So though they'd wanted to hear more, they'd forced themselves to avoid the witch-woman's eyes, had pretended not to believe all the ill omens uttered from between her leathery lips.

When they'd finally managed to ushh her away, she'd cursed them all in a brutal foreign tongue, and before disappearing into the parallel lines of the tracks, she'd turned around once more toward them, whistled, and thrown a ripe orange in their direction. The orange hit one boy on the arm, boy seven, then landed in the gravel without rolling.

Though curious and also desperately hungry, they'd dared not touch it. Others like them, after them, perhaps sensed the same dark something in that strange fruit, because days and then weeks passed and the orange remained there, round, untouched, molding green and showing white rings on the outside, fermenting first sweet and then bitter inside, then gradually blackening, shrinking, shriveling, until it disappeared into the gravel during a long midsummer rainstorm.

The only yard people who didn't curse, didn't trick, didn't ask for anything in return were three young girls with long obsidian braids who carried buckets of powdered magnesium. For free, the three girls offered to tend to the children's ravaged feet, the heels and balls pulpy and bursting open like boiled tomatoes. The girls sat beside them and reached their cupped hands into metal buckets. They powdered the children's soles and insteps, and later used tattered cloths or scraps of towels to wrap ripped skin. They used pumice stones to reduce tough calluses, careful not to rub the skin raw, and massaged contracted calf muscles with their small but firm thumbs. They offered to puncture bellying blisters using a sterilized needle. "See the small flame of this match?" one of them said, and then explained that when the flame touched the needle, the needle got clean. And last, the youngest of the bucket-girls, the one with the best eyes—big black almonds—showed the children a set of contorted metal hangers and a pair of large clippers that she pulled from inside her bucket, and with them offered to relieve the deeper, more desperate pain of ingrown or half-hanging toenails.

Only one boy, boy six, said yes, yes please. He was not one of the younger ones, nor was he the eldest. He had seen the large clippers offered to him and had remembered the lobsters. He remembered his grandfather walking out of the sea on unsteady twiggy legs, carrying the lobsters inside a net mended twice or thrice with double knots and drops of candle wax. The old man would stand by the shore, his back curved forward to balance the weight of the catch, and call out his name. Always he had run to the shore at his grandfather's call, offered to carry the net for him. And as they made their way from the hard, wet sands nearer to the shore toward the dry, higher dunes, and then crossed the road and boarded the passenger bus, he would peek now and then into the net. He'd observe that death-nest of lobsters crawling over lobsters, speculating how much will we earn, counting how many did we catch, watching the little beasts opening and closing their pincher claws as if they were all uttering sad thoughts to one another in sign language.

He had never thought very highly of the lobsters they caught— those slow, dumb, but eager and somewhat sexual sea monsters that they would later sell in the food market for ten coins apiece. Yet now he remembered them and missed their smell of salt and rot, their perfectly articulated small bodies inching pointlessly inside the wobbly, concave net. So when the girl showed him the clippers, he raised his hand and waved, and she came and kneeled in front of him and held the clippers to his toes and looked into his eyes and told him don't worry, though she was worried, and her hands trembled a little. The boy closed his eyes and thought of his grandfather's bony brown feet, their swollen veins and yellowing toenails. Then, when the metal instrument pierced first hesitantly, then more firmly into his skin, he wailed and cursed and bit his lower lip. The girl felt the resolve of determination layering over her fear as she pierced the skin, and her hands stopped trembling. She deftly clipped and cut the broken toenail, biting her lower lip, too, in concentration or perhaps with empathy. In his mind, the boy cursed her while she cut and twisted, but in the end, he opened his eyes and wanted to thank her, teary and embarrassed, looking up into her steady black eyes. He did not say anything when she said she was all done, and wished him good luck, and told him to always wear socks, but he smiled.

He searched for her the next morning, when the children finally boarded the gondola and the train departed, but in the sea of faces in the distancing train yard, he recognized no one.

## TOGETHER ALONE

As I get into bed and curl around my husband's sweaty back, I can still hear the echoes of these other children, somewhere. I hear the monotonous sound of thousands of lost footsteps, and a dim chorus of voices, weaving in and out of the sentences, swiftly shifting perspectives in the slow, heavy rhythm of the narrative voice, and as I try to fall asleep, I know that this life is mine, and also, at the same time, irremediably lost.

What ties me to where? There's the story about the lost children on their crusade, and their march across jungles and barrenlands, which I read and reread, sometimes absentmindedly, other times in a kind of rapture, recording it; and now I am reading parts to the boy. And then there's also the story of the real lost children, some of whom are about to board a plane. There are many other children, too, crossing the border or still on their way here, riding trains, hiding from dangers. There are Manuela's two girls, lost somewhere, waiting to be found. And of course, finally, there are my own children, one of whom I might soon lose, and both of whom are now always pretending to be lost children, having to run away, either fleeing from white-eyes, riding horses in bands of Apache children, or riding trains, hiding from the Border Patrol.

As my husband feels my body close to his, deep in his sleep, he inches away, so I turn the other way and curl up around my pillow. A kind of future self looks at all this in quiet recognition: what I once had. No self-pity, no desire, just a kind of astonishment. And I fall asleep with the same question the boy asked me earlier:

What happens if children are left alone?


BEDS

The question comes back, more as a presentiment than as a question, early the next morning, as we pack to leave and prepare for the drive ahead of us to the airport near Roswell. I notice a urine stain on the children's bedsheets before we check out of the inn and jump in the car, but I don't ask the boy or the girl whose it is.

I wet my bed until I was twelve. And I wet it, especially, between the ages of ten and twelve. When I turned ten years old, exactly the boy's age, my mother left us—my father, my sister, and me—to join a guerrilla movement in southern Mexico. The three of us moved to Nigeria for my father's work. For many years after that day, I hated politics, and anything to do with politics, because politics had taken my mother away. For years, I was angry with her, incapable of understanding why politics and other people and their movements were more important to her than us, her family. A couple of years later, right after my twelfth birthday, I saw her again. As a birthday present, or maybe just as a general reunification present, she got my sister and me plane tickets to travel to Greece with her, which I guess was kind of halfway between Mexico and Lagos. Our father helped us pack our bags and drove us to the airport: our mother would be waiting for us in the Athens airport. On our first day in Athens, she told us she wanted to take us to the Apollo Temple at the Oracle of Delphi. So we jumped on a local bus. As we found our seats, complaining about the lack of leg space and the heat, she told us that in Greek, the word for being taken somewhere by a bus was μεταφέρω, or metaphor, so we should feel lucky about being meta-phored to our next destination. My sister was more satisfied than I was with the explanation that we had been given.

We traveled many hours toward the oracle. All the while, on the way there, our mother spoke to us about the strength and power of the Pythonesses, the priestesses of the temple, who in ancient times served as the vehicles of the oracle by allowing themselves to be filled with ενθουσιασμός, or enthusiasm. I remember the definition my mother gave of the term, breaking it down into its parts. Making a kind of cutting gesture with her hands, one palm as board and the other as knife, she said: "En, theos, seismos," which means something like "in, god, earthquake." I think I still remem-ber it because I didn't know, till that day, that words could be cut up into parts like that to be understood better. Then she explained that enthusiasm was a kind of inner earthquake produced by allowing oneself to be possessed by something larger and more powerful, like a god or goddess.

As we rode on toward the oracle, my mother spoke to us about her decision, some years earlier, to leave us, her family, and join a politi-cal movement. My sister asked her difficult, sometimes aggressive questions. Although she loved my father, my mother explained, she had been following him around all her life, always putting her own projects aside. And after years of doing that, she had finally felt an inner "earthquake," something that stirred her deeply and maybe even shattered a part of her, and had decided to go out and find a way to fix all the brokenness. Perhaps not fix it, but at least understand it. The bus wound up and down the mountain road toward Delphi, and my mother tried to answer our questions as best she could. I asked her about where she had slept all that time she had been gone, what she had eaten, if she'd felt afraid, and if so, afraid of what. I wanted to ask her if she'd had lovers and boyfriends, but I didn't. I listened to her speak, looking up at her face and studying the many lines of her worried forehead, her straight nose and her big ears, from which hung long earrings, dangling back and forth with the rocking movements of the bus. At times, as the bus climbed on, I closed my eyes and rested my cheek against her bare arm, smelling it, trying to take in all the old scents of her skin.

When we finally got to Delphi and got off the bus, the access to the temple and oracle was already closed. We had arrived too late. That often happened if you traveled with my mother: you arrived too late. She suggested we break in, climb over the fence and see the oracle anyway. My sister and I obeyed, trying to pretend that we enjoyed this kind of adventure. We all climbed over the fence, and started walking through a forest. We didn't get too far. Soon, we started hearing a terrifying dog-bark, and then more barks, all getting closer to us, from multiple dogs, surely a large pack, savage. So we ran back to the fence, climbed back out, and waited on the side of the road for the night bus that would take us back to Athens. Behind us, on the other side of the fence, five or six mean-looking dogs barked at us still.

That encounter with our mother, although it was a failed adventure, planted a seed in me that would later, as I grew older, flower into a deeper understanding of things. Of things both personal and political and how the two got confused; and about my mother in particular and about women more generally. Or perhaps the right word is not understanding, which has a passive connotation. Perhaps the right word is recognition, in the sense of re-cognizing, knowing again, for a second or third time, like an echo of a knowledge, which brings acknowledgment, and possibly forgiveness. I hope my children, too, will forgive me, forgive us, one day, for the choices we make.

## TRIANGLES

On the radio, we listen to a longer report on child refugees. We had decided not to listen to any more news about this, not when our children were awake. But the recent developments, and in particular the story about the children to be deported near Roswell, now thrust me back into the urgency of the world outside our car.

They are interviewing an immigration lawyer, who is trying to make a case to defend the children who will be sent back to Tegucigalpa later that day. I listen for any hint, any bit of information on exactly when and where the deportation will take place.

They don't give any details, but I use the back of a receipt to take down the lawyer's name, a name they've repeated a few times already. Then I search for her on the internet while she explains that if the children are Mexican, they are immediately removed, deported back. But if they are Central American, she says, immigration law has it that they have a right to a hearing. So this deportation is illegal, she concludes. I find the lawyer's name and email address on a page of a small nonprofit organization based in Texas, and I email her. Polite introduction, a few sentences about why I'm contacting her, and my only urgent question:

Do you know where the children will be deported from?

Prompted by the interviewer, she continues to explain that once they reach the border, the children know their best bet is to be caught by Border Patrol officers. Crossing the desert beyond that border, alone, is too dangerous. But some of them do. My mind drifts to the lost children in the little red book, all walking alone, lost now and forgotten in history. The interviewer explains that the children also know that if they do not surrender themselves to the law, their fate will be to remain undocumented, like most of their parents or adult relatives already in the United States. The children who will be deported today have been in a detention facility near Artesia, New Mexico.

I look for airports in or near Artesia, and find one, and note down the location. Artesia is not far from Roswell, I tell my husband, so that must be it. If the lawyer doesn't reply to this email, our best bet will be to drive to that airport. We'll just have to trust, and perhaps we'll get lucky.

### SALIVA

As we drive forward, my husband tells the children a long, winding story that perturbs me and fascinates them, about a woman called Saliva. She was a medicine woman, a friend of Geronimo's, who cured people by spitting on them. Saliva, he said, removed their bad luck, illness, and melancholy with her powerful, salty drops of spit.

### SHUFFLE

I don't know, when the boy suggests a poll as we take a left on Route 285, south out of Roswell, if my favorite song on this trip is Kendrick Lamar's "Alright," which the boy knows by heart and loves, or Laurie Anderson's "O Superman," which the girl always wants to listen to again and again, or a song quite outside my generational listening habits, called "People II: The Reckoning," by a band from Phoenix called Andrew Jackson Jihad—a name we hope is somehow ironic, though we're not sure in which way it could or should be ironic.

We haven't discussed the lyrics of the songs in detail yet, the way the four of us usually do, but I think they're songs about us four, and about everyone else in this big country who doesn't own a gun, cannot vote, and doesn't fear God—or who at least fears God less than he or she fears other people.

I like a line in Anderson's song, about the airplanes coming—"They're American planes, made in America," she says in a robotic voice. The planes always getting closer, always hovering in our consciousness, always haunting people who have to grow up to fear America.

In Lamar's song, I like catching up to the line "Our pride was low, lookin' at the world like, 'Where do we go?'"

I always sing it loud, looking out the window of the car. The boy, from the backseat, sings the rest of the stanza even louder.

And finally, I like a line in "People II" that I maybe don't fully understand, about being in "firefly mode." Now we listen to the song, and I ask the children what they make of it:

What do you think "firefly mode" means?

It means on and off, on and off, says the girl.

She's right, I think. It's a song about switching oneself on and off from one's own life.

For the next twenty minutes or so, we're all silent inside the car, listening to the songs that shuffle and play, looking out our windows at a landscape scarred by decades or maybe centuries of systematic agricultural aggression: fields sectioned into quadrangular grids, gang-raped by heavy machinery, bloated with modified seeds and injected with pesticides, where meager fruit trees bear robust, insipid fruit for export; fields corseted into a circumscription of grassy crop layers, in patterns resembling Dantesque hells, watered by central-pivot irrigation systems; and fields turned into non-fields, bearing the weight of cement, solar panels, tanks, and enormous windmills. We're driving across a strip of land dotted with cylinders when the "firefly mode" song comes up again. The boy suddenly clears his throat, and says he needs to say something:

I'm sorry to break it to you, but the lyrics in that song you keep playing and singing say "fight-or-flight mode" and not "firefly mode."

He sounds like a teenager, talking to us like this, and I'm not ready to accept his correction, though I know he's probably right. Even though he's still a child, he's so much more culturally attuned to this country, and to the times. I dismiss his opinion, unfairly asking him for proof—which he of course cannot give, because I won't lend him my phone to search for lyrics right now. But from this moment on, as the song is played on repeat on our car speakers, he makes a point of singing that part of the chorus especially loud: "fight-or-flight mode." His sister and father, I notice, pause in silence and don't sing that part of the song, at least in the next few rounds. I, in turn, make a point of singing the words "firefly mode" especially loud and clear. The boy and I have always met as equals on this sort of battlefield, notwithstanding our age gap. Maybe it's because our temperaments are so alike, even though we do not share blood-bonds. Both of us will defend our stances to the end, no matter how senseless they eventually reveal themselves to be.

He shouts:

Fight-or-flight mode!

Just as I sing at the top of my voice:

Firefly mode!

Inside the car, I've grown accustomed to our smell, to the intermittent silence between us, to instant coffee. But never to the road signs planted like omens along the road: Adultery Is a Sin; Sponsor a Highway; Gun Show This Weekend! Never habituated, either, to seeing the cemeteries of plastic toys abandoned on front lawns on reservations, or the melancholy adults waiting in line, like children, to refill their large plastic cups with bright-colored sodas in gas station shops, or those resilient water towers in small towns, which remind me of the equipment we used in school during science lab classes. All of that leaves me in firefly mode.

## FEET

Mama! the girl calls out from the backseat.

She says she has a splinter in her foot. She cries and cries and cries, as if she'd lost a limb or broken something.

A saguaro splinter! she claims.

I turn around from my seat, lick the tip of my finger, and place it softly on the—most likely imaginary—splinter. The heel of her foot is soft and smooth, and as I hold my finger against it, I remember the feet of that lost boy being cured by the girl in the train yard.

The reply to my email arrives around noon, when we are just a few miles from Roswell, buying coffees and juices at a gas station. The lawyer says she does not know the exact time, though she thinks it will be during the early afternoon, and confirms our deduction:

the planes will leave from the Artesia Municipal Airport. I check the map. The airport is only forty miles south of Roswell. If the planes are scheduled to take off in the early afternoon, we will easily get there in time.

## TRANSFERALS

As we speed toward the airport near Artesia, I listen for more news on the radio, find nothing. I switch it off and listen to our two children playing in the backseat. Their games have become more vivid, more complex, more convincing. Children have a slow, silent way of transforming the atmosphere around them. They are so much more porous than adults, and their chaotic inner life leaks out of them constantly, turning everything that is real and solid into a ghostly version of itself. Maybe one child, alone, by himself, cannot modify the world the adults around him or her sustain and entertain. But two children are enough—enough to break the normality of that world, tear the veil down, and allow things to glow with their own, different inner light.

I efface myself for a while, and simply let their voices fill the space of the car and the space in my head. They're participating in a verbal choreography that involves horses, airplanes, and a spacecraft. I know their father is also listening to them, although he's concentrating on the road, and I wonder if he feels the way I do—if he senses how our rational, linear, organized world dissolves into the chaos of our children's words. I wonder and want to ask him if he, too, notices how their thoughts are filling our world, inside this car, filling it and blurring all its outlines with the same slow persistency of smoke expanding inside a small room. I don't know to what degree my husband and I have made our stories theirs; and they, their stories and backseat games, ours. Perhaps we mutually infect each other with our fears, obsessions, and expectations, as easily as we pass around a flu virus.

The boy shoots poisoned arrows at a Border Patrol officer from a big horse, while the girl hides from American bluecoats under some kind of desert thornbush (though she finds mangoes growing on its branches and stops to eat one before she jumps out to attack).

After a long battle, the two children sing a song together to resuscitate a fellow child warrior.

Listening to them now, I realize they are the ones who are telling the story of the lost children. They've been telling it all along, over and over again in the back of the car, for the past three weeks. But I hadn't listened to them carefully enough. And I hadn't recorded them enough. Perhaps my children's voices were like those bird songs that my husband helped Steven Feld record once, which function as echoes of people who have passed away. Their voices, the only way to listen to voices that are not audible; children's voices, no longer audible, because those children are no longer here. I realize now, perhaps too late, that my children's backseat games and reenactments were maybe the only way to really tell the story of the lost children, a story about children who went missing on their journeys north. Perhaps their voices were the only way to record the soundmarks, traces and echoes that lost children left behind.

I think about that persistent question:

Why did you come to the United States?

And why are we here? I wonder.

What are you thinking, Ma? the boy suddenly asks me from behind.

Just thinking that you're right. It's "fight-or-flight" and not "firefly" mode.

AIRPLANE

On a strip of gravel, we pull over. To our right is a long wire mesh fence, and on the other side of the fence, there's a runway where a small airplane stands still, an airstair attached to its only door. It's not a commercial plane but not a military aircraft either. It indeed looks like a private plane (an American plane, made in America). We step out of the car, into the dense heat, the midday sun beating down on us. The girl is asleep in the backseat, so we leave two doors open to allow air to blow through the car.

There is no one on the runway except a maintenance man, driving a kind of golf cart in loops. I have my recorder with me, and tuck it into my left boot, pressing Record before I do and making sure the mic is sticking out, ready to trap at least the sounds closer to us. We lean against the car while we wait for something to happen— but nothing does. My husband lights a cigarette and smokes it with long, strained puffs. He asks if he can record some sounds, asks if I mind. I tell him to go ahead; that's why we're here, after all. I watch the maintenance man, who now steps out of the little cart, picks something up from the pavement—a rock? a penny? a wrapper?— deposits it into a black bag hanging from the back of the golf cart, then steps back into his seat and resumes his route until he eventu- ally disappears into the hangar at the right end of the airstrip.

I ask the boy for his binoculars, to get a closer look at the plane parked on the runway. He fetches them from the backseat, and also fetches his camera and the little red book from my box.

The two of us walk across the gravel strip, and stand right up against the fence. I adjust the binoculars to my eyes. Their metal rims feel hot. I zero in on the small plane, but there's nothing to see. As I fiddle with the binoculars' lenses, I hear the boy next to me preparing his camera. There is a suspended silence as he holds his breath while he tries to bring the plane into focus, then there's the click of the shutter button, and then the sound of the rollers turning as they slide the photo out. With the binoculars, I scan the area under and around the plane, catch a bird in flight, and follow it until it disappears. I see the sky, clouds gathering in the distance, an occasional tree, steam rising above the tarmac at the far end of the runway. I hear the boy mumble as he concentrates on protecting the photograph from the blazing daylight, tucking it between the pages of the book so it can develop there, and wonder what sounds my husband's microphone is capturing right now and which ones will be lost. I'm slowly sweeping the runway with the binoculars, left, then right, then up almost vertically toward the unvarying sky, and then down, angling them back closer to me until I see my own two feet blurred against the gravel. I hear the boy walking to the car to put his camera away again, and I hear him as he steps across the gravel back again to the fence, where I'm standing. He asks me for a turn at the binoculars, and I hand them over to him. He fixes the rims of the oculars to his eye sockets, and squints into the lenses the same way his father looks at the highway when he's driving.

What do you see? I ask.

Just brown hills that are blurry and the sky that is blue, and the plane.

What else? Look harder.

If I look too hard, my eyes burn. And I see those little see-through things that float in the sky, sky-worms.

They're not worms. Eye doctors call them floaters, but astronomers call them superstrings. Their purpose is to tie up the universe together. But what else besides superstrings?

I don't know what else.

Come on. So many years of schooling? You can do better.

He pauses, and smiles back at me, acknowledging my teasing, and then maybe trying a little too hard to give me a patronizing glance. He's still small enough to wear sarcasm and condescension like a suit several sizes too big. He looks back through the binoculars, and suddenly he says:

Look, Mama! Look over there!

I slowly walk my eyes on the tightrope laid out between his steady eyes and the line of small figures now stepping out of the hangar and onto the runway. They are all children. Girls, boys: one behind another, no backpacks, nothing. They march in single file, looking like they've surrendered, silent prisoners of some war they didn't even get to fight. There aren't "hundreds," as we'd heard there would be, but we count fifteen, perhaps twenty. It must be them. The night before, they were bused from a federal law enforcement training facility in Artesia to this small airport on State Road 559. Now they walk toward the plane that will take them back south. If they hadn't gotten caught, they probably would have gone to live with family, gone to school, playgrounds, parks. But instead, they'll be removed, relocated, erased, because there's no place for them in this vast empty country.

I snatch the binoculars back, and focus. Several officers march at their side, as if the children might try to escape now, as if they could. I know they are not there, and that even if they were, I wouldn't recognize them, but of course I look for Manuela's daughters, trying to spot any two girls wearing matching dresses.

The boy tugs on my sleeve:

It's my turn!

Mirages rise from the hot pavement. An officer escorts the last child onto the airstair, a small boy, maybe five or six, sucking his thumb as he climbs into the plane. The officer closes the door after him.

My turn to look, Ma.

Wait, I say.

I turn around to check on the girl inside the car. She's asleep, thumb in her mouth, too. Inside the airplane, that boy will sit still in his seat, buckled up, and the air will be dry but cool. The boy will make an effort to stay awake while he waits for the departure, the way my daughter does, the way children his age do.

Mama, he might think.

But no one will answer.

Mama! the boy says, tugging on my sleeve again.

What is it? I reply, losing patience.

My binoculars!

Just wait a second, I tell him sternly.

Give them to me!

I finally hand them over again, my hands shaking. He focuses calmly. I look around anxiously, my jaw tense and my breathing getting quicker and shallower. The plane is standing in the same place, but the officers who escorted the children now walk back toward the hangar, looking like a football team after practice, joking around, slapping one another on the back of the head. Some of them spot us, I think, but they couldn't care less. If anything, it seems like our presence, behind the fence that divides us, encourages them. They turn around to face the plane as its engines are switched on, and clap in unison as it slowly begins to maneuver. From some dark depth I didn't know was in me, a rage is unleashed—sudden, volcanic, and untamable. I kick the mesh fence with all my strength, scream, kick again, throw my body against it, hurl insults at the officers. They can't hear me over the plane's engines. But I continue to scream and kick until I feel my husband's arms surrounding me from behind, holding me, tight. Not an embrace but a containment.

When I regain control of my body, my husband lets go of me. The boy is focusing on the plane through his binoculars, and the plane is positioning itself on the runway. I don't know what the boy is thinking and what he'll eventually tell himself about this, or how he'll remember the instant I am letting him witness. I have an impulse to cover his eyes, the way I still sometimes do when we watch certain movies together even though he's older now. But the binoculars have already brought the world too close to him, the world has already projected itself inside him—so what should I protect him from now, and how, and what for? All that's left for me to do, I think, is to make sure the sounds he records in his mind right now, the sounds that will overlay this instant that will always live inside him, are sounds that will assure him he was not alone that day. I step closer to him, wrapping an arm around his chest, and say:

Tell me what you see, Ground Control.

The spaceship is moving toward the runway, he answers, catching on.

Okay. And what else?

The astronauts are inside the ship now.

Good.

We're almost ready for launch.

Good. What else?

Personnel clearing launch area. Helium and nitrogen pressurization under way. Launch vehicle switching to internal power.

What else? What else?

Wait, Ma, please, I don't know what else.

Yes, you do. Just look hard and tell me everything. We are all counting on you.

For a moment he looks away from the binoculars, looks at me, then at his father, who is holding up his boom again, and then at his sister, asleep still, and then again into the binoculars. He takes a deep breath before he speaks, his voice firm:

Blast danger area cleared. Range has reported go for launch. Sixty seconds. Launch enable switch set to on position. Thirty seconds. Liquid oxygen fill and drain valve closed now. Ten seconds. Arm launch vehicle ignition system check. Nine, eight, seven. Go for main engine start. And six, five, four. Command main engine start. Three, two, one, lift-off . . .

Then what? I ask.

That's it. Lift-off.

What else?

It's hard to focus now. The ship is up in the sky and going faster, it's too hard to focus now, I can't.

We see the plane vanish into the enormous blue—fast and fading, soaring up and away into the now slightly clouded sky. It will soon fly across unpeopled cities, across plains and industrial cancers sprawling endlessly, over rivers and forests. My husband is still holding up his boom, as if there were anything left to record. The end of things, the real end, is never a neat turn of the screw, never a door that is suddenly shut, but more like an atmospheric change, clouds that slowly gather—more a whimper than a bang.

For a long time, I've been worried about what to tell our children, how to give them a story. But now, as I listen to the boy telling the story of this instant, the story of what we are seeing and the story of how we are seeing it, through him, a slow but solid certainty finally settles in me. It's his version of the story that will outlive us; his version that will remain and be passed down. Not only his version of our story, of who we were as a family, but also his version of others' stories, like those of the lost children. He'd understood everything much better than I had, than the rest of us had. He'd listened to things, looked at them—really looked, focused, pondered—and little by little, his mind had arranged all the chaos around us into a world.

The only thing that parents can really give their children are little knowledges: this is how you cut your own nails, this is the temperature of a real hug, this is how you untangle knots in your hair, this is how I love you. And what children give their parents, in return, is something less tangible but at the same time larger and more lasting, something like a drive to embrace life fully and understand it, on their behalf, so they can try to explain it to them, pass it down to them "with acceptance and without rancor," as James Baldwin once wrote, but also with a certain rage and fierceness. Children force parents to go out looking for a specific pulse, a gaze, a rhythm, the right way of telling the story, knowing that stories don't fix anything or save anyone but maybe make the world both more complex and more tolerable. And sometimes, just sometimes, more beautiful. Stories are a way of subtracting the future from the past, the only way of finding clarity in hindsight.

The boy is still pointing at the empty sky with his binoculars. So I ask him once again, this time just whispering:

What else do you see, Ground Control?

PART II

*Reenactment*

# DEPORTATIONS

# DEPARTURE

Calling Major Tom.

Checking sound. One, two, three.

This is Ground Control. You copy me, Major Tom?

This is the story of us, and of the lost children, from beginning to end, and I'm gonna tell it to you, Memphis.

We were there, and the lost children had disappeared on a plane into the sky. I was looking through my binoculars for them but couldn't see anything else, and that's what I told Mama. Just like you won't see much in the picture I took of the plane before it departed. The important things that happened only happened after I took the picture, while it was developing in the dark, inside a little red book where I stored all my pictures, inside a box, inside the car where you were sleeping.

And what happened, so you know it and so you can see it the way I do, too, when you look at the picture later one day, was that the lost children walked out of a hangar in a single line, and all of them were very quiet and looking down at their feet the way children look when they have to walk onto a stage and have stage fright, but of course much worse. They were all taken inside the plane, and I fixed my eyes on it with my binoculars tight against my sockets. Ma started swearing at the soldiers, then screaming like I never heard her before, and then just breathing, saying nothing. I focused hard, and had to focus again when the plane started moving slowly on the runway. Then it was harder to follow the plane speeding and angling up, and impossible to find it once it was up in the air, fast and fading. I buried my eyes deeper into the rims of my binoculars as if I was covering my ears except it was my eyes. Until finally I unstuck my eyes from them because there was nothing to see in the sky, no airplane anywhere up in the sky. It had disappeared, with the children. What happened that day is not called a departure or a removal. It's called deportation. And we documented it.

## FAMILY LEXICON

Officially, Pa was a documentarist and Ma was a documentarian, and very few people know the difference. The difference is, just so you know, that a documentarian is like a librarian and a documentarist is like a chemist. But both of them did basically the same thing: they had to find sounds, record them, store them on tape, and then put them together in a way that they told a story.

The stories they told, although they were sound-stories, were not like the audiobooks we listened to in the car. The audiobooks were made-up stories, meant to make time disappear or at least easier to get through. "When he woke in the woods in the dark and the cold of the night . . . ," the car speakers said whenever Ma turned on the radio, if her phone was connected to it. I knew the line by heart and said it out loud whenever it sounded inside the car, and you would sometimes slip your thumb out of your mouth and repeat the line out loud with me, and you were so good at imitating. We'd both say the rest of the line even if Ma stopped the recording before it was over: ". . . he'd reach out to touch the child sleeping beside him." Then Ma would press Stop, and look for the audiobook of *Lord of the Flies,* or turn on the radio, or sometimes play music.

When we went back inside the car after the airplane took off with the children, though, Ma didn't turn the sound system on at all. She and Pa were in their front seats, you and me in the back. She unfolded her crumpled old map, and Pa concentrated on the highway. We were speeding away like we were running from something chasing us. Everyone and everything was silent. It felt like we were all lost. It wasn't something I saw but something I knew, the way you know some things when you are just waking up but can't explain them because your mind is full of cloudiness. And this can't be explained either, but I think one day, you will know what I mean.

When we were finally far enough from that airstrip in Roswell where the lost children got flown away to who knows where, I asked Pa what would happen next. You were still asleep and I was holding on to the back of Papa's driver's seat and trying to pull myself closer to it, against the itchy pull of my seat belt. I was waiting for Papa to say something, waiting and waiting like I was still focusing on something through my binoculars, but just waiting for his words. Pa was holding on to the steering wheel with his two hands, squinting at the highway as he always did. He kept silent, as he almost always did.

I asked Ma what she thought was going to happen to the children in the airplane. She said she didn't know, but said that if those lost children hadn't got caught the way they got caught, they would all have spread out across the country, and she was showing the big map from her seat like always, and moving her finger around it like she was drawing with her fingertip. All of them would have found a place to go, she said. And when I asked where to, where would they have gone to, she said she didn't know where, exactly, didn't know which dots on the map exactly, but they would have all gone somewhere to live in different houses with different families. Gone to schools? I asked. Yes. And playgrounds? Yes. And parks and all the rest? Yes.

Once upon a time, every morning, we also walked to school with our parents, and they went to work, but they always picked us up later, and sometimes took us to parks in the afternoons, and on weekends we rode our bikes together next to the big gray river, even though you were always sitting in your baby seat and so not really riding, and always fell asleep at some point. That was the time we were together even when we were not, because that was the time we all lived inside the same map. We stopped living in that map when we left on the road trip, and even though inside the car we were sitting so close together all the time, it felt like we were the opposite of being together. Pa would be looking at the highway in front. Ma would be looking at her map, on her lap, and telling us names of places we were going to visit like Little Rock, Boswell, and now Roswell.

I asked Mama questions, and she answered. Where were the children coming from and how had they got here? And she said what I already knew, which was that they had come on a train, and before that they'd walked miles and miles and had walked so much their feet got sick and had to be cured. And they'd survived in the desert, and had had to keep safe from bad people, and had got some help from better ones, and had made it all the way here, to look for their parents and maybe other brothers and sisters that lived here. But instead, they all got caught and put on a plane so they could be removed, she said, disappeared from the map, which is like a metaphor but also not. Because it's real they got disappeared.

Then I asked Ma why she was so angry, instead of sad, and she didn't answer right away, but Pa finally said something. He said don't worry it doesn't matter anymore now, it's over. And then she spoke. She said, yes, exactly. She said she was angry exactly because things could just be over like that, finished, and no one cared to even look. I understood her when she said that, because I also had seen the plane disappear with the children, and I had also seen the names on the tombs of the Apache cemetery, and then their names erased in my pictures, and I had also looked out the window when we drove through some places, like Memphis. Not you, Memphis, but Memphis, Tennessee, where I saw a very, very old woman, almost a skeleton, dragging a heap of cardboard along a sidewalk, and also a group of children, no mother or father, sitting on a mattress in an empty lot next to the road.

I thought I should say all that to her, that I did understand what she meant, and I was also angry like her and like Papa, but it was impossible to say, to find the right words, so instead, I reminded them that we were supposed to go see the UFO museum now, they had promised. They just kept quiet like they were not even listening to me, like I was a fly buzzing in the backseat. And when I said again, I think we should go to the UFO museum because look at my sister, look, she needs to be put on a spaceship and returned to space like those children on the airplane because, look, she's an alien, Ma turned around looking furious and was about to scold me real bad, I think, but then she saw you asleep with your mouth wide open, drooling, your head dangling to one side, looking totally like a Martian, and she smiled a small, difficult smile, and just said okay, maybe you're right about that.

FAMILY PLOT

Before we left on this trip, if I try hard to remember, Pa and Ma used to laugh a lot. When we moved into our apartment together, even though we didn't know one another well, we all laughed a lot together. While you and I were at school, Pa and Ma would be working on some long recording about people talking all the different languages that existed in the city. Sometimes they'd play samples of the recording at home and you, Memphis, you would stop doing whatever you were doing, and you'd stand in the middle of the living room near the speakers. You'd get serious, clear your throat, and start imitating the recorded voices talking in strange languages, making no sense at all but also sounding very similar to those voices. You were good at imitating, even when you were tiny. Both Ma and Pa would be standing around the corner in the kitchen, listening to you, and though they tried to hold it, and even held their hands to their mouths, they'd always start laughing at the end. If you caught them, if you heard them laughing, you always got angry, because you thought they were making fun of you.

When you finally woke up inside the car, and of course asked if we were already at the UFO museum, I told you we'd gone there but it was closed for the summer, but that we were driving to someplace even better, which was the place where Papa's Apaches had actually lived, which was true, even though it took you some time to get used to the new plan, and you sulked for a while.

Ma was looking at her big map and asked if we wanted to stop in the next town, called La Luz, or if we wanted to drive all the way to a town farther away, called Truth or Consequences. You and I voted two against two to drive only to the next town, La Luz. So it was decided: we would drive to Truth or Consequences. When I complained, Pa said those were the rules and that was called democracy.

## INVENTORY

I had a Swiss Army knife, a pair of binoculars, a flashlight, a small compass, and a Polaroid camera. Pa had a boom pole and mic, which recorded everything, and Ma had a small hand recorder, which recorded only some things, mostly the ones that were close up. They had zeppelins and blimps, and I don't know what those were for, exactly. Whenever we stopped in motels, Pa sat for hours on the floor, unknotting cables and waiting for the batteries of his little recorder to recharge. Then he'd make some notes in a small notebook he always carried in his pocket, put his big headphones around his head, and walk outside to the parking lot holding up his pole. Sometimes, if he let me, I would follow him and help him carry things. You'd stay inside with Mama, and I don't know what you'd be doing. Maybe she'd be untangling your hair, which was always tangled, just like Pa unknotted cables. I'd be outside with Papa, both of us busy recording stuff. Though really most of the time the only sounds we recorded were the cars that were passing and the wind that was blowing, so I never knew what he'd be able to make with all those sounds. Once I came up with a kind of joke and asked him if he was recording the sounds of boredom, and I was sure he was going to laugh, but he didn't.

COVALENCE

You knocked on the window and said:
　　Knock-knock!
Who's there? we all answered at the same time.
Cold.
Cold who?
Cold Arms!
You told the worst knock-knock jokes in the universe, they made no sense, but still Pa and Ma pretended they were funny, and fake-laughed.
Mama fake-laughed like ha-ha.
Papa's was more like he-he.
I fake-laughed all silent, just patting my hand on my tummy in slow motion, like in a muted cartoon.
And you, you hadn't learned how to fake-laugh yet.
Even though you couldn't tell jokes properly, and even though you were such a bad reader, like you skipped letters and confused b and d, and also didn't know how to write properly, you were sometimes really smart. One time, you and I both caught a cold, so Ma

gave us some flu medicine, which made us feel even more sick. And when she asked us later how are you two feeling now, I could only come up with the word worse, but you thought about it more carefully and then said, I feel haunted.

## FOUNDATIONAL MYTHS

We finally got to the town called Truth or Consequences, which I thought was a stupid name. Ma found it charming and Pa found it brilliant, and I think that's the only reason we stopped there. The motels we were driving past were so abandoned that even you noticed it and said to the rest of us, look, there are motels for trees in this town. And no one understood what you meant, only I did. You said they were motels for trees because there was no one who stayed there and only branches and leaves could be seen through all the broken windows and broken doors of those motels, so those trees looked like guests there, waving their branches at us driving by.

The motel we found was not as bad as the ones we'd seen before. We settled in, and Papa went out, said he was going to interview a man who was a real blood descendant of Geronimo's, said he'd be back late. Mama lay on her bed, concentrated on reading her book, the same small red book where I stored my pictures, and was paying no attention to us, which I kind of expected but still made me frustrated. That little red book was called *Elegies for Lost Children*, and when I asked her to read out loud to us so we could fall asleep, like she sometimes would, she said, okay fine, just one chapter.

She climbed out of her bed and into ours, in the middle, and we huddled next to her, each of us under one of her arms like she was some kind of eagle. You said, we are the bread and Ma is the butter. I smelled her skin, right at the bend between the forearm and the upper arm, and it smelled like wood and like cereal, and maybe a little like butter. She opened the book, being very careful because there were pictures I'd taken stuck between some of the pages like bookmarks, and she didn't want them to fall out. Then she began reading to us with her sandy voice.

( T H E   F I F T H   E L E G Y )

Long vines hung from low branches, brushed their cheeks and shoulders. Sitting or lying down, aboard the leprous roof of a gondola, they crossed acres of tropical jungle, where they had to be vigilant of men, but wary also of plants and beasts. Even the train crawled more slowly than usual here, as if it too were cautious not to stir the undergrowth awake. Mosquitoes covered the seven of them in pink welts that later turned bruise-purple, later brown, and then vanished but left behind all their dengue poison.

The jungle was lightless and full of hidden horrors. It choked them with the longing to escape but offered them no foreseeable relief. Their heads filled with heavy air and fever. The colors of the jungle, its fetid vapors, ignited their open eyes with wild visions. Nightmares flowered in all their dreams, filled them with humid tongues and yellow teeth, and the big, dry hands of older men. One night, sleepless and shivering despite the heat, their bones rattling, they'd all seen it, the fleeting silhouette of a body hanging from a rope strung to a branch. The man in charge told them the hanging man was a man no longer, said they shouldn't be concerned for him, shouldn't pray for him either, for he was nothing now but meat for the insects and bones for the beasts. The man told the children that if they made any mistake, any false move, they would also be no more than meat and bones, corpses, severed heads. Then he did a head count. He shouted: "Lieutenant, a head count! Count all your corpses!" And he replied to himself: "Yes, sir!" and started counting, slapping each child across the head as he called out a number: one, two, three, four, five, six, seven.

Here Ma quit reading and said maybe she should read something different to us. But you had already fallen asleep, and so I said, no, Ma, come on, look, she's asleep. And I'm old enough. Even comic books are more violent than this. So she cleared her throat and continued:

As they rode across the jungle on top of the train car, the seven, trying to sleep but also fearing to fall asleep, they heard stories and rumors.

"Was full of thugs and murderers," people said. "Everyone will have his heart out, set on a pike spike," a woman atop a boxcar said. "One man had both his eyes torn out, and all his goods sequestered," they said. And they also said, "Here stripped, here made to stand." The words traveled across the train roof faster than the train itself, and reached the seven children, who tried to not listen but were unable. The words were like those mosquitoes, injected thoughts into their heads, filling them, creeping up everywhere inside them.

One boy, boy number six, the boy whose feet had been cured by the bucket-girl, coiled into a fetal position every night, to wait for sleep. He tried to remember his grandfather, but the old man was not anywhere in his mind, and neither were his lobsters. Everything was becoming erased. He'd coil and then unwind to lie faceup toward the sky, shuffling and shifting and looking for sleep. Then he tried to remember the girl's soft hands fixing his feet with her clippers, tried to summon her black eyes, and wished them there with him, her eyes and bare hands, inching around his body and into darker crevices. But hard as he tried, his mind forced him back to the larger metallic pincers of the beast now crawling rhythmically along the train tracks.

The children dared not shut their eyes too long at night, and when they did, they were not able to dream of what lay ahead. Nothing beyond the jungle was imaginable while they were inside its grip. Except one night, when the eldest of the boys, number seven, offered to tell them a story.

You want to hear a story? he asked.

Yes, said some of the younger ones, yes please. The older ones said nothing, but also wanted to hear it.

I'll tell you a story, but after I tell it, you all have to shut your eyes and think about it, about what it really means, and not think about the train or the man in charge or the jungle or nothing.

Okay, said one. Fine, said another. Okay, yes, they said.

Promise?

They all promised. Everyone agreed.

Tell it, they said. Tell it.

Okay, the story is this: "When he woke up, the dinosaur was still there."

That's no story, said one of the older boys.

Shhh, said one of the girls. We promised. We said we'd just keep quiet and think about the story.

Can you tell it again? asked boy number three, his eyelids heavy, puffy.

Okay, just once more, and then you're quiet and go to sleep.

And as boy three listened, trying to fall asleep, he gazed up at the sky through the dark leaves, the constant black-deep above him, and wondered, do gods float up there, and which gods do we worship where? He looked long and hard for them up there, but there were none.

## MOTHER TONGUES

I asked Mama for just one more chapter. She said no, she had said only one, and that was that. She went back to her bed and turned off the lights. I forced myself to stay awake, pretending to sleep, and when I was sure she was finally asleep, I switched on the bedside lamp, took the book, and opened it.

The picture I had taken earlier that day, of the airplane standing there, slipped out from the pages of the book. I looked at it, hard, like I was waiting for the children to appear in it, but of course they didn't. There's nothing in the picture, if you look at it, except that stupid plane, which makes me so frustrated. But as I tucked the picture back in between some pages toward the end of the book, I realized something important, which is this: that everything that happened after I took the picture was also inside it, even though no one could see it, except me when I looked at it, and maybe also you, in the future, when you look at it, even if you didn't even see the original moment with your own eyes.

Finally, being more careful this time and holding the sides of the book tighter so that the other pictures wouldn't fall out, I opened it to the beginning. I read the first lines of the story, which I'd heard Mama read out loud once but which were harder to understand if I read them myself:

(THE FIRST ELEGY)

Mouths open to the sky, they sleep. Boys, girls: lips chapped, cheeks cracked, for the wind whips day and night. They occupy the entire space there, stiff but warm, lined up like new corpses along the metal roof of the train gondola. From behind the rim of his blue cap, the man in charge counts them—six children; seven minus one. The train advances slowly along tracks parallel to an iron wall. Beyond, on both sides of the wall, the desert stretches out, identical. Above, the swart night is still.

## TIME & TEETH

I read those lines over and over, and tried to memorize them, until I thought I understood them. I was a level Z reader. You were not even level A because you confused the letters b and d, and also the letters g and p, and when I showed you a book and asked you what do you see here on this page? you said, I don't know, and when I said what do you at least imagine? you said that you pictured all the little letters jumping and splashing like all the kids in our neighborhood when they finally opened the swimming pool and let us swim there. I read the first page of Ma's red book over and over, until I heard Pa's footsteps coming back from the street, stopping outside the room, and then the door handle turning, so I threw the book on the floor and pretended to be sleeping, opening my mouth a little.

## TONGUE TIES

That night, I dreamed that I killed a cat and that afterward, I walked out into the desert all by myself and buried its parts: tail, feet, eyes, and some whiskers. Then a voice was asking me if the parts of the cat were the cat. But of course I didn't actually do any of this, I only dreamed it, which was lucky and relieving, but which I only realized when I woke up and remembered that we were in a town, which was called Truth or Consequences.

## PROCEDURES

The next day, we woke early and went out to play on a patio while Pa and Ma were still asleep, and the patio was full of cats sleeping on benches and chairs and under tables, which made me feel a little guilty, as if I had really killed one of them, and not just dreamed it. So I made up a game about rescuing cats, and we played for a while, but you never got the rules right, so we ended up fighting.

In the car we didn't fight so much, but sometimes we got bored for real and sometimes we pretended to be bored. I knew they didn't know the answer, but still I asked Ma and Pa, maybe just to annoy them:

How much longer?

And then you asked:

When will we get there?

To distract us, and keep us quiet, Pa and Ma would sometimes play news on the radio or play audiobooks. The news was usually bad. The audiobooks were either boring or too adult for us, and at first Pa and Ma kept on changing their minds about which one to listen to, jumping from one to another, until one day they found the *Lord of the Flies* audiobook and stuck with it. You said you hated it and complained you didn't understand a word, but I noticed that you tried to pay attention to it anyway, whenever it played, and so I forced myself to pay attention, too, and pretended to understand everything, even though at times it was difficult to understand.

## JOINT FILING

If we got lucky, they would turn the car's sound system off and tell us stories and histories. Mama's stories were always about lost children, like the news on the radio. We liked them, but they also made you feel strange or worried. Papa's histories were about the old American southwest, back when it used to be part of Mexico. All of this was once Mexico, Ma always used to say when he started speaking about that, and moved her one arm across the entire space around the car. Pa told us about bluecoats, about Saint Patrick's

Battalion and Pancho Villa. Our favorite histories, though, were the ones he told about Geronimo, the Apache. And even though I knew his histories were all just a trick he did to distract us while we were in the car, whenever he started speaking about Geronimo, every time, I fell for it, and so did you, and we both forgot all about being in the car, and having to pee, and about time and how much time was left in front of us. And when we forgot about time, time passed much quicker, and we also felt happier, though this can't be explained.

You'd always fall asleep listening to those histories. I usually didn't, but I was able at least to close my eyes and pretend to sleep. And when they thought we were both sleeping, they'd sometimes fight, or keep silent, or else Pa would play bits of his inventories, which he'd been recording along the way and wanted to discuss with Ma. He was making inventories for something he called his inventory of echoes. And if you're wondering what inventories of echoes are, this is what they are. Inventories of echoes are things made of sounds, sounds that got lost but were found by someone, or that would get lost unless they were trapped by someone, someone like Pa, who would make an inventory with them. So they were like a collection, or like a museum of sounds that did not exist anymore but that people would still be able to hear thanks to people like Papa who made them into inventories.

Sometimes his inventories were just wind blowing and rain falling and cars passing, and those were the most boring of all. Other times they were conversations with people, interviews, stories, histories, or just voices. Once he even recorded our voices talking in the backseat of the car, and then played them for Ma when they thought we were both sleeping and not listening. And it was strange to listen to our own voices around us, like we were there but also not there. I felt like we'd disappeared, thought, what if we are not actually sitting back here but only being remembered by them?

## ALONE TOGETHER

We would ask Papa for more Apache stories. My favorite story, even though it was also the one that made me saddest and angriest, was the one about the surrender of the last Chiricahuas. For days, they walked, Pa told us: men, women, girls, boys, one behind another, sad faces, no bags, no words, no nothing. They walked in a single line, held as prisoners, like the lost children we saw in Roswell.

The last Apaches walked from Skeleton Canyon toward the mountains to the north. There was a white-eye general and his men. They were head-counting the prisoners of war all the time to make sure none escaped. They counted one Geronimo plus twenty-seven more. They advanced slowly through the canyon under the terrible sun, he said. And he didn't say it but I was thinking all the time that in their minds, those prisoners were probably scared and full of angry words, though in their mouths there was silence only.

Ma kept silent most of the time when Pa was telling his histories, maybe thinking about her own lost children story and picturing them in her head being put on that airplane in Roswell, or maybe just listening to what Pa said and thinking nothing.

Pa told us about how Geronimo and his band were the last people on the entire continent to surrender to the white-eyes. Fifteen men, nine women, three children, and Geronimo. Those were the last Indians who were free, he said, and told us we had to always remember that. Before they surrendered, they'd wandered the big mountains called Sierra Madre, broken out of reservations, raided settlements, killed many evil bluecoats and many evil Mexican soldiers.

You listened and looked out the window. I listened and held on to the back of Pa's pilot seat and sometimes pulled myself closer to him. He held on to the steering wheel with his two hands, and he was always looking straight at the highway. Before he fell off his horse and died, Pa said, Geronimo's last words were: "I should have never surrendered. I should have fought until I was the last man alive." That's what Pa told us. And I think it's probably true that Geronimo said that, though Pa also said no one could really ever know because there was no recording or anything to prove it. He said that after Geronimo's surrender, the general and his men set forth on the godless desert in Skeleton Canyon and herded Geronimo's band like they were herding sheep aboard death ships. And he said that after two days, they reached Bowie and there they were crammed into a train car and sent east, far from everything and everyone. I asked him what happened later, and I was thinking about Geronimo's band, but also I was thinking about Mama's lost children, who had also been riding on trains, not knowing where or why or what was going to happen to them.

While Pa spoke, I was sometimes drawing a map of his history with my finger on the back of his driver's seat, a map mostly full of arrows, arrows pointing everywhere, arrows shot, whoosh, from horseback, arrows crossing rivers, half arrows disappearing like ghosts, arrows shot from dark mountain caves, and some arrows dipped into rattlesnake poison pointing at the sky, and no one could see any of my finger-maps, except me and you.

Finger-maps were something I'd invented and perfected way before our trip. In second grade, when I was sitting at my desk, working on number bonds or cursive letter practice, I liked to imagine where Ma and Pa were, maybe because I felt alone and missed them, but I'm not actually sure why. When I finished a section of number bonds or a line of a's or h's, I sometimes slid the tip of my pencil from the edge of the sheet of paper and drew with it on the desk. It was completely prohibited to draw on the desks. But I closed my eyes and imagined Ma and Pa getting on the subway, moving in a straight line for five stops uptown, then walking out, and walking three blocks east. And while I imagined all that, the tip of my pencil followed, five up, three to the right. I drew those imagined maps for weeks, and after a while, my desk was all full of beautiful routes that I knew exactly how to refollow, or kind of. Until one day the teacher told the principal I was drawing doodles all day on my desk instead of getting my work done, and then the principal told Ma and Pa that I had damaged school property. In the end, we had to pay a fine of fifty dollars, which Pa said I had to pay back with chores. After that, I still drew maps on my desk anyway, but I changed to using only my fingertip, so no one would see them now except me. And that is called finger-mapping.

I knew you could see my finger-maps perfectly, because when I drew them on the back of Papa's seat, you'd stare at them with your long, long way of looking at things when you were trying to understand them. And in understanding finger-maps, like in many other things, we were alone together.

What happened a few years after, Papa told us, was that the Apaches were crammed back into a train car and sent to a place called Fort Sill, where most of them ended up dying, and were buried in the cemetery. I listened to that part of the story but didn't draw it 'cause that part was undrawable. You won't remember, Memphis, but we all went to that cemetery together, and I took pictures of Apache graves: Chief Loco, Chief Nana, Chief Chihuahua, Mangas Coloradas, Naiche, Juh, and of course Geronimo and Chief Cochise.

Later, when I looked at the pictures again, I noticed that the names on the tombstones hadn't come out at all. So when I showed Ma and Pa the photos, Pa said they were perfect because I'd documented the cemetery the way that it exists in recorded history, and at first I didn't understand him, but then I did. He meant, I think, that my camera had erased the names of Apache chiefs the way they are also erased in history, which is something Pa was always reminding us of, and that's why it was so important that we memorize all those names, because otherwise we would forget, like everyone else had already forgotten, that the Chiricahuas were the greatest warriors there were on the continent, and not some weird species that lived in the Museum of Natural History next to the petrified animals, and in cemeteries like that one, also alone together, as prisoners of war.

## ITEMIZATION & BOXES

During the trip, Ma's job was mostly to study the map and plan our route for the day, though a few times she also would drive. Pa's job was to drive, and to record sounds for his inventory. Your job was easy, you had to help Pa make sandwiches or help Ma clean all our boots, or help anyone do whatever. My jobs were harder. For example, I had to make sure the trunk of the car was neat and tidy before we started driving, every time, after any stop. The hardest part was making sure the boxes were in place. There were seven boxes in the trunk. One was yours and was empty, another was mine and was also empty. Then, Pa had four boxes and Ma had one box. I had to make sure they were all in place, together with the rest of our stuff in the trunk. It was like having to solve a puzzle, every time.

We were not allowed to dig around in the boxes at all, but I earned permission to open one box, Mama's box, which was labeled Box V. I had earned permission to open Ma's box, I think, because when I started taking Polaroid pictures with my camera, Ma discovered we had to use a book to store the photographs in while they were developing, otherwise they'd burn and would come out all white, though it's difficult to explain why this happens. The point is that before I took a picture, I'd be allowed to take a book out of her box, the book that was at the very top, which was the little red book about lost children. I was allowed to use it to store my pictures in, to tuck them between pages. And each time I opened the box to take the book out, I'd shuffle the things inside it around, to get a quick look. In her box there were some books, all with dozens of little Post-its that flagged the special pages. Mama kept those especially far from your reach, I think because when we still lived back home, you were always stealing the Post-its from her books to make draw-ings and then sticking them on the walls all over the apartment. So she made sure you didn't even get near her box.

Inside the box were also some newspaper cutouts, maps, files, and pieces of paper in all different sizes with notes she had written. I'm not sure why, but I was always curious about all the things in that box. I think maybe because it made me feel the way I felt one day when you and I made up a game while we were playing in the park, making little clay figures that we decided to bury under trees so that some scientist in the future could find them and think they were made by members of an ancient tribe. Except, with Ma's box, I was not the one who had made the clay figures but the scientist who had found them centuries later.

APACHERIA

The roads toward Apacheria were long, and we were driving there in a straight line, but it was like we were driving in circles.

There was that voice in the car speakers from the audiobook that always came back, saying: "When he woke in the woods in the dark and the cold of the night he'd reach out to touch the child sleeping beside him." Sometimes I pretended to be sleeping behind them, too. I tried. Especially when they were fighting. Not you. When they were fighting, you would come up with jokes or sometimes even say, Papa, you go smoke your cigarette now, and Mama, you focus on your map and on your news.

Sometimes they listened to you. They'd stop fighting, and Ma would play music on shuffle, or else turn on the radio. She always told us to be quiet when news about the lost children came on, and she always got all strange after hearing it. She either got strange and started telling us about that little red book she was reading about lost children, and their crusade, about them walking across deserts or riding trains through empty worlds, all of which we were curious about but could hardly make sense of. It was either that or she got so sad and angry after hearing the radio news that she didn't want to talk to us anymore, didn't even want to look at us.

It made me so angry at her. I wanted to remind her that even though those children were lost, we were not lost, we were there, right there next to her. And it made me wonder, what if we got lost, would she then finally pay attention to us? But I knew that thought was immature, and also I never knew what the words were to tell her I was angry, so I kept quiet and you kept quiet and we all listened either to her stories or just to the silence in the car, which was maybe worse.

## COSMOLOGY & PRONOUNS

I don't think you understood any of the news or any of her stories. I think you didn't even listen. But I listened. I didn't understand all of it, only parts of it, but whenever the radio voices started talking about the refugee children or Mama started talking about the children's crusade, I would whisper to you, listen, they're talking about the lost children again, listen, they're talking about the Eagle Warriors that Pa told us about, and you would open your eyes and nod and pretend you were understanding everything and agreeing.

I don't know if you will remember what Pa told us about the Eagle Warriors. He said the Eagle Warriors were a band of Apache children, all warriors, led by an older boy. He said the boy was about my age. The Eagle Warriors ate birds that they hunted in midflight by throwing rocks at them, all with their bare hands. They were invincible, he told us, and they lived all alone in the mountains without parents and even so were never afraid. And they were also a little bit like small gods, because they had learned the power to control the weather, and could either attract rain or push a thunderstorm back. I think they were called the Eagle Warriors because of this sky power they had, but also because if you ever got to see them from far away, running down a mountain or in the desert plains, they ran so swift and fast they looked like eagles floating rather than people stuck to earth. And sometimes while Pa was telling us all this, we would both be looking out the car window at the empty sky, wishing we could see eagles.

You asked, one day in the car, if we were going to live in the car forever. Though I knew the answer, I was so relieved to hear Pa say, no, we're not. He said we would arrive, in the end, soon, at a beautiful house made of big gray stones, where there was a porch and a garden so big we'd get lost in it. And you said, I don't want to get lost. And I said, don't be silly, he just means it's the biggest garden you've ever seen. Though later, I kept wondering if it was possible to really get lost in a garden and wished we were back in our old apartment, which was already big enough for the four of us.

The house we were going to, Pa said, was between the Dragoon and Chiricahua Mountains, not far from a place called Skeleton Canyon, in the heart of Apacheria, near where Geronimo and the other twenty-seven members of his band had surrendered. I asked if it was called that because there were real skeletons there, and Pa said maybe yes, and dried his forehead with his hand, and I thought he was going to carry on with the story, but he just got silent and looked into the highway. I think maybe when Geronimo and the other people walked along that canyon, they were also silent all the time, and listening hard and squinting, to make sure that their feet would not step on bones of skeletons of before, and if we ever go to that canyon, you and I will do the same.

## PASSING STRANGERS

Soon after the beginning of the trip, aside from keeping the trunk neat and tidy, I knew my duty was to keep track of stuff, take pictures of everything important. The first pictures came out white and I got frustrated. Then I studied the manual and I finally learned. Professionals have to do this kind of thing, and it's called trial and error. But for a while after learning how to do it, I still didn't know what my pictures had to be of. I wasn't sure what was important, what wasn't, and what I should focus on and photograph. For some time, I took many pictures of whatever, with no plan, no anything.

One day, though, while you were asleep and I was pretending to sleep but actually listening to Ma and Pa arguing about radio, about politics, about work, about their future plans together, and then not together, about us, and them, and everything, I came up with a plan, and this was the plan. I'd become a documentarist and a documentarian. I could be both, for a while, at least on this trip. I could document everything, even the little things, however I could. Because I understood, even though Pa and Ma thought I didn't, that it was our last trip together as a family.

I also knew that you wouldn't remember this trip, because you're only five years old, and our pediatrician had told us that children don't start building memories of things until after they turn six. When I realized that, that I was ten and you were only five, I thought, fuck. But of course I didn't say so out loud. I just thought, fuck, silently, to myself. I realized that I'd remember everything and you maybe wouldn't remember anything. I needed to find a way to help you remember, even if it was only through things I documented for you, for the future. And that's how I became a documentarist and a documentarian at the same time.


## FUTURE

I turned ten the day before we left home. And though I was already ten, I still felt lost and unsure sometimes and asked how much longer, and where will we stop. And then you'd ask, where are we going exactly, and when will we get all the way to the end? Ma sometimes pulled out her big map, which was way too big to unfold all the way, and with her finger she circled a part of the map, saying, this, this is the end of the trip. Pa would sometimes remind us, though we already knew it, that all of that had once been part of Apacheria. There were the Dragoon Mountains, and the Wilcox dry lake, and then the Chiricahua Mountains, and Ma would read names of places aloud in her low, raspy voice: San Simon, Bowie, Dragoon, Cochise, Apache, Animas, Shakespeare, Skeleton Canyon. When she was done, she'd put the map in front of her, under the slanted windshield, and then she'd put her feet on top of the map. Once I took a picture of them, and the picture was a good one, though in real life her feet looked a little bigger, browner, and more worn out.

# MAPS & BOXES

This whole country, Papa said, is an enormous cemetery, but only some people get proper graves, because most lives don't matter. Most lives get erased, lost in the whirlpool of trash we call history, he said.

He spoke like this sometimes, and when he did, he was usually looking out through a window or at some corner. Never at us. When we were still back in our old apartment, for example, and he got mad at us for something we'd done or maybe not done, he would look straight at the bookshelf, not at us, and say words like responsibility, privilege, ethical standards, or social commitments. Now he was talking about this whirlpool of history, and erased lives, and was looking through the windshield at the curvy road ahead as we drove up a narrow mountain pass, where there were no green things growing, no trees, no bushes, nothing alive, only jagged rocks and trunks of trees split in half as if old gods with giant axes had got angry and chopped this part of the world apart.

What happened here? you even asked, looking out the window, though you didn't usually notice landscapes.

Papa said: Genocide, exodus, diaspora, ethnic cleansing, that's what happened.

Ma explained that there had probably been a recent forest fire.

We were in New Mexico, finally in Chiricahua Apache territory. Apache was the wrong word, by the way. It meant "enemy," and that's what the Apaches' enemies called them. The Apaches called themselves Nde, which just meant "the people." That's what Pa told us as we drove on and on in that lonely mountain pass, higher and higher, everything around us gray and dead. And they called everyone else Indah, he said, which meant "enemy," and "stranger," but also meant "eye." They called all the white Americans white-eyes, he told us, but we already knew that. Ma asked him why and he said he didn't know. She asked him if eye and enemy and stranger were all the same word, Indah, then how did he know that the Americans were called white-eyes and not actually white-enemies? Pa thought for a while, stayed silent. And maybe to fill in the silence, Ma told us that Mexicans used to call white Americans hueros, which could either mean "empty" or mean "with no color" (now they still call them güeros). And Mexican Indians, like Ma's grandmother and her ancestors, used to called white Americans borrados, which meant "erased people." I listened to her and wondered who were actually more borrados, more erased, the Apaches that Pa was always talking about but that we couldn't see anywhere, or the Mexicans, or the white-eyes, and what it really meant to be borrado, and who erased who from where.

## MAPS

Ma's eyes were usually fixed on her big map, and Pa looked ahead toward the road. He said, look there, those strange mountains we're getting closer to are where some of the last Chiricahua Apaches used to hide, during the very hot summer months, because otherwise they'd die from heat exposure in the desert plains to the southwest. Or, if the heat and sickness and thirst didn't kill them, then the white-eyes always did. Sometimes I couldn't tell if Pa was telling stories or if he was telling histories. But then, driving on that curvy road in the mountain, suddenly he took off his hat and threw it in the backseat without even looking where it would land, which made me think he was telling us real histories and not stories. His hat landed almost in my lap and I reached out to touch it with the tip of my fingers, but I didn't dare put it on my head.

He told us about how the different Apache bands, like Mangas Coloradas and his son Mangus and Geronimo, who were all part of the Mimbreño Apache band, were fighting against the cruelest white-eyes and the worst come-and-goes, which is what they called the Mexicans. They joined up with Victorio and Nana and Lozen, who were part of the Ojo Caliente band and were fighting more with the Mexican army, and then also joined with another one of our favorite Apaches, Chief Cochise, who was invincible. The three bands became the Chiricahuas, and were all lead by Cochise. This all sounds confusing, and it is, it's complicated, but if you hear it carefully and maybe draw a map, you might understand it.

## ACOUSTEMOLOGY

When Pa stopped talking, I finally put on his hat, and whispered to you like I was some old Indian-cowboy, said, hey you, hey Memphis, imagine we had got lost here in these mountains. And you said, just you and me alone? And I answered, yes, just you and me alone, do you think we'd join the Apaches and fight against the white-eyes? But Mama heard me, and before you could answer me, she turned around from her seat and asked me to promise that if we ever got lost, I would know how to find them again. So I said, of course, Ma, yes. She asked me if I knew her and Papa's phone numbers by heart, and I said, yes, 555-836-6314 and 555-734-3258. And if you were out in the open country or desert and there was no one to ask for a telephone? she asked. I said we'd look for her and Papa in the heart of the Chiricahua Mountains, in that place where echoes are so clear that even if you whisper, your voice comes back the same way your face looks back at you when you stand in front of a perfectly smooth, clean mirror. Papa interrupted, saying, you mean Echo Canyon? And I was so glad he was listening to me and was helping me out with Ma's difficult questions that always felt like tests. Yes, I said, exactly, if we got lost, we would look for you in Echo Canyon. Wrong answer, Ma said, as if it really was a test. If you get lost out in the open, you have to look for a road, the larger the better, and wait for someone to pass, okay? And both of us said, yes Ma, okay, okay. But then I whispered to you, and she didn't hear me, I said, but first we would go to Echo Canyon, right? And you nodded, and then whispered back, but only if I get to be Lozen for the rest of the game.

## PRESENTIMENT

For a while after Ma's test, I kept on thinking, would we really be able to find our way alone to that Echo Canyon? I thought if only, if only we had a dog, there would be no risk of getting lost. Or less risk, at least. Papa once told us a story, a real one that had even been on the radio and in the newspapers, about a little girl who was only three or four years old and lived in Siberia and left her house one day with her dog, looking for her father in the forest. Her father was a fireman, and he had left earlier that day, because there were wildfires spreading. The girl and her dog disappeared into the forest, but instead of finding him, they got lost. They were lost for days, and rescue teams were looking all over.

On the ninth day after they had gone missing, the dog returned to the house, on his own, without the girl. At first everyone was worried and even angry when they saw him come back, wagging his tail and barking. They thought he had abandoned the girl, maybe dead, and had come back selfishly for food. And they knew that if she was still alive, she was not going to survive without him now. But a few hours later, inside the house, the dog started barking at the front door, would not stop barking. When they let him out, thinking maybe he needed to poop, he ran from the door of the house to the first row of trees in the forest, and then back to the house, over and over. Finally, someone understood that he was trying to say something, not just barking and running like a crazy beast, so the girl's parents and also a rescue team started following him.

The dog took them into the forest, and they walked for many hours, across streams and up and down hills, and then, on the morning of the eleventh day after they had got lost, they found her. She was huddled up under tall grass, which is called tundra or taiga, or maybe just grass, and the dog had showed them the way to her. She had survived thanks to her dog because he kept her safe and warm at night, and they ate berries and drank water from the rivers, and were not eaten by wolves or by bears, which was lucky for them because there are thousands of bears and wolves in Siberia. And now he had shown the adults all the way to where he had left her. I felt like crying every time I thought of this story. I didn't cry, but I kept on thinking what it would feel like to wake up one morning after so many days alone with my dog, but suddenly even more alone, my dog gone.

You were drawing something on the window with saliva, a new disgusting habit since Pa told us about the witch-doctor woman called Saliva who was Geronimo's friend and cured people by spitting on them. What would you do if we lived in a village next to a forest and we had a dog, and we went into the forest one day and suddenly got lost there with our dog only? I asked you. And all you said was, I would stand next to you and make sure the dog didn't lick me.

## JUKEBOXES & COFFINS

We finally stopped and had a real breakfast in a diner, which had a jukebox. And it was perfect, except there was an old man in the booth in front who was wearing a tie with a picture of Jesus Christ stuck with nails to the cross, and on top of the tie he was wearing a silver chain with another cross hanging but with no nails and no Christ on it. I was nervous because I thought you might say something about Jesus Fucking Christ, which you had discovered made Pa and Ma laugh every time you said it. But luckily you didn't say anything about that, I think because the man made you a little scared. I was also a bit scared of him and took a picture of him without even looking into the lens, just resting the camera on our table and calculating the focus. He didn't even notice when the shutter went who-ching because he was talking nonstop to the waiter and to us and to whoever would listen to him. He ordered pancakes and kept on wanting to talk to Pa and Ma about salvation, and then told the two of us jokes, one after the other, horrible jokes about Indians and Mexican people and Asian people and brown people and black people, and basically all people except people like him. I wondered if he didn't notice that we were not like him. Maybe he was a little blind. He was actually wearing very thick glasses. Or maybe he did notice and that's why he was telling us all those ugly jokes. When his breakfast came, he finally shut up. Then he cut a huge square of butter, rubbed it on the pancakes using his fork, and asked us where we all were from. Ma completely lied and said we were French and from Paris.

Back in the car, you made up your absolute best knock-knock joke ever, which Pa didn't understand, 'cause it was half in Spanish, but Ma did, and so did I 'cause I also understood Spanish:

Knock-knock!

Who's there?

Paris!

Paris who?

Pa-re-ce que va a llover!

And Ma and I laughed so hard that you wanted another go, and then you told your second-best joke, which was this:

What did the knock-knock joke say to the other kind of joke?

And we all said: What?

And you said: Knock-knock.

So we said: Who's there?

And you said: Knock-knock!

So we said: Who's there?

And again you said: Knock-knock!

It took us all a minute, but then we got it, and we all laughed, with real laughs, and you smiled out the window looking all proud of yourself and were about to slip your thumb into your mouth but didn't this time.


## CHECKPOINT

That day after breakfast, we drove so long without stopping, I thought I would die. But I was glad to leave that town full of cats and that old man with the cross on his tie, so I didn't complain, not even once. In the car, Ma read the news on her phone and read something aloud to Pa about the lost children arriving safely back in their country, where people in the airport had given them balloons. And Ma sounded angry about them getting balloons, and I didn't get why. She used to give us balloons, too. We would walk down the street to the store and we would get a balloon each, a real one filled with helium, and she'd write our names across them with a marker. I'd hold on to the thread of my balloon as we walked back home, and I always played a game, though I don't know if it even counts as a game, which was that I wasn't holding on to the balloon but rather the balloon was holding me. Maybe it was just a feeling and not really a game. After a few days, no matter what we did to try to save them, our balloons would start to get smaller and would drift around the house by themselves, just like Mama's mom, who you don't remember because you were tiny and she only visited us in New York once, and then she died. But before she died, she also used to drift around the house, from room to room, complaining and sighing and moaning but mostly being silent and kind of getting smaller. The balloons we got would drift lower and lower in that same way as she did, closer to the ground, until one day, they were under a chair or in some corner and our names on them were wrinkled up and small.

We finally stopped to buy food in a city, because that night and possibly the next night, we would sleep in a house in the Burro Mountains that Ma had found on the internet and had rented. The city where we stopped for shopping was called Silver City, which Pa told you was made of real silver except it had been hidden by coats of paint so that enemies would not come and take parts of the city away. You got obsessed with this, and while we walked around the streets, then into a supermarket, and up and down the aisles, you thought you saw hints of that hidden silver everywhere, including in all the canned beans, and a bottle of Windex, and even a box of Froot Loops, which you called frutilupis, the same thing Ma called them, though I suspected you were only pretending to see hints of hidden silver in the frutilupis because you wanted Ma and Pa to buy them for you, which meant you were sometimes smarter than they thought.

We drove a little farther after that, and when we arrived in the Burro Mountains, it was still daytime, which was good for a change, because when we arrived to rest or sleep in places it was usually sunset or nighttime, which meant we had to be in bed soon, which made me think Pa and Ma always wanted to spend as little time as possible with us. But this time, we arrived in full daytime. Two very old grown-ups, a lady and a man with cowboy hats, showed us into a small and dusty house, made of clay, I think. Then the man and woman showed us the two bedrooms, and the little bathroom between them, and then the space with the kitchen, living room, and dining table. They walked so slow and explained so much, you and I were getting antsy. They gave Pa and Ma the keys, and told us how things worked and what not to do, and showed us where the trail maps were, and the walking sticks for hikes, and asked us if we needed anything else or had questions, and luckily Ma said no, so they finally went away.

Pa and Ma got to pick their bedroom, and we complained that we had to share a bed in ours while they each got their own bed in their room, but they scolded us, and we didn't complain more. We were happy to not be in a motel for a change, or in a creepy inn or a bed-and-breakfast. We helped them unpack some things, and then they gave us water and snacks, and opened beers and sat out on the porch with a view of the mountain ridge. You and I explored the inside of the house on our own for a while, but it was small, so there was little to explore. We found two flyswatters behind the refrigerator in the kitchen and took them back outside to the porch, where Ma and Pa were. We offered to kill all the flies so they could relax, said we'd only charge a penny per fly, and they accepted. Hunting flies was harder than we thought, there were so many. We'd kill one fly and ten new flies would appear from nowhere. It was like a vintage video game.

Pa and Ma said they needed a nap, and went inside, and meanwhile you and I collected rocks and pebbles from around the house, being careful when we picked up rocks in case there was a scorpion, wanting to find a scorpion but also not wanting to find one. We put all the rocks and all the pebbles into a bucket we found next to the trash cans at one side of the house, and we spread them on the table. When we'd finished arranging them all on the table, you looked at everything and said that it was like the turtles in the Sargasso Sea that I'd told you about. I asked you why, 'cause I was not understanding you, and you said because, because look at all the turtles floating there, and you were right, the pebbles looked like turtle shells from above.

Then when we got bored and got hungry we went into the kitchen and found tomatoes and salt, and I showed you how to bite into tomatoes, salting them before each bite, and you loved it even though you usually hated tomatoes.

ARCHIVE

Later in the afternoon, you killed a dragonfly by mistake and started crying like a waterfall. I tried to convince you that you hadn't killed it, that it just had died at exactly the same time you caught it inside the glass jar, which was possibly true because the dragonfly had just frozen in there, and it was still beautiful even though it was completely dead, its wings still spread like it was flying without moving. It didn't look like it had been hurt. It was not missing any parts of its body or anything like that. Still, you cried like a madchild. So to stop you from crying, because Pa and Ma were still taking a nap inside the house and I knew if they heard you they would wake up and come blame me, I told you to be quiet and said, listen, let's bury it, and then I'll show you an Apache ritual so that its soul can get unstuck from its body and fly away, which I know is stupid, but I still felt inside me that the idea was good and also even true, though I'd just made it up. So we took spoons from the drawers in the kitchen and a glass full of water to wet the ground if needed, and we walked to a shady spot in front of the house under the shadow of a large red rock and got down on our knees.

The ground was harder than I thought with all those roots clutching to the powdery sand, and even the water we poured on it did not make it much softer, and we hit and dug so hard that we bent the spoons till they were ruined and you were laughing so loud, saying the spoons looked like question marks, which you'd been practicing to draw in school when we were in school still. But in the end, we had a hole big and deep enough to bury the dragonfly, the two spoons, and even a penny, which you threw in for good luck, because you are superstitious like Ma. After that, I had to come up with the ritual because I hadn't thought of that part yet.

I told you, you go pick up pebbles, and I will go inside and steal a cigarette and matches from Pa's jacket. And so we did that and then we met again in front of the little grave, where you were making a circle of pebbles around the covered hole. You were doing a good job, but anyway I told you to try to make it nicer, and when you finished, we sat crisscross applesauce in front of the grave and I lit the cigarette and blew some smoke into the grave and managed not to cough and then put the cigarette out with my shoe on the stony rubbish the way Pa and Ma do. To finish, I threw a handful of dust on the grave, and then I tried singing an ancient song I'd heard Pa playing once, maybe an Apache song, that went ly-o-lay ale loya, hey-o ly-o-lay ale, but you kept giggling instead of being serious.

So then we tried singing something we both knew, like "Highwayman," and we sang words like "sword and pistol by my side, sailed a scooter round the horn of Mexico, got killed but I am living still, and always be around, and round, and round." But we had forgotten half the words and were just humming most of them, so finally we decided we needed to sing the only death song we knew by heart, which was in Spanish. Mama had taught it to us when we were both littler and it was called "La cama de piedra." Finally, you got serious, and we both stood up like soldiers and began: "De piedra ha de ser la cama, de piedra la cabecera, la mujer que a mí me quiera, me ha de querer de a de veras, ay ay, ¿Corazón por qué no amas?" We sang, louder and louder, until we got to the last part, which we sang so loud and so well, I felt the mountains were standing up to listen: "Por caja quiero un sarape, por cruz mis dobles cananas, y escriban sobre mi tumba, mi último adiós con mil balas, ay ay, ¿Corazón por qué no amas?" When we finished, you said maybe we should kill more insects and bury them and create an entire cemetery.

SAMPLES

In the evening, Pa made dinner, and you fell asleep with your head on the table before we even finished. After dinner, he carried you to our bed, then said he was going on a night walk and left with his recording equipment. I helped Ma clear the table, and said I'd wash the dishes. She thanked me and said she'd be out on the porch in case I needed anything.

When I'd finished washing up, I joined her outside on the porch, where she was reading her red book out loud, speaking into her sound recorder. There were many moths flying around the lightbulb above her, and when she saw me there, she switched off her recorder, looked a little embarrassed, like I'd caught her doing something.

What you up to, Mama? I asked her. Just reading and recording some bits of this, she said. I asked her why. Why? she repeated, and thought a little before answering. Because it helps me think and imagine things, I suppose. And why do you read out loud into your recorder? I asked. She told me that it helped her concentrate better, and I made a face like a question mark. So she said, come here, sit down, try it out. She was pointing to the empty chair next to hers, where Pa had been sitting earlier that day. I sat down, and she handed me the book, opened to a page. Then she switched her recorder back on, and stretched her arm toward me so that the recorder was near my mouth. She said, go on, read this bit, I'll record you. So I started reading:

(THE SIXTH ELEGY)

The yard where the children had boarded the first train, and the dark jungle after it, were long gone. Aboard that first train, they'd crossed the dark wet jungles of the south, making their way up toward the mountains. In a small village, they'd had to jump off and catch another train that came only a few hours later. On this new gondola, better somehow, less grim, painted brick red, they climbed to the cold cusps of the mountains in the northeast.

The train rose high above the clouds there, almost floating, it seemed, above the thick milky blanket of clouds that stretched far toward the eastern sea. It carried them up along the winding mountain path above ravines and next to plantations laboriously crafted by many human hands into hostile rocky ridges.

Far from towns and checkpoints, human and inhuman threats, but also somehow closer to death, the children were able to sleep unshaken by night terrors for the first time in many moons. They were all asleep and did not hear or see the woman who, also asleep, rolled off the side of the roof of their gondola. Tumbling awake as she went down the jagged ridge, she'd torn open her stomach on a broken branch, and kept on falling, until her body thumped flat, into abrupt emptiness. The first living thing to notice her, the next morning, was a porcupine, its spines erect and its tummy ballooned on larch and crab apples. It sniffed one of her feet, the one that was unshod, and then circled around her, uninterested, sniffing its way toward a bunch of drying poplar catkins.

Only one of the two girls aboard the gondola, the younger one, realized that the woman was missing. The sun had risen, and the train was passing through a small town perched on the western edge of the range when all of a sudden a group of strong, stout women, with well-kept long hair and long skirts, had appeared next to the tracks. The train had slowed down a little, as it often did when crossing more populated areas. The people aboard the gondola were startled at first, but before they could say or do anything, from below, these women started to throw fruit and bags of food and water bottles up to them. Good fruit: apples, bananas, pears, small papayas, and oranges, which everyone peeled fast and almost swallowed whole but which the girl kept, tucked under her shirt. She had wanted to wake the woman up to share the news of the free food. But she was not aboard the train anymore, it seemed. She wondered where the woman had gone, and thought maybe she'd just jumped off at a stop to join her family in one of those misty towns while everyone was asleep. The woman had been kind to her. One night, when the girl, shaking with jungle tremors, had screamed and wailed and cursed for water, the woman had given her the last sips from her canteen.

The girl remembered the missing woman again a few mornings later, when the train was passing through another town in the lower valleys. The tall mountains were now far on the eastern horizon, and the children saw some people standing beside the tracks in the distance. They gathered along the edge of the gondola's roof— hands ready to catch flying food—but instead received rocks and insults. Whispering, as if she were praying to some fallen angel, the girl said: You were lucky, dear flying lady, to miss this part of the ride, because we almost got killed by stones, and I wish you had taken me with you, wherever you are, and good luck.

The beast pierced and puffed smoke, in and out of dark tunnels long ago dynamited and carved into the layers of the black heart of the range. The children played in these tunnels—held their breath as the train sped into the darkness, only allowed to breathe again when their gondola had made it across the arched threshold back into the light, and the valley opened up again, like an abysmal, blinding flower, under their eyes.

## MAPS & GPS

We play this game, too! I told Ma. And she nodded as she turned her sound recorder back off.

We used to play it when we were riding inside the car, driving on mountain roads where there were tunnels. We all held our breath as soon as the car went into the tunnel, and were only allowed to breathe again when we reached the other side. I usually won. And you always, always cheated, even if the tunnel was short and the cheating not even worth it.

Can we read a bit more? I asked Ma. She said no, that was it for today. We were going to wake up early the next morning and walk down to the creek, and maybe farther into the valley, so we better go to sleep. She handed me the car keys and asked me to put the book back in her box, Box V, so I did. And then the two of us went inside. She left the keys on top of the fridge, which is where she always left keys, and poured me a glass of milk. Then we went to the bathroom and brushed our teeth together, making monkey faces in the mirror at each other, and finally we each went into our bedrooms and said goodnight, goodnight. You were taking up all the space on our bed, so I pushed you as far as possible to your side. But as soon as I turned the light off, you inched right back to me and threw your arm around my back.

## NO U-TURN

I had heard echoes before, but nothing like the ones we heard that next day when we all walked out into the Burro Mountains. Near where we used to live, back in the city, there was a steep street that went down to the big brown river, and the street had a tunnel above it because on top of that street, and on top of that tunnel, there was another street going across the other way. Cities are so complicated to explain because everything is on top of everything, with no divisions. On weekends when the weather was warm, we used to ride our bikes from our apartment on Edgecombe Avenue, first up and then downhill until we reached that steep street and went under that tunnel under the other street to reach the bike path that went along the river, the four of us, each on our own bikes except you, Memphis. You sat in a child's seat at the back of Papa's bike. Always when we reached the tunnel, I held my breath—partly because I knew it was good luck to hold my breath, partly because under the tunnel it smelled of wet dog fur and old cardboard and pee. So I kept silent and held my breath in the tunnel. But always, every time, Pa shouted the word echo as soon as we reached the tunnel, and then Ma I think smiled at him and also shouted echo, and then you copied them and shouted echo from behind, and I loved the sound of the three short echoes bouncing off the walls of the tunnel while we came out through the other side and I finally breathed again and only then I shouted echo though there was never any reply because it was too late.

But the echoes we heard against the rocks that morning in the mountains were real echoes and nothing like the ones in our old tunnel in the city. That day Mama and Papa had woken us up before sunrise and given us mush, which I hate, and boiled apples, which I like, and we'd taken long walking sticks from a basket outside the house and walked down the path to the creek and slowly back up another mountain, and then halfway down the other side of the second mountain, until we'd found long flat rocks, where we lay for a while and then sat for a while, the sun getting higher and heavier on our hats. I took my camera out of my backpack and told Papa to stand up, which he did, and I took a picture of him with his hat on and smoking the way he smokes when he's worried, his forehead all crumpled up and his eyes looking somewhere like they're looking at something ugly, wishing I knew but not knowing what he was thinking or what he was always worried about. Later, I gave him that picture as a present, so I didn't get to keep it for you to see and keep and I'm sorry for that.

We sat down again and ate cucumber sandwiches on buttered bread that Ma had packed in her small sack, and she said we were allowed to take our heavy boots off while we ate. For a moment, I was happy knowing we were all like this together. But then, while we were eating, I realized Mama and Papa were not talking to each other, saying nothing, again not talking not at all, not even to say pass me the water bottle or pass another sandwich. When Papa Cochise got moody, you and I would tell him to go have a cigarette, and usually he'd go and have one. He smelled disgusting afterward, but I liked the sound of him blowing out smoke and the way he squinted when he did. Ma said he furrowed his brow like he was squeezing out thoughts from his eyes, and that he did it so often, one day there would be no thoughts left in there.

Now they were not even looking at each other or nothing while we ate, so I thought hard and decided I should either tell a joke or start talking louder because although I liked some kinds of silence, I hated that sort of silence. But I couldn't think of any jokes or funny words, or anything loud to say like that, just because. So I took off my hat and put it on my lap. I thought hard what to say and how and when. Then, looking at my hat on my lap, I got an idea. I looked around and made sure no one was watching, and then with one hand I flung the hat up high in the air, and it flew up and then down, falling and then rolling down the side of the mountain, bouncing off rocks, and finally getting caught in a bush. I took a deep breath and made a face and pretended to sound worried when I shouted very loud into the wind, shouted the word hat.

That's when it happened. I shouted the word hat, and you all looked at me, and then looked back at the mountain, because we all suddenly heard hat hat hat hat coming back at us from the mountain, my voice bouncing off all the mountain rocks around us, all the rocks repeating hat.

It was like a spell, a good spell, because all of a sudden, the silence between us was filled with smiles, and I felt the same feeling growing in my stomach that I know we all used to feel each time we were riding our bikes so fast down that steep street downhill toward the tunnel toward the river, and suddenly now Papa shouted the word echo and Ma shouted echo and you shouted echo and all around us the echoes multiplied, echo, echo, echo, and even I shouted echo, and for the first time I heard my own echo coming back, bouncing back to me so loud and clear.

Papa put his sandwich down and cried, Geronimo! And the echo said onimo, onimo, onimo.

Mama shouted, you hear me? And the mountain bounced back ear me, ear me.

So I shouted, I'm Swift Feather! And it came back eather, eather, eather.

And you looked around kind of confused and said softly:

But where are they?

Then we stood up one by one, all of us barefoot on the surface of the long flat rock, and tried different words like Elvis, words like Memphis, like highway, and moon, and boots, hello, father, away, I'm ten, I'm five, I hate mush, mountain, river, fuck you, you, fuck you too, too, tooshie, ooshie, fart, airplanes, binoculars, alien, goodbye, I love you, me too, too. And then I shouted, auuuuu, and we all howled like a pack of wolves and then Pa tried clapping his hands against his mouth, saying, oooooooo, and we all followed him like an ancient family, and then Ma clapped her hands together and the claps came back to us clap clap clap, or maybe more like tap tap tap. And when we'd all run out of things to say and all run out of breath, we sat down again, the three of us except you, who cried one last cry.

But where are you, are you, are you?

And then you looked back at us and said, now whispering, I don't see them, where are they, are they hiding from us? Pa and Ma looked at you looking confused and then back at me like wanting a translation. I understood your question perfectly, so I explained it to them. I was always the one standing between you and them, or between us and them. I said, I think she thinks there's someone on the other side of the mountain who is answering us. They both nodded and smiled at you and then at me and then even looked at each other still smiling. I explained, Memphis, there's no one out there, Memphis, it's just our own voices. Liar, you said. You called me a liar. So I said, I'm not lying, you idiot. And Mama scolded me with her eyes, and told you, it's just an echo, baby. It's just an echo, Papa also said. They didn't know but I knew that that was no good as an explanation for you, so I said, remember, remember the bouncy balls we got from that round machine in the diner where you cried afterward? Yes, you said, I cried because you kept getting all the colorful balls and me, I kept getting only plastic bugs. That's not the point, Memphis, the point is the balls, the point is, remember how we played with them outside the diner afterward, throwing them against the wall and catching them again? Now you were listening and said, yes, I remember that day. Our voices are like those bouncy balls, even if you can't see them bouncing now, I said. Our voices bounce off this mountain when we throw our voices at it, and that's called echo. Liar, you said again. I'm not lying, he's not lying, it's true, baby, that is echo, that's what echo is, he's not lying, I'm not lying, we all told you.

You're so proud and so arrogant sometimes, you still didn't believe us. You stood upright very serious on the flat rock and straightened out your pink hat and then your T-shirt like you were about to pledge allegiance to a flag. You cleared your throat and cupped your hands around your mouth. You looked into the mountain rocks like you were giving someone an order and took a deep breath. And then, then you finally shouted hard, you shouted, people, shouted, hello, people, shouted, we're here, up here, here, here, Jesus Fucking Christ, Christ.

## BIRDS

Back in the house that afternoon, I helped Papa cook. We prepared the grill outside. Papa threw some coal in the grill and lit it, and I went to the kitchen to get the meat from the fridge, buffalo meat, which is my favorite kind. I got to help him by holding the tray with the meat. One by one, he'd fork a piece of meat and carefully put it on the grill. I stood there and was still thinking in my head of echoes, and everything around me reminded me of the echoes we'd heard earlier on the mountain, Pa's back-and-forth movements, back and forth, the fire whispering inside the grill, some big birds slapping their wings above us, and even your voice back in the kitchen inside the house, where you were helping Ma wrap vegetables in tinfoil, wrapping potatoes, onions, garlic, and also mushrooms, which I hate.

I asked Papa if the echoes we had heard earlier that day were like the ones in Echo Canyon he'd told us about. He said yes but no. In the Chiricahua Mountains, in Echo Canyon, he said, the echoes were even stronger and more beautiful. The most beautiful echoes you ever heard, he said, and some of them have been bouncing around there for so long that if you listen carefully, you can hear the voices of the long-departed Chiricahua peoples. And of the Eagle Warriors? I asked him. Yes, of the Eagle Warriors, too.

I wondered for a while how that was possible, and then I asked Ma and Pa to explain echoes to me more clearly, more professionally, as we all set the table, a long wooden table outside the house, bringing plates, forks, knives, cups, water, wine, salt, bread. I understood the basics. They said an echo is a delay in sound waves. It's a sound wave that arrives after the direct sound is produced and reflected on a surface. But that explanation didn't answer all my questions, so I kept insisting, asking more and more, until I think I got them both a bit annoyed, and Pa said:

Food's ready!

We sat around the wooden table, and Papa wanted to make a toast, so he let me and you try some drops of wine in our cups, although he also poured a lot of water into them, to make the taste softer, he said. He said kids in this country were usually not allowed to taste wine, said their taste buds were completely ruined by puritanism, chicken fingers, ketchup, and peanut butter. But we were now kids in Chiricahua Apache territory, so we were allowed to have a tiny taste of life. He raised his cup, said Arizona, New Mexico, Sonora, Chihuahua were all beautiful names, but also names to name a past of injustice, genocide, exodus, war, and blood. He said he wanted us to remember this land as a land of resilience and forgiveness, also as a land where the earth and sky knew no division.

He didn't tell us what the real name of the land was, but I suppose it was Apacheria. Then he took a sip from his cup, so we all took a sip from our cups. You spat it all out onto the ground, said you hated it, this waterwine. I said I liked it, though really I didn't that much.

TIME

We finished eating quickly because we were so hungry, but I didn't want that evening to end, ever, though I knew it would end and so would all our evenings together, as soon as the trip ended. I couldn't change that, but for tonight, at least, I could try to make the night longer, the way Geronimo had the power to stretch out time during a night of battle.

QUESTIONS & ANSWERS

I decided to ask questions, good ones, so that everyone forgot about time. That way I could make time stretch longer.

First I asked the three of you what you wished for the most right then. You said: Frutilupis! Pa said: I wish for clarity. Ma said: I wish for Manuela to find her two daughters.

Then I asked Pa and Ma: What were you like when you were our ages and what do you remember? Papa told us a sad story about when he was your age and his dog got run over by a tram and then his grandmother put the dog in a black plastic bag and threw him in the trash. Then he said that when he was my age, things got better for him and he used to be the director of the children's newspaper in the building where they lived. He was in charge of leading an expedition every Friday after school to the stationery shop, where there was a machine called the Xerox that made copies of whatever they wrote or whatever they drew but without there being computers or anything. One time, because they had not written anything or drawn anything for the newspaper, they just put their hands, then their faces, then their feet on the machine and the machine printed copies of that, and then when no one was looking, one boy pulled down his pants and sat on the machine and made a copy of his butt. You and I laughed so hard that the waterwine I had just taken a sip of came all out through my nostrils and stung.

Then it was Mama's turn, and she remembered that when she was five years old like you, she was in a living room in a house with her mother and her mother's friend, and there was a huge fish tank with many fish that she was looking at. At some point, she turned around and her mother was not there, only her mother's friend, so she asked her, where is my mother? and the friend said, she's in there, look, she became a fish. And at first Mama was really excited and trying to make out which of the fishes was her mother, but then she started getting scared, thinking, will my mother come back and ever stop being a fish? And so much time passed that she started crying for her mother to come back, and I think that while she was telling this story, she almost started crying again, and I didn't want that, so I asked her what about when she was my age, what was her favorite game when she was ten.

She thought for a moment, and then she said her favorite thing when she was ten was breaking into and exploring houses that were abandoned because the neighborhood where she lived was full of abandoned houses. And she said nothing else, though you were curious to know more about those abandoned houses. For example, were there ghosts in them and did Ma ever get caught by anyone like the police or her parents? But instead of telling us more, she asked us, what about you two, how do you think you will be when you are our age and grown up?

You raised your hand to speak and so got to speak first. You said, I think I will know how to read and write. And then you said you would have either a boyfriend or a girlfriend but that you'd never marry anyone so you didn't have to tongue kiss, which I thought was smart. Then because you didn't say anything else, I got to speak. I said I would travel a lot, and have many children, and would cook buffalo meat for them every day. For a job, I'd be an astronaut. And as a hobby, I would document things. I said I would be a documentarianist, and I said the word so quick that I think maybe Pa heard documentarist and Ma heard documentarian, and no one minded.

## CREDIBLE FEARS

That night, when everyone was asleep and I couldn't sleep, I snuck out of our bedroom, took the car keys from the top of the refrigerator, and went outside. I crossed the porch, walked slowly to the car, opened the trunk, and looked around in the dark for Ma's box. I wanted to read what happened next in the lost children's story, in the red book, but this time I wanted to read out loud and record some more, like I'd done with Ma the day before. I didn't want to make a racket looking for the recorder in the box, so I just took the entire box with me. I was about to go back inside the house when I remembered that Ma kept her recorder in the glove compartment most of the time, and not in the box. So I walked back to the car, opened the passenger door, put the box down on the seat, and looked in the compartment. It was there. Ma's big road map was also there. I took both things, the road map and the recorder, opened the box's lid just enough to sneak them inside it silently, then tiptoed back to the house, and across the house into our bedroom carrying everything. You were fast asleep and snoring like an old man, Memphis, and occupying most of the space. I put the box on the floor for a moment, pushed you to your side, being extra gentle, and switched on only the little bedside lamp so I wouldn't wake you up. You stopped snoring, turned around, belly facing the ceiling. Then your mouth opened a little and you started snoring again. I climbed into my side of the bed and sat there, with Ma's box in front of me.

Very carefully, I opened it. I took out the road map, the recorder, and the red book with my pictures inside its pages, and put all three things on the bedside table, under the lamp. I was about to close the box again and get ready to read when something came over me, which I cannot explain. I felt like I needed to see what else was in that box, look at all the things that I knew were always under the little red book, things I wasn't allowed to look at so never did. But no one was watching me now. I could shuffle the things in the box around all I wanted. As long as I put everything back in its place after, Ma would never even notice.

One by one, I started taking things out of the box, slowly, making sure I put everything in order on the bed, so I could put it back later exactly the same way. The first thing I took from the top of the box I put on the left-foot corner of the bed, which was my corner, the second thing next to it, then the third, fourth.

It was more stuff than I thought. There were a lot of cutouts and notes, and photographs and a few tapes. There were folders, birth certificates and other official things, maps, and some books. I put each thing on the bed, one next to the other. At some point, I had to get out of bed and walk around the edges, so I could reach everything better. By the time I took out the last thing, I'd taken up most of the space in the bed, and even though I didn't want to put anything on top of you in case you moved between the sheets and messed everything up, I ended up having to put some maps and some books on top of you.

I spent a while looking at all of Mama's stuff, all laid out, walking around the bed, back and forth, until my head was spinning with feelings. Finally, I took a folder labeled "Migrant Mortality Reports" and opened it. It was full of loose pieces of paper with information, and I looked through them, I tried to understand what they were saying but couldn't, there were many numbers and abbreviations, and it was so frustrating to not understand. I decided to focus on the maps, because at least I knew I was good at reading maps. I took one that was right on top of your knees, or maybe your thighs, I couldn't tell, 'cause of the sheet. The map was strange. It showed a space, like any map, but in that space there were hundreds of little red dots, which weren't cities because some of them overlapped with others. When I looked at the map key, I realized the red dots stood for people who had died there, in that exact spot, and I wanted to vomit, or cry, and wake Ma and Pa up and ask them, but of course I didn't. I just breathed deep. I remembered Ma and Pa making five-hundred-piece puzzles walking around the dining table in our old apartment, how they looked serious, worried, but at the same time in control, and that's how I decided I should stand in front of all that stuff lying on our bed.

There was another map similar to that one, which I'd put right on top of your belly. It also had many red dots, and I was about to skip it because it made me feel sick, but then I realized it was a map of exactly where we were going to go in Apacheria. The map was missing most names of places, but I was able to make out the Dragoon Mountains in the west. Then, in the east, the Chiricahua Mountains, where Echo Canyon was. And between the two ranges, the big dry valley where there was a dry lake called Wilcox Playa, though on this map the name didn't appear. Papa had shown me other maps of this same part of Apacheria many times, pointing to places and telling me their names. I had to repeat them after him, especially the names that were important in Apache stories, like Wilcox, San Simon, Bowie, Dos Cabezas Peaks, and Skeleton Canyon. I felt proud of it now, that I knew my way around Apacheria so well without even having been there yet. In Ma's map, for example, even if the names weren't written on it, I think I spotted the town called Bowie, north of the big dry valley, right on the railroad tracks, which is where Geronimo and his people had boarded a train after their final, final surrender. I also spotted Skeleton Canyon, south-east of the Chiricahua Mountains, which was where Geronimo and his people were captured before boarding that train in Bowie, and of course Dos Cabezas Peaks, which is where the ghost of Chief Cochise still walks around.

Then I noticed that on this map, right in the center of the valley between the Dragoons and the Chiricahuas, Ma had marked XX with a pen, and then made a big circle around the two X's. It was the only map where she'd made any markings. I wondered what that meant. I thought about it for a long while, and out of all the possibilities I came up with, I think this was the one: Mama had made those marks because she was sure that some lost children were there. Two children: XX.

Then I realized: maybe the two X's were the two girls Mama often spoke about, Manuela's daughters, who had gone missing. Mama had good instincts, she was Lucky Arrow, after all. So if she was looking for them there, they were probably there, or somewhere near there. And then I had an idea that felt like an explosion in my head, but a good explosion. If the girls were there, maybe we could help Ma find them.

## ELECTRICITY

So this is what I decided. The next morning, before Ma and Pa woke up, you and I would leave. We'd walk for as long as we could, like the lost children had walked, even if we might get lost. We'd find a train and board it, heading toward Apacheria. We'd walk into the valley where Ma had circled those two X's. We'd look for the two lost girls there. If we got lucky and found them, we'd all head together to Echo Canyon, where Pa had always told us we could be easily found if we got lost, thanks to all the echoes. And if we didn't find the girls, we'd still head to Echo Canyon, which, according to Ma's map, was not too far from the place where she'd marked XX. I knew, of course, I'd get into big trouble for this. Ma and Pa would be so angry when they realized we had run away. But after a little while, they'd be more worried than mad. Ma would start thinking of us the way she thought of them, the lost children. All the time and with all her heart. And Pa would focus on finding our echoes, instead of all the other echoes he was chasing. And here's the most important part, if we too were lost children, we would have to be found again. Ma and Pa would have to find us. They would find us, I knew that. I would also draw a map of the route you and I would probably follow, so that they could find us at the end. And the end was Echo Canyon.

It was silly of me to have broken a promise and looked inside Ma's box. But also I finally understood some important things after looking at all that stuff, understood them with my heart and not only with my head. Though my head was spinning, too. But I'd finally got it, and that's what matters, 'cause now I can tell you about it also. I finally got why Mama was always thinking and talking about all the lost children, and why it seemed like she was farther and farther away from us every day. The lost children, all of them, were so much more than us, Memphis, so much more than all the children we ever knew. They were like Pa's Eagle Warriors, maybe even braver and smarter. I also finally understood what you and I had to do to make things better for all of us.

## ORDER & CHAOS

I got so excited about my plan that I even felt I should wake every-one up to share it with the family, which of course I didn't do. I breathed deep and slow, trying to keep calm. I put all of Ma's things back in her box, in the right order, or almost, because you had turned around on your side and made a bit of a mess.

Before I closed the box, using the lid for support, I drew the map of my planned route. I based my map on one of the maps in Ma's box, the one where she'd made the circle around the two X's. First I drew the map, in pencil. Then I drew the route you and I would take, in red. Then, in blue, I drew the route that I imagined the lost children in Ma's book might take. And the two routes, red and blue, met at a big X, which I made in pencil, and which was kind of at the same spot where Ma had marked XX on her map.

When I was finally finished, I looked at the map, and rubbed my stomach butterflies. It really was a very good map, the best I'd ever made. I put it at the top of the pile of things inside Ma's box, right on top of her map with the two X's. I knew she would find it there. Before closing the box, I thought maybe I should also leave a note in case my map was not clear enough to them, though it was clear enough to me. So I unstuck a blank Post-it from between the pages of one of the books in the box, a book called *The Gates of Paradise*, and wrote a note like old telegrams in stories, saying, went out, will look for lost girls, meet you later at Echo Canyon.

I still had to take the box back to the trunk, and I did. I crept outside, opened the trunk, put the box in its place. And when I went back inside, I felt like I was a finally almost a grown man.

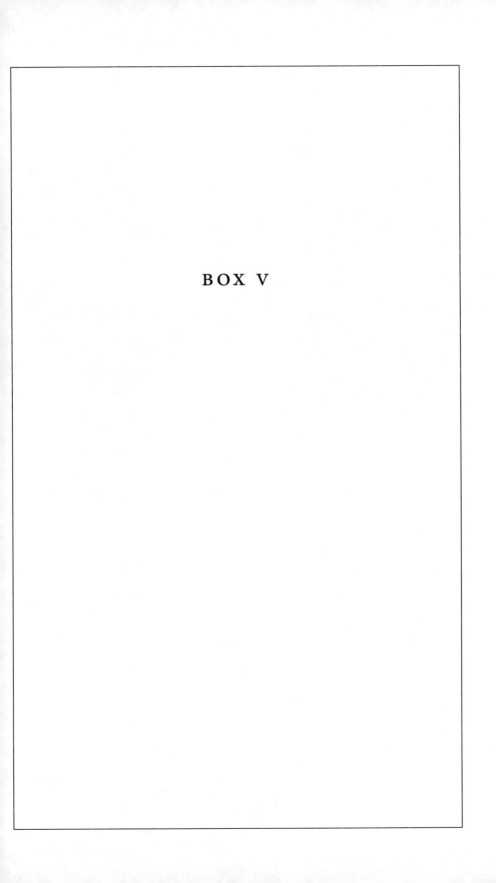

BOX V

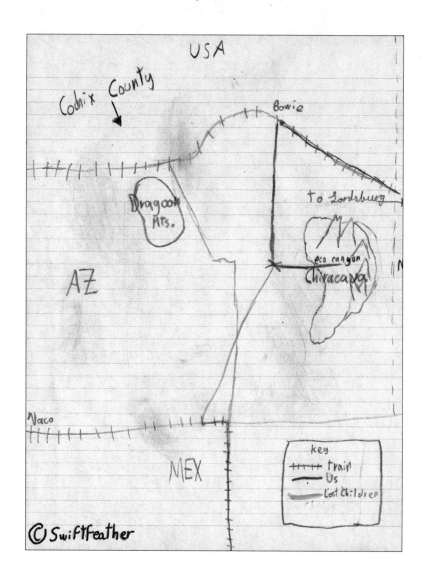

§ MAP

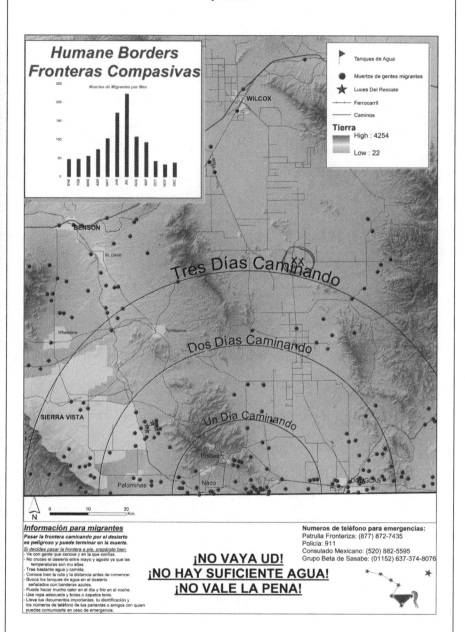

Humane Borders
Fronteras Compasivas

Muertes de Migrantes por Mes

Tanques de Agua
Muertos de gentes migrantes
Luces Del Rescate
Ferrocarril
Caminos

**Tierra**
High : 4254
Low : 22

WILCOX

BENSON
St. David

Tres Días Caminando

Whetstone
Tombstone

Dos Días Caminando

SIERRA VISTA

Un Día Caminando

Bisbee

Palominas
Naco
DOUGLAS

0    10    20 Km.
N

**Información para migrantes**
Pasar la frontera caminando por el desierto
es peligroso y puede terminar en la muerte.
Si decides pasar la frontera a pie, prepárate bien.
- Ve con gente que conoce y en la que confías.
- No cruces el desierto entre mayo y agosto ya que las
  temperaturas son muy altas.
- Trae bastante agua y comida.
- Conoce bien la ruta y la distancia antes de comenzar.
- Busca los tanques de agua en el desierto
  señalados con banderas azules.
- Puede hacer mucho calor en el día y frío en la noche.
- Use ropa adecuada y botas o zapatos tenis.
- Lleva tus documentos importantes, tu identificación y
  los números de teléfono de tus parientes o amigos con quien
  puedes comunicarte en caso de emergencia.

¡NO VAYA UD!
¡NO HAY SUFICIENTE AGUA!
¡NO VALE LA PENA!

Numeros de teléfono para emergencias:
Patrulla Fronteriza: (877) 872-7435
Policía: 911
Consulado Mexicano: (520) 882-5595
Grupo Beta de Sasabe: (01152) 637-374-8076

Name: HUERTAS-FERNANDEZ, NURIA
Sex: Female
Age: 9
Reporting Date: 2003-07-09
Surface Management: Private
Location: SMH
Location Precision: Physical description with directions,
    distances, and landmarks (precise to within 1mi/2km)
Corridor: Douglas
Cause of Death: Exposure
OME determined COD: COMPLICATIONS OF
    HYPERTHERMIA WITH RHABDOMYOLYSIS AND
    DEHYDRATION
State: Arizona
County: Cochise
Latitude: 31.366050
Longitude: −09.559990

Name: ARIZAGA, BABY BOY
Sex: Male
Age: 0
Reporting Date: 2005-09-19
Surface Management: Pima County
Location: ARIVACA RD MP19
Location Precision: Vague physical description (precise to
    within 15mi/25km)
Corridor: Nogales
Cause of Death: Nonviable
OME determined COD: STILLBORN NONVIABLE MALE
    FETUS
State: Arizona
County: Pima
Latitude: 31.726220
Longitude: −111.126110

Name: HERNANDEZ QUINTERO, JOSSELINE
  JANILETHA
Sex: Female
Age: 14
Reporting Date: 2008-02-20
Surface Management: US Forest Service
Location: N 31′ 34.53 W 111′ 10.52
Location Precision: GPS coordinate (precise to within
  ca. 300ft/100m)
Corridor: Nogales
Cause of Death: Exposure
OME determined COD: PROBABLE EXPOSURE
State: Arizona
County: Pima
Latitude: 31.575500
Longitude: −111.175330

Name: LÓPEZ DURAN, RUFINO
Sex: Male
Age: 15
Reporting Date: 2013-08-26
Surface Management: Private
Location: INTERSTATE 10 MILEPOST 342.1
Location Precision: Physical description with directions,
    distances, and landmarks (precise to within 1mi/2km)
Corridor: Douglas
Cause of Death: Blunt force injury
OME determined COD: MULTIPLE BLUNT FORCE
    INJURIES
State: Arizona
County: Cochise
Latitude: 32.283693
Longitude: −109.826340

Name: VILCHIS PUENTE, VICENTE
Sex: Male
Age: 8
Reporting Date: 2007-03-14
Surface Management: Private
Location: 2 MILES WEST OF 12166 EAST TURKEY CREEK
Location Precision: Street address (precise to within
    ca. 1000ft/300m)
Corridor: Douglas
Cause of Death: Undetermined, skeletal remains
OME determined COD: UNDETERMINED (SKELETAL
    REMAINS)
State: Arizona
County: Cochise
Latitude: 31.881290
Longitude: −109.426741

Name: BELTRAN GALICIA, SOFIA
Sex: Female
Age: 11
Reporting Date: 2014-04-06
Surface Management: Private
Location: UMC MORGUE
Location Precision: GPS coordinate (precise to within
    ca. 300ft/100m)
Corridor: Douglas
Cause of Death: Exposure
OME determined COD: COMPLICATIONS OF
    HYPERTHERMIA
State: Arizona
County: Cochise
Latitude: 31.599972
Longitude: −109.728027

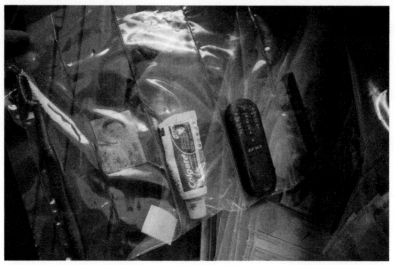

*Objects found on migrant trails in the desert, Pima County*

§ LOOSE NOTE

A map is a silhouette, a contour that groups disparate elements together, whatever they are. To map is to include as much as to exclude. To map is also a way to make visible what is usually unseen.

§ BOOK

*The Gates of Paradise,* by Jerzy Andrzejewski

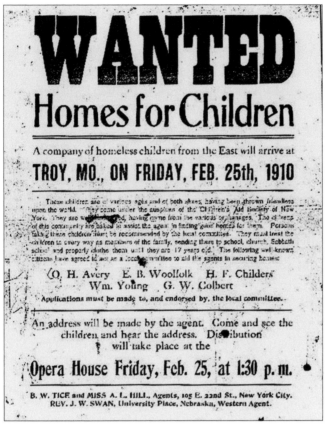

*Homes for Children. Orphan Train Movement, 1910*

§ NOTE

In the year 1850, there were around thirty thousand homeless
    children in New York.
They ate out of trash cans, roamed the streets in packs.
Slept under the shadows of buildings or on sidewalk heating
    grates.
They joined street gangs for protection.
In 1853, Charles Loring Brace created the Children's Aid
    Society, to offer them help.

But there was no way to offer sustained relief.
A year later, the Aid Society came up with a solution.
Put children on trains and ship them to the West.
To be auctioned off and adopted by families.
Between 1854 and 1930, more than 200,000 children were
    removed from NY.
Some ended up with good families, which took care of them.
Others were taken in as servants or slaves, enduring
    inhumane living conditions.
Sometimes unspeakable abuse.
The mass relocation of children was called the Placing-Out
    Program.
The children became known as the Orphan Train Riders.


§ FOLDER (FROM BRENT HAYES EDWARDS'S WORKING
    BIBLIOGRAPHY: "THEORIES OF ARCHIVE")

"What Is Past Is Prologue: A History of Archival Ideas Since
    1898, and the Future Paradigm Shift," Terry Cook
"The End of Collecting: Towards a New Purpose for Archival
    Appraisal," Richard J. Cox
"Reflections of an Archivist," Sir Hilary Jenkinson
*Owning Memory: How a Caribbean Community Lost Its
    Archives and Found Its History,* Jeannette Allis Bastian
*Dwelling in the Archive: Women Writing House, Home, and
    History in Late Colonial India,* Antoinette Burton
"'Othering' the Archive—from Exile to Inclusion and
    Heritage Dignity: The Case of Palestinian Archival
    Memory," Beverley Butler
*Dispossessed Lives: Enslaved Women, Violence, and the
    Archive,* Marisa J. Fuentes
*Lost in the Archives,* Rebecca Comay, ed.
*Archive Fever: A Freudian Impression,* Jacques Derrida
"Ashes and 'the Archive': The London Fire of 1666,
    Partisanship, and Proof," Frances E. Dolan
"Archive and Aspiration," Arjun Appadurai

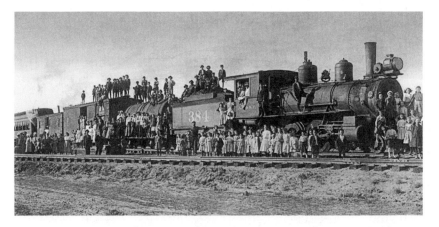

*Orphan Train*

§ BOOK

*The Children's Crusade,* Marcel Schwob

§ LOOSE NOTE / QUOTE

"Until the 18th century most trading companies had little or no desire to purchase children from the coast of Africa, and encouraged their captains not to buy them. . . . By the middle of the 18th century, however, planters economically dependent on the slave trade came to depend on children and youth. As the abolitionist movement increasingly threatened their slave supply, planters adopted the strategy of importing younger slaves who would live longer. As a result, youth became an attractive asset on the auction blocks of the slave markets. Ironically, abolitionist sentiment changed 18th-century definitions of risk, investment, and profit. As the plantocracy purchased more breeding women and children in order to save their economic interests, traders modified their ideas of profit and risk and ideas of child worth changed throughout the Atlantic World."

—COLLEEN A. VASCONCELLOS, "CHILDREN IN THE SLAVE TRADE," IN CHILDREN AND YOUTH IN HISTORY

## § LOOSE NOTE / QUOTE

THE DOLBEN'S ACT OF 1788:

"II. Provided always, That if there shall be, in any such ship or vessel, any more than two fifth parts of the slaves who shall be children, and who shall not exceed four feet four inches in height, then every five such children (over and above the aforesaid proportion of two fifths) shall be deemed and taken to be equal to four of the said slaves within the true intent and meaning of this act. . . ."

ANNOTATION: "THE DOLBEN'S ACT OF 1788 WAS PROPOSED BY NOTED ABOLITIONIST SIR WILLIAM DOLBEN BEFORE THE ENGLISH PARLIAMENT. WHILE IT WAS MEANT TO RESTRICT THE SLAVE TRADE, IT ACTUALLY HAD AN ADVERSE EFFECT ON CHILDREN."

—ELIZABETH DONNAN, DOCUMENTS ILLUSTRATIVE OF THE SLAVE TRADE TO AMERICA, ANNOTATED BY COLLEEN A. VASCONCELLOS, IN CHILDREN AND YOUTH IN HISTORY

*Geronimo and fellow prisoners on their way
to Florida, September 10, 1886*

§ BOOK

*Le goût de l'archive,* Arlette Farge

§ LOOSE NOTE

Euphemisms hide, erase, coat.
Euphemisms lead us to tolerate the unacceptable. And,
   eventually, to forget.
Against a euphemism, remembrance. In order to not repeat.
Remember terms and meanings. Their absurd disjointedness.
Term: *Our Peculiar Institution.* Meaning: slavery. (Epitome of
   all euphemisms.)
Term: *Removal.* Meaning: expulsion and dispossession of
   people from their lands.

Term: *Placing Out.* Meaning: expulsion of abandoned children from the East Coast.
Term: *Relocation.* Meaning: confining people in reservations.
Term: *Reservation.* Meaning: a wasteland, a sentence to perpetual poverty.
Term: *Removal.* Meaning: expulsion of people seeking refuge.
Term: *Undocumented.* Meaning: people who will be removed.

§ LOOSE NOTE / QUOTE

On Saturday, November 19, 2002, sixty people incarcerated in a camp for illegal immigrants *sew their lips together.* Sixty people with their lips sewn reel around the camp, gazing at the sky. Small muddy stray dogs scamper after them, yapping shrilly. The authorities keep postponing consideration of their applications for leave to remain.

—FROM *BELLADONNA*, BY DAŠA DRNDIĆ

§ LOOSE NOTE

Words, words, words, where do you put them?
Exodus
Diaspora
Genocide
Ethnic cleansing

§ BOOK

*Belladonna,* by Daša Drndić

ANNE CARSON

*Father's Old Blue Cardigan*

*Now it hangs on the back of the kitchen chair*
*where I always sit, as it did*
*on the back of the kitchen chair where he always sat.*

*I put it on whenever I come in,*
*as he did, stamping*
*the snow from his boots.*

*I put it on and sit in the dark.*
*He would not have done this.*
*Coldness comes paring down from the moonbone in the sky.*

*His laws were a secret.*
*But I remember the moment at which I knew*
*he was going mad inside his laws.*

*He was standing at the turn of the driveway when I arrived.*
*He had on the blue cardigan with the buttons done up all the way to the top.*
*Not only because it was a hot July afternoon*

*but the look on his face—*
*as a small child who has been dressed by some aunt early in the morning*
*for a long trip*

*on cold trains and windy platforms*
*will sit very straight at the edge of his seat*
*while the shadows like long fingers*

*over the haystacks that sweep past*
*keep shocking him*
*because he is riding backwards.*

CONTINENTAL DIVIDE

Outside our window, the sky had got red and pink and orange the way the sky in the desert always gets before the sun comes out, before it suddenly turns blue, which is a natural phenomenon you wouldn't understand now even if I explained it.

I climbed out of bed and quietly packed all my useful stuff in my backpack. I had a lot of useful stuff I got because I had turned ten years old the day we started the trip. As a birthday present, you made me a card that said, Today I will always love you more than yesterday. Though only I could make out your terrible spelling, which was probably something like, Tday I wll owaz lov you mre than yustrday. I put that in my backpack. Pa gave me a Swiss Army knife, a pair of binoculars, a flashlight, and a small compass, and Ma gave me my camera. I put all those things in my backpack. Then I realized that Ma's sound recorder, her big map, and the little red book were still lying on the bedside table, I'd forgotten to put them back in the car the night before. So I just put them in my backpack, too.

I tiptoed to the kitchen and got two bottles of water and a lot of snacks. Also, at the last minute, I decided to take a small map that came with the house and that I'd found earlier in a basket next to the door. That map was called Map of Continental Divide Trail, and it included the walking trails in the Burro Mountains area, so it could come in handy. Finally, I emptied your backpack on the floor behind the bed, and put only *The Book with No Pictures* back in. I didn't want to pack anything else in your backpack because I knew if it was too heavy, I'd end up carrying it for you.

Out our window, I noticed that the sun was just coming up from behind the mountains, and so I hurried to wake you up. I woke you up nicely, Memphis. You hated being woken up loudly or too fast. You smiled, sleepy-eyed, then said you were thirsty. So I tiptoed quickly back to the kitchen, poured you a glass of milk, and fast-walked back to our room holding the glass a bit away from me and making sure not to spill. You sat up on the bed and gulped the milk down. When you handed the empty glass back to me, I told you, hurry, get up, we're going on an adventure and I have a surprise for you. You got up, refused to get out of your nightgown and get properly dressed, but you at least put on a pair of jeans under your nightgown, and socks, and your good shoes, and we walked out of the room, very quiet, and then out to the porch.

The morning felt warm and full of stories, like the ones Pa told us. We walked out onto the Continental Divide Trail, went down the steep hill from the house toward the dry creek. And when we reached the creek, you stopped to look up toward the house, and asked if Ma and Pa had given us permission to walk this far, all alone. I told you a lie I had already planned. I told you yes, Pa and Ma had given us permission to go explore on our own. I said they'd told me that you and I had to go and find more echoes, all the way in Echo Canyon. Really? you said. And for a moment I worried you weren't going to believe this story. Yes, I told you, Ma and Pa said so. And they also said they'd catch up with us later in Echo Canyon.

After thinking about it for a moment, you finally said, that's so nice of Ma and Pa. And that's the surprise you had for me, Swift Feather! Right? Yes, exactly, I said, and I felt relieved that you had gone along with it, but it also made me feel a little guilty that you believed anything I said.

We walked in silence for a while, the way street dogs walk together like they're on a mission, the way all dogs walk in packs like they're on a mission. We weren't a pack, it was just you and me, but it still felt like that, and I howled like a dog-wolf, and you howled back at me, and I knew we were going to have fun on our own. I thought then that even if we got lost forever and Ma and Pa never found us, we would at least still be together, which was better than being separated from each other.

## STORIES

It wasn't even noon when you said you were starving and hot, because the sun wasn't even right on top of us. But I didn't want you to get too tired too quick, so I said, time for a picnic. I chose a shady spot and we put our backpacks under a small tree. I realized I'd forgotten to bring a cloth to sit on. But I told you that Apache children needed no cloths or anything, they would sit right on the ground, and you agreed. We ate some of our snacks and drank a little water, three gulps each from our bottles.

I studied my Continental Divide Trail map, like Ma studied her map, and I knew we were probably near a place called Mud Springs under the Sugarloaf Mountain and had to walk toward Spring Canyon and then Pine Canyon. I was in control of the situation and proud to be able to follow a map as well as Mama did. Then I asked you if you wanted me to read you a bit from the story of the lost children, not because I really wanted to read to you but because I wanted to know what came next in the story. But you said no thanks, very politely, maybe later.

## BEGINNINGS

We started walking again, one behind the other like we formed part of a line, and we walked for so long, talking about how we'd find echoes. You kept on coming up with ideas about how to trap echoes and said, if only we still had that glass jar that was empty where we trapped the dragonfly back some days ago.

I don't know exactly when, but suddenly I thought, perhaps now we are actually lost, and I told you, Memphis, maybe we're lost. And I felt excited but also a little worried. We turned around, but we couldn't make out anything except the same rocky hills and desert woodland everywhere in front of and behind us. When I noticed that you looked worried, but not too worried, I said, this is all part of the plan, trust me. And you nodded, and asked for water, and we drank so much, we finished our two bottles.

The cowpath rose and fell along the creek. We stopped to look back and look forward, trying to look at it like our parents would look at a path and know how much longer and how much farther. You kept on asking how much farther, how many more blocks, which is also what you would ask Ma and Pa in the car on the way here and it would make them giggle and would make me annoyed. This time, though, I understood why it was a little bit funny for a serious question, but I didn't laugh or giggle, and took you seriously and just said, one more uphill one more downhill and then we'll get there, though really I had no idea, even though I'd studied the map so hard. I started to get really worried suddenly, and thought we should maybe turn back.

## NARRATIVE ARC

Finally, when the sun was a little lower, we noticed the creek next to the path had a bit of water and we rushed down to wet our mouths and drank the water though it was green and slimy on our tongues. We took off our shoes also and walked on the watery stones, feeling the fresh and the slipperyness.

We called for Ma and Pa now and then, but our voices got drowned in the air as soon as we cried out. Not an echo, not anything. That's when we really realized, like inside our stomachs, that we'd got lost. We called Mama, Papa, louder and louder, and there were no echoes, and we tried other words like saguaro, Geronimo, but nothing came back.

We were alone, alone completely, much more alone than we sometimes felt we were at night when the lights got turned off and the door got shut. I started to have thoughts of many bad things with each step we took. And later, I thought nothing but looked around us for wild beasts, thinking if the beasts found us, they would notice we were lost and attack us. Nothing around us looked familiar, and when you asked the name of that tree, that bird, that kind of cloud, I just said, I don't know, I don't know, I don't know.

Once, when we were still all in the car together, we had said yes when Ma said if you ever get lost, can you promise me you will know how to find us again? I promised, yes, Mama, of course. But I never really thought after that question how I would keep that promise—not until now. And I kept on thinking as we walked maybe back to them, maybe farther away from them, how will I keep my promise and how will we find them again? But it was impossible to concentrate on this problem because our boots on the gravel along the dry cowpath beside the creek made a sound like teeth grinding cereal, which was distracting and also made me hungry. The sun was hitting us in the forehead now through the short trees, and the white wind blowing brought so many worldsounds, it made us scared. Sounds like a thousand toothpicks falling on the ground, sounds like old ladies scratching in their handbags for things they never find, sounds like someone hissing at us from under a bed. Black birds were making triangles and then lines and then again triangles above us in the sky and I thought maybe they were trying to make arrows and pointing us someplace, but no, who could ever trust birds? Only eagles were to be trusted. Next to a big rock, I decided we should stop and rest a little.

ALLEGORY

If I concentrated, I could picture all of it in my head, Echo Canyon, a large shimmering plain on a hill, and there, our parents waiting for us, probably angry but also happy to see us again. But all I could see in the very far distance were many hills and the up and the down of the path, and beyond it, the high mountains above the gray haze. Behind me always was the sound of your little steps grinding the gravel and also your moaning, your worrying, your thirst and hunger. When night began to fall and I was feeling worried, I remembered that story about the Siberian girl and her dog, which had kept her safe and then rescued her. I told you I wished we had a dog. And you said, yuck, no. And then after a little silence, you said, well, maybe yes.

Once, still with Pa and Ma, we'd walked into a secondhand store, which is something Ma loves to do even if she never buys anything, and we'd seen an old dog dozing, looking like a cozy rug spread out on the floor. We'd gone to pet it while Papa looked at things and Ma talked to the shop owner, which she also loves to do in small shops. And I petted the dog and talked to it and you started asking the dog really funny questions, like, would you rather be taller, would you rather be orange, would you want to be a giraffe instead of a dog, would you love to eat leaves, would you rather live out in the wild like next to the river? And I could swear under oath that every time you asked a question like that, the dog nodded, saying yes, saying yes, yes to every question. So when we were in the river walking on those slippery green rocks, I thought of the dog and thought that if it was here with us, we might not be scared ever at all. Even when the night fell later, it would be okay because we'd have the dog to cuddle with, and you would curl up under its leg and I would spoon it on the other side only keeping my mouth shut to not get hairs on my tongue, which would make me gag. And if at night we heard other dogs barking in faraway ranches in the valley, or if we thought we heard wolves howl up in the mountains, or sidewinder snakes slithering on the ground toward us, we would not be frightened, would not have to crawl under fences or hold rocks in our hands while we slept.

I took out my Continental Divide Trail map to study it once more and memorize the route. We had to reach a place called Jim Courten Ranch, then go past the Willow Tank, and the Still Tank, and then the Big Tank, and I knew we would find water in the tanks, so I wasn't worried. After the last tank, it was not a long walk to the first real town, which was Lordsburg, and we'd have to pass the Davis Windmill and then the Myers Windmill, and as long as we passed those windmills, I'd know we hadn't lost our way completely. Once we passed the last windmill, there would be a cemetery, and then finally Lordsburg. There we would find a train station and jump on a train, although this part I didn't have so well planned out yet. I was trying to explain all this to you, and you just nodded and said okay, and then you asked if I could read a little bit to you while there was still some light and promised not to fall asleep and to keep me company. So I opened my backpack to get Ma's red book, shook it inside the backpack so that the pictures would slide out, and then took it out to read this to you:

( THE SEVENTH ELEGY )

The mountain train came to a final halt in a large open yard surrounded by smoldering factory sites, half-abandoned, and empty storage bodegas. There was no one and nothing inside the buildings around the yard, except for a few owls and cats and families of rats scavenging for scraps of earlier days. The children were told to get off. They'd have to wait there for the next train to pass, the man in charge said. Two, maybe three nights, maybe four. He knew, but did not tell them, this was halfway, they had made it halfway already. Had they known, they would have felt some relief, perhaps. The only thing the man in charge did tell them was that what would follow was the desert, and that the next train would not stop, would only slow down a little to change tracks, so while they waited, they'd practice train-jumping, memorize instructions, learn to jump aboard a moving train, unless they wanted to be crushed under its wheels.

During the days that they waited, whenever the man in charge was gone or was asleep, one of the boys took out a map he had been given earlier along the route. He'd unfold it, spread it out on the gravel, and another boy would light it, striking matches. The other children sat around it like it was a bonfire. They studied it, smiled at sonorous names, halted before names unlikely, repeated names strange or beautiful, and finally a foreign name, right on the other side of the thick red line. Pressing his index finger against the crumpled piece of paper, the boy drew a line from that name into the desert plains and valleys between two mountains, a line that ended in a town, another strange name. The boy said:

Here. Here is where we walk to, and here is where we jump on the next train.

And then? another boy asked.

What next? asked a girl.

Then we'll see what happens next.

The night sky above the train yard, quiet and black, could be overlaid with many thoughts: thoughts of before and especially thoughts of the future beyond. Looking up into the dark, one of the littler ones, the fourth boy, whispered this question into the eldest one's ear:

How do you imagine it, across the desert, after we cross it, the big city I'm going to?

The older one thought for a second and told him there would be one long iron bridge hanging over blue waters that were still and smooth. He would not cross this river in floaters, not cross this bridge aboard train tops, but in a good car. All around him would be beautiful cars, all of them new, each moving slowly and in an orderly way across this bridge. There would be great buildings made of glass rising up to meet him.

When the older boy paused for breath, the little one asked:

And then?

And then he tried to imagine further, but he could not picture anything and could only think back to the putrid jungle, aboard the blue roof of the old gondola, his thoughts like an ocean receding, accumulating destruction and fear in a great wave. In his mind, the impeccable future, the summoned waters, smooth and still, flooded suddenly with the brown wave of earlier rivers, and is covered with the debris of creepers and vines crawling under dark tunnels, like the ones carved into the high mountains he saw from the roof of the brick-red gondola.

He made an effort to retain the thought of glass buildings and gleaming cars but saw only ruins, imagined only the liquid sound of millions of hearts pumping blood into veins, pumping hearts of wild men and women, all throbbing at the same time under city ruins. He could almost hear them, a dozen million hearts pulsing, pumping, palpitating in that future city in some ways identical to the dark jungle they had left behind. He raised his hands to his head and placed his index and middle fingers on his temples, locating the beat of his heart thrusting blood there, feeling the waves of thoughts relentless, and the fears forming slowly there, crashing against some deeper unknown place.

## POINT OF VIEW

By the time I had finished reading, you were asleep and I was a little scared to fall asleep, and I remembered those lines we used to repeat in the car, "When he woke in the woods in the dark and the cold of the night he'd reach out to touch the child sleeping beside him," and for the first time I understood exactly what the author had meant when he wrote them.

I also felt that we were getting closer and closer to the lost children. It was as if while I listened to their story and their plans, they also listened to ours. I decided to read aloud just one more chapter, which was very short, even if you were already asleep.

## (THE EIGHTH ELEGY)

The boys relieved their bladders together, making a circle around a dead bush near the tracks in the train yard. Before they had come to the train yard, it was a difficult task, and now they had almost forgotten how simple it was. Aboard the trains, in the early mornings, the boys were allowed to relieve their bladders only once. They stood by the edge of the gondola's rooftop, in pairs or alone. They saw the yellow arch of urine first jetting forward, then spraying sideways, broken into countless little drops. The girls had to climb down the side ladder, jump onto the small platform between cars, and, holding on to bars, squat into the emptiness, spraying or soiling the gravel beneath them. They closed their eyes, trying to not see the moving ground. Sometimes they looked up and saw the man in charge looking down at them, grinning under his blue cap. They looked past him, and sometimes they saw high eagles crossing the bluer sky above, and if the eagles did pass, the girls knew they were being watched over and were safe.

## SYNTAX

I realized I also had to pee. I used to pee only in toilets, but I had learned to do it in the open, just like the lost boys did from the top of the gondola. And now I think I could only ever pee in the open. I learned to do it one day when we were outside the Apache cemetery. You all got in the car to wait for me and I asked you to look the other way and Ma and Pa did, but you, Memphis, you covered your face with your hands but didn't really cover your eyes. I knew you were peeking and would look at my butt and think that my tooshie was ugly, and maybe laugh at me, but I couldn't have cared less because anyway you always used to see my butt when we'd shower together, and you'd even see my penis, which you called yo-yo, so sometimes I call it yo-yo, too, but only in the shower, because it's the only place I'm not shy about words like that, 'cause there we're alone together.

That time in the cemetery, I peed so strong, I was bursting. And it was so much pee coming out of me that I wrote my new initials on the dust: S for Swift and then F for Feather, and then I even underlined them both.

When I was pulling up my pants, I remembered a joke or a saying Pa had told us where someone says, you can piss on my face, just don't tell me it's raining, and I was going to laugh or at least smile, but then I also remembered that Geronimo was buried there beyond the wall because he fell off his horse and died and now was buried in the cemetery for the prisoners of war, and I felt proud to be peeing there on the stupid wall that kept the prisoners of war locked up and removed and disappeared from the map, just like Ma used to say about the lost children, who had traveled alone and then were deported and wiped off the map like aliens. But later, inside the car looking back at the cemetery, I just felt angry because peeing on the wall wouldn't have mattered to the people who had built the wall around the dead prisoners, and then I was angry for Geronimo and for all the other prisoners of war, whose names no one ever remembered or said out loud.

And these names I remembered every time I peed out in the open like a wild beast. I remembered their names and imagined they were coming out of me, and I tried to write their initials in the dust, different ones each time, so I wouldn't ever forget their names and so that the ground would also remember them:

CC for Chief Cochise
CL for Chief Loco
CN for Chief Nana
S for the priest woman called Saliva
MC for Mangas Coloradas
And a big G for Geronimo.


RHYTHM

We opened our eyes again when the sun was up, and I heard a motor, which at first I ignored because I thought it was dream noise. But you also noticed it, so we decided to walk toward that sound. We followed it for a little while, down a rocky slope, until we saw a man at the bottom of a road, a man with a white straw hat sitting on his tractor pushing hay into a neat pile. My strategy was clear from the beginning. When we approached him, you had to keep quiet and I was to do the talking and would fake an accent and sound in control of the situation.

So the first thing I said when we were finally a few steps from him was, hello sir, and can I take a picture of you dear sir, and what's your name sir, and he looked a little surprised but said the name's Jim Courten, and sure thing young man, and then after I took the picture, he asked us our names and where we were going and where were our parents this fine morning. When I heard his name was Jim Courten, I almost cried out with joy, because that meant he was the owner of the Jim Courten Ranch I had circled on my Continental Divide Trail map, and so I knew we were on the right path. But I didn't show any feelings, and I knew we couldn't seem lost because I wasn't sure we should trust him yet, so I lied, told him our names were Gaston and Isabelle and repeated the line I had already made in my head before he even asked the question: I said, oh, they're just at the ranch back there, Ray Ranch, and are busy with stuff 'cause we just moved here. We moved here from Paris 'cause we are French, I said, all in a convincing French accent. He was still looking at us like he was waiting for more words, so I said, French children are very independent, you see, and our folks told us to walk around and explore to keep us busy, you know, and asked us to take pictures to send back to our French relatives, and when he nodded, I said, could you maybe give us a ride to the Big Tank so we can take pictures of it? Also, we said we'd meet our folks there. I'm not sure if he believed us, and I think he was a little drunk because he smelled strong, like gasoline almost, but he was nice and he took us to the water tank, where we waved goodbye, pretending we knew our way and pretending, especially, we were not nearly dying of thirst.

When he was gone and the motor sounded like the memory of something far away, you and I looked each other in the eyes and knew exactly what the other was thinking, which was, water, and we ran for the water, and we got down on our bellies by the shore of the running river and first tried to cup our hands, but it was no use, so we made an O with our mouths like we were insects and drank the gushing gray water directly from the river as if our lips were straws. I could see your little teeth and your tongue coming out and disappearing back in as you sucked in the water.

## CLIMAX

According to the Continental Divide Trail map, we were only ten miles from the next town, which was Lordsburg, where there was a train station that I hoped would have trains that went west toward the Chiricahuas and Echo Canyon. I tried to explain this to you, excited and proud of how well I was following the map, but you weren't really interested. Later, sitting by the shore, still hungry but not thirsty at least, I was trying to figure things out, and I took things out of my backpack, like some matches and my book and my compass and my binoculars and also some of my pictures, which were all in a mess inside the backpack, and put everything on the mud all lined up next to one another. There was the picture I'd just taken, of the rancher on his tractor. You said the rancher looked like Johnny Cash, which I thought was really elevated for your age, and I told you, you're so smart.

It was an okay picture, except the rancher looked like he was fading under a bright fountain of light that I didn't remember had been there at all when I took it. And then I remembered also that I'd taken some pictures of Pa where he looked like he was disappearing, under too much light. So I scratched through my stuff to find those pictures, and I did. One of them was of one day when we drove on many roads and crossed Texas and Papa stopped the car in the middle of the highway, which was empty anyway, and we both got out and I took a picture of him next to a sign that said Paris, Texas, and then we got back in the car. And the other one was of one day when we went to the town called Geronimo on our way to the Apache cemetery and Papa parked the car again next to the sign that said Geronimo City Limits and I took a picture.

Now, lying there on the mud by the shore of the tank, you and

I, I realized these three pictures looked so much like one another, like pieces of a puzzle I had to put together, and I was looking at them, concentrating hard, when you suddenly came up with the clue, which was good and smart but also terrifying. You said: Look, everyone in these pictures is disappearing.

## SIMILES

It was late afternoon when we finally reached Lordsburg, and we'd been walking for so long though I'd thought we had been so near, and we were thirsty again because there had been no other water tanks on that part of the way, just two old windmills, which were abandoned, and also closed or abandoned shops like Mom and Pop's Pyroshop, and a huge billboard-like sign that just said Food, which I took a picture of, and later the cemetery, and when we had finally left the Continental Divide Trail, there was an abandoned motel called End of Trail Motel, which I also took a picture of. When we reached the big highway that would take us straight to Lordsburg Station, there were also strange road signs saying things like Caution: Dust Storms May Exist and another one saying Zero Visibility Possible, which I knew meant something about bad weather conditions, but I smiled to myself thinking it was like a good-luck sign for us because we'd have to be invisible now that we were going to enter a town full of strangers.

The Lordsburg train station looked more like a train yard than a station. There were a few old train cars parked there but no real station with people coming and going with suitcases and other things you normally see in stations. It looked like a place where everyone had died or simply vanished, because you could feel people and almost smell their breath around you, but there was no one to be seen. We walked along the tracks for a little while, heading west, I think, because we had the sun in our faces, though it didn't bother us because it was already low in the sky. We walked along the tracks until we had to step around a parked train, and as we walked around it, we spotted an open diner, and the diner was called the Maverick Room. We stood looking at it for a long time, with our backs against the parked train, wondering if we should walk over and go in. It was just some steps from the tracks, right after a strip of gravel. I was scared to go into the diner, but I didn't say it. You really wanted to go in, because you were thirsty. I was, too, but I didn't say that either.

To distract you, I said, hey, I'll let you take a picture of the train, and you can hold the camera all by yourself. Of course you agreed immediately. We took a few steps away from the train, stood midway between the train car and the Maverick Room. I took out the camera and Ma's red book from my backpack, the way I always prepared before a picture. Then I let you hold the camera, and you looked through the eyepiece, and just as I was telling you to be patient and make sure you'd focused well, you pressed the shutter, and the picture slid out. I caught it just in time, quickly put it inside Mama's red book to develop, and threw the camera and the book back in my backpack.

You asked, what's the plan now, Swift Feather?, so I told you that the plan was to wait for the picture to develop. Then, again, you said you badly needed water, which I knew, because your lips were all chapped. And I could tell you were close to throwing a tantrum, so I said, okay, okay, we'll go into the diner. And what's the plan after that? you asked. I told you the plan was to jump back on that train car after we got something to drink at the diner. I said we'd sleep on the roof of that train, and that the train would probably depart the next morning, heading west, which was the direction to Echo Canyon. I didn't know what I was talking about, of course, I was just making everything up, but you believed me because you trusted me, and this always made me feel guilty.

I thought: The plan for now is, we will go inside and we will ask for water sitting at the long counter and pretend that our parents are coming any minute, and after drinking the water, we will run away. It won't count as stealing because glasses of water are free anyway. But I won't tell Memphis this part, I thought. I won't tell her we will have to run away after drinking the water, because I know it will scare her and she doesn't need to be scared.

## REVERBERATIONS

The sun was low in the sky when we walked into the diner. As soon as we walked in, I knew we shouldn't stay too long in there or we'd start looking suspicious, like we were alone, no parents. We sat at the long counter on high stools with bouncy foam. Everything around us was shiny, the napkin holders, the big loud coffee-makers that smell so acid, the spoons and forks, even the face of the waitress was shiny. You, Memphis, asked the waitress for crayons and paper, which you got, and I asked for two waters and said we'd wait for our mom and dad to come to order real things. The waitress smiled and said, sure thing, young man. The only other person, aside from us and the waitress, was an old man with a round pink face. He was standing a few feet from us, dressed in blue. He was drinking a tall glass of beer, and was eating chicken wings and sucking the stuck meat from between his long teeth. I could see you wanted some chicken, too, 'cause your eyes got all tear-swollen and mad like birds fighting for space on branches.

But we weren't going to risk it. I said, focus on your picture, and so you drew a girl figure and wrote Sir Fus in Love, and then said it said Sara Falls in Love. I didn't want to correct your spelling because it really didn't matter that much, because who was going to see the drawing except us anyway?

The man went to the bathroom and left his dish full of chicken wings right there. The waitress was in the kitchen, and when I was sure no one was watching, I reached over and snatched two chicken wings from his plate and handed you one, which first you held tight in your hand, and then, when you saw I was quickly eating mine, you did the same. And when we'd eaten the last bit of meat on them, we threw the bones under the counter.

Then the waters came, with a lot of ice. I took sugar packets and emptied them into our waters and then I put a bunch of them in my pocket, for later. And the waters were so good and sweet, we drank them so quickly, so quickly that I was all of a sudden ashamed to leave. My legs felt heavy and embarrassed, for the waters and also for the evidence of the chicken-wing bones under the counter. We sat there in silence for a while, and I helped you with your drawing and made a heart around Sara Falls in Love, and we both made shooting stars around her and some planets. But even when I was concentrating on coloring in the planets, I knew in my mind I couldn't pretend for much longer to still be waiting for our parents to come in.

I was about to not know what to do next and mess everything up when something happened that was lucky for us. I think you brought us the luck. Mama always said you had a good star above you. The man next to us with the round pink face and long teeth stood up and went to the jukebox in the corner. I think he was drunk because he took a long time messing around with it, pressing buttons, and his body moved a bit from side to side.

Finally, a song came up—and this was the lucky part for us. It was one of our very own songs, yours and mine, one of the songs we knew by heart and had been singing in the car with our parents before we got lost or they got lost or everyone got lost. The song was called "Space Oddity," about an astronaut who leaves his capsule and drifts far away from Earth. I knew we both knew the song, so I started up a game for you to follow right there. I looked at you and said, listen, you're Major Tom and I'm Ground Control. Then slowly I put imaginary helmets on both of us, and both of us were holding pretend space walkie-talkies. Ground Control to Major Tom, I said into the walkie-talkie.

You smiled so wide, I knew you understood my game immediately because also you usually do. The rest of the instructions came from the song, but I was lip-singing them, looking straight at you so you wouldn't get distracted by something else, because you're always distracted by tiny things and details.

Take your protein pills, I said. Put your helmet on, said the song, and then ten, nine, eight, commence the countdown, turn the engines on. You were listening to me, I knew. Check ignition, said me and the song. And as the countdown for space launch went down, seven, six, I slid off the stool and started walking backward toward the door still looking at you and lip-singing really clear. Five, four, and then you also slid off the stool holding the picture you'd drawn with Sara falls in love, three, two, and then came one, and right on one, we were both on the ground and you started following me, walking slowly on tiptoes and opening your eyes like when you're looking at me underwater. You could be so funny sometimes in your face. You were moonwalking, but forward, and smiling so wide.

No one in the diner noticed us, not the pink man, not the waitress, who were talking up close to each other, almost touching noses across the bar. We had already reached the swinging doors, exactly when the song gets louder, this is Ground Control the astronaut shouts into the microphone in the song. And I knew we'd made it when I held the door open for you and suddenly we were stepping through it and were both outside, safe and free outside, not having been caught by the waitress, or the man who was eating those chicken wings, or anyone.

We were invisible, like two astronauts up in space, floating toward the moon. And outside, the sun was setting, the sky pink and orange, and the freight trains parked on the tracks were bright and beautiful, and I ran for it so fast across the gravel and around the train in front of the Maverick Room, and beyond the train tracks, and laughing so hard my bladder almost exploded from all the icy water we'd drank. And I ran more, crossed the big road and then ran along smaller streets until I reached the desert shrub, where there were no more houses or streets or anything, just shrubs and sometimes tall grass. I kept on running 'cause I could still hear the song, but only in my head, so I sang it in pieces out loud as we ran, like I'm floating, and like the stars seem different, and also my spaceship knows which way to go.

I ran so fast for so long. I was still shouting, can you hear me, Major Tom? And I turned around to look behind me, but you were not there anymore. Major Tom? I shouted many times all around me. You weren't there at all. I must have run too fast for her, I thought inside my head. I must have run too fast, too fast for her little legs, thinking you were keeping up, and you just didn't. She's so useless sometimes, I thought then, but of course I don't think that for real. You probably got distracted by something small and stupid like a rock in a funny shape or a flower that was purple.

You were not anywhere. I kept on looking, shouting, Major Tom, and then Memphis, for minutes or hours, till I noticed there were

longer shadows growing slow under things and I got angry thinking maybe you were hiding and then scared and guilty thinking
maybe you'd fallen and were crying for me somewhere and I was
also nowhere for you to see me.

I walked back toward the Maverick Room diner, where we'd last
been together. But I stayed some feet away from it, by the train
parked outside it, because the area outside the diner was full of
adults, men and women, tall and strange and not trustable. Later, I
climbed up to the roof of a train wagon, the same train wagon I had
taken a picture of earlier that day. I climbed to the top of it, using
one of the side ladders. Up there on the train-top, I knew, no one
would be able to see me, no matter how tall they humanly were.

I opened my backpack and took some of my stuff out to keep me
company. I took out the binoculars, the Swiss Army knife, and the
Continental Divide Trail map, and I hit the map with my fist and
spit on it, because I realized that by following that trail, the only
thing I had managed to do was to get you and me divided, and I felt
so stupid, like I'd walked straight into a trap no matter all the warn-
ings. I put everything back into the backpack. It was no use, having
my things there, they were no company now. From the roof of the
train car, the sky looked almost black. A few stars showed up in the
sky. The song about the astronaut kept coming back to me in my
head. Except now the part about the stars that looked very different
felt like a curse that the sky had cursed us with.

LOST

Where were you, Memphis? Did you know we were lost? When I first realized that we were lost, I thought that if Pa and Ma never found us, we would still be together, and that was better than not ever being together again. So all the while as we were getting more and more lost, I was never scared. I was even happy to get lost. But now I'd lost you, so nothing made sense anymore. I just wanted to be found. But first I had to find you.

And where were you? Were you scared? Hurt?

You were strong and mighty, like that Mississippi River we had seen in Memphis. That I knew for sure. You'd earned your name because of that. Do you remember how you earned your name? We were in Graceland, Memphis, Tennessee, in a hotel that had a swimming pool in the shape of a rational guitar, like the guitar in the song called "Graceland" that Ma and Pa sang aloud together, they knew all the words, even if they sang off-key. We were all lying on the beds in the motel room, with the lights off, when Pa started telling us how Apaches earned their names. He told us that names were given when children got more mature and had earned them, and they were like a gift given. The names were not secret but also they couldn't be used just like that by anyone outside the family because a name had to be respected, because a name was like the soul of a person but also the destiny of a person, he said. Papa named me Swift Feather, which I liked because it sounded like an eagle and at the same time like an arrow, which were two fast things I liked. I gave Papa his name. I think it was the best name because it was based on a real person. It was Papa Cochise, which he had earned because he was the only one who knew about real Apaches and could tell all of their stories whenever we asked him to and even when we didn't ask him to. And he named Ma Lucky Arrow, and I thought that suited her well, and she didn't complain, so I guess she also thought so.

And you. You, who wanted to be called either Guitar Swimming Pool, which we didn't let you get called, or Grace Landmemphis Tennessee, like in the song. So you got Memphis, and that's why you're Memphis now. Ma also told you then that Memphis was once the capital of Ancient Egypt, a beautiful and powerful place by the Nile River, protected by the god Ptah, who had made the entire world just by thinking or imagining it.

But where in the world were you now, Memphis?

## ERASED

This you should know about yourself. On long drives, you always could sleep. I'd close my eyes and pretend to sleep, thinking that if I pretended long enough, I would fall asleep. Same thing at night, no matter where or what, you'd dig your head into any pillow and suck your thumb and fall asleep like it was easy. Most nights I couldn't sleep no matter how hard I tried, and I would just lie there hearing our voices the way they'd sounded inside the car all day, but kind of broken or far away, like echoes, but not good echoes.

Ever since I was very small, I could never fall sleep. Mama tried many different things. She showed me how to imagine stuff. Like, for example, I had to imagine my heart beating in the dark space of my body. Or other times, to imagine a tunnel, which was dark, but from where I could see light on the other side, and imagine how my arms slowly transformed into wings, and tiny feathers grew out of my skin, my eyes always focused on the tunnel, and as soon as I reached it, I'd be asleep and that's when I would be able to fly out the other side. Mama had shown me all these techniques, and even on the worst nights, after a while of trying, they worked.

But that night, lying on top of the boxcar in front of that diner, thinking maybe you were in there with those strangers, or maybe lost in the desert getting farther from me, it was the opposite. I didn't want to fall asleep even though my eyes kept closing. The rooftop of the train car was a good lookout point, and I knew I shouldn't move from there, because of course I knew the rule: that when two people get lost, the best thing is for one to stay in the same place and for the other to do the looking. I thought you would be looking, because you probably did not know this rule. So although I wanted so much to go out looking for you, I stayed right there, lying on my belly, my face facing the diner, my arms crossed by the edge of the gondola. I took out the lost children's book, shaking it inside the backpack to make sure there were no pictures stuck inside it, and holding my flashlight, I tried to read a little.

While I read, I forced myself to think, imagine, remember. I had to understand where we'd gone wrong, where the continental divide curse had cursed and divided us. I tried to think the way I know you think. I thought, what would I do if I were Memphis and we got divided? She's smart, I thought, even though she's small, so she will come up with a plan. She wouldn't have gone back into the diner, no way. She wouldn't have got near the adults there. But where were you, Memphis? I had to stay put for the rest of the night, looking up now and then at the neon lights spelling Maverick Room. I had to be patient and not lose hope, and concentrate on reading about the lost children, with my flashlight, until the sun came back and my thoughts were not so dark and confused like they were then.

## (THE NINTH ELEGY)

Before the first siren sounded across the train yard, like the bugles calling reveille on camps where he'd been trained, the man in charge was awake and ready. Anticipating the siren, he'd woken the seven children, one by one. He'd lined them up from youngest to oldest, ten steps apart from one another along one side of the track. The train would be approaching at the sound of the third siren, he'd told them, and when it blared, they were to stand guard and repeat in their heads the instructions he had given them. It would not stop, he told them. It would only slow down a little while it changed tracks. Stand still looking toward the approaching train, in the direction of the caboose, he told them. Don't talk, breathe slowly. Only boxcars and gondolas had side ladders. Some tank cars had side ladders, too, but these should be avoided. This they already knew. Make sure hands are not sweaty or arms limp. First wait for the person at the end of the line to jump aboard. Then focus on the next approaching boxcar or gondola and spot a side ladder. Keep your eyes on the ladder; zero in on a single bar as it comes closer. Reach out, clasp the bar with one hand, run with the train, don't step too close to the track and the spark-spitting train wheels. Use accumulated momentum and leg strength to push against the ground, leap up, clasp a lower bar with the other hand, swing inward, and pull body weight toward the side ladder using arm strength.

Most of the children had forgotten all these details. He told them he would stand behind each one of them as one by one they gripped onto a side ladder bar. He'd run with each of them and push from behind as they pulled themselves up, starting with the first child, the youngest, and working his way forward toward the seventh. Once on the ladder, they'd have to hold tight and stand still. He would catch on last and climb to the top of a car, and once the train reached full speed, he would go from car to car to collect each of them from their ladders, help them up, and take them to a gondola. If someone hesitated, if they failed, if they fell, they would get left behind.

So at the sound of the third siren, they'd stood still, feeling the hot gravel below them, trying not to think, not to remember, not to pray. But time passed quicker than their minds could wonder or flake, and so did the train. The first, the second, and the third child were on board before the fourth could spot a ladder. He'd missed two ladders, and had almost missed a third, but the man in charge had slapped him across the head, and he'd finally reacted. He'd darted after the ladder, both arms held out "like a sissy playing tag with a motorbike"—as was later recounted to the others by the man in charge. The fifth and sixth children had managed as well as the first three had, even though the man in charge had pushed them so hard against the ladder bars they'd almost bounced off back to the ground speeding below them.

And there at last stood the seventh boy. He was the oldest, and the only one who could read well and do numbers. While the man in charge was working his way up the line toward him, he'd checked off in his mind first boy, second boy, third boy, and he'd also begun reading the strange words written on the train passing before him: Car Equipped, Gross Weight, Container Limit, End, Inch, Tread Con, Shoes On, Container Limit. Then, when he noticed the fourth boy was having trouble and maybe would not make it aboard, he started to read the words aloud, openly disobeying the instructions given by the man in charge, Noninterchange Cars, Equipment

Register, Container Guides Must Be, Inch, Tread Shoes, Jack Lift Here, Jack Lift Here, Hand Brake Only Applies on the End Track, Interchange Cars. He read them louder and louder as the man in charge approached him: Equipment Register, Plate H, Containers Max Weight, Plate I. They sounded to him like the pages of a strange and beautiful book: Container Guide, Remove All Debris, Dock Here, Minor Inch Tread, Container Guide, Exceeds Plate, Container Guide. And when it was finally his turn, he spotted the upcoming, still blurry side ladder, reading Use Shoes, Pull Release Load, Trucks, Controlled Interchange, Car Equipment. He was now screaming the words out and the man in charge was running behind him, asking what the fuck was wrong with him, to which he only replied with more train-words, Special Break Beam, See Badge, Special Break Beam, See Badge. He was sure he would not make it, but suddenly, like a bird spreading out its new wings, he opened his arms outward, Plates, Container, Special Break Beam, Carrier Net, 20 Feet Container Limit, and then grasped and gripped a bar, flung closer, Special Break Beam, Next Load, felt a push on the bottom of his right sit bone, Any Load, Break Beam, Container Guide, and pulled himself inward, pulled hard against an unexpected kind of centrifugal force, thinking and no longer speaking the last spotted words: Remove All.

The siren blared again, and the train reached full speed. All seven of them were now clinging to ladders on different train cars. A dark exhaustion overtook the seventh boy, still clinging on to a bar by the inner bend of his elbows. The wind was beating fresh on his face, and he forgot for a moment there were others he needed to look after. He forgot there were six others who were gripping bars like he was, some closing their eyes, some smiling softly, the two girls howling at the sky in a wave of relief and maybe joy—because they had made it, they had all made it.

The seventh boy suddenly remembered the man in charge, who was running breathless behind the caboose. He looked back and spotted him, running behind the train looking like a terrified rabbit. He was sure, for a second, that the man in charge would not make it, not ever come back up to their gondola, and he hoped so hard that he almost started praying, but he remembered that strange wise man in the first train yard who had told them they should never pray to any god when they were riding trains. So he just bit his lower lip and watched.

The man in charge kept running behind the train—thinking, as he ran, "Always be ready"; hearing, in the back of his mind, the far echoes of bugle blares in early morning; telling himself, "I was always the first one up, always awake before daybreak, motherfuckers," knowing he could not spell or read the words bugle or blare or reveille, but could run after trains like no one else. And as the man in charge sprinted the last final steps, he promised himself that once he was atop that gondola, he would find that smart-ass boy, the seventh one, the little reader of words, the fucker. And oh, how slowly he would damage him, first his mind, then his body. He'd squeeze all the smart words out of his mouth, then cut his tongue off; he'd force him to see nightmares with his sharp little eyes, then scoop them out of their sockets; with his bare hands, he'd rearrange the boy's nimble bones and derange his pretty face until there was nothing recognizable left of him. Then, finally near enough, the man in charge clung onto a metal handle, and flung himself up, as the train sped through the barrenlands toward the northern deserts.

ITEMS

I dug my face into my crossed arms and shut my eyes. I did not want to read the next elegy, and I did not. I was too afraid to read more, afraid that the man in charge would find the seventh boy and punish him. What would he do to him? I thought, in my mind, of what I would do if I were that boy, and how I'd try to get away from the man in charge. I made escape plans, imagined ways out, jumping off the train, or pretending I was already dead so he wouldn't kill me again. Until, I think, I fell asleep and started dreaming similar dreams.

I'm sure I was dreaming because I had a pipe in my mouth, and of course I don't smoke, even though I have wondered about it before. I had a pipe, and you slept next to me and sucked your thumb. I didn't have a lighter or matches so I didn't actually smoke, not even in the dream. I only wanted to smoke. It wasn't so much like a dream but like a thought or feeling that kept coming back to me, needing to be solved but staying not solved. What I kept thinking in the dream was: Where will I find the matches or the lighter? Pa and Ma always had one or the other, in his pocket and in her bag. So I looked in my pockets in my dream but there were only rocks, coins, a rubber band, crumbs, no matches. Then I looked in my backpack and instead of all my stuff, there was only *The Book with No Pictures*. In real life, you used to laugh when we read it to you. So in the dream I woke you up and read it to you. And when I read to you, still in the dream, you laughed so hard it woke me up for real.

When I woke up, what I thought was there was not there anymore. I looked around for the neon lights spelling Maverick Room, but none of that was there. The sun was rising. It took me a moment, but I realized that the boxcar of the train on which I had been reading, and dozing off now and then though I tried not to, was moving. I felt the wind blowing against my face, and then my blood rushing to my cheeks, and a hollow inside my stomach. I felt horror.

I forced myself back into my mind. I forced myself to think again. To imagine. To remember. To rewind that train that was moving so fast, to rewind it in my mind, and understand. I took my compass out of my backpack, and the needle showed the train was moving west, which was the right way. Then I remembered I had told you, right before we'd gone inside the diner on that day we'd got divided, that the plan was to climb atop the train outside the diner and ride that train to the west toward Ma and Pa in Echo Canyon, and all of a sudden I knew. I knew you had to be there, too, somewhere, on that same train, which actually was moving. And though I couldn't see you, I knew you were okay 'cause I'd heard you laugh inside my dream. I knew I would have to wait for the sun to come out first, but I'd find you.

LIGHT

And when the sun was up, higher than the peaks of the mountains far away, I knew I had to start looking.

You wouldn't be on any of the gondola rooftops, because it was too hard to climb the metal ladders. Also, because I was up on the roof of a gondola, I could see across the rooftops of all the other ones, and I took my binoculars out of my backpack and looked through them, to double-check, and they all were empty. Nothing in the many gondolas in front of me, toward the train engine, and nothing in the three gondolas behind me, toward the caboose. This train was different from the lost children's train, because it was people-less. If you were going to be anywhere on it, it was either going to be on one of the connecting platforms or inside one of the gondolas. But you'd probably be too afraid to climb into a gondola, even if you'd found one that wasn't locked, because who knows who or what was inside those dark spaces. So I thought if you'd be anywhere, it had to be on a connecting platform between two gondolas.

I had to choose between walking toward the back of the train, across only a couple of gondolas, or walk around ten gondolas toward the front.

Ma had a silly superstition, which was that when we rode trains or subways, she'd never sit on a seat that faced the back of the train. She thought that facing backward on a train was bad luck. I always told her I thought her superstition was ridiculous, and unscientific, but one day I started doing the same thing, just in case. Ma's superstitions were like that, they were contagious. You and I, for example, collected pennies we found on the sidewalk and put them inside our shoes, like she did. We didn't miss a single penny. Once I got into trouble at school because I was walking strangely, limping across the classroom all day, and the teacher made me take off my shoe, and she found like fifteen pennies in there. At pickup time, when she told Ma what had happened, Ma told her she would talk to me about it, but then, when we were far enough down the block, she congratulated me and said in all her life she'd never met a more serious and professional penny collector.

I decided to head toward the front of the train and slowly started walking on the roof of the gondola where I'd slept. The train wasn't moving that fast, but it was still difficult to walk there, it was true that it felt like walking on the spine of an enormous worm or a beast. I wasn't too far from the edge of the first gondola, and when I reached it, I decided not to try to jump to the other gondola, like the lost children did sometimes, which may have been cowardly of me, but who would even know. I stood there, looking down at the gravel that was moving underneath the train like a fast-forwarded movie, and had to sit down for a moment on the edge to catch my breath, because my heart was beating hard inside my chest but also inside my throat and head, and maybe also my stomach. After a little while, I still felt my heart everywhere, but I took a last deep breath, and then inched on my butt toward the ladder in the right-hand corner of the gondola's rooftop, put my feet on the second step, turned my whole body around until I felt the hot edge of the roof pressing against my chest, slid down a tiny bit more, holding on tight to the sides of the ladder, and finally started climbing down, slowly, toward the connecting platform. The whole beast rocked from side to side as it moved forward, and it rocked especially hard on the connecting platforms.

The first few gondolas were very difficult. I walked across the roofs, taking slow steps and opening my legs apart for balance, like I was a walking compass. When the train jerked and I lost balance, I let myself fall to my knees and crawled the rest of the way. The sounds the train made were scary, like it was about to fall into pieces. When I reached the edge of a gondola and was either on my knees or on all fours and looked down to the connecting platform, I could see in my mind the face of the seventh boy, and I was afraid to see his body sweeping past underneath me, even though I knew he wasn't going to be there. But at the same time, when I reached the edge of a gondola, I got hopeful, then I looked down to the connecting platform, and it was empty.

I don't know how many gondolas I crossed, I don't know for how long, it was so hot and I was getting desperate, and especially I was dizzy, maybe trainsick, because everything looked blurry and tilted, and I felt like throwing up except there was nothing to throw up.

I don't know how to explain it to you, what I suddenly felt when I reached the end of one of the gondolas and was about to sit on the edge and repeat the same looking down, inching, turning, climb-downing, but then I saw something beneath me, on the connecting platform, first a heap of colors like rags bundled together, but then I focused and made out feet, legs, body, head, all curled up into a ball. I screamed so loud: Memphis! Memphis!

You didn't hear me, of course, because of the sound of the train. I realized then it was so loud, much louder than my voice, and also the wind was blowing in my face and snatched my words right out of my mouth, and they flew backward toward the caboose. But I had found you, Memphis. I was right, and my dream was right! You are so damn smart! More than smart, you are wise and ancient, like the Eagle Warriors.

I had found you, and I was so out of my mind and felt so strong and fearless that I forgot all about the dizziness. I started climbing down the ladder to you too fast and almost slipped, but I didn't. I made it all the way down and stepped on the last step, then put my two feet down on the connecting platform, and took a few steps to kneel down next to you. You were fast asleep like nothing had happened, like you always knew everything was gonna be all right. I wanted to shout in your ear and wake you up, saying something like Found! Like we'd been playing hide-and-seek all along. But I decided to wake you up gently, instead. I crawled around you and sat with my backpack resting against the metal wall of the gondola. Your head was touching my leg. Then I lifted your head slowly with my two hands and slipped my leg under it, and it felt like the world was coming back together.

I realized that I was riding backward on the train now, and shadows, haystacks, fences, and bushes kept sweeping past me, shocking me a bit each time, but I decided not to care about it, 'cause I'd found you, so there was no way that riding backward could mean bad luck this time, right now. I scratched your head a bit, your wild curls all tangled, until you opened your eyes, and looked at me sideways. You didn't smile but said, hello there, Swift Feather Ground Control. So I said, hello there, Major Tom Memphis.

SPACE

When you finally sat up, you asked me where I'd been. I lied and said I was just out getting food and water. Your eyes opened wider and you said you wanted some, too, so I had to say I hadn't found any yet. Then you asked where we were, how many more hours or blocks to Echo Canyon, and I told you we were almost there. To distract you for a while, I suggested we could climb up to the roof of the gondola together and play the name game, said if you could spot any saguaros, I'd pay you a penny for each. But you said, no, I'm thirsty, my stomach is burning, and then flopped down again like a dog, your head on my leg. The train moved on, and we were quiet for a while, and I rubbed your belly, making circles with my hand, clockwise, the way Ma did when we had bellyaches.

Finally, the train stopped. You sat up again and I tiptoed to the edge of the connecting platform. Holding on to the wall of the gondola, I leaned out to check if I could see anything, and I did. There was a bench, and behind it a small ice-cream stand, which was closed. But between the ice-cream stand and the bench was a sign, and it said Bowie. I looked back at you and said, this is it, Memphis, here is where we get off! You didn't move, you just looked at me with your black eyes, and asked me how come I knew we had to get off at this place. I said, I just know, that's the plan, trust me. But you shook your head. So then I said, remember, Memphis, Bowie is the author of our favorite song. You shook your head again. So then I told you the only thing I actually knew, which was that Bowie was the place where Geronimo and his band were forced to get on a train that deported them someplace far away, and Pa had told us about it. You didn't shake your head this time, maybe because you also remembered that, but you didn't get up or move either. So I had to make up the rest of the explanation, said Pa had told me that to get to Echo Canyon, we first had to jump off the train in Bowie.

He said that? you asked. I nodded. You got up and walked to the edge of the connecting platform, dragging your backpack behind you. I jumped off and helped you down, and then helped you put on your backpack. The gravel was hard and hot under our feet, and though we weren't moving anymore, it felt like we still were, like we were still on the train. We walked over to the bench and sat down, with our backpacks on our backs. Just a few seconds later, the train whistle sounded and slowly the train took off again. I wasn't sure if we should be glad we'd got off in time or if we had messed up, and before I'd made up my mind, you asked again where Echo Canyon was. So I took my backpack off my back and took Ma's big road map out, and you asked, what are you doing, and I said, shhh, wait, let me study the map for a moment.

I concentrated hard, looking for names I recognized. After a while, I found the name Bowie and the names Chiricahua Mountains and Dragoon Mountains all in the same fold in Ma's enormous map, so I knew at least we had to be looking at that fold. From Bowie, I finger-walked a route down south, across the big dry valley, and then east to the Chiricahuas, but also I realized that the walk was longer that I'd imagined.

I told you, okay, we have to get up and walk a little more now. You looked at me like I had punched you in the belly. First, your eyes got teary, a red line around the bottom edge. But you held in the tears and you looked at me with a kind of crazy look, full of angry thoughts. I knew it was coming, and it did. You had a meltdown. No, no, Swift Feather! you shouted, sitting up from the bench. Your voice was trembling, roaring. And then you said, Jesus Fucking Christ, and I almost laughed but I didn't because I could tell you were being serious about this and using the expression like an adult, that you finally understood it, or maybe had understood it all along. You told me I was the most terrible guide, and a terrible brother, that you would not move until Ma and Pa came to find us there. You asked me why I had even gotten us here. I replied the way Ma and Pa used to, said something like, when you're older, you'll understand. That made you even more angry. You kept on screaming and kicking the gravel around. Until I stood up, too, and took you by the shoulders and told you that you had no choice, said I was all you had right now, so you could either accept that or stay on your own. You were probably right, I was a terrible brother, and even more terrible guide, not like Ma, Lucky Arrow, who could find anything and never get lost, and not like Papa Cochise, who always took us everywhere and kept us safe, but I didn't say that part. I just looked you in the eyes, trying to look angry and at the same time kind, like they sometimes looked at us, until you finally wiped your face and said, fine, okay, fine, I trust you, though for a long time after that, you refused to look me in the eyes.

## LIGHT

We walked along the train tracks for a while, and I had Ma's big map under my arm and also now my compass on my palm. We passed a strange corral where men with shotguns dressed old-fashioned were either about to kill each other or acting out a scene. We didn't stay to watch, but I thought I'd take a picture of them. When I reached into my backpack for the camera, I realized I had forgotten the little red book on the train. I thought I had put it back, but I hadn't. At least I'd taken out my pictures from inside it; they were all in a mess in my backpack. I still took the picture, but this time I put it inside the folds of Ma's map, then threw the map in the backpack and zipped it up.

We walked a little farther and refilled our water bottles in a bathroom in an abandoned gas station, and also peed a few drops in a toilet with a broken seat, and then noticed that there was no roof above us. From there, we left the tracks and went south into the desert plain, following the compass. In the distance, we saw clouds.

You gave me your hand, and I held it tight. We walked into the unreal desert, like the lost children's desert, and under their blazing sun, you and me, over the tracks, and into the heart of light, like the lost children, walking alone together, but you and me holding hands, because I was never going to let go of your hand now.

# PART III

## *Apacheria*

# DUST VALLEYS

During the hours after our children disappeared, my husband and I sped along back roads and across valleys: Animas, Sulphur Spring, San Simon. The light is blinding in those desert flats. Under the oppressive arch of their pristine skies, straights of land stretch long, their ground cracked and saline. And when the wind speeds across the dry lake beds, it wakes up the dust. Slender columns of sand spiral upward and move across the surface almost choreographically. Locals call them dust devils, but they look more like rags dancing.

And as we drove past them, every dust rag looked like it could spiral the girl and boy back into existence. But no matter how hard we looked behind the whirling confusion of sand and dust, we found not our children but only more sand and dust.

I had first realized they were not in their room in the morning, when I'd gotten out of bed to go to the bathroom and, as I often did in our old apartment, where we had separate rooms, I peeked into theirs to check on them. Their bed was empty, but I didn't think much of it. I assumed they were outside the house we'd rented, were exploring the area, picking up stones and sticks, doing the things they usually do.

I got back into bed, but I was unable to fall asleep again. I felt a kind of electric vacuum in my chest, and I should have listened to these early signals. But many mornings I had woken up with a similar feeling, and I interpreted those undercurrents of doubt and unease running through me as just a slight variation on an older, deeper anxiety. I read in bed for a while, as I'd taught myself to do from a young age whenever I felt unready to face the world, and I let the morning ripen, until the room was flooded with new light, and the air was thick with the steam of body vapors and the smell of warm sheets.

In his bed next to mine, my husband shifted and rolled, his breathing becoming shallower until he finally awoke—with a startle, as he always does—wrenching himself out of bed with a sense of urgency and readiness that I've never understood or shared. He left the room, and then came back a few minutes later, asking where the children were. I said they were probably outside somewhere.

But the children were not outside, not anywhere in the perimeter of the cottage.

We explored the area around the cottage stupidly, clumsily, and still in a kind of disbelief, as if we were looking for a set of keys or a wallet. We looked under bushes, up in trees, under the car, opened the refrigerator more than once, turned the shower on, then off, and then went back outside, farther out into the valley and creek—what is our rescue distance now? I thought—calling out their names, our voices expanding in waves of horror, crashing, breaking, our screams more and more like the calls of apes, guttural, intestinal, visceral, desperate.

What, where next?

Next was all lumped together in an alternation of executive decisions and irrational turns. Shoes, keys, car, Twitter, phone calls, sister, Highway 10, breathe, think, Road 338, decide, follow the train tracks, don't follow the train tracks, take back roads. The exact sequence of events is blurred in my memory. What did they know and what did we know? What did we think the boy would do in this circumstance? Where would he head to, once he realized he and his sister were lost? And the question most dreaded, which kept coming back, paralyzing my entire body:

If they are lost in the desert, will they survive?

After some hours of driving aimlessly, we headed to the Lordsburg police station, where a policeman took down our information and asked us for a description of the two children.

Child one. Age: 5. Sex: Female. Eye color: Dark brown. Hair color: Brown.

Child two. Age: 10. Sex: Male. Eye color: Hazel Brown. Hair color: Brown.

We stayed in the waiting room of the police station until we were given directions to the nearest motel, where we could rest and wait and continue looking the day after. We took turns lying on the bed, though of course we did not sleep. Where would the boy decide to head once he knew they were lost?

We spent the next morning and afternoon driving around the Lordsburg area, returning to the police station every few hours. But nothing seemed to be moving in any direction, so during the second night, taking turns lying down on the still-made motel bed, and perhaps sleeping in intervals of ten or twenty minutes, we decided that as soon as the sun rose the next day, while the police continued to search the area, we would drive farther west. We called the police station to tell them, and they took notes, gave us a few instructions.

The children had been missing for almost forty hours when we climbed into the car again the next morning at sunrise. As a reflex, I opened the glove box to take out the map, but it wasn't in its place, nor was my recorder. So I got out of the car again, opened the trunk. I thought I'd look in my box for my map. Everything was out of place in the trunk, a mess. I called my husband over, and he came around to the back of the car to join me. My box was open. My map wasn't there. Instead, at the top of the open box, there was a map, a map the boy had drawn by hand, and stuck on it was a Post-it note, saying: "Went out, will look for lost girls, meet you later at Echo Canyon."

We both stood next to the open trunk, looking down at the map and the note stuck on it, both holding on to the sheet of paper like it was a last bastion but also just trying to decipher what it meant. My husband said:

Echo Canyon.

What?

They're going to Echo Canyon.

Why? How do you know?

Because that's what we've been telling them all this time, and that's what the map shows, and that's what the note says, that's why.

I was not convinced, despite the clarity with which the boy's message spelled it out for us. I was not entirely reassured, despite my husband's conviction. I was not relieved, though I should have been. There was, at least, somewhere we could drive toward, even if it may have been a mirage, even if we were following a map drawn by a ten-year-old boy. Immediately, we were back in the car, speeding in the direction of the Chiricahua Mountains.

Why? Why did they leave? Why had I not seen the signs earlier? Why hadn't I looked in the trunk sooner? Why were we here? And where were they?

We sped out of Lordsburg, southbound, parallel to the New

Mexico–Arizona border, across the Animas Valley, past a ghost town called Shakespeare, past a town called Portal. Why? I could not stop thinking.

Why don't you call the Lordsburg police and tell them we're on our way to the Chiricahuas? my husband said.

I called and was told they'd send someone over.

We drove on in silence along a dirt road until we reached a town called Paradise—a few scattered houses—where the road ended abruptly. There we left the car. I took my phone out and searched for a signal, but there was none.

The sun was still low when we began climbing up the eastern slope of the Chiricahua Mountains, looking for the trail toward Echo Canyon, the slopes and jagged cliffs of the desert multiplying around us like a question impossible to answer.

# HEART OF LIGHT

*(Last Elegies for the Lost Children)*

(THE ELEVENTH ELEGY)

The desert opens out around them, wide and invariable, as the train advances westward, parallel to the long iron wall. The sun is rising far to the east, behind a mountain range, a grand mass of blue and purple, its contours jagged lines, like hesitant brushstrokes. They are silent, the six children, more silent than usual. Locked up in their terrors, the six.

Some sit on the edge of the train gondola, facing the east, dangling their legs, spitting out saliva balls just to see whose gets farther, but mostly gazing down at the ground that sweeps beneath them, white, brown, speckled with thornbushes, rubbish, strange rocks. Some sit cross-legged, facing the front of the train, more alone than the others, letting the wind brush their cheeks and tangle their hair. And a couple more, the two littlest, remain lying down on their sides, their cheeks against the roof of the train gondola. With their eyes, they follow the monotonous line of the horizon, their minds threading thoughts and images into a long meaningless sentence. The desert is an enormous, motionless hourglass: sand passing by in time detained.

Then, the sixth boy, who is now the eldest of the group, reaches into his jacket pocket and feels the cold, concise edges of a mobile telephone. He had found the phone tucked under a track in the last yard while he was practicing train jumping with the others and had hid it. He had also found a good black hat and was now wearing it. The man in charge had not objected to his wearing the hat he'd found, but the boy knew he'd confiscate the telephone if he caught him with it, even though it was broken and could not be used.

He makes sure the man in charge is still sleeping, and he is. The man in charge is as if in a coma, far away, breathing deeply, huddled under a tarp. So the boy takes out the telephone. Its glass is smashed like a window hit by a bird or a bullet, and the battery is dead, but still he shows the object to the rest of the children as if he were showing them a treasure found after a shipwreck. They all respond with gestures, silent but acknowledging.

Then he suggests a game, tells all of them to watch him and listen carefully. First he hands the dead phone to one of the girls, the older one, and says: "Here, call someone, call anyone." It takes her a moment to understand what he's suggesting. But when he repeats his words, she smiles, and nods, and looks around at all of them, one by one, her tired eyes suddenly looking enormous and ablaze. She stares back down at the phone in her hand, takes the collar of her shirt and stretches it outward, looking at something stitched in its inner folding. She pretends to dial a long number, and then holds the phone up tight to her ear.

Yes? Hello? We're on our way, Mama, don't worry. We'll be there soon. Yes, everything's okay.

The others observe, each understanding the rules of this new game at their own pace. The older girl quickly passes the telephone to her little sister and prompts her with a whisper to follow the game. The little one does. She dials a number—only three digits— noticing the embarrassing sand and soot deep under the nail of her index finger, knowing her grandmother would have scolded her if she saw her nails. She holds the phone up to her ear.

What did you have for dinner?

Others wait for her to say more, but this is the only sentence she delivers. The boy sitting next to her, one of the older ones, boy number five, takes the phone from her and also dials, but he places it to his mouth as if it were a walkie-talkie.

Hello? Hello? I can't hear you. Hello?

Self-consciously, he looks around him, holds the phone to his mouth, and burps into it. Then he laughs with the awkward, uneven waves of puberty. Some of the others laugh with him, and he passes the phone down.

Another boy, boy four, receives the phone now. It trembles in his hand, and he does nothing with it. He passes it to the next boy, the third boy, who pretends it is a bar of soap and cleans his body with it, silent.

Some children laugh, some force themselves into laughter. Next to him, the youngest of the children, boy three, smiles, shyly, under his sucked thumb. He slowly unplugs his thumb from his mouth. It's his turn to take the phone, and he does. He looks at it, cradled in the cup of his hands, and then looks up at the rest of the group. He knows by the eyes of the others, by the eyes they look at him with, that he has to say something, that he cannot just keep quiet like he always keeps quiet. So he takes a deep breath and, looking at the phone still cradled in his palms, starts whispering into it. He speaks for the first time, and speaks more than he's ever done before:

Mama, I haven't been sucking my thumb at all, Mama, you'd be so proud, and proud to know we've rode on the back of many beasts for many days and weeks now, I'm not sure how long, but I've become a man, and a lot of time has passed, but I still can remember the stones you used to throw into the green lake, when we were there, some of them dark, some of them flat, others small and shiny, and I have one of the stones, the one I didn't throw, in my pocket, and my train brothers and sisters are good people, Mama, and all of them are brave, and strong, and have all different faces, there's a boy who's always angry, he talks in a strange language in his sleep, and when he's awake, he talks in our language but is still angry, and there's another boy who's almost always serious though sometimes does funny things, but when he is serious, he says we are ready for the desert, Mama, and I know he's right, and there are two girls who are sisters and look almost the same, except one is bigger and the other is smaller, and the smaller one is missing some teeth, like I will soon, because I can feel one or two moving already in my mouth, the two girls never get scared, though, not even the smaller one, they are both gentle and brave, they never cry, and wear shirts that they keep clean no matter what, and on the collars of the shirts their grandmother sewed the telephone number of their mother, who's waiting for them on the other side of the desert, they showed the numbers to me once and they looked just like the number you'd also sewn on my shirt so I can call my aunt when I cross to the other side of the desert, I promise I'll be strong when we have to climb over the wall with the rest, and won't be scared of jumping, won't be afraid of any beasts either and won't ask to stop for a rest or something to eat once we cross, I promise I will cross the desert and get all the way to the big city, and across the bridge in a beautiful new car, across the bridge to where there'll be buildings made of glass rising up to meet me, which is what the seventh boy told me, because there used to be seven of us, and the seventh was the oldest boy, he was the only one who was not afraid of the man in charge, and kept us safe from him, the man in charge looked like he was a little scared when the boy was watching him, with his big dog eyes, always watching over us with dog eyes, still now he is, I know, although he's gone now, not on the train with us anymore.

He suddenly stops talking and plugs a thumb back into his mouth, the phone resting now in only one of his hands. The sixth boy takes his phone again, knows he has no words left to say.

After a few moments, he tells the rest of the children that the phone is also a camera, and now they all have to huddle together for a portrait, and they do. They come together, but very carefully, without standing up. The train rocks constantly and sometimes jerks a little, and they have learned to listen to its movements with their entire bodies. They know when they can stand up and when they need to move across its surface without standing. Finally huddled together, some tilt their heads to one side or the other, some make peace signs or horn signs, smile or stick out their tongues, contort in grimaces. The boy says:

When I count to three, we all say our names.

He pretends to focus.

They stare straight into the telephone's eye with a strange, powerful gaze. Behind them, the sun is rising higher in the sky. The five of them look serious, mighty. The boy adjusts his black hat, then counts to three, and on three, they all shout out their names, including him:

Marcela!

Camila!

Janos!

Darío!

Nicanor!

Manu!


( T H E   T W E L F T H   E L E G Y )

A ruffle of murmurs hovers in the sullen air and the train stands still on the tracks. Sitting up, the now eldest boy, boy six, looks around and notices that the man in charge is now awake, sitting cross-legged and looking not at him, not at the rest of the children, but into his empty smoking pipe.

The boy scans the other travelers, grown-ups most of them, in groups of threes and fives or sixes, all huddled tightly together, maybe more tightly than usual. The sky is pale blue, and the sun is milky behind the screen of haze on the horizon. The older girl, sitting cross-legged, looks up toward the sky, braiding her hair. And the youngest one, boy three, lying sideways, sucks his thumb again, his right cheek and ear resting on the leprous surface of the train car. All around them, barrenlands stretch shadowless.

The six children notice a man climbing up a side ladder and standing tall near the edge of their gondola. He does not look like a priest. Perhaps he is a soldier. He is bending over a group of men and women. They see a woman grapple with the possible soldier for her sack. They hear her dull, dry wail when the soldier snatches the sack away from her and flings something overboard. She lets out a second cry. Her voice rises from her chest, up her esophagus, like the cry of a caged animal. The children hear it and they all sit up now, alert. An electric discharge travels from some vague nerve inside the muscles of their hearts, which pump a message into their chests and down their spines, and as fear settles in the bowls of their bellies, their limbs tremble slightly. They confirm the man is, indeed, a soldier. In a nearby branch, a trio of vultures stands guard or perhaps simply sleeps.

Between the soldier and the children, men and women huddled and squeezed against one another along the gondola murmur and whisper, but the ripples of their words do not reach the children, who are waiting for a cue, waiting for instructions from the man in charge, waiting. Even the older boys in the group are silent and look scared and don't know what to tell the rest. The man in charge fidgets with his pipe, unengaged, far away somehow. As the soldier approaches the children, his heavy boots polished black over black thumping against the roof of the train car, they understand that he is not going to ask for passports, not for money, not for explanations. The youngest boy maybe doesn't understand, but he shuts his eyes and wants to suck his thumb again and is about to but instead bends over his crossed legs and bites the strap of his backpack.

They'd all brought with them a single backpack. The man that would lead them through forests and plains and now through deserts had told their parents before leaving:

No unnecessary belongings.

So they had packed mostly only basics. At night, atop the train, they used the backpacks as pillows. By day, they hugged them to their stomachs. Their stomachs were always sick with rocking and angry with hunger. Sometimes, when the train was about to cross near one of the police or military posts that mushroomed silently along the way, they were told to jump off, leaping off the ladder onto the ground, scratched and bruised by stones and branches, always holding on tight to the backpack. They'd walk in a single line amid thornbushes and pebbled dirt, always parallel but far enough from the tracks. They'd walk silently, sometimes whistling alone, sometimes together, their backpacks hanging. The older boys wore them on one shoulder like when walking to school, and the younger children thrust their small bodies forward to balance the heavy weight of toothbrushes, sweaters, toothpaste, Bibles, bags of nuts, bread buns smeared with butter, pocket calendars, spare change, and extra shoes. They walked like this until the man in charge signaled it was time, and then they cut through the bush, walking perpendicular and then parallel to the tracks, and caught up with the slow-moving train again some miles ahead.

But this time they had received no warning and had slept through a stop at a military post, where the train had boarded soldiers.

Now, on the roof, the silhouette of the soldier against the pale sky looms directly above them. He stretches an arm and knocks with his fist twice on the skull of the boy who is biting the strap of his backpack. The boy raises his head and opens his eyes, fixing them on the soldier's good boots as he hands the backpack over to him. Slowly the soldier opens it and pulls out its contents, studying and naming each object before he throws it back over his shoulder. He collects all their backpacks, one by one, meeting no resistance from this group of six. No wails, no cries from any of them, no struggles as he takes the backpacks and reaches into each one, roams with his hand, and flings things high into the air, punctuating their names with question marks as they fly and crash or sometimes feather into the ground below: Toothbrush? Marbles? Sweater? Toothpaste? Bible? Underwear? A broken telephone?

Before he can move on to the next group of backpacks, the train blows its whistle. He scans the children, and nods at the man in charge. The men exchange glances and a few words and numbers that the children cannot make sense of, then the soldier takes a large folded envelope from inside his jacket and hands it over to the man in charge. The train blares a second whistle, and the soldier, like the rest of the soldiers atop the beast, all performing a similar operation on contiguous train cars, slowly climbs down the side ladder of the train and hops onto the ground, dusting his thighs and shoulders as he strolls back to the post.

The whistle blows for the third time and the beast jerks once, twice, and then resumes its forward course, all its screws and draw-bars shrieking awake again. Some travelers look over the edge of the roof to the ground scattered with personal belongings, the desert sand like an ocean flowing backward after a shipwreck. Others prefer to look farther away into the northern horizon or up into the sky, thinking nothing. The train gains speed upon the tracks, almost lifting a little like a ship setting up mast and sailing forth. From his booth, a lieutenant watches the train disappear into the haze, thinking haze, thinking spray, thinking ships cutting through the waste of seaweed: the heaps, the broken, the beautiful rubbish, all the colors of stuff beaming now under the sun.

( THE THIRTEENTH ELEGY )

Under the desert sky, they wait. The train moves in perfect parallel to the long iron wall, forward yet somehow also in circles, and they do not know that the next morning, the train will come to a final halt. Caught in repetition, trapped in the circular rhythm of the train wheels, tucked under the umbrella of the invariable sky, none suspect that it will finally happen the next day: they will arrive somewhere, and get off the train at the first sign of dawn.

They had heard stories about it for so long. For months or years, they formed pictures of places and imagined all the people they would finally see there again: mothers, fathers, siblings. For so long, their minds had been filled with dust, and ghosts, and questions:

Will we make it safely across?

Will we find anyone on the other side?

What will happen on the way?

And how will it all end?

They had walked, and swam, and hidden, and run. They had boarded trains and spent nights sleepless atop gondolas, looking up at the barren, godless sky. The trains, like beasts, drilled and scratched their way across jungles, across cities, across places difficult to name. Then, aboard this last train, they had come to this desert, where the incandescent light bent the sky into a full arch, and time had also bent back on itself. Time, in the desert, was an ongoing present tense.

They wake.

They watch.

They listen.

They wait.

And now they see, above them, an airplane flying across the sky. They follow it with fixed gazes but don't suspect that the plane is full of boys and girls like them, looking down toward them, though none see each other. Inside the plane, a little boy peers out the oval window and plugs his thumb into his mouth. Far below him, a train advances on a railroad track. Sitting next to him is an older boy, his teenage, pimple-scarred cheeks similar to the almost lunar industrial landscapes over which they will fly. The little boy's thumb, in his mouth, tucked between his tongue and his palate, makes his throat less hungry, his belly less empty with angst. A resilience will start settling in him, thoughts slowing and dissolving, body muscles yielding, respiration layering quietude over fright. The boy's thumb, plugged, sucked, pumped, swollen, will slip out as he sinks into sleep, erased from his place in his seat, on this plane, erased from the fucked-up country below him, removed. Finally he shuts his eyes, dreams spaceships. The plane will sweep above vast stretches of land, over peopled cities, above the stones and the animals, over meandering rivers and ash-colored ridges, a long powdery white line trailing behind it, scarring the sky.

## (THE FOURTEENTH ELEGY)

It starts at sunset, when storm clouds are gathering above and in front of them. The beast screeches through the continuous desert, always rocking and shaking on the tracks, threatening to fall apart, derail, suck them into its insides. The man in charge has drunk himself to sleep again, holding to his half-bare chest a plastic bottle of something he got in exchange for one of the boys' empty backpacks. He is so deep inside his sleep, dreamless or full of dreams, no one knows, that when the younger of the girls shoves a bird feather she collected days earlier deep into his nose, he only grunts, shuffles, and continues to breathe like nothing. She giggles, toothless here and there, and looks up at the sky.

Suddenly a single, tepid, fat drop falls on the surface of their gondola. Then a few more drops plop down on the roof. The sixth boy, sitting cross-legged, clears the space in front of him and hits the roof of the gondola with his fist. The thump echoes inside the empty space bellow. Another raindrop falls, and another, beating against the metal rooftop. The boy hits the roof again with the same hand, and then with the other—thud, thud—and again: thud, thud. Drops now fall more eagerly, more rhythmically, on the tin roof. The older girl, squatting on the surface of the roof, looks up at the sky, and then down at the space in front of her frogged legs. She hits the gondola with her fist once, and again, twice. Others follow her, with palms or fists, pounding, knocking, thwacking. One boy uses the bottom of a half-empty water bottle to whack the train roof. Another takes off his shoes and pounds on the roof with them. At first he struggles, but then he manages to find his beat inside the beat of the others, everyone hitting the beast with all their accumulated strength, fear, hatred, vigor, and hope. And once he's found the beat and stayed on it, he cannot suppress a deep, visceral, almost feral sound, which begins in a howl, travels around the group of children contagiously, and ends in roaring laughter. They beat and laugh and howl like mammals of a freer species. They dip their fingers into the dust turned to sudden streams of mud on the surface of their train car and paint their cheeks with it. Aboard other train cars, some travelers hear the beat and the howls and wonder. The train travels through the curtains of water, across the thirsty desert cracking open a little to receive the unexpected shower.

When the rain subsides, the children, exhausted, wet, relieved, lie faceup on the gondola, mouths open to catch the last drops. The man in charge still sleeps, wet and oblivious to the rumpus. It's the oldest of the six children who sits up and starts speaking, saying:

Warriors had to earn their names.

He tells them that in the old times, names were given out to children when they got more mature.

They had to earn them, he says.

He continues to explain that names were like a gift given to people. The names were not secret, but they also couldn't be used just like that by anyone outside the family because a name had to be respected, because a name was like the soul of a person but also the destiny of a person. Then, getting up, he slowly and carefully walks to each of them, and into their ears he whispers a warrior name. They feel the train rocking beneath them, hear its wheels slicing the heavy air of the desert. The boy whispers a name and they smile back into the darkness, in acknowledgment of what they are being given. They smile perhaps for the first time in days, receiving his whispered word like a gift. The desert is moonless dark. And slowly they fall asleep, one by one, embracing their new names. The train moves slowly, in perfect parallel to the long wall, moving forward through the desert.


(THE FIFTEENTH ELEGY)

Mouths open in the night, they sleep. The train advances slowly along tracks parallel to the wall. From behind the rim of his blue cap, the man in charge counts them—six children in total, seven minus one. Boys, girls: lips chapped, cheeks cracked. They occupy the entire space there, stiff but warm, lined up like new corpses along the metal roof of the train gondola. Beyond, on both sides of the wall, the desert stretches out, identical. Above, the swart sky is still.

But the great ball of the earth keeps turning, always constant, always spinning, bringing east toward west, west toward east, until it catches up with the moving train, and from the last gondola, the first signs of daybreak are spotted by someone, someone in charge of keeping vigil, and as instructed, that person alerts another, and the alert is passed on, between men and women, from lips to ears, in whispers, mutters, cries, until it reaches the conductor in the engine car, sitting on a rickety stool, worming a finger inside his ear for wax-crust, thinking of beds and women and bowls of soup, and he sighs, twice, deep sighs, finally scoops out the incrustation from his ear and pulls the emergency lever, and one by one in chain reaction the brake pistons shove inside their cylinder cavities, compressing air, and the train sighs loudly, skidding and screeching to a final halt.

Ten train cars back from the engine car, the man in charge hurries the six children down the side ladder, one by one, and lines them up against the iron wall. Other men in charge of other children and other adults, on different gondolas and boxcars, do the same. Wooden ladders, ropes, improvised props, prayers, and good wishes are passed on, horizontal to the wall. And over the wall—quick, invisible—bodies climb and cross to the other side.

(THE SIXTEENTH ELEGY)

Unreal desert. Under the brown fog of a desert dawn, a crowd flows over the iron wall, so many. None thought the trains would bring so many. Bodies flow up the ladder and down onto the desert floor. It all happens too quickly after that.

The children hear men's voices calling out instructions in another tongue. They do not understand the words, but they see others lining up along the wall, foreheads pressed against the iron, so they do the same.

Far away, a dead, sharp sound blasts into the emptiness. Men and women, girls and boys, hear it. It travels from ear to ear, spreading fear in their bones. And then, again, the same sound, now multiplying in a continuous hail. The children stand still, exhale brief, infrequent sighs. Their eyes are fixed on their feet; their femurs locked into the sockets of their heavy hips.

The man in charge suddenly cries, run, follow me. The children recognize his voice and begin to run. Many others run, too, all in different directions, dispersing, despite the orders yelling them back to a halt, back to the line. They run. Some of those who run soon fall down when bullets pierce their livers, intestines, hamstrings. Their few belongings will outlive their corpses, and will later be found: a Bible, a toothbrush, a letter, a picture.

The man in charge again yells, run, run and don't stop running, and now lets them overtake him, ushering the six children on from behind, like a sheepdog, running behind them, yelling, go on, don't stop! One boy, the fifth, falls down, not dead, not hurt, but too exhausted, lips soft against hard dust. The man in charge shouts, go on, go on, leaving him behind but still guarding the back of the small pack, which runs onward in a closed horde, five children, two girls and three boys, and he continues to run behind them for a few more steps until a small bullet hits his lower back, rips easily through a thin layer of skin, then through thicker muscle, and finally bursts his sacrum bone into tiny pieces.

Once more he yells, go, go, as he falls to the ground, and the children continue running, as fast as they can for a while, then slower and slower, and finally start walking when behind them no more bullets and no more footsteps follow. They carry on and on, the five of them. In the distance, they see thunderclouds gathering, and they walk in that direction. Toward what now, they do not know. Away from the darkness behind them. North into the heart of light they walk.

# ECHO CANYON

A nd south into the heart of light we walked, Memphis, you and
me, close together and quiet, like the lost children walked
somewhere, too, under the same sun maybe, though I kept feeling
all the time that we were walking on the sun's surface and not under
it, and I asked you, don't you feel like we're walking on the sun, but
you didn't say anything in return, you weren't saying anything,
nothing at all, which made me worry because it felt like you were
disappearing and I was losing you all over again, even though you
were right next to me, like a shadow, so I asked you if you were tired
just to hear you say something, but you only nodded yes you were
tired but said nothing, so I asked you if you were hungry, and you
said nothing but nodded yes you felt hungry, which I felt, too, felt
hunger ripping me from inside, ripping me apart and eating me
from the inside out because I could not feed it anything, though
maybe it wasn't that, maybe it wasn't hunger, that's what I suspected
sometimes, that it wasn't hunger, but I didn't tell you that, I didn't
say so out loud because you wouldn't understand, I thought maybe
it was not hunger but more like a sadness or like an emptiness, or
maybe some kind of hopelessness, the kind of hopelessness that
seems like it will never get repaired no matter what, because you're
trapped in a circle, and all circles are endless, they go on forever,
round and round this round endless desert, always the same, in a
loop, and I told you, you know how we used to fold pieces of paper,
me and you, when we made origami fortune-tellers, and you said
hmmm, so I said this desert is just like our origami fortune-tellers,
except that in this one, when you open the paper flap in the corner,
your fortune is always desert, every single time, desert, desert, desert, same thing, and when you said hmmm again, I realized that
what I was saying made no sense, that my brain was just going
round and round, empty and full of hot air only, though sometimes
when the desert wind came, it cleared my thoughts for a moment,
but mostly there was just hot air, dust, rocks, bushes, and light,
especially light, so much of it, so much light pouring down from
the sky that it was hard to think, hard to see clearly, too, hard to see
even the things we knew by name, by heart, names like saguaro,
names like mesquite, things like creosote and jojoba bushes, impossible to spot the white heads of teddy bear chollas right in front of

our eyes before they clawed out to scratch and prick us, impossible
to see the outlines of the organ pipes farther away in the distance
until they were right in front of us, everything invisible in that light,
almost as invisible as things are by night, so what was it for, all that
light, for nothing, because if light had been useful, we wouldn't
have got lost inside of it, so lost inside light that we were sure the
world around us was slowly fading, becoming unreal, and for a
moment it did disappear completely and all that was there was the
sound of our mouths breathing thin air, in and out, and the sound
of our feet, on and on, and the heat on our foreheads burning out
our last good thoughts, until the wind came again, a little stronger
than before, blew on our faces, brushed our foreheads, whirled into
our ears, reminded us that the world was still there around us, that
there was still a world somewhere, with televisions, and computers,
and highways and airports, and people, and parents, the breeze
brought back voices, it was full of whispers, it brought voices from
far away, so we knew again there were people somewhere, real people in a real world, and the wind blew some more and shook the
real branches around us, the real branches rattling like sidewinder
snakes, which were also real, so in my head I was able to make a list
of real things that existed around us in that desert, the sidewinder
snakes, the scorpions, coyotes, spiders, creosotes, teddy bear chollas, jojobas, saguaros, and suddenly you said saguaro, like you'd
read my mind, or maybe I'd been saying these words out loud and
you heard me and repeated one, said look there, look, a saguaro,
and of course there wasn't a saguaro, but there was a nopal cactus
right in front of us, a nopal where six fat prickly pears had sprouted,
full of sweetness and water, Mama called them tunas, and they were
real, we picked them all, dug our nails into them, peeled their thick
skin off in chunks no matter if our fingers were getting pricked by a
thousand tiny thorns, they were real, and ate them like we were
coyotes, the juice bursting out and trickling down, through our
teeth gaps, down round our chins, down along our necks, and disappearing under my dirty torn shirt and your nightgown, I realized
now that they were torn and dirty, and only barely covering our
chests, but who would care, at least our chests were there, and our
lungs were finally breathing better, filling our bodies with better air,

our minds with better thoughts, our thoughts with better words, words you finally spoke out loud, said would you, Swift Feather, would you tell me more about the lost children, where are they now, what are they doing, will we see them, and as we walked on, I tried to imagine things to tell you about the lost children so that you could hear them the way I did in my mind and also imagine them, I said yes I'll tell you more about them, they're coming to meet us and we'll meet them over there, look, and then I took out my binoculars from my backpack and said here, hold these tight and look through the lenses, look over there, see, focus, look far away over there, toward those black thunderclouds gathering over the valley, can you see them I asked you, do you see those clouds, yes, you said yes, did you focus, I asked, and you said yes I focused and yes I can see the clouds and I can see the birds, too, flying around the clouds, and you asked me if I thought those birds were the eagles, so I looked through my binoculars and then said yes of course they are, those are the eagles, the same eagles the lost children now see as they walk north into the desert plain, beating muscled wings, threading in and out of black thunderclouds, they see them with their bare eyes, the five of them, as they walk onward, under the sun, keeping close together and silent, in a tight horde, deeper and deeper into the silent heart of light, saying nothing and hearing almost nothing, because nothing can be heard except the monotonous sound of their own footsteps, on and on across these deadlands, never stopping because if they stop, they will die, this they know, this they've been told, if someone stops in the deadlands, they never come out, like that boy among them, the fifth, who didn't make it, and the man in charge, who was gone, and also like the sixth boy, who tripped on a root or a rock or a ditch once they were already out of sight of the men who guarded the wall, he had tripped on a root or a rock, no one saw exactly what, but he fell to the ground, his knees unlocking, his hands meeting the hard ground, so tired, while the rest kept walking as he crawled on fours, one step, two steps, so tired, resisting the hard ground, fighting against the wave of fatigue surging from inside him, three steps, four, but it was no use now, it was too late, he knew he should not stop but did, even though one of the two girls, the older one, had said get up, don't stop, even though he heard her voice saying get up now, and felt her hand tugging at his shirt from his sleeve, looked up and saw her arm, her shoulder, her neck, her round face that told him no, do not stop, get up right now I'm telling you, she'd pulled him from his sleeve, which stretched until it ripped half an inch or so, and as he wrapped the palm of his hand around her small clenched fist that tugged at his sleeve, he squeezed her hand just a little to let her know that it was too late now, but that it was okay, and that she needed to let go of him and carry on with the others, and he almost smiled at her as he gave her the black hat he was wearing, and she received it and did, finally, let go of him and she walked on, first trotting a little to catch up with her younger sister, who'd stayed behind too to wait for her, and once she'd caught up, she took her sister's hand and continued walking more slowly, limping a little, one foot half shod in a tennis shoe, the other unshod, bloated and bloody, the sole of which was the last thing the boy saw before he allowed his eyes to close, his mind to shift inward, his thoughts to call up the image of his grandfather's bony brown feet, with their swollen veins and yellow toenails, then a bucket full of clenching lobsters, the metal clippers a girl holds to his own feet, relieving him from the pain that bound him to this body, to this life, and then the never-ending train tracks unraveling behind him and fading into hollow light, so much light, until his elbows gave in and bent deep, so tired, and his chest spread on the sand, so tired, and his lips, half parted, touched the sand, so tired, until the fatigue slowly faded from him, a relief, a final whimper, like a tide at last retreating, he could stop resisting, fighting, trying, finally he could just lie there, completely still, in the same spot where one morning, months later, two men who patrol the borderlands will find the bones that were his bones and the rags that were his clothes, each item of his collected in transparent plastic bags by one of the two men who found him, while the other man takes out a pen and a map, and marks a spot on the map with the pen, one more spot among a few other spots on the paper map that will later be handed over, that same afternoon, at 4:00 or 4:30 p.m., to the methodical old lady who was born many years ago in a house near a smoky lake in the Annapurna Valley, was relocated as a teenage girl to this desert, and now sits in front of a computer in a small office, every weekday, sipping iced coffee from a reusable straw while she waits for the monitor to boot up, her eyes fixed on the screen, which first lights into a generic blue, then slowly pixelates into the custom background of the Annapurna range, snow-covered at sunrise and pristine, and finally freckles with file icons, popping and scattering into successive visibility, while the palm of her hand is wrapping itself around the mouse, squeezing it a little and shaking it awake until the cursor arrow appears from a corner of the screen and is dragged across her desktop snow-covered mountain, is swept over baby-blue file icons labeled Animas Valley Deaths, San Simon Valley Deaths, San Pedro Deaths, and finally stops and is double-clicked on Sulphur Springs Valley Deaths, which opens up and spreads out across the screen, covering the lovely snow-covered mountain on her screen, layering dirty brown sand over clear white snow, dirty sand and red death spots over everything, death marks over fucking everything, the lady mutters between her teeth, because the map of that desert valley, the Sulphur Springs Valley, which is exactly the same but also not the same desert valley right outside her small, dark, but well-air-conditioned office, is speckled with hundreds of red dots, all of them added manually, one by one, by her, the lady who is never late for work, and sips from reusable straws in order not to pollute, and sits up straight in front of the computer monitor while she listens on her earphones to an only mildly pornographic but rotundly moralistic lesbian romance novel written by author Lynne Cheney, titled *Sisters,* not at all oblivious to the fact that the author of the novel is the wife of the ex–vice president Dick Cheney, who, under President George W. Bush, directed "Operation Jump Start," during which the National Guard was deployed along the border and a twenty-foot cement wall was erected across part of the desert, passing just a few miles from her office, which itself is nothing but a small rectangle walled off from that disgusting desert by just a meager adobe wall and a thin, single-leaf aluminum door, under the crevice of which the hot, relentless wind drags the last notes of all the desert worldsounds disseminated across the barrenlands outside, sounds of twigs snapping, birds crying, rocks shifting, footsteps trudging, people imploring, voices begging for water before

fading into silence with a final whimper, then darker sounds, like
cadavers diminishing into skeletons, skeletons snapping into bones,
bones eroding and disappearing into the sand, and none of this the
lady hears, of course, but somehow she senses all of it, as if sound
particles were stuck to the sand particles blown by the desert wind
into the faux grass of her welcome mat, so that every day before
stepping into her office, she has to take her mat and hit it against the
external adobe wall of the office, dust it off with three or four hard
slaps against the wall, until all those annoying sand particles are
blown back into the desert air, back to the streams and currents of
the desert air's unfiltered sounds carried eternally across empty valleys, sounds unregistered, unheard, and finally lost unless by chance
they happen to spiral into the small conch-shaped sockets of human
ears, such as those of the lost children, who now listen to them and
try to name them in their minds but find no words, no meanings to
hold on to, and continue to walk, the sound of the slow flow of footsteps thumping beside them, their eyes always fixed on the ground
below them and only once in a while directed up toward the horizon, where they see something happening, though they cannot say
exactly what, maybe a rainstorm, clouds gathering, far away over
there, black thunderclouds gathering over the valley, over there,
look, can you see them they ask each other, over there, those birds,
maybe eagles, can you see them, and yes one of the boys says, yes
says another, yes we see them, and yes I think they are eagles, you
and I saw them, Memphis, those eagles, though we could not hear
them, because around us we heard too many other sounds, strange
sounds, so strange that I didn't know if they were in my mind or in
the air, like the bells of a church, and many birds scattering, like
animals moving around us quick but invisible, and maybe the
sound of horses approaching, and I wondered if we were hearing
the sound of all the dead in the desert, all the bones there, and
remembered that time Papa had read us a story about a body some
people found in a field and just left there, and that body in that
story had got stuck to some part of my brain and kept coming back
to me, because stories can do that, they stick in your head, so that
when we were walking in the desert, I would keep thinking about
that body in a field, and was scared to think maybe we were going

to walk over someone's bones buried under us, but still we just kept on walking, on and on, the heat always getting heavier and the sun on our foreheads stinging us like a thousand yellow bees even though it was a bit lower now and making small shadows around everything, stones, bushes, cacti, and on and on we went, until I tripped on a root or a rock or a ditch and fell, and my hands hit the hard ground and my palms were full of tiny pebbles and dust and maybe thorns, and I felt like just lying there and putting my cheek to the ground and falling asleep, just a short nap, maybe, but you started pulling me by my shirt, tugging at my sleeve, saying stand up right now, I'm giving you an order, Swift Feather, and though you were younger, you suddenly sounded like you had to be obeyed, so I stood up and said yes ma'am, Major Tom Memphis, which made you laugh first, and then you were crying, then laughing again, round and round like in a circle, all our feelings and bodies changing like the wind, and in that instant, we heard the sky roaring, and we looked up and saw the storm clouds gathering in front of us, they were still far away but closer now than before, and then we saw lightning cracking the huge sky like it was an egg, and the eagles, again, which we could now see with our bare eyes, even though they still looked like tiny dots, they look like lost mittens in the sky looking for their mate down on earth, you said, and then we saw another strike of lightning, even brighter this time than the first, the lost children see it, too, as they continue marching in the desert, the radiant and repetitive desert, trying to listen for the sound of thunder that should follow lightning but hearing only the monotonous thump of their footsteps in the sand, on and on as they continue forward, and though the path across the desert plains is always straight, they feel that they are somehow descending, especially now that they have left the hot wind behind them and are sinking into an airless heat, into the lowest point of the basin-shaped valley, where they reach an abandoned village at the hour when the sun is low and children would normally come out to play, only there is no one in the village and nothing can be heard, except their own footsteps, echoing against walls stained yellow by the fat, low sun, nothing but old forgotten houses, some of which have walls that are cracked, and broken windows through which they

can see empty bedrooms, pieces of broken furniture, some abandoned belongings, the sole of a shoe, a broken bottle, a fork, and
one of the boys, the youngest of the bunch, sees a pink cowboy hat
and picks it up, he doesn't care that it's dirty and worn, and puts it
on his head as the four children continue to walk among a scatter of
broken adobe blocks overgrown with few weeds, some of which
they pull out with their hands and put into their mouths, the sour
taste making them spit and gag, and as they do, the youngest girl
starts to hear something different, a sound like whispering voices,
hears voices all around her whispering words, but where are the
mouths that whisper them, and the other boy, younger than her,
who now wears the pink hat, hears them, too, though he says nothing and only thinks to himself listen, listen, heart, listen like only
the saints have listened before, and in that murmurous silence, both
of them, girl and boy, the youngest of the four, hear the deeper
echoes of the things that were once there and were no longer, the
chiming of church bells, mothers heavy with weeping, grandpar-
ents dispensing instructions and scoldings at the breakfast table,
blackbirds scattering into high trees in town squares filled with
music, the uninterrupted murmur of other children who had died
there before them, where one voice says here we will find the doors
to paradise because the doors to paradise exist only in the inanimate desert, here on the earth scorched by the sun where nothing
else grows, and another says no, we will not find anything here,
because the desert is a tomb and nothing else, the desert is a tomb
for those who need to cross it, and we will die under this sun, this
heat, a murmur says, this is nothing, another answers, wait till we
get to the valley of San Simon, they say it feels like it sits at the doors
of hell, it's hot here, the older girl now says, and her voice sounds so
loud and clear, so real, as the four children pass the limits of this
abandoned village and nothing is left for them to hear, nothing
except the sad sound of wind breathing while they continue to walk
together in a closed horde, deeper into the valley, above which the
sky is filling with clouds, thick clouds gathering swiftly, with the
redeeming promise of change, of water, of shade, far away still but
not too far now because there is another flash of lightning, this time
followed by the distant rumble of thunder, and the four children

look up toward the storm that will come when they reach the very heart of the valley, where the eagles are now flying in strange patterns like writing a sky-message in a foreign alphabet, and for the first time, they hear their whistling and piping, and high-pitched calls, listen, you said, listen, Swift Feather, you said you could hear voices, good voices, maybe like in a playground or a park somewhere nearby, good and real voices, and I tried to listen, but I couldn't hear anything except for the blood in my heart pumping, and thought heart, listen, heart, shut up and try to listen to the voices and try to follow them, stop and listen, and when we both stopped and went under the shadow of a red rock, I did hear the sound of the wind breathing, and the sound of space shifting, but I heard nothing that sounded like human voices, just hollow, empty sounds, it was so hot, it's so hot here I said, and aren't you hot I asked, but you said nothing, answered nothing, so I didn't know if I had thought a thought or spoken real words, and when we got up again and carried on walking, all I could hear was the sound of your little feet thumping on the ground, the sound of your feet like a sound-shadow next to me, and my own feet, and then, farther away, the sound of other footsteps, moving in front of or behind us, across the desert, identical, it must be hard to be dead, you said, and I asked what do you mean, though I knew what you meant because also I felt like I was dead and thoughts were bouncing off every rock, back to me, only interrupted by threatening thunder now and then, from heavy clouds in front of us, which were getting much closer to us, or us closer to them, and closer also to the eagles, which we could finally hear, their whistling and piping, high-pitched, sounds that the lost children confuse with the sound of laughter and cries, children-laughter and children-cries, like in a playground where many children gather to play, except there is no playground and no playing, and nothing can really be heard on the ground where they walk except for the sound of little footsteps shuffling, their own footsteps walking in the inanimate desert, on sand scorched by the sun, and maybe hundreds or thousands of other lost footsteps, it must be toilsome to be dead, one boy thinks, hard to be dead here, he thinks, and remembers something his mother said to him one day, she said that angels never know if they are alive or not, that angels forget if they live among the living or among the dead, but the four lost children know they are still alive, although they walk among the echoes of other children, past and future, who kneeled, laid down, coiled into a fetal position, fell, got lost, did not know if they were alive or dead inside that vast hungry desert where only the four of them now keep walking in silence, knowing they might also soon be lost, thinking who can we call upon now, no one, knowing they cannot call upon anyone, not men, not angels, not beasts, especially not the beasts who, silent but sly and astute, notice that they are lost, and know that soon they will be meat, see their awkward shuffles upon this desert, on this uninterpreted world where everything is unnamed for them, the birds, the rocks, the bushes and roots, a world completely foreign, which will swallow them into its namelessness, as it swallowed each of the other children, but the four continue to walk, silent, trying to ignore these dark thoughts, until the younger of the two girls suddenly says look, look up there, look at those eagles floating right above us, look, and the other three children look up at the sky and see a thick blanket of rain clouds before them, not too far, and indeed, those strange eagles, flying in a tight flock instead of alone, which is how eagles usually fly, but why, you asked me, Memphis, why are those eagles flying like that, Swift Feather, why this and why that, why, you kept asking such difficult questions as we walked toward the thunderclouds, getting closer and closer to them, why, where, what, you asked, but how, how could I answer all of your questions, Memphis, questions and more questions, how are swamps made, what is the purpose of thorns, why don't I laugh when I tickle myself, why can't I laugh anymore at all, why does the air here smell like chicken feathers, and why, look, why are there all these eagles flying together above us now, do you think they are following us, do they want to eat us or are they protecting us, and why, I don't know, I don't know, I don't know, Memphis, but no, the eagles won't eat us, no way, I said, they're taking care of us, don't you remember the Eagle Warriors Pa always told us about, I asked, and you said yes, you remembered, and then said let's follow them, let's pretend the eagles are kites and we have to follow them like when we follow a kite, which was a brilliant idea, so we did just that, we started following them, clutching invisible holders, attached to invisible strings, and walked for a while like that, looking mostly up toward the sky, our eyes on the eaglekites, taking slow steps forward, until suddenly, very suddenly, an abandoned train car was in front of us, some fifty yards from us, and we noticed the eagles stop moving forward and start just circling above the empty space where the train car lay, how it had got there we had no idea, but we stopped our march and stared at it, I took a picture of it, and we stared some more, and then we looked up at the thick clouds getting ready to burst into rain, and at the eagles above us, which were now flying in a perfect circle over the train car, under those clouds, and the four lost children see them, too, circling low in the sky, under the rain clouds, and decide to walk straight toward them, straight ahead, walking much more swiftly now that the sun is sinking in the sky, walking until they spot an abandoned gondola, still small but clear in the distance, and walk straight to it, stopping right under its shadow, their four backs against the rusted metal side, not daring yet to go inside it though the sliding doors are wide open, because whenever they hold their ears to the warm metal wall of the gondola, they hear something shuffling about inside, a person or a large animal, maybe, and decide they will not risk it, unless they have no other choice later, no other place where they can take refuge from the imminent storm, because the threatening, heavy rain clouds are now right above them, and it is almost sunset, it was almost sunset and the heavy rain clouds were right above us, and we were tired, and also there was fear coming at us, Memphis, like during all the other sunsets, so we walked slowly toward the train car, wondering was it empty and was it safe and hoping maybe we would find old food in there, stored in boxes, because I knew those train cars all transported boxes of food from one edge of the country to the other edge of the country, and then you stopped a few steps from the train car and said I had to go and look inside before you would take another step, so I did, I walked slowly and my feet were making more noise than ever against the thorny, pebbly ground, toward the train car, which was large and had been painted red, but the paint had peeled off in parts and there was rust underneath, and the sliding doors were wide open on both sides so that when I stood in

front of the train car, it looked like a window I was looking through
from our side of the desert to the other side, which was exactly the
same as ours except for the higher mountains on that other side at
the end of the stretch of desert, and the sun was setting behind us
on the flat horizon, and in front of us, through the train car doors,
were the high Chiricahua Mountains, and I picked a rock up from
the ground and held it tight in my hand, noticed that my palm was
sweating, but I took three more steps, small steps, and swung my
arm back and then slowly forward, and let go of the rock so it would
rainbow across the air and fall into the train car, slow and soft, like
I was throwing a ball for someone your age to catch, and the rock
hit the metal surface of the train car floor, thumped, echoed once,
then was followed by a flutter that got louder and then louder so I
knew it wasn't an echo but a real sound, and then we saw it, enormous, its huge wings spread out, its curved beak and small feathered head, it paddled in the air, out of the train car into the sky until
it was a smaller object up there, and joined the circle of eagles hovering above us, and we were looking up at them like we were hyp-
notized by their circles when a rock came suddenly flying back at
us, a rock the older girl has just thrown from behind the rusted wall
of the gondola and through its open doors, a real rock that the boy
and his sister would have mistaken for an echo, confused as they
were about cause and effect as the normal link between events, were
it not for the fact that the rock thrown back at them hits the boy on
his shoulder, so very real, concrete, and painful that his nerves wake
up, alert, and his voice breaks out into an angry hey, ouch, hey,
who's there, who's there I said, who's there, he says, and hearing the
sound of his voice, the four children look at one another in relief,
because it is a real voice, finally, clearly not a lost desert echo, not a
sound-mirage like the ones that had been following them all along,
so they smile at one another, and first the older girl and then the
younger one, and then the two boys, peek their faces around one
side of the open door of the gondola, four round faces were looking
right at us from the other side of the old train car, so real I didn't
believe they were real, thought can this be or am I imagining things,
because the desert fools you, and we both knew that by now, and I
still couldn't believe they were real, even though the four of them

were standing right there in front of us, two girls with long braids, the older one wearing a nice black hat, and then two boys, one of them wearing a pink hat, none of them seemed real until you opened your mouth, Memphis, you said Geronimoooo from just a step behind me, and then we heard the four faces say Geronimoooo back to us, Geronimoooo, the two children say to the four of them from the other side of the abandoned gondola, a boy and a girl, and it takes them all some seconds to realize that they are all real, them and us, us and them, but when they do, they all, the four, the two, the six in total, step into the empty, abandoned gondola while slowly, outside, the sound of gathering thunder becomes more constant, reverberating like an angry tide at sea, and bolts of lightning, all around them, start pounding down on the dry sand, sending sand grains into upward-spiraling whirls that remind the six children of the dead, the many dead, ghosts jumping out from the desert floor to haunt them, torment them, and the sky was getting darker, I noticed, night was coming, why don't we make a fire, I said to the five of you, una fogata, I said, and we all agreed it was the right thing to do, so we quickly gathered sticks and twigs and pieces of dry cacti from around the train car, and though they were all too wet already, we started to make a pile with them in the center of the train car, they make a pile right in the middle of the gondola while the older girl walks over to the big nest that the eagle had made in the corner of the train car, on top of two parallel wooden planks, and carefully plucks some dry twigs and grass from it, handing them to the other children, who are still sorting twigs and cacti pieces for the fire, saying things to one another like here, take this, and be careful, this one has thorns, and this twig is longer and better, until they all see the older girl step up on a wooden barrel, she looks into the eagle's nest, scoops something up from inside it, and then looks back at the rest of the children like saying, here, here it is, with a big smile, and in her hand she is holding an egg, still warm, she holds it high above her head like a trophy and then carefully hands it to her sister, who passes it on to the new girl, who gives it to one of the boys, who then passes it to the other boy, the one who is wearing the pink hat, they pass the egg from hand to hand like in a ceremony, feeling that almost-alive thing palpitating in their hands, and then the girl scoops up another egg and another, three eggs in total, which three of the children, the two younger girls and one of the boys, hold in their cupped palms, and at the very end the older girl scoops up the entire nest into her bare arms, carries it, stepping down from the barrel, a nest made of inter-twined sticks perfectly knitted together, which she deposits in the middle of the empty gondola next to the little pile of twigs that the children had managed to gather, and they all stare into it, not know-ing exactly what to do next, until the new boy takes out a matchbox from his backpack, strikes a match, and throws it into the nest, where it dies, then strikes a second match, but nothing, and only at the third try, when he huddles over the nest and holds the lit match to a twig, does he manage to light the dry edge of one, the rest of the children looking at it attentively like they are wishing the flame to spread, and it finally does, it spreads to the rest of the twig, which transports the flame to a thicker stick, and then another, until the entire nest is ablaze, and when there is a proper fire burning before them, the two girls and the boy who are holding on to the eggs let them roll out of their hands back into their burning nest, the flames licking them, scorching them, boiling them, the eggs cook in the fire until, some minutes later, using a long enough stick that she finds on the floor, the older girl rolls them out onto the surface of the train car, just outside the circle of fire, and orders the rest of the children to blow on the shell-surface of the three large eggs, and they do, until they are able to crack them open, peel off the shell, and bite into them with their hungry teeth, taking turns, first the youngest girl, then the boy with the pink hat, then the new girl, then the other boys, and at the end the older girl, who is probably the same age as the new boy, she was my age but was more of a leader than I was, with her big black hat, and while I bit into my part of the soft egg and chewed on the rubbery outside and then into the powdery inside, I kept on remembering the eyes of the big eaglemother that had looked me straight in the face before it flew away out the open door of the train car right after I'd thrown the rock inside, and suddenly you screamed, Memphis, and we all looked at you, and you spit something into your hand, and then pinched it with your other hand's fingers, and you showed us a tooth, you'd finally lost your second tooth, and you gave it to me to keep, for later, and after we finished eating, I said why don't we all tell stories before we go to sleep, and we did, we made an effort to stay awake, and for a while, we filled the space of the train car with stories that sometimes became wild laughing like the thunder rolling and rumbling outside, but we were all tired, getting cold, and the storm was strong still, rain falling almost inside the wagon through the open doors and leaks in the rusty roof, and we ran out of things to tell and to laugh at so we all slowly went silent, and cuddling into my lap, you tugged at my sleeve and looked into my eyes like saying something and then you did say something, softly like it was a secret, said Swift Feather, and I said what, and you said promise you will take me to Echo Canyon tomorrow, and I said yes, Memphis, I promise, and again you said Swift Feather, what is it, Memphis, nothing, Swift Feather, I like being with you and want to always be with you, okay, so I said yes, okay, and the other two girls were still awake, too, but the boys were asleep, I think, because they had gone silent and were breathing slowly, and the older girl asked you and me if we wanted to hear a last story, and yes, yes, yes, we all said, yes, please, so she said I'll tell you a story, but after I tell it, you three have to close your eyes and at least try to fall asleep, and we all said okay, so she told this story, said only this, and when they woke up, the eagle was still there, and that was the end of the story and you didn't fall asleep, I think, but you pretended to and so did the youngest girl until you both did finally fall asleep, but I didn't and neither did the oldest girl, we stayed awake while we poked the fire, which was dying, and she asked me why we were there, you and I, so I told her we'd run away, and when I told her why, she said that was such a stupid thing to do, why would I decide to run away if we didn't really need to run from anything, and she was right, I knew, but I was too ashamed to tell her that I knew she was right so instead, I told her that aside from running away, we were also looking for two girls who'd got lost, two girls who were the daughters of one of our mother's friends, lost where she asked, lost in this desert I said, do you know them, she asked, the two girls you're looking for, no I said, so how are you going to find them, I don't know, but maybe I will I said, but if you do find them, how will you know it is

them if you don't even know their faces, so I told her that I knew the
girls were sisters, knew they were going to be wearing matching
dresses, and knew that their grandmother had sewn their mother's
telephone number on the collars of their dresses, that's so stupid she
said again and laughed with a laugh that wasn't mean at all, more
like a mother laughing at her children, what are you laughing at I
asked her, and she told me that many children who had to cross this
desert had telephone numbers sewn by grandmothers or aunts or
cousins on their collars or inside their pockets, she said that the
youngest boy who was there, sleeping next to you, had a phone
number stitched on his collar, that even she and her sister had numbers on their collars, and she took off her black hat, leaned over
toward me a little from across the ashes, and tried to show me the
underside of the collar of her shirt, see she said, yes I see I said,
though I didn't see much, just felt all my blood rushing to my cheeks
and forehead, luckily the night was dark, everything was dark
except for some ashes still orange in the place where we'd made the
fire, well, goodnight she said and good luck, yes good luck I said
and goodnight, and the night is perhaps not good but is silent, the
six children curled into sleeping positions around the dying fire,
feet touching head touching feet, most of them maybe dreaming,
except the eldest boy and eldest girl, who are still slowly sliding into
sleep when they hear it clearly behind the last crackle of twigs, the
distant cries of a lone eagle, calling for her eggs, and the boy cries
and cries, like he has never cried before, perhaps, and whispers I'm
sorry, eagle, I'm sorry, we were so hungry, and the girl doesn't cry or
say she's sorry but thinks thank you, eagle, until the two finally fall
asleep like the others, and the boy dreams he is the young Indian
warrior girl called Lozen, who, one day when she'd just turned ten,
climbed up one of the sacred mountains in Apacheria and stayed
there alone for four days, until, after the fourth day, before she went
back down to rejoin her people, the mountain gave her a power,
which was that from then onward, by looking at which veins had
turned dark blue after she walked around in a circle lifting her
hands up, she would know where the enemy was and be able to
steer her people away from danger, and in his dream he was she,
and she was leading her people away from a band of what could

have been soldiers or paramilitaries dressed in nineteenth-century traditional bluecoats but holding wild guns, and huddling them all into an abandoned train car, where he starts hearing, with the repetitive obsessiveness of nightmares, a line delivered histrionically, when he woke in the woods in the dark and the cold of the night, over and over again, the same sentence never completed, when he woke in the woods in the dark and the cold of the night, until the boy opens his eyes suddenly, wrenches himself up, and reaches out to touch his sister sleeping beside him, feeling a deep relief at confirming that she is there, next to him, there you were, Memphis, your curls all damp, I remembered Mama used to smell your head like she was smelling a bunch of flowers and I never knew why but now I knew why, I bent down to smell you and you smelled like warm dust and pretzel, salty but also sweet at the same time, and so I kissed your curls and when I did, you said some words like eagle and moon, or maybe eaglemoon, and then you were sucking your thumb again, and seemed far away, while I looked around in the dark, still no sunrise, and knew in my heart though not my head that the Eagle Warriors had been there with us all this time, the storm had almost died out and we were safe thanks to them, I knew, they had been protecting us from everything, so I curled up again on my side, listening to the other four children breathe, asleep, and to you, sucking your thumb, and imagined the sounds you made were the thumps of footsteps, dozens, the Eagle Warriors, marching around us, your thumb sucked, thump, and the flutter of eagle-wings, and thoughts like eaglemoon, thunder-lightning swelling in the sky, until I finally shut my eyes again, thought about eagles, fell asleep into eagledreams, and dreamed nothing, slept deep, finally, so deep that when I woke up, it was bright out, and I was alone in the abandoned train wagon, so I rushed to my feet in a panic, and leaned out the wide-open doors of the wagon, and noticed the sun was above the mountain already, and you were there, I saw you, was so relieved, you were sitting on the ground some steps from the wagon, patting mud, I'm making mud pies for breakfast you said, and look I have a bow and arrow so we can hunt something, too, you said, and lifted up a plastic bow and arrow from the ground by your side, where did you get that and where are the other four children I asked, and you said they had left, they'd left right before sunrise, and you said you'd got the bow and arrow in a trade, told me you'd traded some stuff from my backpack with the older girl, and in return she gave you the bow and arrow, what, I asked you, what are you talking about, I repeated, looking around the wagon for my backpack and then shuffling things inside around it to see what was missing, Ma's big map was missing, the compass was missing, the flashlight, the binoculars, the matches, and even the Swiss Army knife were missing, so I jumped off the wagon with my light backpack around one shoulder, walked over to you, stood right above you, why did you do that I screamed, because we're going to meet Ma and Pa today so we don't need that stuff anymore Swift greedy Feather, you said, talking so calmly, and I was so angry at you, Memphis, furious, how do you know we will meet them today I asked you, and you said you knew because Pa had told you that the end of the trip was when you lost your second tooth, and though that was silly and made no sense, it made me feel some hope, maybe we would find them today, but I was still furious, you'd given away my stuff, at least you didn't give away my camera and my pictures I said, then you turned your head up to look at me and said well I also traded my book with no pictures and my backpack, oh yeah for what, I asked you, for hats you said, one for me and one for you, and you pointed your finger to two hats on the ground a few feet from you, a pink one and a black one, the pink one is yours and the black one is mine you said, so I breathed deep trying to not get more and more angry, and sat down on the ground next to you, thought you were probably right, or at least hoped you were right, we didn't need that stuff anymore if we were going to find Ma and Pa soon, or be found by them, sometime soon, I could see the Chiricahua Mountains close by in the east and now that the morning had come they looked smaller and closer and less difficult to climb than what they'd seemed the day before under the storm, it would probably take us just a few hours to get to the highest point, where Echo Canyon was, I was squinting my eyes trying to make out which the highest peak was, following the jagged line of the mountains, wishing I still had my binoculars, when you said want some mud pie for breakfast or what, so I smiled at you and said yes, please, just one slice, and reached over to grab the hats that you'd traded our stuff for, handed you the pink one, and no you said, the black one is mine, so we tried them both on, back and forth, and true the pink one felt good on my head, and yours tilted weirdly to the front, almost covering your eyes, but it looked good, and you looked serious as you cut the mud pie into big slices, which then we pretend-ate with sticks, where were the four children heading to exactly I wondered while I pretend-chewed, would they make it, would the map be useful, I hoped it would, if they walked in a straight line, they would be able to make it to the train tracks before sunset, I'm sure they will, I kept saying to myself while you and I got ready to go and as we started walking toward the mountains ahead, I'm sure they'll make it to the tracks soon, we were also moving easier and faster than I thought because the sun was still low, the air wasn't hot yet, and we had eaten and rested, so we weren't getting tired and thirsty like the day before, so soon we had reached the slope of the mountains and started climbing up a steep trail, past the tall stone columns of the Chiricahuas that looked like totems or skyscrapers, and higher up, toward the highest peaks, and up and up we went, walked on and on, till we reached the high valley, red and yellow in the sun, a high valley that Pa had described to us once but that was even more beautiful than he had said, and we reached the highest point there was to reach, from where we could see the rest of the valley, and there we found a small shallow grotto and decided to rest there for a while, because we knew we were on the right path, because Pa had also described these kinds of grottos to us, small and not dangerous, no bears or animals there because they were not deep enough for big animals to hide in, and after we'd rested a little, because we had the hats and we also had the bow and arrow, we decided to play the Apache game we used to play with Pa, so I hid behind a rock in the grotto, and you hid somewhere else there, too, and you would look for me, and I would look for you, and whoever spotted the other first would shout Geronimo, and that person would win, those were the rules, and I was still hiding when you came around slyly from behind me and shouted Geronimo, so proud of winning, shouted so loud that your voice quickly traveled and then came back to us, clear and strong, eronimo,

onimo, onimo, so I shouted Geronimo again, to test the echo, and we heard it bouncing back even stronger and longer, Geronimo, eronimo, onimo, onimo, and we both got so crazy with relief or joy or both, because this was it, this was the heart of Echo Canyon, we'd found it, and we were suddenly so restless with good restlessness that next we shouted our names at the same time so what came back was something muddled like etherphis, etherphis, phis, shhhh, shush, I said, and I made a sign with my index finger on my lips so you'd keep quiet a second because it was my turn now, why you said, because I'm older I answered, and I was just pulling in air so I could shout out my name, Swift Feather, when suddenly, before I was able to say my name, we both heard something else, loud and clear and familiar, coming from far away but straight at us, and then bouncing off every rock in the valley, ochise, cochise, ochise, and then, right after that, we heard arrow, arrow, row, and it was hard to pull the next word out from my stomach because it was suddenly full of thunder-feelings, my stomach, and full of lightning, my head, full of joy, they had found us, finally, and I felt I would be unable to even say anything, but I did, I pulled in air and shouted Swift Feather, and we heard it bouncing back, feather, eather, and we heard them saying we're coming, oming, oming, and probably something like stay where you are, are, are, and you stood there and it took you a moment, but you also breathed in all the air around you, your belly ballooning out, and called it out, your beautiful name, and it came back mighty and powerful all around us, Memphis.

PART IV

*Lost Children Archive*

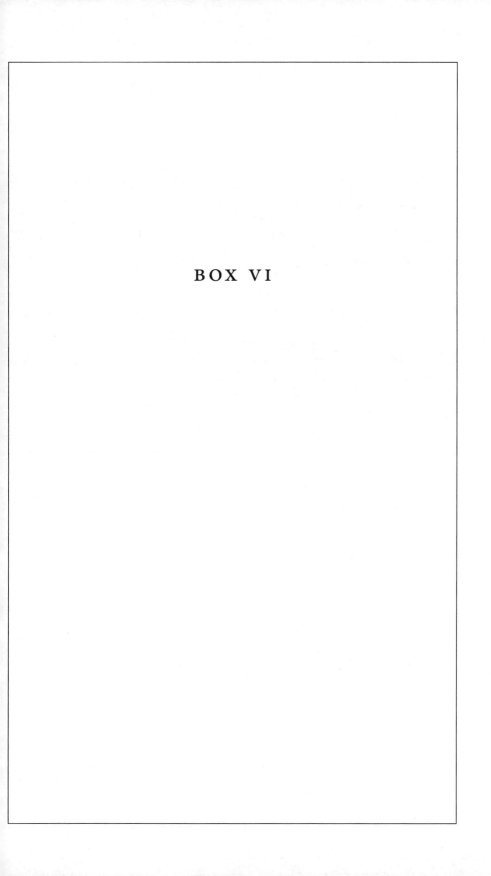

BOX VI

## § ECHO ECHOES

Mem mem mem mem
Eather eather eather
Wa wa wa wa wa
Em em em em em
Ow ow ow ow
Eas eas eas eas
Eist eist eist eist

## § CAR ECHOES

Cow, horse, feather, arrow, ow, ow, us playing
No no no, yes yes yes, us fighting
Rrrrrr, chupe, chupe, srlssnnn, us sleeping, me thumb-
    chuping, you snoring
Blah blah blah blah, bad news, the radio, the radio, more
    radio
Stop, go, no, more, less, Jesus Fucking Christ, ist, ist, Ma and
    Pa talking, arguing, whooooo, hhhhh, hhhhh, all of us
    breathing, silence
He-he, ha-ha, heeee, all you fake laughing
When he woke in the woods in the dark and the cold of the
    night . . .

## § INSECT ECHOES

Teetoo, tootoop, tooop, two ants talking
Bzzzzz, bee buzzing
Bzzzz, wachink, bee stinging (you)
Bzzzzzzzzz, bye-bye, bee

## § FOOD ECHOES

Rumch rumch, us eating cookies
Tuc tic tuc tic, crumbs falling on the car seat

Swish, woosh, us wiping up the mess
Shhhhhh, don't say anything

## § STRANGER ECHOES

Over-easy, milk or no milk, more ice, ice ice, diner
    conversations
Fill it up, up, up, gasoline station conversations
Two double beds yes, yes, yes, motel conversations
License, please, police conversations
Stop, stop, stop, military post conversations
Papers, passports, where are you from, why are you here, ere,
    Border Patrol conversations

## § LEAVES ECHOES

Whooosh, whoosh, leaf falling
Crrp, crrp, leaf crunching

## § ROCK ECHOES

(Silence)

## § HIGHWAY ECHOES

Fffffffffffffhhh, cars driving past on highways
Fffhhhhhhhhhhhhh, cars we hear from inside the motel

## § TELEVISION ECHOES

Not allowed!

## § TRAIN ECHOES

Rishktmmmmbbbbggggeeeeek, train arriving in station
Tractractracmmmmmmshhhhhh, train leaving station

## § DESERT ECHOES

Tac, took, tac, our footsteps in desert
Waaaaahhhh, nooooo, ahhhhhh, me crying
Wwwwwwzzzzzzzzz, wind blowing across a dry lake
Shrrrrrr, ssssssssss, hsssssss, sss, hhhhh, dust-clouds appearing
    and disappearing
Waaaaahhhh, nooooo, ahhhhhh, me crying
Tac, took, tac, shrrrrrr, ssssssssss, walking across a dry lake,
    footsteps on dust
Kikikiki . . . kuk . . . kuk . . . kuh, eagles flying
Slap, flap, blap, plap, wings flapping, slapping
Tsssssss, fsssss, wind through saguaros
Creek, croook, cccccrrrr, abandoned train car, metal creaks
Aaaeeee, aeeeeee, oooooh, wind-cries
Waaaaahhhh, nooooo, ahhhhhh, me crying

## § STORM ECHOES

Brrrrrrhhhh, krrrrrrrhhhh, thunder far away, storm coming
Zlap, boooom, rrrrtoooom, thunder all around
Tictictictictictictictic, rainstorm
Tictictic . . . tictictic . . . tictictic, less rain

## § TOOTH ECHOES

Crrrakk, shmlpff, blurpm, my tooth cracking and coming out
    slowly

# DOCUMENT

This is Ground Control. Calling Major Tom.

Checking sound. One, two, three.

This is Ground Control. You copy me, Major Tom?

This is the last recording I'm making for you, Memphis, so listen carefully. You and Mama will leave tomorrow morning at sunrise from the house in the Dragoon Mountains, in Apacheria, and will take an airplane back home. This recording is just for you, Memphis. If anyone else is listening to it, including you, Mama, it's not for you. But you probably have already listened to most of it, Ma. After all, it's your recorder. Maybe I should say now, I'm sorry I used your recorder without permission. And I'm sorry that I messed up the order in your box. It was a mistake, an accident. Also, I'm sorry I lost your map, Ma, and took your book about the lost children, and then went and lost it, too. I left it on the train that took us from Lordsburg to Bowie. Maybe someone will find it one day and read it. And maybe a train was the right place for it to end up. At least I recorded some parts of it in this recording, so not everything is lost. I know you also recorded other bits, so perhaps we have almost all of it on tape. I'm not trying to make excuses, I really am sorry, and also, I don't mind if you listened to my recording, just as long as you keep it safe for Memphis. As long as you keep it safe and let her listen to it one day, when she's older. Maybe when she turns ten. Okay, deal, yes? Okay.

This is the last bit of tape I'm recording for you, Memphis, because this is where the story ends. You always want to know how all stories end. Today is the day it ends, at least for now, for a long time. After Ma and Pa found us in Echo Canyon, a bunch of park rangers came with space blankets to cover us both, and brought apple juice and granola bars, and they carried us back across the canyon to a little office full of posters of bears and trees and some really bad hand-drawings of Apaches. Someone drove Pa to where he'd left our car, and when he came back, he and Ma carried us to it, though we didn't really need to be carried, and Ma climbed into the backseat with us, held us tight, kissed our heads, and rubbed our backs while Pa drove slowly, very slowly, to the house in the Dragoon Mountains. The house is a rectangle made of stone, with two bedrooms, and a living room and an open kitchen. It has a front porch and a back porch, a tin roof painted green, and big windows with shutters to keep the light and heat of the desert out.

Today, at sunrise, you and Ma will wake up and leave. I have to keep this last recording short so you don't wake up before I finish. And I have to put the recorder back into Mama's bag before you both leave, so she can take it with her. She'll take it back with her, and then, one day, when you're older, Memphis, you will listen to this recording. You will also look at all the photographs I put neatly inside my box, labeled Box VII, which Ma will also take back with her because I just left it on top of all your stuff, basically bags and backpacks, which she lined up next to the door of the house, ready for when you have to head out. Pa and I will be sleeping inside the house when the car service comes to pick you up to take you to the airport. Pa will be in his room and I will be in my new room.

After we got lost, and then were found, I think Ma and Pa did think about staying together, not separating. I think they tried, maybe even tried hard. When we first got to the house after we'd been found again, we tried to go back to normal again. We all painted walls and listened to the radio together; I helped you write out the echoes we'd collected on little pieces of paper and put them in your box, Box VI, which you wanted Pa to keep. Another day, we helped Ma repair a window and also a lamp, we went grocery shopping with Pa and barbecued dinner with him, and we even played Risk, two nights in a row, you in charge of rolling dice, and me and Ma fighting over Australia.

But I think in the end, it was impossible for them. Not because they didn't like each other but because their plans were too different. One was a documentarian and the other a documentarist, and neither one wanted to give up being who they were, and in the end that is a good thing, Ma told me one night, and said someday we will both understand it better.

Remember I told you one day, which seems kind of long ago now though it isn't, that I wasn't sure if I was going to be a documentarist or a documentarian, and that I didn't tell Ma and Pa about it at first because I didn't want them to think I was trying to copy them or had no ideas of my own but also because I didn't want to have to choose if I'd be a documentarian or a documentarist? And then

I thought maybe I could be both? I kept on thinking about that, about how to be both.

I thought this, though it was all a bit confused: maybe, with my camera, I can be a documentarian, and with this recorder where I've been recording, which is Mama's, I can be a documentarist and document everything else my pictures couldn't. I thought about writing stuff down in a notebook for you to read one day, but you are a bad reader still, level A or B, still read everything backward or in a mess, and I have no idea when you'll finally learn to read properly, or if you ever will. So I decided to record sound instead. Also, writing is slower and reading is slower, but at the same time listening is slower than looking, which is a contradiction that cannot be explained. Anyway, I decided to record, which was faster, although I don't mind slow things. People usually like fast things. I don't know what kind of person you will be in the future, a person who likes slow things or one who likes fast things. I kind of hope you are the type of person who likes slow things, but I can't rely on that. So I made this recording and took all those pictures.

When you look at all the pictures and listen to this recording, you'll understand many things, and eventually maybe you'll even understand everything. That's also why I decided to be both a documentarian and a documentarist—so you could get at least two versions of everything and know things in different ways, which is always better than just one way. You'll know everything, and slowly start to understand it. You'll know about our lives when we were with Mama and Papa, before we left on this trip, and about the time we were traveling together toward Apacheria. You'll know the story of when we first saw some lost children boarding an airplane, and how it broke us all into pieces, especially Mama because all her life was, was looking for lost children. She got even more broken one day, when we were all back together again in the house in the Dragoon Mountains, because she got a phone call from that friend of hers, Manuela, who had been looking for her two girls who'd got lost in the desert, and her friend told her that her daughters had been found in the desert, but they weren't alive anymore. For days Ma hardly spoke, didn't get out of bed, took showers that lasted hours, and all the while, I wanted to tell her that maybe the girls who had been found were not her friend's daughters, because I knew for a fact that many children had telephone numbers stitched on their clothes when they had to cross the desert.

I knew this, and you'll also know this, because you and I were with the lost children, too, though only for a little while, and that is what they told us. We met them, and were there with them, tried to be brave like them, traveling alone on trains, crossing the desert, sleeping on the ground under the huge sky. You have to always remember how, for a while, I lost you and you lost me, but we found each other again, and carried on walking in the desert, until we found the lost children inside an abandoned train car, and we thought they were maybe the Eagle Warriors that Pa had been telling us about, but who knows. You have to know all of this, and remember it, Memphis.

When you get older, like me, or even older than me, and tell other people our story, they'll tell you it's not true, they'll say it's impossible, they won't believe you. Don't worry about them. Our story is true, and deep in your wild heart and in the whirls of your crazy curls, you will know it. And you'll have the pictures and also this tape to prove it. Don't you lose this tape or the box with the pictures. You hear me, Major Tom? Don't you lose anything, because you're always losing everything.

This is Ground Control speaking. Can you hear me?

Put your helmet on now. And remember to count: ten, nine, eight, commencing countdown and engines on. Check ignition. And, seven, six, five, four, three, and now we're moonwalking.

This is Ground Control. Can you hear me?

Do you remember that song? And our game? After the moonwalks comes the part we love the most. Two, one: and you're launched into space. You're up in space, floating in a most peculiar way. Up there, the stars look really different. But they're not. They're the same stars, always. You might feel lost one day, but you have to remember that you're not, because you and I will find each other again.

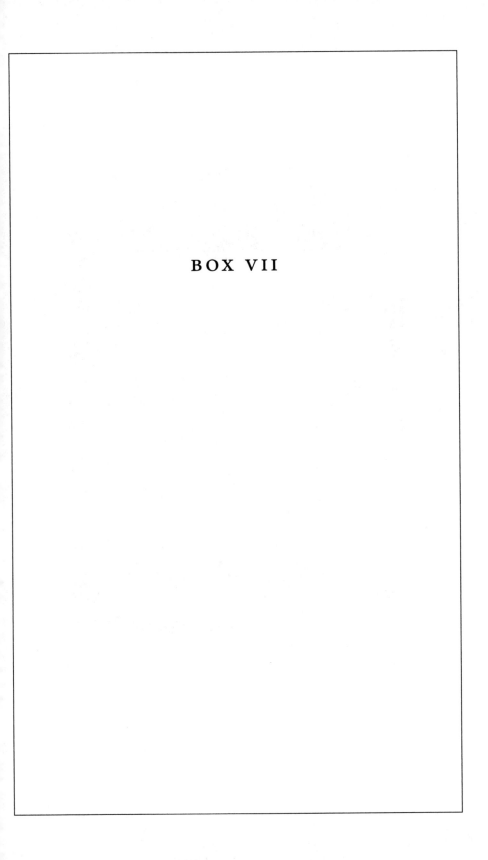

BOX VII

§ POLAROID

§ POLAROID

§ POLAROID

§ POLAROID

§ POLAROID

§ POLAROID

§ POLAROID

§ POLAROID

## ACKNOWLEDGMENTS

I began writing this novel in the summer of 2014. Over time, a large number of people and institutions have helped it come into being. I am deeply thankful to all, but I especially want to thank the following:

The Akademie der Künste, in Berlin, which offered me a fellowship and residence in the summer of 2015, and where, after a year of note-taking, I finally began typing.

Shakespeare & Co., in Paris, and especially Sylvia Whitman, who in the summer of 2016 generously offered me a roof and bed above the bookstore, where I was able to devote many hours to the manuscript.

The Beyond Identity program, at the City College of New York, where I was a visiting fellow between the fall of 2017 and the spring of 2018, and thanks to which I had time to finish and edit the manuscript.

Philip Glass, who exists, and whose *Metamorphosis* I listened to approximately five thousand times while writing this novel.

My agents and sisters-in-arms, Nicole Aragi and Laurence Laluyaux, as well as their wonderful assistants, Grace Dietshe and Tristan Kendrick Lammar.

My brilliant editors: Anna Kelly, at Fourth Estate; and Robin Desser, at Knopf, as well as Annie Bishai—the best editorial assistant I have worked with.

My editor and longtime interlocutor at Coffee House Press, Chris Fischbach.

My friends—generous early readers during different stages of the manuscript—N. M. Aidt, K. M. Alcott, H. Cleary, B. H. Edwards, J. Freeman, L. Gandolfi, T. Gower, N. Gowrinathan, R. Grande, R. Julien, C. MacSweeney, P. Malinowski, E. Rabasa, D. Rabasa, L. Ribaldi, S. Schweblin, Z. Smith, A. Thirlwell, and J. Wray.

Miquel and Ana.

And my parents, Marta and Cassio.

WORKS CITED

*(Notes on Sources)*

Like my previous work, *Lost Children Archive* is in part the result of a dialogue with many different texts, as well as with other nontextual sources. The archive that sustains this novel is both an inherent and a visible part of the central narrative. In other words, references to sources—textual, musical, visual, or audio-visual—are not meant as side notes, or ornaments that decorate the story, but function as intralinear markers that point to the many voices in the conversation that the book sustains with the past.

References to sources appear in different ways along the novel's narrative scheme:

1. The fundamental "bibliography" appears within the boxes that travel in the car with the family (Box I–Box V).

2. In the parts narrated by a female first-person narrator, all sources used are either cited and quoted or paraphrased and referenced.

3. In the parts narrated by the boy first-person narrator, works previously used by the female first-person narrator are "echoed," while others are quoted or paraphrased and referenced.

4. Some references to other literary works are spread nearly invisibly across both narrative voices as well as the *Elegies for Lost Children* and are meant to appear as thin "threads" of literary allusion.

One such thread alludes to Virginia Woolf's *Mrs. Dalloway*, wherein the technique of shifting narrative viewpoints via an object moving in the sky was, I believe, first invented. I repurpose the technique in point-of-view shifts that occur when the eyes of two characters "meet" in a single point in the sky, by looking at the same object: airplane, eagles, thunderclouds, or lightning.

5. In the parts narrated by a third-person narrator, *Elegies for Lost Children,* sources are embedded and paraphrased but not quoted or cited. The *Elegies* are composed by means of a series of allusions to literary works that are about voyages, journeying, migrating, etc. The allusions need not be evident. I'm not interested in intertextuality as an outward, performative gesture but as a method or procedure of composition.

The first elegies allude to Ezra Pound's "Canto I," which is itself an "allusion" to Homer's Book XI of the *Odyssey*—his "Canto I" is a *free* translation from Latin, and not Greek, into English, following Anglo-Saxon accentual verse metrics, of Book XI of the *Odyssey.* Book XI of Homer's *Odyssey,* as well as Pound's "Canto I," is about journeying/descending into the underworld. So, in the opening Elegies about the lost children, I reappropriate certain rhythmic cadences as well as imagery and lexicon from Homer/Pound, in order to establish an analogy between migrating and descending into the underworld. I repurpose and recombine words or word-pairings like "swart/night," "heavy/weeping," and "stretched/wretched"—all of which derive from lines in "Canto I."

Sources in the *Elegies* embedded in the third-person narrative follow a similar scheme as above, and include the following works: *Heart of Darkness,* by Joseph Conrad; *The Waste Land,* by T. S. Eliot; *The Children's Crusade,* by Marcel Schwob; "El dinosaurio," by Augusto Monterroso; "The Porcupine," by Galway Kinnell; *Pedro Páramo,* by Juan Rulfo; *Duino Elegies,* by Rainer Maria Rilke; and *The Gates of Paradise,* by Jerzy Andrzejewski (translated by Sergio Pitol into Spanish, and retranslated by me into English).

Below is a list of exact lines or words alluded to from each work, roughly in the order in which they appear in the *Elegies* sections of the novel:

Ezra Pound, "Canto I"
· And then went down to the ships
· Heavy with weeping, and winds from sternward
· Swartest night stretched over wretched men there

Joseph Conrad, *Heart of Darkness*
· lightless region of subtle horrors
· Going up that river . . . It looked at you with a vengeful aspect.
· There was no joy in the brilliance of sunshine.

Ezra Pound, "Canto I" and "Canto II"
· impetuous impotent dead,
· unburied, cast on the wide earth
· thence outward and away
· wine-red glow in the shallows
· loggy with vine-must

Ezra Pound, "Canto III"
· his heart out, set on a pike spike
· Here stripped, here made to stand
· his eyes torn out, and all his goods sequestered

Augusto Monterroso, "El dinosaurio"
· When he woke up the dinosaur was still there.

Galway Kinnell, "The Dead Shall Be Raised Incorruptible"
· Lieutenant! / This corpse will not stop burning!

T. S. Eliot, *The Waste Land*
· A heap of broken images where the sun beats

Galway Kinnell, "The Porcupine"
· puffed up on bast and phloem, ballooned / on willow flowers,
  poplar catkins. . . .

T. S. Eliot, *The Waste Land*
· Looking into the heart of light, the silence
· Unreal City,
  Under the brown fog of a winter dawn,
  A crowd flowed over London Bridge, so many,

I had not thought death had undone so many.
Sighs, short and infrequent, were exhaled,
And each man fixed his eyes before his feet.

Juan Rulfo, *Pedro Páramo* (retranslated by me from the Spanish
   original)
· Up and down the hill we went, but always descending. We had
  left behind hot wind and were sinking into pure, airless heat.
· The hour of day when in every village children come out to play
  in the streets
· Hollow footsteps, echoing against walls stained red by the
  setting sun
· Empty doorways overgrown with weeds

Rilke, *Duino Elegies* (loosely retranslated from Juan Rulfo's free
   translation of *Duino Elegies*)
· knowing they cannot call upon anyone, not men, not angels,
  not beasts
· astute beasts
· this uninterpreted world
· voices, voices, thinks listen heart, listen like only the saints have
  listened before
· how strange it feels to not be on earth anymore
· angels forget if they live among the living or among the dead
· toilsome to be dead

Jerzy Andrzejewski, *The Gates of Paradise* (loosely translated from
   Pitol's Spanish translation of the Polish original, and retranslated
   by me into English)
· they walked without chants and without ringing of bells in a
  closed horde
· nothing could be heard, except the monotonous sound of
  thousands of footsteps
· a desert, inanimate and calcined by the sun
· he touched the sand with his lips
· the sky was stained with a violet silence

· in a strange country, under a strange sky
· far away, as if in another world, thunder resonated heavily

To the best of my ability, I have quoted, cited, and referenced all works used for this novel—aside from the boxes, embeddings, retranslations, and repurposing of the literary works in the third-person narrative thread of the novel, which I cite above.

## ILLUSTRATION CREDITS

243: Courtesy of Humane Borders
250: © Felix Gaedtke
251: By J. W. Swan (public domain), via Wikimedia Commons
253: Courtesy of Kansas Historical Society
255: *Geronimo and fellow Apache Indian prisoners on their way to Florida by train.* 1886. State Archives of Florida, Florida Memory.
257: Image courtesy of the *Hofstra Hispanic Review;* poem © Anne Carson

## A NOTE ON THE TYPE

This book was set in Minion, a typeface produced by the Adobe Corporation specifically for the Macintosh personal computer, and released in 1990. Designed by Robert Slimbach, Minion combines the classic characteristics of old style faces with the full compliment of weights required for modern typesetting.

*Composed by North Market Street Graphics, Lancaster, Pennsylvania*

*Printed and bound by LSC, Crawfordsville, Indiana*

*Designed by Iris Weinstein*